FIELD OF BLOOD

MARKUS HEITZ

DO!RS

FIELD OF BLOOD

Jo Fletcher
BOOKS

First published as *Doors ! Blutfeld* by Verlagsgruppe Droemer Knaur, Germany, in 2018
First published in Great Britain in 2021 by

Jo Fletcher Books, an imprint of
Quercus Editions Ltd,
Carmelite House
50 Victoria Embankment
London EC4Y 0DZ

An Hachette UK company

A CIP catalogue record for this book is available
from the British Library

PB ISBN 978 1 52940 232 2
EB ISBN 978 152940 231 5

10 9 8 7 6 5 4 3 2 1

Typeset by CC Book Production
Printed and bound in Great Britain by Clays Ltd, Elcograf S.p.A.

MIX
Paper from
responsible sources
FSC® C104740

Papers used by Jo Fletcher Books are from well-managed forests
and other responsible sources.

Some say history is made by the winners.
Sometimes, it's rewritten by an author.

If you would like to know how Viktor von Troneg and his team of experts came to be tasked with rescuing Anna-Lena van Dam and how they managed to enter the cave system beneath the van Dam estate, read from the beginning.

If you would like to go straight to the door marked with !, please start with Chapter IV on page 97.

INTRODUCTION

FIRST DEAD END

Trepidation.

Trepidation and a sinking sense of hopelessness were all she could feel in the darkness as she wandered endlessly through the stone labyrinth, refusing to succumb to fear.

The smell was one known only to ancient buildings, of cold stone, damp dust and the millennia of abandonment. The leather soles of her high-heeled shoes scraped over rocky ground and slipped on the loose stones rattling around her, but there was no chance of her giving up.

She knew this place; she had heard plenty about it and now she had to find a way to leave – or remain there for ever. Death was coming for her more quickly than she could have imagined: she understood that now.

She tried to keep her breathing as quiet as possible as the LED light on her mobile phone glimmered into life for a promising second, before immediately switching off again, as if out of spite. It continued to flicker on and off, emanating a frantic, cold glow like a stroboscope.

The young woman swiped and tapped the display with her broken fingers again and again, but to no avail. The indifferent message remained: No Service.

If she had been less afraid, she might have felt the

energy all around her, as pervasive as the air she was breathing. It was not electrical, nuclear or even thermal, but rather the sort of energy that might accumulate at a spiritual site: churches, monasteries and sacred places in the middle of forests were full of this kind of energy.

As her phone continued to flash on and off, the young woman swore quietly to herself. 'Stay on!' she whispered, infuriated.

Then the little light lit up and illuminated her face, tearing it out of the darkness. Her features were striking: pure, bright, freckled skin with a light layer of make-up, her coppery hair artfully arranged in a weather-beaten up-do. She wore a small stud in her left nostril and a pair of expensive diamond earrings that glittered in the light as if she were seeking to impress a congregation of the great and the good.

But there was no one around to be impressed by her distinctive appearance.

Dazzled by the light, the young woman screwed her eyes shut and her phone slipped out of her usually well-manicured fingers: the last few hours had clearly taken their toll.

As the mobile fell to the ground, the beam of light passed down her body, briefly illuminating her dark green silk dress, now torn and flecked with mud. It revealed scratched and filthy forearms, the shattered glass of her eye-wateringly expensive watch, a small handbag clutched under her right arm and, finally, the black evening courts, the soles and uppers now covered with scratches. There was nothing practical about this attire for such an environment: her visit here was entirely unplanned.

The phone skipped across the floor and the cold white LED beam brought the stony, dusty ground out of the darkness and illuminated several empty cartridge cases, for use in a modern military weapon. The sound of the impact echoed around the room, the full size of which was beyond the reach of the small light.

After one final rattle, the phone settled on the ground with its light facing downwards. Blackness descended.

'Kcuf.' The young woman quickly bent down and picked up the device. 'Gnikcuf lleh!'

She was fully aware that words were coming out of her mouth backwards: she'd discovered it was just one of the many idiosyncrasies of this place. At first she had doubted her own sanity, then gradually she'd managed to suppress that fear. There were worse things down here.

She picked up the mobile and flashed the light all around her, illuminating walls made of grey concrete and reddish-brown brick that receded into the distance. Eddies of whirling dust danced their way through the artificial brightness like tiny moths attracted to the glow.

Then the beam passed over a series of doors made of stone and weathered wood. Three of them bore wrought-iron knockers and two were bare. The ring that should have been held in the mouth of the beautifully crafted creature adorning the second door was missing. The doors were embedded in the rocky wall as if their existence in this godforsaken place was entirely natural.

'On erom,' she whispered in frustration. 'Please, no more doors!' Her prayer was purely rhetorical.

She walked forwards slowly and cast her light over the

five doors. She had realised long ago that she was not the first visitor to try to unlock the secrets of this mysterious place. There was more than a kernel of truth to her mother's stories after all.

That knowledge was of no help whatsoever.

Markings both old and new were carved into the stone and wood; some had been scratched in, others added in pen, and they were mostly written in languages the young woman did not understand. Some of the characters might have been decipherable by archaeologists or experts in ancient and pre-history; some might even have been of interest to cryptologists or etymologists or those with knowledge of Eastern studies.

What stood out. however, were the thick red question marks on the first three doors, drawn on in lipstick and clearly new.

'Pull yourself together,' she whispered to herself, wiping a dirty strand of hair from her green eyes. Her forehead glistened with sweat and her deodorant had long since given up on her. It was not at all cold in the maze and running had become increasingly more of an ordeal with each futile escape attempt. She was ravaged by hunger and thirst and she could feel the blisters on her feet rubbing with every step she took, but she dared not walk around barefoot. 'Come on now!'

She tried to slow her breathing as she stepped up once more and withdrew a red lipstick from her handbag.

As she walked off the step, the now familiar feeling of a world being turned upside down grabbed her from behind her navel and flipped her over. The first time it had happened, she'd panicked and injured herself on the wall next to her. The second time the world turned on its axis, she found herself half drifting and had managed to manoeuvre herself so she was half pressed up against the wall in an attempt to offset the worst of the damage when gravity reasserted itself. This time she carefully raised her arms in order to remain upright.

She floated, waiting for her inevitable painful return to the stone floor.

Everything loose on the ground started to rattle and clatter around; fine particles of dust swam through the lamplight, accompanied by pebbles, bones and pieces of metal and fabric that had belonged to previous visitors.

After ten seconds, everything crashed to the ground.

She scrambled to her feet and took a few steps, stopping in front of the furthermost of the five doors: the one made from weathered oak. Instead of a knocker, it had a sliding bolt and a box lock. Her grandmother had once told her a story about this door, but she couldn't remember any of the details. The metal was thin, with inlays of gold, tarnished silver and some sort of copper alloy. Using her mobile light as a guide, she pulled out her lipstick and painted a large exclamation mark on it.

A noise suddenly erupted from the surrounding darkness. All she could hear was the pounding of heavy paws and the grinding of claws. She didn't even notice smearing lipstick on her palm as she instinctively covered the light with her hand. The beam scattered through her fingers, framing her face and eyes as if she were in a silent film.

She didn't dare turn off the light, in case she couldn't make it turn back on again.

Listen. Hold your breath. Just one more time.

She hadn't yet caught sight of her pursuer, but she knew this creature was on her tail. Perhaps it was there to guard this place? Or perhaps it was just a being who had heard her moving around and wanted to put a stop to it.

She inched towards the fourth door, which was made of stone with a knocker in the centre, the only one without a marking, and stood silently with her back against the wall, so as not to be ambushed in the darkness.

The quiet scuttling stopped abruptly.

Almost there, she thought as she placed her hand carefully on the latch and tried to push it down. Nothing happened.

She tried the door again while she carried on looking around her, before stopping to listen once more.

All was quiet.

'Kniht,' she muttered, taking a chance and illuminating the door knocker. 'Emoc on, think!'

A heavy silver ring with a bulge at the bottom could be seen in the elaborately carved ebony wolf's mouth resting imposingly on the metal plate in the centre of the door. The stone was dark grey with black grain, with inlays of white marble and onyx forming incomprehensible symmetrical symbols.

She hesitantly stretched out a hand, grabbed the ring and knocked hard against the stone, leaving behind some of the red lipstick that had stuck to her hand.

The noise was metallic, hollow and far too loud, filling the entire room with a deafening *boom*, as if someone had simultaneously played all the notes on an organ in a cathedral. An iridescent flickering accompanied the eerie yet welcoming clamour above the door. All the worlds and planets and creatures of the known and unknown universe now seemed to gather to witness her arrival.

The flickering light leaped to the other doors, illuminating them briefly, the markings on the walls gleaming as if they'd been written in gold and giving off a warm light that betrayed the presence of a fine vein in the rock. It was visible for no more than the duration of a heartbeat. A crackle and a crunch flew through the room before mutating into a whisper and a rustle.

The young woman suddenly felt as if a giant were pressing down hard on her shoulders, the gravity in the room becoming overwhelming, forcing her to her knees and compressing her vertebrae and joints so hard that she cried out in agony – but it stopped as suddenly as it had started.

The darkness returned; the weight was lifted.

'What on earth . . . ?' she muttered, rising to her feet.

She put her hand gently back on the latch, which this time offered no resistance.

Relieved, she slowly opened the door.

She was met with the presence of a soft, silvery light, accompanied by the sound of owls hooting and foxes barking, intermingled with the peaceful whoosh of falling leaves. A fresh, cleansing wind began to dance through her coppery hair. It felt as if she were being offered the freedom she had been hoping for the whole time she had been wandering through the maze.

She wanted nothing more than to step across the threshold into a world that could soothe her ills – then the growl of a predator cut through the idyll like a knife, stopping her in her tracks. It was followed by the lingering, mournful howling of a wolf: a pack was being summoned for the hunt. She drew her foot back carefully: this was a freedom she would pay for with her life. She knew she wouldn't stand a chance against such skilled hunters.

The silvery light lit up the area behind her, revealing an empty cavernously high room with only one entrance: the one she had come through. As well as the scribbled inscriptions, notes and memos from previous visitors, the brick and concrete walls were also decorated with rusty brown splodges and ancient flecks of spilled blood. Some had used it to write a final message or curse before succumbing to their anonymous deaths.

The broken ring of the destroyed door knocker lay on the ground, alongside all manner of broken grey bones and the scattered remains of skeletons.

The light also revealed something else.

A man – a *dead* man – could be seen just at the edge of the light's reach, through the haze, where silver became ghostly grey, crouching in an unnatural position. He was wearing grey-white camouflage gear with a Kevlar vest over the top; in his right hand he clutched a sub-machine gun. Empty magazines and dozens of bullet casings littered the floor around him. His throat had been slit and the blood that had poured out of it had dried and plastered his body.

Panting, the young woman quickly shut the door and using her phone, once again the only source of light, saw a large red X marked on it. 'Not there,' she whispered. 'I can't . . .'

The sound of heavy paws could be heard again, coming ever closer, accompanied by a scratching noise, as if there were several beasts approaching, all manner of beings who, in her imagination at least, would do all manner of terrible things to her if she ever found herself in their clutches.

'Go away!' The young woman shone the light all around her as if its weak glow suddenly had the lethal cutting power of an industrial laser. 'Evael em enola! I've got a gun!' she lied. 'Stay yawa morf em!'

For an instant, an enormous shadow could be seen in the trembling cone of light – then everything went dark.

'Kcuf! *Fuck!*' She frantically pulled on the door knocker and the gleam of the wood lit up the room. With a cry of anguish, she yanked the door open again.

The silvery light struck her once more as the wind blew through her hair as if to welcome her in.

The young woman hurriedly crossed the threshold and entered a world she knew would not offer her the freedom she desired. Perhaps she had merely exchanged a quick death for a slow one.

Giving up was out of the question, however.

She armed herself with a branch from the ground and ran off into the unknown.

CHAPTER I

Germany, Frankfurt am Main

Viktor headed straight through the 'Nothing to Declare' doors. The white duffle bag slung over his right shoulder and his casual sporty attire rendered him utterly inconspicuous amid the throng in the arrivals hall.

The plane had been stacked for more than an hour as a result of bad weather, turning what ought to have been a forty-minute flight into a two-hour débâcle as they waited for a runway to become available. It had made Viktor's mood somewhat sub-optimal, and it was only exacerbated by the rumblings in his stomach.

He looked at his phone and read the message from his prospective client once more:

DEAR MR VON TRONEG
LOOKING FORWARD TO MEETING YOU AND GLAD TO HEAR YOU'RE
WILLING TO START SOON. MY CHAUFFEUR MATTHIAS WILL PICK YOU
UP FROM ARRIVALS. KEEP AN EYE OUT FOR HIM THERE.
REGARDS
WALTER VAN DAM

Viktor looked around.

There were several people milling around at the exit holding pieces of cardboard, mini whiteboards or tablets bearing the names of the passengers they were waiting for, although his name was nowhere to be seen.

He decided to carry on through the hall to track the man down. His blue eyes were concealed behind a pair of sunglasses and on his head he wore a white baseball cap. He was in his mid-twenties, in excellent shape, and hardly seemed to notice the weight of his waterproof bag; one of the reasons it had taken him very little time since leaving his previous job to become one of the finest potholers in the world.

'Where is this chap?' Viktor muttered, pulling out his phone again to give his client a ring, when he spied a man in a dark blue suit with a cap and black leather gloves. He was holding a printed card that read 'Cave Tours' and carried himself in a manner reminiscent of a gentleman's valet.

Van Dam should have called him Jeeves as his work pseudonym, Viktor thought. He turned around and waded through the crowd towards Matthias; as he did so, he thought about Walter van Dam, about whom there was disconcertingly little information to be found online.

He'd been born in the Netherlands and was the head of a global import/export company founded for overseas trade in the eighteenth century. Very little was known about the man himself; he shied away from the public gaze and for the most part sent proxies to his official engagements. The van Dam family had allegedly branched out further, but Viktor had not been able to find out much beyond that. That was understandable, as there was quite a trade in kidnapping and ransoming the very rich. The less the public knew about you, the better.

It was ultimately irrelevant to Viktor, as long as the Dutchman did not attempt to drag him into any criminal activity. The first payment had already landed in his account and was substantially higher than anything the German state had paid him for far more dangerous jobs.

Next to the chauffeur stood a gaunt man about fifty years old, wearing a bespoke checked suit and highly polished brown shoes that made him look a bit like an Oxford professor. His foot was resting on an expensive-looking aluminium case, as if he were trying to stop it escaping, and he was reading a newspaper. The designer glasses gave him an arrogant demeanour.

'Good afternoon, gentlemen.' Viktor removed his own sunglasses, catching a glimpse of his three-day-old beard in the reflection as he did so. 'Mr van Dam is expecting me. My name is Viktor Troneg.'

'Welcome to Frankfurt.' The chauffeur inclined his head in greeting. 'My name is Matthias. The rest haven't arrived yet.' He gestured towards the other man, who was still absorbed in his reading and did not react. 'May I take this opportunity to introduce you to Professor Friedemann, renowned speleologist and geologist.'

Viktor inclined his head and Friedemann, whose long grey hair was drawn up in a ponytail, nodded in reply without looking up from his newspaper; Viktor thought his angular face had more than a passing resemblance to a skull.

'This is Mr von Troneg, a potholer and free-climber,' Matthias said. 'From what I gather, he's got quite the international reputation.'

'Very good.' Friedemann turned the page and busied himself in the next article.

Viktor already knew which one he liked the least. 'Were we all on the same flight?' he asked.

'You were indeed, Mr von Troneg.'

'No need to keep the *von*. I'm not overly keen on my ancestral name.' Then he broke into a grin. 'Whatever would you have done if it had crashed?' he asked.

'The plane? Highly unlikely,' replied Matthias. 'In any case the clairvoyant wouldn't have boarded.' He laughed drily.

'Clairvoyant? Well, that's something, I suppose.' Viktor lifted up his baseball cap and slicked his long black hair back before replacing it. 'And what if she *had* got on?'

'She'd have suffered a tragic death, and rightly so,' commented Friedemann, without looking up. He carefully adjusted his glasses.

Viktor grinned and was about to respond when he noticed a particular woman out of the corner of his eye – and he clearly wasn't the only one: practically all the passengers appeared to have turned their gaze in her direction.

She was dressed in a tight-fitting, cream-coloured designer dress and pushing a large, outrageously expensive designer suitcase in front her. With a fashionable handbag hanging artfully from her right arm and large sunglasses hiding her eyes, she had the aura of an haute couture model. She held a vanity case in her left hand. Her curly long blonde hair had a theatrically black strand at the front.

Viktor stood there, admiring her. 'Impressive entrance.'

'I hope you're being ironic.' Friedemann finally looked up from his paper and turned his eyes towards her. 'Dreadful person. Sat behind me on the flight and kept ordering champagne. They must have wanted to drown her in it by the end.'

'That is Ms Coco Fendi,' the chauffeur clarified, raising his arm to catch her attention. 'Our clairvoyant, gentlemen.'

'Really? *Coco Fendi?*' Viktor had to laugh. 'Perfect name for a performer.'

'Coco Fendi: a cross between a handbag and a fashion brand. I'm assuming she's really called Sabine Müller or something,' Friedemann added. 'A double fraud, if you ask me. Only frauds need to dress up like that much of a cliché to be able to perform.'

As Ms Fendi was walking through the hall in search of her welcoming party, the lock on her vanity case snapped open, scattering the contents all over the floor. Pendulums, crystals, tarot cards, bone cubes and runestones rattled and rolled around as if a magician's box had exploded. All that appeared to be missing was a white rabbit, a black candle and a painted skull.

'She didn't see that coming.' Friedemann looked back down at his newspaper. 'Not a good sign at all, gents.' The lenses of his glasses flashed in the light, as if to underscore his statement.

Coco Fendi swore so loudly that she could be heard from the other side of the hall: not the sort of attitude her initial appearance suggested. She let go of her suitcase and bent down to pick up her paraphernalia, which was made all the more difficult by her tight dress.

Viktor was about to walk over and help her when a thickset man in a tight jacket, baggy jeans and crumpled shirt approached from the magazine stand. He acknowledged her briefly before putting his own bag down and lowering himself to his knees to assist in the clean-up operation.

'The white knight has come to rescue his fair medium,' observed Friedemann, who had become a rather acerbic commentator.

'By your leave, that's Doctor Ingo Theobald,' explained Matthias. 'He's part of the team as well.'

'Ah, a doctor? Good.' Viktor folded his arms, happy not to intervene now that Fendi and Theobald were doing such a good job of clearing up. 'Still a shame, though. I'd hoped we'd have another young woman in the group.'

'I bet you'd regret that almost immediately,' barked Friedemann with the pomposity of a snobbish fifty-year-old. 'There's not much that can beat the wisdom that comes with age. Knowledge is power and this woman has neither years nor knowledge on her side.'

Viktor wondered how the man was able to see what was going on around him without moving his eyes. *A master of peripheral vision*, he thought.

Coco Fendi was so engrossed in the recovery of her belongings that she only belatedly noticed the helper kneeling beside her.

'Thank you – that's most kind of you.' Her tight dress

was hindering her movements somewhat, but that was the price one paid for beautiful, expensive clothing, which she could well afford. Her bright hair obscured her vision, the curls hanging like a curtain in front of her eyes. 'A true gentleman.'

She positioned her enormous suitcase as a shield, preventing anyone from absconding with her possessions. The small group of people around the chauffeur disappeared behind it.

Coco turned towards her saviour, stroked her hair out of her face and recognised Ingo Theobald, a man in his early forties with greying blond hair falling down to his neck. A pair of youthfully nerdy nickel glasses perched on his unshaven face.

'You?' she laughed, kissing him on the mouth.

Ingo let it happen more out of surprise than anything else. 'What are you doing here?' he asked in astonishment.

'Working,' she responded curtly, bridling at his obvious discomfort at meeting her here. She picked up the tarot cards. 'And you? Investigating a case?'

'Working.' He examined her, then looked over her suitcase at the uniformed chauffeur waving at them. 'Don't tell me . . .'

Coco raised her eyes and understood. 'No! You as well?'

Ingo sighed and took her free hand in his. 'Don't do this, Beate. It's going to be incredibly dangerous!'

'It's well paid,' she retorted. 'And don't call me that. I am Coco Fendi, the acclaimed clairvoyant and medium, known for my work on the radio, television and online. Do you know how many followers I've got?'

She stuffed her scattered belongings back into the case; there would be time to sort everything out later.

Ingo had not expected to see Beate again, and certainly not to learn that they had been commissioned by the same company. He looked at her reproachfully, wanting to say something back – something cruel, like, being a clairvoyant, she must have known they were going to meet again at the airport. Instead, he said, 'That outfit's a bit much, isn't it? You're pretty much confirming every prejudice under the sun about people in your line of work.'

'It's all part of my brand. I'm like Elvira, Mistress of the Dark. Only more stylish.'

'You do realise that Elvira was satirising the whole gothic horror genre?'

'I don't care. I'm giving people what they expect, and that makes them happy – people love clichés. You know I tried doing it differently before and how much of a failure that was. So now they're getting the mother of all extravagant psychics.' Coco kissed him again behind the suitcase and caressed his cheek. 'Play along. Please. Once we're upstairs you can fuck me like it's going out of fashion, I promise.' She looked at him intensely. 'Please, Ingo – it was only your expertise that got me this job.'

'We're not talking about one of your shows where all you've got to do is entertain your followers,' he responded, concerned.

'Just let me do me, okay?' she asked, her voice noticeably cooler. Her kisses had failed to win him around, which annoyed her greatly. She slammed the case closed and snapped the locks shut. 'Just one more time. Then I'll have got enough money together.'

Ingo frowned, remaining silent as they stood up. Thanks to her love of the high life, Beate was always in dire financial straits. She viewed herself as being from the tradition of divas in the Roaring Twenties, although there weren't many men nowadays willing to bankroll a spiritualist. The fact that she looked like a garish walking cliché didn't bother her in the slightest. He found her explanation plausible, but she was giving little away. Beate was old enough to decide how she wanted to come across.

'Wrong bag?' came a stern female voice from behind them.

Ingo and Coco turned around to see a woman in her mid-thirties standing two feet away. She was dressed in city camouflage trousers and a fine rib vest with a brown, scuffed leather jacket over it and holding a steaming coffee cup in her right hand.

The words were not intended for them, but rather for a young man wearing a wide-brimmed fishing hat, who frowned guiltily. She had stopped his bag with her right foot – which was in fact Ingo's bag.

'Hey! That's mine,' protested Ingo.

'It's so easy to pick up the wrong bag at the airport,' said the stranger. With her mid-length blonde hair tied up in a braid, her appearance was the absolute opposite of Coco's: one could win wars, while the other was only good for entertaining the troops.

'Let go of me!' exclaimed the thief as he tried to escape her clutches and make off with his stolen goods. Greed had clearly overridden sanity.

The woman stepped back, then struck him in the

solar plexus. He crumpled to the floor and remained there, panting and clutching his stomach.

She grinned down at him and took a sip of her coffee. Not a single drop had been spilled. 'It's pretty slippery here, so be careful not to lose your footing. Good job you haven't broken anything.' She raised her hand. 'My fist is harder than your sternum. Shall we find out together what that means?'

Two security guards approached with caution. 'Can we help you?' announced one of them, withdrawing his radio to call the security post.

The unknown woman turned to face Ingo with a wicked grin on her face. 'This is a security announcement. Please do not leave your luggage unattended.'

He smiled and extended his hand. 'Thank you! I'd have been lost without you.'

'Lucky you were here.' Coco explained what had happened to the security officers, while they picked up the thief and secured his hands with cable ties.

'Ah, it would appear everyone from the Cave Tours group has managed to find one another,' said the chauffeur, who had appeared alongside the two guards without either of them noticing him. 'My name is Matthias. Mr van Dam has sent me to pick you all up.' He gestured around him and started to introduce everyone. The militant coffee drinker was apparently one of them.

'And this most attentive lady here is Dana Rentski, a renowned free-climber,' Matthias said, concluding the introductions. A flurry of handshakes followed.

'But we're not at full capacity yet,' he continued. 'There's still one missing. Then we can make a move. Mr van Dam will explain the rest to you.' Matthias turned to the two airport officials and handed them a business card, in case there were any further questions that weren't covered by their statements and the security cameras, then the men took the captured thief away.

'Quite the show,' said Viktor to Dana. He couldn't help but notice both her firm handshake and athletic physique.

'Thank you.' She drained the last of her coffee and tossed the cup confidently into the nearby paper recycling bin. 'I like to be of use when I can.'

A silence fell upon the disparate group; apparently nobody wanted to be the first to start a conversation. Friedemann returned to his newspaper.

Meanwhile, an overweight man in a pair of bright jersey trousers and a garish shirt hurried across from the check-in desks. He had clearly tried to emulate the beard and haircut of the comic superhero Tony Stark, but the rest of his look and his physical appearance were utterly unsuitable for the role, making him look more like a caricature of Magnum, PI, than Ironman.

Viktor guessed this was the final person hired by van Dam. The man cut rather a ludicrous figure at first glance, even more so than Friedemann.

The fag-packet Magnum caught sight of the group, raised his arm in greeting and clumped his way over to them.

'Watch where you're going,' he snarled at a little boy walking hand-in-hand with his mother, ruthlessly carving his way towards the people awaiting him. 'Sorry. There was some old biddy taking an age to get her bag off the luggage belt.

I had to wait yonks for mine. She didn't want to let go of her Zimmer frame and took for ever to hobble off with the ancient piece of crap that passed for her suitcase.' He nodded to those around him. 'Pleased to meet you. Carsten Spanger's the name, but you can call me Tony.'

'Helping her might have speeded things up,' remarked Dana coolly.

Carsten scratched his head. 'And then who would have helped me?' he added, before laughing to show that he had clearly misunderstood her. 'Well? Am I the last one here?'

'Yes, you're the last,' replied Dana.

'Don't bite my head off,' Spanger retorted. 'Next time I'll be a very good little Boy Scout and help every old lady I come across.'

'Right, that's everyone then.' Matthias took control of the situation before this minor tussle could go any further. 'If you'd all like to follow me?'

They left the hall together and were soon standing in front of a black Mercedes people carrier. They got in, with Viktor and Dana stopping to help the chauffeur load the cases into the storage area.

'Thanks, that's very kind of you. More than can be said for the other lot,' said Matthias, reaching up to shut the boot.

'The other lot?'

Matthias realised that he'd been blabbing. 'The others, Mr Troneg.' He closed the boot, smiled and gestured to him that he should get in as well, before hurrying over to the driver's seat.

'After you, Ms Fendi.' Carsten allowed her to get on

ahead of him and immediately stood to admire her back-side as she bent over, then wiggled his eyebrows like a sleazy ventriloquist's dummy. 'I'm already your biggest fan.'

Viktor ruminated over what Matthias had said. 'The other lot,' he repeated to himself softly. So they weren't the first group van Dam had hired.

Unknown to Viktor and the rest of the so-called Cave Tours group, an inconspicuously dressed man in his mid-forties was sitting on a bench not far from where the incident with the vanity case had taken place. He had a small laptop resting on his knee, but there was nothing to distinguish him from the dozens of other people milling around, apart from the unusually concerned expression on his face – as if he had just learned about an event that would change the course of history for ever.

The man occasionally looked over the screen to check the arrivals board, then turned his piercing gaze to the right again and looked at the people who were introducing themselves to one another. Frown lines began to form on his forehead.

In the open chat window could be seen the message he had written:

ARRIVED WITH TRONEG AT FFM.

HAS BEEN MET AT ARRIVALS.

PART OF A TEAM. WILL SEND PHOTOS OF THE GROUP SHORTLY.

INSTRUCTIONS?

The man reached for his paper cup and tasted the drink that had ostensibly been sold to him as an espresso. It looked more like a brown slurry that had been forgotten about and simply heated up again because someone had neglected to throw it away.

The answer arrived with a beep:

FOLLOW THEM.
KILL TRONEG IF YOU CAN.
COLLATERAL DAMAGE ACCEPTABLE.

Next to the chat window, the man had opened a photograph showing Viktor in front of a tumbledown shack, holding a fully-equipped G36 rifle. It was not clear where and when it had been taken, but the colour of his camouflage suggested it was in Iraq or Afghanistan, or another desert country. He had been there with a German unit that had no official reason to be there.

But this was not the reason why Viktor von Troneg was on the hit list. German Special Forces were constantly moving through forbidden terrain without governments or any other regulatory bodies being aware of them.

There was a second photograph underneath, far grainier, that had clearly been enlarged, showing an antique-looking stone door with a door-knocker made from black metal, shaped like a lion's mouth and bearing a golden ring between its white teeth. The signs and symbols carved into it were too pixelated for them to be deciphered. The door belonged to the hut Viktor had been kneeling in front of in the first photo, casting his eyes around for enemies without once looking behind him ... which might have been a lethal error with a door of this kind.

The man responded in acknowledgement and, as the chauffeur led the sextet across the hall, lifted up his smartphone to take photos of the group and send them off.

Calmly, the middle-aged man stood up and slinging a rucksack over his shoulder and carrying his laptop under his arm, began to follow them, just one of countless anonymous business travellers making their way through the terminal. No one could possibly guess what he was up to or what organisation he worked for.

The man left the building and leaned against a pillar a few yards back from the black Mercedes people carrier, looking around for a taxi. There was only one car in the rank.

The group had finished getting in; the vehicle's indicators blinked and it drove off.

The man strode purposefully towards the last taxi. 'Hello. I'd like to go to—'

'Sorry. I've just had another booking come through on the radio,' replied the driver through the window with a regretful gesture. 'One of my colleagues will be with you shortly.' He turned on the ignition and drove off.

Shortly wasn't soon enough. There were no other taxis as far as the eye could see.

Cursing, he turned around and took out his phone, keeping his eye on the Mercedes as it faded into the distance. 'It's me,' he said to the gruff voice at the other end. 'I need to find the owner of a black Merc people carrier.' He recited the model and registration number.

In a matter of seconds he knew where he had to go to find Viktor von Troneg.

Instead of waiting for the next taxi to come along, the man walked over to the closest car hire kiosk. His orders were clear and had to be carried out to the letter.

SECOND DEAD END

After her courageous step across the threshold, the young woman in the dark green evening dress wandered a few yards forwards before stopping and gazing around at the dark forest; it was disconcertingly peaceful.

She was surrounded by ferns and the ethereal glow of the silvery moonlight dappling through the giant trees. The earthy cry of a screech owl rang in her ears, accompanied by the barking of a fox. The wind coursed playfully through the branches and foliage, creating a rustling sound all around her.

The young woman was not going to be fooled again, not when everything she had read about in the stories had been proved right. She stood still, casting her eyes all around and listening out for signs of danger while clasping the branch ever more tightly in her right hand.

The ominous rumbling of the predators inhabiting this world had died away for now. She hoped that the creatures had found other prey, preferably this invisible creature from the labyrinth.

It was only when she was certain that there was nothing moving near her that she decided to press on slowly. She looked down at her smartphone.

No Signal.

'For fuck's sake,' she muttered, looking back at the door she had just come through.

On this side, the passage belonged to the remains of an old bunker which had become embedded into the landscape and overgrown with greenery. The markings on the door were illegible and the signs themselves gave away no clues as to their meaning. It was clear, however, that this was not a place that had anything to do with the world she knew. There was nothing reminiscent of the cavernous hall with its five enigmatic doors.

She'd known that would be the case, though.

The sound of an electronic beep suddenly rang out and she looked at the display.

The signal bar started to flit rapidly between showing one and two bars.

'Yes! Please!' she cried out in relief. 'That must mean . . .' She stretched her arm upwards in an attempt to find more reception and strode cautiously forwards.

She had been wrong after all. *Thankfully!* This wood was part of good old Planet Earth, with its mobile phone masts and boosters that would help her to escape. Perhaps she had opened a door to a nature reserve or a wolf enclosure. That would explain the howling.

She slipped through a dense field of lush green ferns, constantly looking for an even better signal. She caught her high heels repeatedly on the soft ground and kept having to avoid unhelpfully located boulders, but finally she emerged in a clearing bathed in moonlight. The celestial body looked considerably larger and closer than normal.

She made her way cautiously into the centre of the clearing and held her phone up as high as she could. 'Come on,' she whispered imploringly. 'Take me home.'

A faint crackling could suddenly be heard and the ferns swirled all around her.

The young woman remained stationary but looked around, listening attentively, her branch thrust out in front of her to ward off any potential attack. Her nose-stud and one of her earrings glimmered icily in the starlight. The other one must have fallen off at some point; she certainly wouldn't be going back to look for it.

At that moment, the display on her phone showed a full bar of signal as her reward. 'Yes!' she screamed with joy.

Her scratched fingers flitted over the device to start dialling.

She kept looking around, trying to avoid becoming something's dinner just before being rescued. She looked at the ferns suspiciously as they swayed in the breeze. A distant howling erupted once more, far enough away for her to not have to fear it, but close enough to remind her that the animals had not altogether gone.

She ducked down reflexively so as not to be discovered; she would have preferred to crawl out of the exposed area and head towards a tree in order to wait for the park ranger or official to rescue her from the compound.

As if to punish her, the signal bar went back to how it had been before.

She stood up again and pressed the phone to her cheek. After what felt like an eternity, it started to ring.

Three, four rings.

A click. Someone had answered.

'Papa – can you hear me, Papa?' she exclaimed joyfully. 'Listen to me! I was at Great-grandad's house—'

A distorted, unhuman voice emanated from the speaker, nothing but unintelligible babbling.

She looked at the display. She had definitely dialled the right number. 'What on earth—?'

She hung up and dialled the emergency services.

Her phone tried to get through again.

The howling returned, much closer than it had been a few seconds earlier, while the ferns suddenly moved in the opposite direction to the wind. Something was running directly towards her, protected under the cover of the green canopy.

'Fuck!' The young woman ran back towards the door through which she had just come. Her prospects of survival felt greater on the other side of this forest, even if there was something else waiting for her in the chamber. At least now she was armed with a branch.

The bar had returned to zero. No Service.

The ruined bunker appeared between the tree trunks; the door was now wide open.

Moonlight shone into the room beyond, illuminating the markings on the concrete and brick walls; it was the closest thing to temporary safety she was likely to get. She could see the broken door knocker on the floor, as well as the skeletal remains and the dead man in his camouflage gear. The sub-machine gun in his hand looked tempting, though she had no idea how to use it. It would at least give her something more robust than the branch to defend herself with.

She'd started panting with exertion but still managed to keep her speed up. She stumbled on the steep ground but just about stayed on her feet.

The rumbling approach of the beasts came ever closer.

I'm going to make it, she kept thinking. She wasn't even ten yards away now. *I'm going to make it!*

A man in a pin-striped suit, his white shirt and black tie arranged immaculately, emerged from inside the bunker and stood in the entrance. His abrupt arrival had something of the surreal about it. His face wore a curious expression as he watched the young woman running for her life.

Then he raised his right arm, revealing a ring on his finger that shimmered in the moonlight. He placed his hand on the door and pushed it shut before she was able to make it to the passage.

'No!' exclaimed the young woman angrily, '*No* – I've got to get in! Listen to me – I've got to—' She threw herself against the door at full speed and reached it while it was still slightly ajar; in her attempt to jam the stick into the crack to keep the door open, it split in two and the wood shattered in her hand. 'No! No, open the door!' She rammed her shoulder against the door repeatedly, tearing her skin and green dress in the process. 'You prick!' Warm blood began to seep from the fresh cuts and scratches she had just acquired.

A deep laugh erupted from the other side of the door and the unknown man pushed back. He was too strong for her. The door closed. The lock clicked into place and at the same time a terrible whirring sound could be heard.

The young woman kicked it miserably. She knew what that noise meant: there was no way back.

Now it was just her, the forest and the monsters.

CHAPTER II

Germany, Near Frankfurt

The journey was made in silence at first, the Mercedes cruising along the motorway, taking them further and further away from the airport. Matthias was a cautious but skilled driver, nipping from lane to lane to make decent progress.

Coco Fendi rummaged in her box of tricks and began to rearrange the stones, runes and other odds and ends that had fallen out so ignominiously earlier, then she opened the case completely, spreading it out on the seat next to her so that the other passengers all had to shuffle up, but nobody complained.

Viktor examined Dana Rentski's face in the reflection in the tinted window. She looked vaguely familiar, but he couldn't think where from. He had taken part in numerous climbing competitions over the years and it was not at all out of the question that they had come across each other at one time or another. As soon as he tried to talk to her, however, she made it perfectly clear from her body language that she had no interest whatsoever in having a discussion. She was reading a book on her smartphone and did not wish to be disturbed.

If his feeling of having met her before had anything to do with his old job, then it probably was not going to be a happy story. It would mean they were not on the same page whatsoever.

Spanger dozed, snorting and grunting every time they went over a bump.

'Now then.' Friedemann was the first to speak. The man folded up his newspaper and placed it in his lap before allowing his mocking gaze to pass over the group. 'What have we here?' He pointed to his chest. 'Rüdiger Friedemann: geologist and speleologist.' Then he pointed to Dana and Viktor. 'Two free-climbers.' He inclined his finger towards Coco. 'And a medium.' His brown eyes turned to Ingo. 'You are our doctor, and you' – he looked towards Spanger, who had opened his eyes at the sound of his voice – 'are our technical support, if I had to guess.' He looked smugly at the man with his curious beard. 'You're a bit too tubby for caving, though. We can't have you getting stuck down there.'

Spanger rubbed his eyelids and cleared his throat to reply, but before he could muster a response, Ingo said, 'I'm not a medical doctor. I'm a doctor of physics and parapsychology, from the Freiburg Parapsychological Institute.'

Friedemann laughed. 'A ghost-hunter? Sweet Jesus, what a team we've got here!'

'I'm not just a climber,' said Dana. 'I also do a bit of martial arts on the side. Just about enough to give thieves a good hiding. Or arrogant tossers. Age makes no difference to me whatsoever.'

'Touché,' replied Friedemann, amused. 'How refreshing it is to see someone with a bit of courage about them.'

'Don't be a dick, Friedemann. Just because you're a professor, it doesn't mean you have to get off on your title,' replied Spanger sourly. 'You look like you'd fall over if someone blew on you. Or—'

'With all due respect, *this* is the strangest group I've ever had to lead.' Friedemann looked around the interior of the vehicle.

'*You?*' exclaimed Dana with disbelief. The look she gave him made it perfectly clear that she did not believe he would last an hour in a climbing harness. '*You're* going to be leading our team?'

Friedemann smiled. He appeared to be enjoying this. 'That's what it says in my contract.'

The surroundings they were whizzing past had started to change dramatically. The Mercedes was now driving through an affluent suburb of old mansions and enormous gardens.

By now, Viktor was certain that Dana's face was not familiar from any climbing exploits. 'Help me out here,' he said to her. 'We know each other from somewhere. But it's not from anything involving caves or climbing, is it?'

She shrugged and carried on reading.

Viktor could not fathom Dana's behaviour. He continued to rack his brains but the story of where or how they'd met was lost in the fog somewhere. Or had he become a victim of his own imagination because she resembled someone he knew?

'Why don't you ask our clairvoyant, Mr von Troneg?' Friedemann smiled at Coco, who was still engrossed in her triage. The car slowed down and stopped with a gentle sway.

'She'll definitely be able to tell you where you've met before. Or in what life.' He rolled up his newspaper and thumped it down on her open suitcase. 'Ms Fendi, give this gentleman a hand. Spiritually, that is. Impress us.'

'I don't provide those sorts of services for free. Nor good impressions, for that matter,' she said coolly before closing the case. 'We've all got bills to pay.' She snapped the locks back into place with a flourish and tossed her blonde curls with that unusual black streak in a well-rehearsed, suitably melodramatic gesture.

Spanger laughed bitterly. 'There's something to be said for that. By the way, I'm not an IT geek, Professor Friedemann. I'm a bodyguard.'

The old geologist's smile turned into a vicious grin. He could think of a million jokes to make about the man's corpulence, but he chose to keep the ones about being a cushion for bullets to himself for the time being. 'I'm sure you're the very best.'

The team climbed out, Friedemann leading.

The Mercedes had stopped in the drive of an imposing Art Nouveau mansion in the middle of carefully curated parkland. The sun was warm on their backs and shone welcomingly through the trees; it smelled of the last days of summer, though autumn was well underway.

Matthias walked around them and opened the boot. 'Don't worry, I'll take care of your luggage.'

'As you did for the others?' replied Dana. Clearly she had also noticed his slip of the tongue earlier.

'Please make sure nothing falls open,' Coco reminded him. 'And don't scratch them! Bags can feel pain too – especially when they're as expensive as mine are.' Keeping hold of the case containing all her paraphernalia, she pulled a golden pendulum hanging from a silver chain out of her coat and pointed it at the mansion. 'There's sorrow in this house,' she muttered darkly.

Ingo looked at her in warning, but she smiled dismissively. She was perfectly happy being a walking cliché.

'Sorrow, yes. And even more money,' added Spanger. 'Good for us – means we'll definitely get paid.'

'Go on in,' Matthias implored with a friendly smile. 'Mr van Dam is keen to meet you all.'

At that moment, the front door opened. The servant who appeared in the doorway, dressed in a uniform similar to the chauffeur's, invited them inside. 'Follow me, please. Everything's ready for you.'

The group passed through an imposing entrance hall, glimpsing a series of elegantly furnished rooms on the ground floor, before heading up the stairs. Viktor looked around in amazement; he felt as if he were in a museum. He was not particularly well versed in art, but the paintings looked as if they might have been from the eighteenth century and would certainly have been worth a small fortune, just like the rest of the treasures adorning every room they passed.

Spanger was mimicking the brisk pace set by the staff, his substantial posterior wiggling left and right as he moved. Coco was holding her pendulum out the entire time, her face set in a mask of concern. Ingo, meanwhile, was walking with his hands behind his back as if he were a philosopher.

'We're here.' The woman knocked on the door and,

upon hearing a voice from inside, ushered them through the impressive set of double doors into their client's office. 'If any of you have got any dietary requirements or allergies, please let me know. I'm here to serve.' After making sure no one needed anything right then, she gestured inside. 'I'll be back soon, ladies and gentlemen.'

They were hit by a smell of a fresh aftershave that somehow complemented the room perfectly. The dark interior was a daring mixture of old and new, Bauhaus and baroque, combining steel, leather and wood to give the impression of having been put together at the whim of some progressive designer. Thick, dusty tomes and antique-looking folders stood on sober, functional shelves, while one corner was taken up by a large, elaborately crafted wardrobe that looked as if it might lead straight to Narnia.

Walter van Dam was seated behind his desk, hunched over a laptop. He was about Friedemann's age, mid-fifties, with greying hair and similarly coloured moustache and sideburns, and was dressed in an expensive-looking dark brown suit. He glanced up and gestured to the six chairs in front of his desk. 'Welcome, ladies and gentlemen.'

They offered their greetings and sat down. The woman who'd met them at the door returned, pushing a trolley on which an assortment of coffee, tea, mineral water and biscuits was laid out, before retiring again.

'I must apologise in advance for the urgency of this matter. I'm running out of time, you see, so please don't be offended if I come across as rude,' van Dam explained. 'Do I need to introduce you to one another, or did you get that out of the way on the journey here?'

'Already done,' Friedemann announced. 'They all know I'm in charge, at any rate.'

'Then I'm sure you also understand that you're a rather special group,' said van Dam, his tones clipped. 'Including a medium.'

'Indeed.' Viktor cocked his head to one side, looking at Mr van Dam, who seemed to be more of a grounded businessman than a fringe lunatic. 'For which I'm sure there's a reason?'

'Desperation, I imagine,' muttered Spanger.

Van Dam's business-like manner faded and he appeared to sink a little behind his computer. 'You're right, Mr Spanger, I am desperate,' he admitted quietly. 'Beyond desperate.'

The group exchanged glances.

Coco looked as if she wanted to say something and began to point the pendulum at him, but Ingo gently touched her arm to stop her. Now really wasn't the time. She relented.

Van Dam cleared his throat and took a sip of water from the glass next to him. A few droplets got caught on his beard, making his face glimmer for a moment. 'My daughter has been missing for a week.' He turned a picture frame around to show them the face of a freckled, red-haired young woman, no older than twenty, with a cheeky smile playing on her lips. 'I suspect she's in an unexplored cave system. Alone.'

'I'm so sorry,' replied Viktor spontaneously. He knew all too well what it felt like to be worried about a loved one. He just about managed to stop himself from asking where she had gone missing.

'The police and fire service would be your best bet, then,' Spanger said, making no attempt to conceal his disappointment. He had been counting on something exciting. 'The emergency services, at any rate.'

'I've got nothing against the authorities,' van Dam said, having regained his business-like demeanour, 'but there are some matters that do not concern the government. The last thing I want is to have hordes of curious firefighters or police officers swarming all over my property.'

'I'll track down your daughter, no matter where she is,' Coco assured him in a theatrical voice, as if she were trying to entertain an audience. She couldn't turn it off, no matter how hard she tried. 'That I promise you, Mr van Dam.'

'I have every faith in you, Ms Fendi. Given that you have passed Doctor Theobald's parapsychological tests, you are clearly predestined to do so.' He clasped his hands together. 'As I've said, I'm running out of time. My daughter . . .' He paused, taking a deep breath as he struggled to maintain his composure.

'How could she get lost when she was on your property?' ventured Viktor.

'And what's our resident ghostbuster here for?' Dana enquired, her voice sounding matter-of-fact. 'Do you really expect we'll have to contend with ghosts?'

'There's no such thing as ghosts,' added Ingo. 'I should know, after more than two hundred investigations.'

'My reason for inviting Doctor Theobald is because . . . because he *is* scientifically very well versed. I need the six of you to be prepared for *anything* on this expedition, ready to deal with any situation that might arise,' said van

Dam quickly. 'It is your job to find out how precisely she disappeared, Mr von Troneg. You'll have state-of-the-art caving equipment, ample provisions, as well as helmet cameras and signal-boosters to make sure images are fed back up to me. I'm afraid my claustrophobia will prevent me from accompanying you, otherwise I would have gone to rescue my daughter myself. But even if I can't be there in person, I'd like to know what's going on underground.' He hesitated briefly, then added, 'Firearms and light body armour will also be provided.'

Spanger laughed, his mood improving. 'Whoa – because?'

'As you may be aware, I am a wealthy man. My daughter is usually protected by bodyguards from the moment she steps foot outside the house. But this was not the case on her last outing.' He glanced down at his laptop. 'There's a very good chance that criminals took this opportunity and are holding my daughter captive down there. That's why Mr Spanger is with you. As a firearms expert.' He stood up and smoothed out his waistcoat and tie. 'As I said, you must be ready for anything.'

Viktor found his explanation rather odd. 'Has anyone sent a ransom note?'

'No. The kidnapping idea is just a guess.' Van Dam pointed at the door. 'Please excuse my lack of manners. And I beg you not to consider me unprofessional because I didn't brief you in advance, but the nature of this matter required the utmost discretion, not least because of my daughter's profile. Your contracts have all been signed and the first instalments have been paid. Feel free to check your accounts.' He walked around the desk, clearly heading for the door. 'Time is pressing, ladies and gentlemen – time my daughter doesn't have. Everything you need to know about the caves and your fellow teammates can be found in the files Matthias has given you. You are to leave immediately. As the most experienced speleologist and geologist, Professor Friedemann will lead the group, as per his request. If you'd be so kind . . .'

Viktor raised his hand, which van Dam deliberately ignored, but Viktor continued regardless, 'Sorry, just a quick question. Have you already sent another team out?'

'No.'

His reply was firm and abrupt, but after the chauffeur's slip-up earlier, everyone now knew that they were the second group to have been despatched and that the first had not returned. Van Dam's unconvincing denial served only to suppress any further enquiries.

Everyone stood up.

Friedemann was looking closely at the cabinet behind van Dam's desk. 'These carvings are exquisite.' His face had acquired an expression that was typical of an expert spotting an anomaly or making a spectacular discovery. 'I've never seen such a specimen before. It must be priceless.'

'Not this one. I got it from a flea market. It's just my cocktail cabinet.' Van Dam pointed emphatically to the exit once again. 'Bring me back my child – alive – and I'll make you all rich beyond measure. The hundred thousand euros each of you has received is just a fraction of what you'll get if you return my Anna-Lena safely to me.'

*

The team got back into the same black Mercedes that had collected them from the airport. They began to drive through a wilderness of sorts, passing increasingly fewer houses and ever-deeper woodland, until Matthias announced that they would arrive in a few minutes. 'Don't worry about how remote it is,' he added. 'It'll make your task a lot easier.'

The ragtag bunch read their dossiers in silence.

They were all wearing dark military clothing, climbing gear and light Kevlar vests and were armed with pistols, holstered on thighs or underarm. The semi-automatic she'd been issued looked like an alien life form to Coco, but Friedemann had insisted that she take something other than clairvoyant trinkets to protect herself. Two light rucksacks were resting in front of him and Spanger.

Viktor considered it rather a bold move to arm people with weapons when they no experience in handling them, nor any legal authorisation to do so. He also doubted whether a civvy with a gun would actually be able to hold their own against potential kidnappers.

Friedemann put his folder to one side and fumbled around as if looking for something, before pulling out a well-thumbed notebook from his right trouser pocket. It looked old, both in terms of style and wear and tear. Clearly relieved, Friedemann looked at it briefly, then stuffed it under his Kevlar vest, something Viktor didn't fail to notice.

'Not much information in here,' Spanger grumbled. 'Just a load of stuff about van Dam's daughter.'

'What were you expecting?' Dana put a piece of chewing gum in her mouth. 'He said the cave system hadn't been explored before.'

Viktor and Coco both gave a quiet laugh, which somehow reinforced his suspicion that the clairvoyant could do more than just predict the future. He had been trying to talk to her about the official investigation by the Parapsychological Institute, as he had never heard of a real, verified psychic before, but she was having none of it, claiming she needed to concentrate as she shuffled her deck of cards. She said she'd be happy to tell him all about it after their assignment, by way of consolation.

'I'm curious to find out more about these caves,' Ingo said as he put his folder to one side. 'I've never come across someone who considers a cavern to be his own private property.'

'I don't like caves,' came Spanger's irritable reply.

'I'd have put money on that. You look like the sort of chap who needs a lot of room. I can't imagine narrow spaces are your thing.' Friedemann looked around intently. 'I don't believe this young lady has been kidnapped.'

'Neither do I,' agreed Viktor, who already knew the information in the file off by heart. 'Otherwise van Dam would have hired people with experience in hostage negotiation. Anyone else would put his daughter in danger. Though I suppose it could be the case that the first team was just that but they weren't able to manage it.'

'I'm so pleased I've got your approval,' said Friedemann, his voice laced with mockery. 'I don't foresee any problems. We'll follow the safety rope mentioned in the handout. Anna-Lena is almost certainly just lying around somewhere, waiting for help.'

'What's so special about you that he's put a geologist

in charge?' Dana had doubted his leadership credentials from the start. 'Just curious,' she added. She smiled coolly.

Friedemann looked at her calmly. 'I suppose you think you should be leading us, just because you can climb like a mountain goat?' He rubbed his thumbs over the tips of his index and middle fingers. 'I can see where the rock is fragile and where it's dangerous; where there are cracks and what you need to look out for. And what routes we shouldn't take. I've led dozens of expeditions to the furthest reaches of the Earth. And everyone has returned safely.' He returned her cold smile. 'Just for your information.'

Dana's smile faded; she was clearly still not convinced.

'What about the first team?' Spanger interjected. 'What do you think happened to them that van Dam doesn't want us to know?'

Coco finished her shuffling. 'They might have had a fall, or just given up, or . . .' She pulled out the ace of spades. 'Oh.'

'Oh?' echoed Spanger.

'This is the death card,' she breathed, giving the bodyguard a long, meaningful look.

Dana snorted contemptuously and pulled her ponytail tighter. 'Good job it wasn't me who picked it then.' She looked out the window. 'What's that? It doesn't look like a cave.'

The Mercedes was stopping in front of an enormous dilapidated house. There was something classical about the façade, which looked like the end of the nineteenth century in style, complete with resplendent turrets and oriels.

The windows were stained glass and would certainly provide a fascinating mixture of colours inside during the day. Despite its shabby condition, the house looked far too magnificent to be haunted.

The remains of what appeared to be a small factory could be seen next it; what was left of the collapsed building suggested it had fallen victim to fire.

Viktor picked up his file and skimmed it to check he had not missed anything about this place, but there was nothing to be found. It concerned itself only with the unknown Anna-Lena, a girl of barely twenty years. One week was enough for a person to die of thirst; it could take maybe three times that to die of hunger – less for a skinny girl. Van Dam was right: there was no time to lose.

A black Black Badge Wraith was parked at an angle in front of the building; judging by the layers of dust, it had been there for rather a long time. The Rolls-Royce, which, according to their dossiers, belonged to Anna-Lena van Dam, was a clear sign that she had been here.

Viktor quickly checked his phone to see if he could find anything about Friedemann online, as Dana's scepticism was proving contagious. This gaunt professor truly was a luminary, though he looked rather different in the photographs – more like a distant relative. *Mind you, these photos are probably ancient*, thought Viktor.

'We're here,' Matthias announced redundantly, before getting out. He had a tablet clutched in his left hand. 'It's up to you now.'

The team climbed out the car. Viktor and Spanger grabbed the backpacks and strapped them on as Dana said, 'Let's go.' She checked her pistol, took out the magazine and pushed the slide back and forth, then secured the trigger and loaded the semi-automatic.

Coco was watching her closely. 'That looked ... well-practised.'

'Gun club,' replied the woman with a grin.

'I'll accompany you as far as the entrance.' Matthias strode towards the door of the building, pulling out a large bunch of keys.

'So the entrance to the cave is in the basement.' Ingo pointed at the Rolls-Royce. 'Why is that still here?'

'Mr van Dam wanted it left in case his daughter managed to find her way out on her own. That way she could just set off straight away or ring for help. It's equipped with a VPN.' Matthias walked up the steps to the door. 'Oh, and don't forget the rifles. They're in the boot.'

Spanger hurried back to the car, removed the parcel shelf and had a look at the G36 automatic rifles, complete with several spare magazines and retractable shoulder supports. 'That's more like it!' He picked one of them up and loaded two magazines. 'We could put these to good use.' He began fiddling with it, looking for the magazine ejector, then pulled on the breech block to no effect. Nothing about the way in which he was handling the weapon gave the impression that he had a clue what he was doing.

Coco and Ingo caught each other's eye, silently agreeing that they wouldn't be taking one. There was no way they'd be able to handle them.

Viktor and Dana were looking at the automatic weapons as if they were souvenirs in a gift shop.

'These are good if you're dealing with terrorists, but they're not going to be much use in a cave system.' Viktor tapped the pistol resting in his shoulder holster. 'These are perfect at short range, though.'

To his surprise, Dana took one of the G36s out of its case. She examined it briefly, swivelled around and adjusted the sight. Then she loaded a full magazine, attached it and checked the safety was on before slinging the rifle over her shoulder. She put two cartridges into the holders on her vest, then still without a word, she turned around and followed Friedemann, Ingo and Coco.

Spanger and Viktor looked on in amazement.

'You can find all sorts of dangerous animals in caves,' she called back over her shoulder. She was fully aware that the two men were looking at her. 'Cave bears, for example.'

Viktor hesitated. No one truly believed this was a kidnapping; rather, that some sort of accident had befallen Anna-Lena. Despite not wishing to come across as paranoid, he nevertheless decided he too would bring one of the automatic weapons with him. He went through the checking and loading process with the same ease as Dana.

'She's right,' he said out loud, before setting off.

Spanger looked even more confused. then began to run, his gait making him look like a clumsy bear. 'Hey, Rentski! Can you show me how to use one of these guns?'

'You're better off not using it at all,' came her spare reply.

The rest of the group laughed. They put on the radio headsets and fastened their helmets, which were all equipped with cameras in special holders that would transmit pictures back to the surface from the cave using a series of signal-boosters. Their backpacks contained all the necessary electronic equipment to operate such a system.

'Can you tell us what sort of magic is going on here?' Coco asked Matthias. Her pendulum had been swinging incessantly. She kept all the other items she intended using for detection in a pouch on her belt. 'I'm getting some very strange energy. Something terrible has happened here.' She came across as far less artificial than she had at the airport or in van Dam's office.

'We can all see the burnt-down shed next to it as well,' Spanger muttered.

'Yes, but you're only looking. I'm listening to the full story.'

'The fire on the woodwork has been there for ever.' Matthias opened the double doors, which were studded with bronze inlay and set in a heavy frame adorned with intricately carved floral patterns. 'This is a very old property; it has belonged to the van Dam family for years. Once the fire destroyed the factory and Mr van Dam's grandfather retired from the board, there's been no use for it. The surrounding woods have been leased to a hunting club,' he added, pushing open the heavy doors. 'You'll need to turn on your helmet lights. There's no electricity down here.'

Using his tablet to create a small pool of light, the chauffeur led the group through the abandoned house.

White sheets had been laid over the furniture and thick cobwebs had formed in the corners, in one of which could be seen the skeletal remains of a dog.

'Hmm, that's not what I'm getting.' Coco pulled out a bottle of fragrant water, which she began to spray around her. 'It hasn't got anything to do with the fire. It's . . . something far worse.'

'Oooooh,' replied Spanger, giggling like a schoolboy.

'Pull yourself together, man,' Friedemann snapped. 'Whatever our talented Ms Fendi is sensing might well be of help to us. It certainly can't hurt to pay attention to the unusual things going on around us.'

The only tracks through the dust and dirt were the lonely footprints made by what Coco identified as a pair of lady's high-heeled shoes, which gave the rest of the group food for thought.

'Tell me, did the first team not come through this house on their way to look for Miss van Dam?' enquired Viktor, ignoring the denial that another group had already been despatched. 'I can't see anything here apart from this pair of size 38 high heels.'

'Forgive me, but that's not something I have any knowledge of,' Matthias responded. He opened another door, revealing a steep stone staircase beyond. 'This is as far as I can go.'

He turned on a monitor, where Messenger was open. Van Dam's moustachioed face appeared on the screen: he looked exhausted but excited at the same time. 'Your mission will begin down there,' came his voice tinnily through the speaker. 'Please get a move on – follow the rope! It's the best way down. And make sure to use the signal-boosters for your helmet cameras so I can see what you see.'

'We will, Mr van Dam. No problem,' Friedemann promised.

Coco took a crystal necklace out of the pouch on her

belt and put it on. 'We'll find Anna-Lena: the cosmic forces are with us.'

'Sure they are. And firepower as well.' Spanger was fiddling in vain with his G36, until Dana snatched it out of his hands and armed it for him.

'For a bodyguard you seem to know very little.' She pointed at the safety catch and raised her index finger to show him he needed to make sure he knew what position it was in.

'I wish you every success. Find my daughter.' Van Dam nodded and the signal switched to stand-by mode.

'Let's be off then.' Friedemann pointed to Spanger, indicating he should start, and he began to move, Dana and Friedemann following, with Viktor and Coco next. Ingo took up the rear.

They made their way down, step after worn step. The beams of light cast by the helmet lamps spun around the room, flitting over old brick walls like the confused rays of tiny lighthouses. It smelled neither musty nor stale, only of cold rock and dust. Carved pillars of the same rock held up the vaulted brick ceiling.

Spanger held his G36 at an angle, his index finger twitching nervously on the trigger as if he were already fearing an attack at this stage of the mission. The light from his helmet fell abruptly on a rust-flecked steel cable stretched horizontally across. 'I've found the rope!'

He looked back along it: the end of the steel cable was wrapped several times around a pillar and held in place by a carabiner that looked disconcertingly old.

Spanger turned his head the other way, the light following.

The finger-thick cable passed horizontally through an inwards-opening door and into the darkness beyond. The beam from his helmet was mostly lost in the darkness, only occasionally illuminating the taut, steel cord in the distance when he twisted his head. There were no walls, no floor and no ceiling to be seen on the other side of the door.

'Holy shit—!' Spanger exclaimed in disbelief. 'Come on – you've got to see this!'

One by one, the others arrived at the bottom. They all looked in astonishment at the open door as they shuffled their way slowly towards it. Coco started to lift up her crystal pendant, but Ingo grabbed her hand and pulled it down.

'Now that's what I call a cave.' Friedemann pressed forward and shone his light into the blackness. Like Spanger's, the beam met no resistance other than the rope. He ran his hand over the door frame and smiled, as if he had found something unspeakably valuable and remarkable.

'I can't hear an echo.' Ingo picked up a stone from the floor and threw it into the void. 'Let's see how deep it is.'

They waited for several seconds, but no sound was forthcoming.

'That's . . . not good,' whispered Coco.

'No it's not,' Viktor agreed. The hairs on the back of his neck were standing to attention. 'I've never seen anything like this before. This cave has got to be . . . enormous.' He looked at Friedemann. 'What do you reckon? Have you ever come across anything like this?'

'No. I fully agree with your assessment.' Friedemann peered uncertainly into the blackness beyond.

Dana took a step past the men, clipped a safety carabiner and a low-friction roller onto the old steel rope and slipped into her harness. 'Van Dam told us to follow the rope.' She took a run-up, leaped through the door and went shooting along the steel cable into the darkness.

'Off you go, Spanger, follow her,' Friedemann ordered.

Spanger swore and hooked himself up to the rope. As Friedemann fiddled laboriously with his own climbing harness, struggling to secure the carabiners to the cable, Spanger too jumped and set off after Dana. Meanwhile, ignoring her complaints, Ingo was helping Coco to lash the last of the straps around her body.

Viktor watched Friedemann's awkward attempts to fasten himself in, which he considered rather peculiar; a speleologist of his renown really ought to be able to do that in his sleep. 'Is this the first time you've used this equipment?' he asked.

'Yes. I haven't needed harnesses on any of my other expeditions,' explained the scrawny geologist between curses. 'Not this sort, anyway. I used to be able to do it, Mr Troneg.'

Viktor bent down to help him. His eyes betrayed his doubts about this statement, but all he said was, 'It could happen to anyone, Professor.'

'Then let's go and save the girl. You bring up the rear.' Friedemann chased after Dana and Spanger, closely followed by the parapsychologist and the clairvoyant.

Viktor could hear the whirring of the rollers through the darkness and caught glimpses of the five lances of light as they flew through the gloom. Instead of setting off straight away, he thought to test the fastening of the rope to the column. Although there were five adults hanging from it, the cable appeared to be completely untroubled by the load.

'There's something very off about this,' he said to himself, screwing up his face. A young woman driving a luxury car to an abandoned house, wandering around with high heels on her feet and sliding down a steel cable? In a cave without a floor or ceiling? Not on your life. A search party who had left no trace of their presence? The dossiers they had been given were useless; there was no map and their client had hidden the fact that he had already sent out a team before them.

But orders were orders – and a hundred thousand euros, increasing to one million if they succeeded, was not something to be scoffed at. He could put that to very good use indeed. He was familiar with the G36, although he had hoped to never have to lay eyes on one again, let alone use one. It appeared he could not shake off his old life that easily.

Viktor examined the carved doorframe in the helmet light. An inlaid stone that reminded him a little of fool's gold reflected the beam.

A door to a cave system, he thought. Who would build such nonsense? He closed the door gently until the edge hit the cable, then spotted a rather puzzling door knocker on the inside: a grotesque face was holding a rusty metal ring between its fangs.

What on earth is this? Viktor touched the skull of this fantastical beast and ran his fingers over its rough teeth. He had seen something like this before, at an old job. Scenes appeared in his mind: the rattle of gunfire, burning wind, blood and screaming.

He quickly started to look for something to focus on to stop him from falling back into the past, back into trauma that could never be defeated. *What would it sound like if I were to use the knocker?* His fingers lifted the ring up carefully.

The hairs on the back of his neck began to stand on end again. Through his gloves he could feel an invisible stream of energy flowing through the metal. *Probably not a good idea.*

'Troneg? Where have you got to?' Friedemann's voice was far away but there was no echo at all. 'Everything all right?'

Viktor slowly lowered the heavy ring, causing it to squeak eerily. He had a bad feeling about what would happen if he brought it down with force – he might not have Coco's abilities, but a quiet little voice at the back of his head was warning him of highly unpredictable consequences if he did so.

'Coming. Just wanted to test the anchoring.' Viktor clicked himself on and took himself as far back as the pillar in order to work up as much of a head of steam as possible. He was breathing very deeply. 'Whatever this is, it's not just a cave,' he muttered, before running forward.

He threw himself onto the rope through the door.

At the same time, Spanger's scream could be heard a long way away. 'Shit, no – *no—!*'

A G36 roared and a bright muzzle flash tore through the darkness.

And the light reflected onto rock.

CHAPTER III

Germany, Near Frankfurt

The man who had secretly followed Viktor von Troneg from the arrivals hall and had photographed the team was sitting in the driver's seat of the BMW X5. He had parked his rental car less than a hundred yards from the dilapidated house, outside which stood the black Mercedes people carrier and the ostentatious Rolls-Royce.

The mini laptop was resting on his lap while he looked over at the estate through his binoculars, which were equipped with night vision. No one from the group had reappeared yet; they were either in the house or in the vault beneath it. Frank Sinatra's 'Strangers in the Night' was coming gently through the car speakers, providing a melancholic accompaniment to the scene playing out before him.

New photographs of the group had come in from headquarters via the car's internal Wi-Fi system. It was impossible these days to keep things secret; nothing was difficult to find if you knew where to look. Thanks to the wonder of the internet and its myriad possibilities, it had been easy enough to track down the sextet and trawl through their backgrounds. And there were several things that did not match what they had told van Dam.

'Those little liars.' His mouth twisting in amusement, he read the most recent report about Coco Fendi, whose real name was Beate Schüpfer. Van Dam had been unimpressed by the tragic past of his psychic, which included a disastrous stage show.

Then he typed into the open chat window:

NEW INSTRUCTIONS?

After a brief delay, the reply appeared:

WAIT.

He gave a short growl of irritation and cast his eyes back onto the estate. It looked as if he would be here for a while.

The beam of his helmet lamp was lost in the darkness. Viktor dragged himself along the rope with his hands, the low-friction roller making it a virtually effortless task. Every now and again he knocked off flakes of rust that were coming loose from the wire.

He could see four beams of light in the distance.

A long muzzle flash emanated from the barrel of one of the G36s as it tapped out a staccato rhythm. Then the shooting ended abruptly.

'Spanger? Spanger, what's happening?' Viktor enquired nervously, preparing himself to intervene if necessary.

'Shit, I'm . . .' came Spanger's incoherent reply.

Viktor slid forwards along the cable towards the group, who had assembled on a plateau several yards wide. Stone walls towered above them all around; there was only rock below.

He landed, scattering the empty ammunition cases at his feet. 'What have I missed?'

Coco held the pendulum in her hand; Dana had her rifle in position, while Ingo was shining his light into the dark corridor opening out next to the ledge.

Friedemann had secured himself to the rope with two carabiners; he and Spanger were standing at the edge, their helmet lamps pointing down into the depths below.

'You won't be getting it back,' said the geologist rather spitefully.

'Shit,' was all Spanger could say in response.

Viktor detached himself and moved over to stand with them. 'What's going on?' he repeated. He stole a glance at the ancient twisted-steel cord that was fastened to a rust-brown bolt that ended at the cliff-face.

Spanger sighed. Staring over the edge, he admitted, 'Utter carelessness.'

'Utter stupidity,' Dana said. 'I told him he should have put the safety on, but he didn't. It's gone – he's dropped it.'

'It happened while we were moving, okay?' Spanger grunted. 'It went *click* and the damned thing moved. My finger slipped on the trigger and—'

Friedemann pulled him back from the edge by his shoulders. 'Now you've just got your pistol to protect us with.'

'We'd better get going,' Ingo shouted, shining his lamp into the passage.

'What's to say that our little van Dam hasn't fallen in?' Dana looked at Viktor. 'We'd never find her body. God knows how long the rope would need to be for us to reach the bottom of this cave.'

Coco held her pendulum out towards the dark passageway and gave a meaningful nod. 'No, she's alive – she's down here!'

'Then let's go and look for her.' Ingo stepped forwards.

'Hey, stop – not without me.' Spanger hurried alongside them as if the incident with the G36 had had nothing to do with him.

Coco followed them.

Meanwhile, Friedemann was struggling with his climbing harness, unable to remove the carabiners from the steel rope.

Viktor walked over to him and released the catch. 'Like this, Professor.'

'I know – I know. I'm just out of practice, Mr Troneg. Too much time sitting at a desk. You get rusty.' Friedemann ignored his suspicious look and followed Ingo. 'Come on, then. If our clairvoyant is saying this young lady is still alive, we need to get her out of danger as quickly as possible.'

'The others are in rather a hurry – and they are surprisingly optimistic. Perhaps Ms Fendi and her superpowers have given them a sense of security.' Dana gestured to Viktor to take the lead, but he refused. 'Fine then.' She took a few steps to the side and shone her light down once more over the sprawling ledge. 'Sure you haven't forgotten anything?'

The beam of her lamp fell upon a black military-style boot poking out from behind a shelf of rock. The foot was trembling slightly.

'What's that . . . ?' As quick as a flash, Dana armed the G36. 'Troneg, can you see that?'

'I can see it. Let's have a proper look.' Viktor moved to join her, his own rifle lowered, the cones of light from their helmet lamps illuminating the ground in front of them.

Someone was lying next to an overhang on a narrow ledge with a vertical drop right alongside. Apart from his boots, he was wearing nothing but a pair of plain grey underpants. He had been shot several times – the state of his chest left little hope for his survival. His body was also covered with scratches and open wounds probably caused by the fall, and there was a hunting knife lodged in his right shoulder. His blood had spread out in a pool all around him, with rivulets running across the stone and dripping over the edge into the black depths.

'Holy shit,' exclaimed Dana.

The mortally wounded man stared blindly into the light, his face etched with pain and horror. He groaned and tried to say something, but all he could manage was to spit out red droplets.

'Van Dam, are you seeing this?' Viktor said over the radio.

'Yeah, I can see it.' The voice through his earpiece sounded agitated.

Dana approached cautiously, knelt beside the dying man and examined his wounds. 'There's nothing we can do for him. It was a nine-millimetre, I reckon. Probably a sub-machine gun.'

The injured man relaxed, as if he were ready to finally move into the light. With a clink, a long tool was released from his slackening right hand, which was lying just outside the illuminated area.

'Do you know him, van Dam?' Viktor asked.

Dana was balancing fearlessly on the ledge. She took off the dead man's boots and searched them, but was unable to find anything inside them that might cast any light on the matter. She walked through his blood and lifted up the object that he had been carrying; the light from her helmet revealed it to be a bolt cutter.

'I've never seen him before in my life,' came their client's curt reply.

Dana and Viktor exchanged glances.

'What was he doing with that?' The blonde woman stood up and examined the steel cable more closely in her lamplight. She ran her fingers along it, then pointed to some furrows she could feel: the spot where the blades of the cutter had been attached. 'Trying to remove all contact from the outside world? Why, though?'

'And an armed stranger prevented him from doing so.' Viktor looked around, wondering if perhaps Dana was wrong in her assessment of it being a nine-millimetre and the man had accidentally been on the wrong end of Spanger's volley. 'Or did he take the bolt cutter off someone to stop them from cutting the rope?' His concern for Anna-Lena grew. 'What's going on here?'

'*Could* it be a kidnapping?' Dana pointed to the coiled

strands. 'Working hypothesis: they follow her for a little while, or even lure her down here under some false pretence or other. Then they bag her up, carry her through another exit and cut the cable – making it impossible for anyone to follow them.'

'But who shot this bloke if we're certain he didn't get in the way of Spanger's salvo? And why?'

Dana put her hand over her microphone and gestured to Viktor to do the same. 'From one of the members of the first team van Dam isn't telling us about,' she said quietly. 'For whatever reason. And it was definitely a nine-millimetre.'

Spanger's head appeared in the passageway, dazzling both of them with his light. 'Where have you two got to, then?'

'We're coming,' called Viktor. 'We were just having a look around.'

'Come on.' Mini van Dam wants to be rescued and I want to be above ground.' Spanger disappeared again.

They both moved off.

'Do you not want to tell Friedemann?' Dana guessed.

'No, only once we've found something that leads to a definitive conclusion.'

'That's a bit risky. We've already got at least one armed stranger on the loose down here.'

'Who could be miles away from here by now. And it's not a good idea to scare the shit out of the others for no reason.' Viktor studied her. 'By the way, you've really got a very good eye for ammunition and bullet holes.'

'I told you all: gun club.' Dana swivelled the muzzle

of her G36 to point at Viktor as if he were her prisoner, gesturing at him to walk ahead of her. 'What do you think of Friedemann?'

'Not all that much. But he's our leader.' Viktor sloped off. The soft click behind him indicated that Dana had carefully switched the gun's safety catch. To *live*.

'That makes two of us.'

It didn't take them long to catch up with the rest of the group and slide into place. Ingo and Spanger were at the front, followed by Coco and Friedemann, then Viktor and finally Dana.

The passage they were hurrying through had been carved out by hand, supported in some places by brick or concrete with rusty iron wires protruding from where the material had been chipped off. The reinforced concrete looked as if the expansion had been undertaken at the end of the nineteenth century – at the earliest.

'This won't have been a mine.' Viktor occasionally stooped to place a signal-booster on the ground, checking each to ensure its diodes were blinking obediently and that he could still hear van Dam. 'Any ideas, Professor?'

'It's not built on any sort of mining structure, not even a mediaeval one. I don't even know what you'd be able to mine here anyway. I'm guessing it used to be some sort of hiding place for smugglers,' Friedemann explained. 'Or perhaps an attempt at a home-made bunker system in the event of Germany being overrun during a war – a precursor to the survivalist movement, if you will.'

Their march was taking them ever deeper into the system. They occasionally came across forks in the tunnel, where they left it up to Coco to decide which path they should take. All the while there were no clear signs or marks on the wall, they were happy to follow the medium's expertise.

'I'm receiving Anna-Lena's signal loud and clear,' she whispered, running forward purposefully, clutching her pendulum in an outstretched hand. 'She's still alive. Yes, I can definitely sense it.'

Ingo threw her the occasional sceptical glance, but she ignored him and he stayed silent. He didn't have the heart to crush her spirits.

Viktor could not help but notice when Friedemann briefly switched off his helmet camera and furtively pulled out his worn notebook from under his Kevlar vest. He was about to start leafing through it when Ingo suddenly stopped in his tracks. Friedemann hastily put it back. 'What is it?'

'Just a sec. I need to get a few things out of my rucksack.' The parapsychologist moved towards Viktor, rummaged around in his backpack and pulled out a tablet and what looked like some gauges. He connected a few wires, then plugged them into the tablet in order. 'This way I can read the results in real time.' With the press of a button he turned on the entire contraption. 'Just in case we need a bit of science.' He studied the display closely.

Spanger watched him, holding his pistol in his right hand. 'What are you measuring?'

'Spanger, keep moving forward,' Dana was hissing when a loud crash erupted, like a heavy door being slammed, or maybe something ramming into a steel bulkhead. The threatening rumble that rolled through the passage and echoed all around them was closely followed by a strong breeze.

Dana immediately dropped to one knee and spun around, ready to fire, while Viktor readied his own G36.

The gauges emitted a series of warning beeps, then fell silent a few seconds later. Ingo stared at the display, babbling something about 'an anomaly' and 'physically impossible', neither of which statements Viktor liked one little bit. It was a fact that 'impossibilities' always spelled trouble. A great deal of trouble.

'A rockslide?' Spanger's face was creased in puzzlement.

'No, it sounded more like . . . a door,' said Friedemann in alarm. 'Or like the sort of large gate you'd find at the entrance to a city. Most unusual.'

'Unusual indeed,' added Ingo distractedly, his gaze still fixed on his readouts.

'There,' whispered Coco. 'Look at that!' She looked at her hand in amazement: the pendulum was floating horizontally in the air, pulling against the chain in an apparent attempt to drag the woman further along the passage.

'How are you doing that?' Ingo lowered his voice so only she could hear him and added, 'Is this some new trick of yours?'

Coco shook her head, her eyes wide with wonder and amazement, as if this were the first time she had truly believed that she actually had clairvoyant abilities.

Friedemann gave a satisfied smile. One hand was resting on the Kevlar vest with his notebook underneath. 'We're spot on,' he whispered delightedly. 'Onwards!'

*

Walter van Dam sat in front of a triptych of monitors, looking over the various helmet-camera feeds. The booming crash that sounded as if someone were banging down the gates of the underworld had made him sit up and take notice.

'Professor Friedemann, what was that?' he asked anxiously. 'What's going on down there?'

'We don't know yet,' he replied, his voice distorted, 'but we've picked up a clear trace of your daughter, thanks to Ms Fendi.'

'If that was a gate or something,' Spanger called out from the background, 'it must be enormous. Why on earth would there be something like that down here?'

'Ingo, have you seen this? The pendulum! It's standing . . . horizontally!' Coco was wittering away, still acting as if this were the first time her gift had ever actually worked.

Van Dam poured himself a drink. 'Well, get on with it then,' he demanded. 'Don't just stand there. Find my daughter.'

'We're going, we're going,' announced Viktor.

'Good – now hurry up.' Van Dam sounded anything but reassured.

Viktor was at the front, his rifle locked and loaded, while Dana stalked along beside him, their helmet lamps lurching from side to side. They could not see anything dangerous in the passageway and the commotion surrounding the loud rumbling had abated.

But they had not forgotten about it.

Ingo, Coco and Friedemann followed, with Spanger

bringing up the rear. The doctor was carrying his gauges, occasionally stealing a quick glance at them. The pace of the group had increased as they trudged along in silence, the only sounds coming from the stamping of their boots and the jingling of Ingo's equipment.

'You're a free-climber then?' Viktor muttered to Dana, who was advancing in the manner of a well-trained soldier. Catching a glimpse of her beside him, he was struck by an image from a very long time ago – and it was at that moment that he remembered where they had met before. 'And a martial arts expert to boot. And a gun-club member. What kind of gun club? It must have been where you—?'

'Not the time,' she growled without looking at him.

'On the contrary.'

She looked at him closely. 'What's with all the questions?'

'As I said, I've seen you before somewhere.' Viktor returned her gaze. 'In Darfur. A report on military reconnaissance that had nothing whatsoever to do with free-climbing. Tell me I'm wrong.'

Dana narrowed her eyes. 'What were you doing in Darfur?'

'I didn't say I was there.'

'But you had access to reports – so you're not just a free-climber either, then, are you?' Dana did not like where this conversation was heading. 'I've got a twin sister who's a mercenary. Not that we get confused for each other much, though.'

Viktor was not prepared to be shaken off that easily. 'I don't know what kind of game you're—'

They both stopped abruptly, their faces wide with amazement at the scene before them.

'What it is?' Friedemann asked from behind them.

'Stop! I'll get some more light.' Viktor removed a flare from his belt, lit it and threw it into the enormous chamber opening out in front of them at the end of the passage. 'I want to have a better look before we go in.'

Dana hurled a second from behind him.

A barren, cavernous room with markings scrawled all over the walls was illuminated in deep red by the hissing, smoking light emanating from the flares. All manner of inscriptions, scribbled notes, arrows, signs and scratched messages could just about be made out, as well as broken pieces of iron and the destroyed remnants of at least one skeleton.

Viktor could see a dead man on the ground. In contrast to the man on the ledge earlier, he was wearing camouflage gear and armour and had a sub-machine gun lying next to him.

Behind him stood five doors embedded into the rock face. They were made of wood and stone, with both old and new markings alike etched onto them. The three doors in the middle had door knockers in the shape of a ring, the second one of which was broken. The two outermost doors were equipped with large box locks. A thickly drawn question mark could be seen on each of the first three doors; the fourth door had an X on it and the last bore an exclamation mark. They were all painted on with red lipstick, and when Viktor touched one of the symbols, he found the lines were fresh and still a little moist.

'What's all *this*?' Spanger exclaimed in disbelief. '*Doors?*'

'Looks like it,' replied Viktor. 'So what's the plan, Professor?'

'We should probably ask our medium.' Friedemann joined them at the front. 'It's beautiful, isn't it? They really are fine specimens.' His gaze drifted to the door in the centre, the one which bore a red question mark. 'That's where the vandals were holing up.' He pointed to the door on the left. 'What a pity the ring has been destroyed – it can't be used any more.'

Dana and Viktor exchanged glances once more. The fact that a geologist was looking at doors as if he had just discovered an extra-terrestrial stalagmite seemed more than a little peculiar to them.

'Doors? In a cave?' Ingo squeezed his way between them into the entrance and was babbling away as if the dead man were not there at all. 'How fantastic! A mystery – I love mysteries. Let's have a closer look.'

'Definitely,' said Coco, exhilaration filling her voice, holding the chain with the energised pendulum firmly between her fingers. 'Anna-Lena is very close by!' She took a step inside the chamber.

Ingo held tightly to her harness.

Only then did Coco spot the dead man with his torn throat. She uttered a low cry. 'By the spirits of the beyond!' She almost let go of the chain. 'Why didn't any of you warn me?' She could not take her eyes off the corpse. Her enthusiasm for their task and this place was fading more and more with every heartbeat. 'I . . . I think I'd rather go back up.'

The flares suddenly rose into the air, along with everything else in the chamber. The sextet looked on in silence: for reasons beyond them all, it looked like gravity had suddenly stopped. Ingo's equipment once again began to emit loud warning sounds.

A young woman entered the foreground, floating up from behind the upside-down armoured corpse; she had apparently been lying against the wall in the man's shadow. Her long red hair enveloped her like a gently blazing flame; her nose piercing and a single earring sparkled in the red glow. She was wearing a badly torn ball gown and high-heeled shoes. Her eyes were closed and her arms and legs were relaxed as if she were underwater.

'There,' Dana shouted, 'that's her – Anna-Lena!'

'Should we go in and get her?' Viktor looked at Friedemann. 'What do you think, Professor?'

The flares, corpse, Anna-Lena and everything else fell back to the ground.

'What ... what was that?' Viktor turned to face the parapsychologist in amazement.

'Not ghosts, that's for sure.' Ingo swiped the display of his tablet. 'That was a—'

Friedemann interrupted him. 'Well, it's stopped now, so we can go and investigate,' he announced, as if this were the sort of thing he encountered all the time on his field trips. 'If your little gadgets pick up anything dangerous again, let us know, Doctor. Let's go and get Miss van Dam out of there.'

The group advanced slowly, plunging into the flickering red light and smoke cast by the flares. Friedemann instructed Viktor and Dana to tend to the young woman lying on the ground next to the dead body; her limbs were somewhat contorted after the fall. 'Doctor, keep an eye on everything else. Make a record of what we've found here. *Everything*. I want to have a look around in peace.'

'Really? Why?' Spanger took a step back towards the passage.

'Because it's all rather exciting.' The professor sidled up next to Dana and Viktor as they were examining Anna-Lena. Looking at Spanger, he muttered, 'You wouldn't understand anyway.'

'Nothing looks to be broken at first glance, nor are there any external injuries,' Dana announced as she lifted the young woman's eyelids and shone a light into her eyes. 'Pulse normal, but no pupil reaction.'

'God, Anna-Lena!' They could hear van Dam's relieved voice. 'Come on, get up – now!'

'Just a moment. We've got to make sure she's physically capable of surviving the journey back,' Dana replied resolutely as she carried on checking the girl over.

Ingo turned off his gauges and pulled out a camera. 'I've never seen anything like this before – not during any of my investigations! Gravity reversal? That's impossible – well, usually.' He began to take endless photographs of the doors, the inscriptions and the symbols. 'You can clearly see magical formulae in the graffiti – some look as if they're hundreds of years old,' he continued enthusiastically. 'Look: there's cuneiform, hieroglyphics, ancient Greek, Persian . . .' He could hardly contain his excitement. 'It's quite possible that our little anomaly had something to do with these.'

Viktor saw Friedemann pulling out his notebook and caught a glimpse of his first entry: *Arc Project // Arkus // Arcus.*

The professor started leafing through it, comparing the markings on the pages with the inscriptions on the doors. Some of them matched.

'I'm here if anyone needs me.' Spanger remained near the entrance, strapped into his harness.

Viktor decided to confront Friedemann about his book later, instead choosing to have a look around. 'Who the hell would build doors in a place like this?'

'What I find far more impressive is their condition and distinctiveness,' Ingo added happily. 'These doors are all from different centuries. The symbols on them . . . are . . . I mean, some of them, well, I don't even know what they're supposed to be. I'm not talking about all the scribbling that's been added later, but what the creators of these doors actually inscribed themselves.'

Spanger had changed his mind. He walked over to the armoured dead man, took his gun from him and began to search his body. 'Sub-machine gun. H&K, MP5, nine millimetre,' he shouted over to the group, adding, 'See? I'm not completely useless.'

'You could learn that just by playing a first-person shooter.' Dana looked at Viktor and raised her eyebrows in triumph. It was this weapon that had most likely done for Underpants Man. The boots belonging to the two dead men were identical in design and tread pattern.

'But he's got nothing on him – no badges or papers or anything. Looks like he could be part of some sort of special unit.' Spanger bent down to examine the wound on the man's neck more carefully. 'Throat slit.' He pointed to the empty sheath. 'And his knife's missing.'

'These your people, van Dam?' radioed Dana after finishing her examination of the unconscious woman.

'I'll tell you again, I haven't sent out another team. Now bring me back my little girl,' he ordered, putting down his glass. 'Tell me, Mr Troneg, have you made sure to put all the boosters down? The picture has suddenly gone all fuzzy and I can barely hear you at all.'

'I have, Mr van Dam,' Viktor replied.

'That sort of thing can be triggered by magnetic fields and radiation,' said Ingo, who was standing next to his equipment and looking at the display on his tablet. 'Oh my God – my devices are going haywire again. I can see . . . measurable differences in the magnetic field and so forth. The gravitational pull is slowly decreasing. A little more and we'll start to feel it.'

'Or it could be a jammer,' said Dana. 'Or someone's found one of our boosters and switched it off. We need to get a move-on. Van Dam, your daughter is in a good enough state for us to bring her out.' She looked at Viktor. 'You can carry her.'

Viktor handed his rucksack to Coco, who in turn handed it to Ingo, and picked up the young woman. He could not believe how light she was – surely no more than seven and a half stone. He laid her gently over his shoulder.

'Pack up your stuff, Doctor,' Friedemann ordered. 'We're leaving.'

Coco looked at her golden pendulum, which was

showing no inclination towards the younger van Dam but was instead pointing at the doors. 'That's . . . odd.'

'Your pendulum must be wrong,' said Ingo, giving her a look to suggest the show was over before he turned back to his gauges and stuffed them into his backpack.

'It can't be.' Coco looked at the doors. 'There are more secrets through there.' She looked at the corpse and shuddered. 'Probably for the best that we're not going to be the ones to investigate them.' She put her pendulum away.

'Right, let's go.' Friedemann shooed Spanger forwards with a wave of his hand. 'We've found what we were looking for.' He gave the doors a curious look.

Viktor thought it was almost as if he had really been there for them and not for the young woman.

The group made their way back through the passages by the light of their helmet lamps. The place was silent, making it feel all the more depressing.

Where are you going? said a voice that appeared to be inside Coco's head. *Stay a while longer.*

She slowed down, prompting Ingo to give her a nudge. She began to shiver all over. 'Can you hear that too?'

He can't hear me. I thought I was talking to you. You're rather special, you know, said the sombre voice. *What if I were to kill the others? Would you stay then?*

Coco felt her throat tightening. 'No,' she whispered.

'No?' Ingo looked at her, confused.

We could have ever so much fun, Beate. That is your name, after all. Or would you rather I called you Coco?

She didn't know what she could say that the unknown voice would not consider as a challenge.

Suddenly her mind was flooded with images: a dog-like beast pouncing on and slaughtering the group; an armed unit that wanted to attack and kill them; a monster made of smoke stabbing them with burning blades. A mounted unit riding into a mediaeval battle, followed by drones chasing their group through an unknown city, and finally a man in an American Second World War uniform with his gun raised, aiming the barrel at her face – and pulling the trigger.

Coco's mouth opened into a scream – and everything around her disappeared.

She found herself standing back in front of the five doors.

They were opening and closing, opening and closing, opening and closing, incessantly. They roared and rattled, creating a loud rumble that shook the walls. Scree and stones tumbled down, crashing onto the ground. Blood poured out of the first door, hissing with steam, while liquid fire rushed out of another, with the one next to it producing some sort of acid that mixed with the scattered pieces of bone that came coursing out of the door alongside it; from the final door came piles of putrid entrails. The hellish conglomeration seized Coco and dragged her below the surface.

The decaying corpses of Ingo, Friedemann, Spanger, Viktor and Dana danced around her, their clawed hands striking her. Their shrill, screeching laughter shook her to her core.

'We're dying in this cave,' they sang. 'We're dying! And you didn't warn us – that's why we're going to kill you!

We're going to kill you!' The five of them then threw themselves onto the clairvoyant and opened their jaws as wide as possible.

Coco began to burn, her body dissolved by the acid as she suffocated, while the drifting bones crushed her. As the group feasted upon her flesh and tore her to pieces, she somehow found the strength to utter the loud cry of anguish that had been stuck in her lungs.

The illusion was shattered immediately.

Panting, she stumbled through the passage in front of Ingo, barely able to stay upright on her trembling legs. Fear constricted her heart as the beams from the helmet lights danced in front of her eyes in double vision.

'Everything all right?' Ingo had spotted that something was amiss. 'What's wrong? Pins and needles?'

Coco didn't dare to speak. Horror had paralysed her voice. She was certain that death would fall upon her the moment she made a peep. How was she suddenly able to see these visions? Should she ever manage to escape from this place, she would never step foot in it again.

'Well, that was easy.' Spanger felt heroic when he held the sub-machine gun, just as he had always wanted – maybe not exactly like Tony Stark, but like a man who had done a good deed. It did not concern him in the slightest that their task had been so easy, or that they had found a dead body. If they should happen to stumble upon any enemies, he was ready: ready to pull the trigger and become even more of a hero. 'What was it killed the other bloke?'

'Let's hope we don't have to find out.' Dana was keeping a close eye on their surroundings. The cones of light rendered them easy targets, which was making her rather uneasy. A decent marksman would simply have to aim just beneath the light and it would all be over.

'Oh, I'm sure we can handle it.' Spanger fiddled with the safety catch. 'We're pros.'

'You certainly are,' remarked Friedemann.

'Didn't we say you were going to be a bit nicer to me?'

'Calm down,' Viktor urged them. 'Even if every man and his dog can see us, that doesn't mean we have make a racket the entire way back.'

His reminder had the desired effect: silence descended upon the team.

Ingo kept looking at the recordings from his measurements, trusting that they were all correct. What other experiments could he do in the hall with the doors? Where did the volatile gravity come from? The dead body made him uneasy, but scientific curiosity pushed those doubts to one side. He had already made up his mind that with another, more appropriate team and van Dam's permission, he would return and astonish mankind with what he had discovered.

Ingo didn't know he wasn't the only one with that idea, though.

'Don't dawdle,' Dana hissed at him. 'You can marvel over your findings once we've reached the surface.'

After a short while they arrived back at the platform.

'Good,' came Friedemann's voice. 'We're nearly there – now we just need to cross.'

They secured the helpless Anna-Lena to the rusty cable and began to make their way back through the darkness, moving forwards in silence until they could see the entrance in the glow of their helmet lamps. One after the other, they arrived in the basement.

As easy as their task had been, and as pleased as he was to have found the missing woman so quickly, Viktor thought their mission had been entirely surreal. If you ignored the abnormalities such as the sudden changes of gravity and the two dead bodies, it had been a walk in the park. It wasn't that he had been looking forward to a shoot-out, but he thought it curious that they hadn't encountered a single serious problem. A bunch of Boy Scouts could have saved the young woman, as indeed could the first military unit who had been sent out. Or was this all some kind of a test?

Viktor carried the unconscious woman up the stone steps and onto the ground floor of the villa, where the chauffeur was waiting for them. They assumed van Dam had informed Matthias of their return.

'I've already re-configured the seating in the car,' Matthias explained, adjusting his cap. 'We can get going straight away.' They hurried through the rooms towards the exit. The chauffeur handed Spanger the spare key for the Rolls-Royce. 'I don't suppose you'd be able to take this back?'

'You're kidding!' Spanger grinned. This was the first time he had ever been allowed to drive a luxury car like this.

'Don't you want to call an ambulance?' Dana said over the radio to her employer. 'I don't know whether she's got any internal injuries tha—'

'No publicity,' van Dam interrupted. 'I've arranged for

a team of specialists to come to my house and examine my daughter thoroughly. Then we can decide what to do next.'

When they reached the exit, Coco wanted to weep with happiness. The black Mercedes was parked with its side door open; as Matthias had said, the seats had been joined together to create a large flat surface in the middle.

'Thank you all once again,' said van Dam through their earpieces. 'You will of course each receive your rewards, as promised. Ms Rentski and Mr von Troneg, you'll go with Matthias, while the rest of you can take the Rolls.'

Not a test, then, Viktor thought with a shrug, his mood improving. He laid Anna-Lena onto the seats and shuffled back to allow Matthias to fasten her seatbelt. Relief suddenly washed over him. 'Good job we managed to find her so quickly.' Saving a human life was a wonderful feeling. He could not resist shaking hands with everyone in the group and congratulating them on a job well done. 'I think you'll find we've done rather well here.'

That same joy was clear onto the faces of his comrades too.

'Easy money, that.' Spanger said callously as he fiddled with the key to the Rolls-Royce. 'A million, right? All for just under three hours' work.'

Coco was standing next to Ingo, who was busy checking the measurements on his displays. 'Yes, but what's the explanation for all this?' She felt liberated; the tremor in her hands had abated.

'There isn't one.' Ingo looked excited. 'Mr van Dam, may

I go back down and have a look around? These physical phenomena are crying out for proper, in-depth research.'

'No way. Nothing can make me go back down that hole again,' Coco said quickly, putting down the equipment. 'It's not a good aura at all. Whoever it was who built that place and those doors – they did *not* have good intentions.' She left out telling them about the voice, her vision and her terror.

'I'd like to join Doctor Theobald,' Friedemann interjected. 'These geological structures are quite unique. As my colleague has said, they absolutely *must* be explored further.'

'Unfortunately, I cannot allow that,' replied their client. 'Let's all just be happy that you've returned to the surface unscathed.'

Dana had also detached herself from the harness. She was trying not to catch Viktor's eye, so as not to jog his memory any more. 'We will need to talk to you about a few things once we're back at your house, Mr van Dam,' she said. 'About what we saw down there.'

'That can be dealt with once you're back with me,' he said. 'What goes on in the caves, stays in the caves. That would be my suggestion. Leave everything else to me and don't allow yourselves to be burdened by it.'

Friedemann glanced back through the front door. Who would try to stop him if he went back down? The chauffeur? He could easily bribe the other five to either go with him or leave him alone. With a bit of cunning he was sure he could convince Theobald to make a second descent. By the time van Dam had found another team to get them back out, he could have explored everything he wanted to. He *had* to. He ventured a first, discreet step back towards the verandah.

'What do you mean by that?' Spanger scratched his back. 'What we saw down there? Do you mean the doors?'

'Mr van Dam!' Matthias picked up his tablet nervously. 'I . . . I don't think this is your daughter.'

The group turned to face the chauffeur, who was sitting next to the supine woman.

'What nonsense is this?' snapped the businessman.

'Her eyes, Mr van Dam.' Matthias turned the tablet around and filmed the sleeping woman with its camera. He carefully opened her eyelids with his thumb and forefinger. 'Can you see that?'

The team all huddled around the car.

'I told you so,' muttered Coco. 'The pendulum – it knew we hadn't found Anna-Lena.' The consequences of this realisation made her heart sink like a stone. They would have to go back.

'Ridiculous,' Ingo whispered to her.

'What about her eyes?' Dana enquired.

'They're blue,' replied Matthias, his face growing pale. 'But Miss van Dam's eyes are . . .'

'Green. She's got green eyes.' Van Dam sounded both startled and anxious at the same time. 'Have you checked she's not wearing contacts?'

'Yes. No lenses.' The chauffeur was continuing to film the girl. 'Even if everything else is identical, Mr van Dam – her figure, her hair, even her jewellery – her eyes tell a different story.'

'Is there anything that could have changed her eye colour?' Spanger threw the keys to the Rolls in the air and caught them. 'Bright light or something?'

'Don't talk rubbish,' Friedemann scolded him. 'You can't change eye colour unless you tattoo the vitreous, but in any case, they wouldn't look like this.' He pushed his way forwards and pulled up the sleeping woman's eyelids to double-check. 'See this, Matthias?'

The chauffeur leaned forwards and swore, then checked the other eye himself. 'Green – they're green again! But I swear they were blue before.'

'This is insane.' Dana looked around at her colleagues.

'Beyond insane.' Coco leaned against Ingo, feeling like she needed human warmth and closeness to ease the ominous feeling inside her. Someone she trusted.

'There's only one thing for it.' Van Dam's voice over the radio sounded agitated. 'You'll have to go back down and look for her. Your job is not complete. I need to know for certain.'

'What are we going to do with … this person?' Dana looked at the sleeping woman. It could still be van Dam's daughter, or someone else altogether.

'Matthias will bring her to me,' the businessman decided. 'I'll have her examined and looked after. In the meantime please find Anna-Lena – *my* Anna-Lena, not this copy or whatever she is.'

'You could always try a DNA test.' Viktor recognised the feeling that had crept up on him. In a matter of seconds his feeling of safety had turned into the very opposite. 'It could still be that this is your daughter,' he pointed out.

'Who knows what happened to her in those caves? There were all sorts of strange things going on down there.'

But Matthias was already reaching out to reclaim the key from Spanger. 'Understood, Mr van Dam. I'll bring the woman to you in the Rolls. The Mercedes will have to stay here because it's got the internet connection.'

'I've got a question.' Spanger handed him the key. 'We will get a million for this one? *Another* million, that is? I mean, technically, we've already got your daughter so—'

'Come on, let's go,' the professor interrupted. 'You're an embarrassment to even ask that.' Friedemann was secretly cheering to himself. He now had a legitimate excuse to descend into the cave again.

'Quite right,' Dana confirmed, putting her own gear back on.

'I don't want to go back down there.' Coco looked at Ingo. 'I'm serious. There's something waiting for us.'

'No, no, it's just a bit of wonky physics.' He patted his instruments. 'And we'll find the real missing girl in no time at all. Just like before. Your pendulum seems to know where she is.'

Coco couldn't detect any mockery in his voice. 'But there's still the small matter of the dead man with his throat torn out. And whoever it was who killed him.' She climbed into her harness as if in slow motion. She still couldn't bring herself to talk about that voice, or her vision. 'It's waiting for us.'

'Nothing's going to happen to us.' Ingo too was looking forward to another opportunity to take some measurements. 'I'm absolutely certain of it. We've just got to be careful, that's all.'

'Departure, take two.' Friedemann sounded like he was in a good mood. 'We've already been successful once. Now let's go and rescue the real Anna-Lena van Dam. Green eyes, everyone: make sure you remember that.'

Viktor and Dana, communicating with their eyes, checked their weapons. They had still not told anyone about the half-naked dying man with the bolt cutter and bullet wounds they had discovered and they wouldn't, not yet, so as not to put a downer on proceedings.

The group set off again immediately, passing through the estate and back into the cellar, readying themselves to slide along the steel cable to the platform once more.

Coco was close to tears.

The unknown man watched the entire scene outside the villa in peace, reporting every detail to headquarters, along with photographs. He had even been able to follow about half of their conversation by lip-reading.

The group surrounding the professor disappeared back into the house; the chauffeur once again opened the side door of the people carrier and lifted the comatose doppel-gänger, carried her over to the Rolls-Royce and laid her down on the back seat.

This time, along with acknowledgement of receipt of his report, he received an order:

IMMEDIATE ELIMINATION OF ALL PARTICIPANTS.
EVEN THE UNCONSCIOUS ONE.

The man closed his laptop and placed it on the passenger seat. He started the BMW and drove along the approach road to the abandoned house, then intentionally stalled. He wanted his arrival noticed.

The chauffeur promptly stepped back from the Rolls and closed the door. He looked at the BMW curiously as it rolled across the fine gravel with a soft crunch.

The unknown man took out a slim boning knife from the glove box. The price tag was still on it – he had bought it after he'd arrived, knowing he would have no chance of getting his own weapons through airport security. With a practised movement he slid it inside his sleeve, then got out of the car and walked towards the dilapidated mansion.

'This is private property,' Matthias called out to him, pointing back down the drive. 'You need to leave immediately.'

'Please excuse me. I've just had a technology omni-fuck-up. First my satnav sent me the wrong way and now my rental car has given out on me. It's a good job there's someone here.' The man approached, smiling. 'I don't suppose you could lend me your phone so I can call for breakdown assistance?'

'Ah, understood.' Matthias sighed and briefly looked over at the Rolls to check the woman, but she was still unconscious. Then he removed a packet of cigarettes from his dark blue uniform. 'What's up with your car? Might be quicker if I just help you.' He lit a cigarette and proffered the pack to him. 'I know what I'm doing.'

The man took a step closer. 'I'm afraid with this kind you need a diagnostic computer to make any headway. The curse of the modern world.' He refused the cigarette. 'Bit of an odd set-up for such a deserted place. Nothing illegal, I'm sure?' He grinned to show Matthias he was joking.

'We're in the process of selling the house. Someone's having a viewing.'

'Luckily for me.'

'You could say that.' Matthias felt for his phone inside his pocket. 'Here, go ahead. But I can still try to have a look under the bonnet for you.'

'By all means.' The man's movements suddenly became clumsy as he took the phone. It slipped out of his fingers and landed on the gravel. 'Oh – forgive me! I'm so sorry. I hope your phone's not broken.'

Matthias didn't allow his irritation to show, instead flicking away his half-finished cigarette and bending to pick up the phone.

The man drew the knife out of his sleeve and held it over the chauffeur's exposed neck.

Matthias saw his attacker's shadow with a blade in his hand and quickly turned, his arm raised to defend himself.

Contrary to what Coco had feared, the group travelled the same way through the labyrinth without incident, arriving unmolested at the cavernous chamber with the five doors. Her pulse was racing and she was sweating with fear.

Dana and Viktor once again lit two flares to give them some light, then began to discuss the plan with Friedemann.

'I'm an idiot. I should have brought another G36 with me.' Spanger looked at the sub-machine gun next to the dead man. 'Now I've got to make do with this child's toy.'

Ingo had unpacked his instruments again and was paying close attention to their displays. 'There it is again,' he said with fascination. 'The first tiny deviations.'

Coco walked slowly past the doors, the golden pendulum in her hand. She felt sick. This whole place was dripping with danger. She would not be staying a second longer than necessary, that was for sure. With each passing moment she expected to hear the voice, to see the visions – to be exposed to that same mental torture again.

And that was not forgetting Anna-Lena's doppelgänger with the wrong eyes. Who knew what sort of being they had brought to the surface?

'It's getting stronger,' she announced with simultaneous awe and anxiety. She could hardly stand it; her skin was itchy and prickly. 'You can do the rest yourselves. I've got to get out of this godforsaken hole!'

'Sorry?' Friedemann gave her a look of consternation. 'And how exactly do you propose to do that?' He was holding his notebook in his hand again, consulting it from time to time as he examined the door frames.

'Ms Fendi,' came van Dam's voice in her ear, 'only you can hear me now. I beg you, please stay with the group. I have confidence in your powers. It may well be that the team will find itself in a situation where only your abilities can help them! You saw what happened to the torches before.'

Coco placed her hand over the microphone so that the only sound was the one transmitted through the helmet speakers. 'There's a dead man down here, Mr van Dam. A dead man and something that . . . that wants to kill us. That was not part of the agreement.'

'I'll pay you two hundred thousand euros extra,' he replied. 'The others are watching you, Ms Fendi.'

Coco cleared her throat. 'Mr van Dam, I . . .'

'Nothing's going to happen to you. Think about my daughter, please!'

His heartbroken appeal softened her slightly and she was about to agree when she remembered the cruel voice in the passage. 'You don't understand – you couldn't, not without feeling what I felt.'

'I'm begging you. Without you, my daughter doesn't stand a chance!'

Her sense of duty calmed her fears and drowned out the voices imploring her to turn back. 'All right. I will.' She turned to face the doors so as not to have to look at the man's remains. 'I'll take you at your word, Mr van Dam.'

'Right, we're all here. What are you picking up, Ms Fendi?' Viktor turned to look at the medium. 'Where's our missing girl?'

Coco paused in front of the fourth door, the one bearing the red cross marked in lipstick. The pendulum was standing out from the chain, facing forwards like a pointer. 'Behind this one.' She placed a hand on the enormous handle and tried to pull it, but nothing happened. Shaking didn't help either, nor did leaning on it with all her strength. She took a deep breath. 'By the grandfathers of the four elements . . .' she said, starting an incantation.

'Slow down,' called out Spanger in alarm. 'Who knows what's behind—?'

'*She's*. Behind. It!' Coco's face bore a strange expression.

'By the grandfathers of the four elements . . .' she began again, her voice drifting away into a quiet invocation.

Friedemann put his notebook away, this time stuffing it into a trouser pocket in order to retrieve it more quickly next time. 'No. She's not.' He walked purposefully towards the door on the far left, which also had its knocker intact. 'We'll find her here. There's an arrow on the ground I recognise—'

'Hang on.' Spanger was shining his light at a glimmering spot on the floor that was reflecting the light. 'There: a diamond earring!' The piece of jewellery was lying in front of the furthest door, which had a heavy mediaeval drawbar and a thick box lock. It was this door that had the exclamation mark painted on it. 'Our little van Dam was wearing a pair just like this in the photo in our files.' He looked from Friedemann to Coco and back again. 'What if you're both wrong and she's behind this one?'

Walter van Dam sat enthralled in front of the triptych of monitors, watching what was happening underground with increasing agitation.

Then he noticed that one of the split screens on the right-hand display was black; he frowned with concern. This was not linked to one of the team's helmet cameras, but rather to Matthias' tablet.

He picked up his phone and called his chauffeur, who was supposed to be on his way with Anna-Lena's double.

It rang.

And rang.

And rang.

The fact that Matthias was not answering made him nervous. He poured himself another drink. His nerves shot to pieces by this rollercoaster ride, he had long since replaced water with whisky. Earlier, when they'd announced they'd found Anna-Lena, he had been so happy, but now his anxiety was increasing with every breath. 'Where is my daughter?' he asked again.

'We need to clarify what's going on first, Mr van Dam,' said Viktor. His words were all distorted.

'Unfortunately, there are three possibilities for where your Anna-Lena might be,' radioed Friedemann, who sounded no less distorted than Viktor. The transmission from the cave system must be more or less at its limit. 'Any decision we make could be the wrong one – or the right one.'

'What about the other two?' Van Dam rubbed his moustache frantically.

'We'll check those once we've ruled out the others,' said the professor.

'Show me these doors, Mr von Troneg,' van Dam asked. He would have liked to send Matthias to check the Wi-Fi connection and the Mercedes' built-in modem.

Viktor filmed the doors, which van Dam enlarged on the second screen, and explained the three clues to him. 'Have you seen this before?' he asked. The connection was becoming worse with every word he spoke. 'Anything that could help us?'

Van Dam did not answer but clicked and zoomed in on the feed, took snapshots of all the details and fanned them out on the third monitor to get a better overview.

Then he stared closely at the symbols.

Looking at them caused vivid memories to flood into his mind: memories he would have sooner never returned to. He could still recall his mother's words – and what she had begged of him in her declining years. He had never had the opportunity to carry out her final wishes, and after her death – until this moment – he had all but forgotten about them. He had added Theobald to the group without really believing that his parapsychological knowledge would ever be required – like a parachute you hoped never to have to use. It had come from just a feeling, nothing more, one whose origins lay in the past, indefinable, yet compelling.

'Van Dam?' Viktor's voice was now almost entirely drowned out by a loud humming noise.

Then van Dam heard him say, 'Professor, the signal's gone. He can't hear me any more. What shall we do? Which door do you think we should take?'

Van Dam rose unsteadily and hurried to his shelves. He searched through the books until he finally found the old tome he was looking for, along with the collection of loose papers that had belonged to his grandfather. He removed it and returned to his desk, then put it down and opened it.

Dozens of old drawings of doors were depicted on the fragile, stained pages, and they all had dates and cryptic markings drawn alongside them. He flicked through the sheaf until he found exactly the five doors he had seen on the third screen. The year '1921' was written next to it.

'It cannot be!' he exclaimed.

'Mr van Dam? What did you say?' he could hear Viktor asking. 'If there's anything you know that could help us, please tell us. We need to decide which door to go through first to find your daughter. We can't agree. Do you understand? Any clue you could give us will allow us to find your daughter faster.'

'One moment, Mr von Troneg.' He wanted to make absolutely certain. In a matter of seconds he had compared the symbols on the monitor with the sketches and illustrations in the book and there was little doubt that he was on the right page. Then he noticed a door knocker missing on one of the doors that he had filmed. If his daughter had gone through that one, the consequences would be devastating.

A notification popped up on his computer alerting him to a new email from Professor Friedemann. In the subject line he was asking precisely what time he would be picked up from Frankfurt Airport.

At first van Dam thought it was a delayed message, for the geologist was now roaming around underground looking for Anna-Lena, then he saw the time at which the email had been sent: two minutes ago.

That was surely impossible. But he'd deal with that later; right now he had more urgent matters to attend to.

'Listen to me, Mr von Troneg.' Van Dam propped his head on his hands and fixed his eyes on the descriptions written underneath each door. 'I—'

With a crack the connection died. The monitors went blank and the sound cut out.

'No!' Van Dam stared at the black displays.

Viktor looked at the third, fourth and fifth doors, each representing one of the three most likely possibilities for where to find Anna-Lena, knowing they were running out of time.

Ingo was calibrating his devices in an attempt to update his measurements. He raised his eyebrows as he read the latest results. 'Unbelievable. This . . . this trumps everything else I've seen so far. As we speak, the gravitational values are changing – they're already slightly above the norm. There are enough physical anomalies down here to keep an entire institute busy!'

'We could split up,' Viktor suggested, 'into two teams.'

'No,' said Dana, pointing to the dead man with his slit throat. 'It's far too dangerous for that. We've got to stay together.' She looked at Friedemann. 'You're leading this mission. Make a decision.'

All of Friedemann's earlier certainty suddenly vanished. He stood stock-still in front of the door he had chosen before – the one with the barely visible arrow drawn in the dust – while Spanger bent down to pick up the diamond earring and Coco, muttering incessantly to herself, struggled to control the pendulum tugging on her chain.

'Professor?' Viktor's anxiety was growing. Should they go through the door with the X, or the door with the question mark and the knocker, or the door with the exclamation mark and the antique box lock?

'Tell us where to go, Professor.'

CHAPTER IV

'Oi, Doctor. Have your devices got anything to say for themselves?' Spanger asked. He held the MP5 by its longer arm, reassured by the presence of the weapon he had confiscated. He felt almost heroic. 'Anything we might be able to understand?'

'No. Well, yes.' Ingo blinked. 'Hang on, I can ees rehtona egrus.' Backwards words again – *inexplicable*. He was pronouncing them correctly and they crossed his lips normally, but the moment the syllables came into contact with the air, they flipped around. People who believed in the Devil might attribute it to something Satanic, but for Ingo, this was a phenomenon he was excited to get to the bottom of.

Dana positioned herself so that she had a good view down the entrance passage. If anyone tried to sneak up on them, she'd spot them immediately. Even so, she felt really uneasy; she wished the team would finally reach a decision about which door to go through to look for Anna-Lena. The smell of smoke from the magnesium torches was wafting through the labyrinth, announcing the presence of visitors to all and sundry. They couldn't have found a better way to draw attention to themselves – apart from Spanger's unwelcome volley before losing his rifle, of course.

'I'm absolutely certain of my choice, Professor.' Coco looked at the hovering pendulum, which was still tugging at its chain and vibrating softly. She was amazed at how unambiguously the pendulum was pointing, marking a single direction, when she thought about the missing Anna-Lena. This chamber had evidently turned her into a real medium.

'Well, I'm *also* certain.' Friedemann turned his helmet lamp towards the floor and adjusted his glasses. A scrap of dark green cloth was lying next to a barely discernible arrow that had been drawn in the dust. 'And here's why: Miss van Dam's left us an actual clue. I think that trumps your pendulum and the earring Spanger found in front of the last door.' He placed his hand on the door-knocker affixed to the middle door. He had nothing against clairvoyant powers, but if he could find a way to carry on without them, he would do so. 'This is the one we need to go through.'

Coco remained stubbornly next to the penultimate door. 'My pendulum and the energy it's harnessing are all speaking with one voice.' She pointed to the cross drawn on in lipstick.

'Careful,' warned Ingo, looking at his devices. 'Something's happening!'

The gravity in the cathedral-sized hall was beginning to recede.

Coco's stomach leaped into her throat as Spanger let out a gleeful laugh, while the others spread their arms out in an attempt to retain their balance and not start spinning around uncontrollably.

The suspension of gravity lasted just long enough for them to drift an arm's-length up from the rock floor – and then immediately fall to the ground at what felt like almost three times the normal force. It took several seconds for gravity to get back to normal.

'We're back in the green range,' Ingo announced as he began bolting together his measuring devices to form a relatively wieldable block, to which he attached a strap; that would save him having to transport them all individually. He grinned broadly. His scientific dreams had come true. And he had come well prepared.

'That was mad.' Viktor shone his own light back down the dark hall through which they had just come. 'All quiet. On sngis . . .' He paused. 'It's happening again, isn't it? I'm talking backwards.'

Ingo rubbed his hands together. 'Madness. Madness that I can actually measure!'

'Madness just about sums it up.' Friedemann considered it madness, how much time they were wasting, so he opened the door with the question mark drawn on it.

It swung outwards.

Behind it was revealed: a wall of rock.

Spanger laughed out loud. 'Oh yes. Much better than a pendulum and an earring. I can see that now!'

'I don't understand!' Friedemann closed the door and opened it again. 'It *has* to work.' It still revealed nothing more than bare rock. 'It was different before!'

'*Before?*' Dana narrowed her eyes. 'When was *before*?'

Friedemann ignored her. He slammed the door shut angrily and walked over to the one with the X that Coco had chosen. He pushed the medium aside and began to shake the handle violently, but to no avail – it was locked.

"This *cannot* be happening!' growled the professor, stalking back and forth in front of the doors, his thin frame making him look like an angry black flamingo. 'This one, then!' he shouted out when he arrived at the last one, which had an exclamation mark drawn on it. It was where Spanger had found the diamond earring.

He jerked it open – and instead of rock, the light from Friedemann's helmet lamp cut into a deep blackness.

He had found what he had been looking for. This was the reason why he had joined the mission. The *only* reason.

'Professor, we need to talk about your previous experiences with these doors.' Ingo hung his block of gauges over his shoulder and followed him. Coco was behind him, still clutching the pendulum, which was still desperately insisting that the door to the left, with the X marked on it, was the correct one to take.

Friedemann stepped quickly and fearlessly into the darkness. 'Come on – follow me! There's a passage here. We can talk about all that later. There's no time to lose. This girl's in grave danger.'

'He knows exactly what's going on with these doors,' said Dana, looking back and forth between Viktor and Ingo. 'He's taking us for mugs. This bloke's only here because he knows something about them. It's nothing to do with geology.'

'Later.' Viktor wedged a stone beneath the door with his foot to stop it from closing behind them.

Together they entered a long, winding passage. Dana could well be right, Viktor thought. For a geologist, the difficulty he had had getting into the climbing harness betrayed a concerning lack of experience. Was this their client playing some sort of trick on them? Or was the professor not who he claimed to be? Viktor resolved to keep a close eye on him.

The beams from their helmet lamps shifted this way and that, striking dry rock and what looked to be hastily constructed brick walls; the dirty floor played host to bone fragments and chunks of stone. There was a stale smell in the air, with notes of strong electrical discharge and fried electronic devices.

The group slowly groped their way forwards.

The passage turned out to be a room with no other exits. The only door available to them was the one they had just come through.

'Damn it! I thought . . .' Friedemann looked around angrily. 'I thought we were on the final stretch.'

'No missing daughter, then,' Coco noted with satisfaction. Her pendulum was still standing horizontally in the air, pointing back at the exit. 'It's like I said before: it's the door with the red X.'

Ingo examined the raised brick wall to his left, brushing his fingers over the ridges caused by the stones having been laid imprecisely. 'This wall looks as if it was built in a hurry. Someone wanted to get out of here fast.'

'We'd be better off getting out of this hole as well,' sighed Spanger reproachfully, still clutching the MP5 instead of wearing it over his shoulder to keep his hands free. He liked his new accessory. 'What's this all about then? Who built—?' He suddenly caught sight of something behind Ingo. 'Stop! The wedge is slipping free. The door's falling—'

The door shut with a bang. A strange metallic sound mingled with the slamming noise, closely followed by a crackle.

The sextet froze, as if rooted to the ground.

The pendulum dropped and began to swing back and forth on its chain, before slowly regaining its previous height and pointing to the rock wall. Coco stared at the artefact as it tugged on the chain. She had no explanation for what was happening. There was no exit any more.

'Aha.' Friedemann looked triumphantly at the medium. 'Your powers haven't worked out quite as you'd expected, have they?'

'I'm assuming it ... it's receiving the girl's vibrations through the wall,' said Coco timidly.

'If that's the case we'll see it on here.' Ingo took out his block of instruments and panned it around. The numbers and curves on the displays were all within regular parameters. 'At least there's nothing physical going on to concern us,' he said disappointedly. He put a hand on Coco's back. 'Well done,' he said softly. 'Whatever it is you're doing.'

Coco gave him a warning look. She was rather afraid that her gift with the pendulum might disappear as soon as she started to doubt it, meaning she would revert to her former state of being an imposter. But the pendulum held its course and didn't move an inch.

Friedemann instructed the group to start tapping on the rock to see if it was concealing any secrets behind it. Inch by inch they knocked on the surface carefully, listening closely for any discrepancies.

After a few minutes had passed and their labours had come to nothing, Spanger impatiently turned his gun around and began to use the sub-machine gun's handle as a hammer. Shards of rock flew off. If there was a secret door behind here, he'd fucking well be the one to find it!

'Christ, Spanger!' shouted Dana, pointing at the automatic weapon. 'Put the safety on if you're going to play around with that thing – I've already had to tell you once today.'

'I have.' He hadn't, but he wasn't about to admit it here. He glanced down at the MP5, his sweaty fingers fiddling with it like a novice and nearly dropping it. 'Whoops, that's . . .' he reacted just quickly enough to stop the gun from falling to the floor, but as he caught it his ring finger set off a volley of gunfire. Yet again.

The MP5 rattled violently. The projectiles tore into the stone wall, the muzzle flashing lighting up the chamber.

'Oh, shit! Take cover!' Spanger shouted, as he desperately tried to remove his finger from the trigger.

The hot shells ricocheted off the wall; one of them crashed into his face. He cried out and there came a stink of singed beard hair.

Then the roaring ended; the sub-machine gun was finally silent.

'You colossal fucking idiot!' Friedemann called out from his position on the floor. 'You're supposed to be our weapons expert?' He adjusted his helmet, which had shifted during his mad scramble to hit the deck. 'Where the *fuck* did you learn *that*?'

Spanger shrugged apologetically, his face bright red with shame. 'I . . . I'm sorry.'

'I'm practically deaf.' Coco removed her hands from her ears. There was still a slight ringing in her right one.

'You can't be trusted with firearms.' Dana stepped angrily towards Spanger. There was a notch on her helmet from one of the 9 mm shells. 'Give me that gun before—'

'There—' Ingo's voice pierced the angry hubbub. 'The wall!'

The five bullet holes that had penetrated the mass of rock was causing the entire structure to disintegrate as if it were made of dry sand; iridescent, unearthly light passed through the gaps into the smoky, dusty chamber.

Ingo's devices suddenly started to reveal some of the anomalies that he had measured earlier. Magnetic fields, temperature – everything was now being subjected to violent fluctuations. 'We've found something.'

'*I've* found something,' Spanger added, hiding the MP5 behind his back to keep it out of Dana's reach.

A second door was gradually revealed; the frame looked Art Deco, made of black marble, with inlays of gold and platinum, while the door itself was covered with dark green leather adorned with floral patterns.

There was no trace of any impact from the projectiles. Instead, a faint glimmer could be seen flitting across the surface, oscillating up and down with a crackle that resembled electrical energy.

Viktor recognised the smell. It was the same as the one he had first noticed when they entered the passage. Had the door been used just before they arrived? He shone his torch around. Were there any other exits behind the brick wall?

Coco looked at her pendulum, which was tugging even harder in the direction of the mysterious, shimmering entrance. She couldn't explain this miracle at all. But there was someone down here who might be able to. 'Does your book say anything about this, Professor?'

Friedemann whirled around, putting his hand protectively

over the Kevlar vest before immediately retracting it, annoyed that his instincts had betrayed him. 'What sort of—?'

'I saw you with it earlier. You were reading it with a funny little smile. Will it help us to get out of here? Let's have a look,' asked Coco.

Friedemann refused her with a cold look. 'That won't be necessary. Your pendulum can tell us about the things that matter.' He pointed at the door. 'Anna-Lena's through there.'

The displays on Ingo's devices showed clear curves, with the values for electricity and magnetic fields skyrocketing. 'No change in gravity, but there are other ... things.' He wished he had a dozen better gauges with him so he could perform some more detailed tests. 'All I can say is that some sort of force field has built up.'

Coco welcomed the prospect of escaping from the oppressive chamber. The whispering creature whose voice had accosted her when she had first entered the passage was not on the other side of that door, so all the more reason to keep advancing.

'Where do you think it'll take us?' Viktor walked towards the doorway, kicking away the empty shells on the floor. 'Looks like it's from the Twenties, doesn't it?' The light was now covering the entire door, for the rock had turned completely to dust.

'We'll find out soon enough.' Friedemann laid a hand on the handle and pushed it down. A faint bluish glimmer flickered within the frame. 'Follow me. The fate of a young woman lies in our hands.'

Spanger gave Coco a friendly push to the side. 'Let me through, Madame. I'm being paid to keep you safe.'

He picked up the MP5, checked the safety once more and stepped across the threshold.

Dana sighed. 'We'd be safest if Spanger were back on the surface, as far away from us as possible.' She followed him through, with Ingo and Coco in close order behind.

Viktor once again assumed the role of rear gunner.

To be on the safe side, he looked around the dark room in the beam of his torch. The entrance through which they had entered the chamber was closed and now appeared entirely unremarkable. He was perfectly happy for it to remain that way – their goal was on the other side of the wall of energy.

'I'd never dreamed I'd end up somewhere like here.' Viktor took a deep breath and stuck his gun through the open door. St Elmo's fire flickered and danced across the metallic parts of his equipment, tickling the fine hairs on his arms and neck. Before he stepped through the force field, he picked up a large bone fragment and wedged the Art Deco door open to stop it from locking behind them. They needed a way back ... to their own time? To their reality? Viktor sensed this was no ordinary passage: he had to be prepared for all eventualities.

After checking several times that the piece of bone was going to do a better job than the stone beneath the first door, Viktor stepped through the shimmering haze.

A moment later, Viktor found himself standing in blazing sunshine. 'Holy shit, that's bright!'

Then he smelled the blood.

Blinded, he raised a hand to shield himself from the sun. Where were the others? He took a few steps forward and immediately stumbled.

At the last moment he felt Dana supporting him. 'No dramas. We're all here now.'

His eyes slowly became accustomed to the glare.

A wide, unpaved path stretched out before him amid a blooming aestival landscape – ruined only by dozens of mangled corpses, of people and horses.

The wagons had been overturned and looted; it was not just the men and women who had been slaughtered, but the animals as well, almost as if every living thing had needed to be eradicated to prevent the spread of something evil.

This gruesome scenario was an island of horror in a sea of peacefulness and idyllic nature, blossoming trees and blooming flowers. Oozing intestines, gaping wounds, bare bones, knocked-out teeth, severed heads, sagging eyeballs and exsanguinated bodies combined to form a bloody potpourri. The victims were mainly of darker skin colour, ranging from light brown to black, just like the people Viktor had encountered in the eastern parts of North Africa. Four men were clearly Caucasian.

An unkindness of ravens cawed around the edges of the pile, feasting on the remains and jabbing the dead bodies with red-smeared beaks.

'What on earth . . . ?' Viktor turned around.

Coco was kneeling in the grass, vomiting repeatedly. The rest of the group remained at a distance from the slaughter, shock, surprise and helplessness etched on their faces; they all looked wildly out of place in their black clothing, climbing equipment and helmets.

It took Viktor a few moments to understand that they

hadn't come through a door, but rather, an ornate wooden frame that was leaning upright against an overturned cart. The force field was still there, so their way back was open.

'Not a clue where we are,' Dana reported. 'There's no reception whatsoever, neither for the helmet cameras nor our phones. No internet.' She pointed to the bodies and their corvid companions. 'Those are real. At first I thought this was a set for a film set in mediaeval times – or something staged by a re-enactment group.'

'I think we've been brought to a different era.' Friedemann looked around. Just like the others, he didn't fit in at all with their surroundings, especially given his height.

Viktor and Dana switched on the scopes on their G36s. Looking through the magnifying lenses, they swung their weapons back and forth.

There was no sign of civilisation. They were surrounded by a few coppices and fields with what looked like a meagre yield of crops growing in them, followed by endless meadows and scattered fruit trees. Cirrus clouds were stringing their way across the blue sky above a slightly hilly landscape. Birdsong rang out from the bushes and hedgerows, and a solitary lark chirped disapprovingly down at them.

'It looks like the pits of the earth.' Spanger took off his helmet and tossed it into the grass alongside the path. He shook his shoulder-length brown hair and walked slowly towards the dead bodies. 'Well, bugger me. These lads have seen better days.' His stomach sent out a few early warnings not to look too closely at the piled entrails. Or their caved-in skills. And torn abdomens. 'The killers must have been pretty angry. Who *does* something like that?'

'In the highly unlikely event that the door actually *has* carried us through time, it looks as if we've ended up in the Middle Ages,' said Ingo as he examined the equipment left on the corpses, also taking care not to not look too closely at any of the wounds. 'But these clothes and items are Moorish.' He gestured to two armed men. 'And the swords and armour belonging to the fair-skinned men are European. They're carrying Frankish longswords.'

'Well, aren't you a clever dick,' Spanger said. 'Have you downloaded an app that's telling you all this stuff? You must have some reception if that's the case.'

'Nope, no app.' Ingo grinned and removed his helmet as well. It made no sense to carry on wearing it. 'It's a clever little thing called *knowledge* and it doesn't run on electricity at all. I took a couple of history modules at university.'

'Aha.' Spanger pulled out his smartphone and after staring at the display for a few seconds, finally admitted there was no service. 'And here I pay for international roaming.'

Dana laughed. She had always thought people like Spanger had to be made up, but it appeared they really did exist after all. She did a full circle of the slaughter site, then picked up a broken spear and used it to shift one or two of the dead bodies to reveal their faces.

Viktor shared the doctor's assessment that the door had brought them to the Middle Ages, though he had no idea how this could even be possible. But if they needed to find Anna-Lena in a world without any modern forms of communication, they had a Joker in the pack: someone who didn't need anything like electricity or satellite transmission to function properly. 'Madame Fendi? Would you—?'

'I've already asked her,' interrupted Friedemann, who was showing no intention of abdicating from his role as expedition leader. 'She's still unable to concentrate.'

'Miss van Dam isn't one of the victims.' Dana had checked the bloody amalgamation of bodies. 'There're no more than twenty people in total, I'd say. Four . . . let's say knights, then a few . . .' She paused and looked at Ingo. 'What did you call those people?'

'Moors,' he ventured.

'Knights and Moors travelling together. And then an ambush.' Dana gestured down the winding path. 'Hoof prints. Quite a few of them.'

Viktor looked at the chests: some were still locked, others had sprung open. 'They haven't been broken into,' he said.

'So the attack was just about killing the travellers, who-ever they were.' Dana watched a crow pecking at an object lying among the dead men. It glittered in its beak as it flapped its wings, about to take off. 'Hey!' She ran towards the bird, waving her arms around. '*Tsssh! Shoo!* Leave it alone!'

The bird fluttered away with a squawk, its plunder aban-doned.

Dana bent down to pick it up. 'I've found something,' she called out, hurrying back to the group. She gazed in wonder at the diamond earring in her hand, which had definitely belonged to Anna-Lena, for its counterpart had been found in front of the door back in the hall. They finally had some proof that she had actually been here.

'Good. Now we need to get changed.' The professor pointed at the bodies. 'Everyone find something they can throw on over their own clothes – I don't want us to stand out. We can break open the chests, see if there's anything useful inside.'

'What about our climbing harnesses?' asked Ingo.

'Take them off and hide them– the helmets and cameras as well. We'll bury them next to the path here. But we'll keep hold of the radios.'

Friedemann walked over to the upturned wagons. 'There must be things here that'll fit us.'

Viktor very much doubted that, given how tall the professor was – and he'd have to take his glasses off if he didn't want to attract attention, especially in an era when people were considerably shorter.

Ingo was staying close to Coco, who was still busy with her world-record vomiting attempt. 'We'll try to find something as well.'

'Ms Rentski and Mr Troneg, would you be so kind as to see if you can find any more traces of our missing girl in the grass?' asked the professor, who had already started to remove clothes from the dead. 'She can't have gone far.'

'Why not?' Dana raised her G36 and once again looked through the magnified scope. She didn't think she had missed anything first time around; she was far too experienced for that.

Viktor shared Friedemann's view. 'I think she arrived after the attack. The corpses are less than an hour old, so she can't have had much of a head-start.'

'Unless she escaped on a horse.' Dana put the gun down. Just as she had suspected, there was no one in sight. 'We need Madame Fendi's help – we don't stand a chance without it.' As soon as horses walked over hard or stony dry ground it would become much harder to track them, and if they came across water – a river or stream – she'd be left guessing altogether.

'Over there – on the right,' said Spanger suddenly. 'Is that smoke? It wasn't there before.'

Friedemann, Dana and Viktor looked in the direction he was indicating.

He was right: more than a dozen plumes of smoke were now rising from the other side of a hill, each separated from one another. The dark smoke impinged upon the blue sky with its fluffy white clouds as if trying to destroy the idyllic picture.

While they were staring, more smoke appeared.

'What do you reckon that is?' Spanger was holding the clothes he had found, although anything other than the widest caftan available would probably be out of the question for him. 'A town going up in flames?'

'Too small.' Dana was horribly familiar with burning settlements. This sort of smoke didn't fit that scenario.

'There were hardly any cities in the early Middle Ages,' said Ingo. 'It could ... could be slash-and-burn farming.' He looked at the green nature all around him. 'Which would admittedly be a pretty stupid idea – it's the wrong time of year for it.'

'Ms Rentski and Mr Troneg, both of you go and check,' Friedemann ordered. He didn't want to encounter any surprises. 'Mr Spanger, you can stay here as our bodyguard.' He had gathered a pile of clothes and now he carried them over to Ingo and Coco. 'These should more or less fit you.'

Viktor gave a lax salute and fell into a light jog alongside

Dana, heading towards the wooded hill. They hadn't covered their modern equipment, but that probably wasn't the worst idea for a quick reconnaissance mission.

The hill and the thicket blocked their view of the base of the fire, so they'd have to push through the branches to see anything. They both had their weapons ready, in case they needed to use them at a moment's notice.

Together they advanced through the wood's light undergrowth, keeping their eyes open for any tracks that might have been left by Anna-Lena, but finding nothing of any use.

'A free-climber, you say?' Viktor tried again.

'Just like you,' Dana snapped back at him. 'Just like you, Troneg.' She glanced at him. 'Can't hurt for our climbers to have some specialist skills, can it?'

'Spot on.' Viktor was determined to get to the bottom of where they knew each other from. Dana's explanation about a twin sister was total horseshit.

The two of them finally reached the top of the hill. They stood peering through the tree trunks down at the plain below, which was where the smoke was coming from.

The sight that greeted Viktor and Dana left them speechless.

Frankfurt, Lerchesberg

Walter van Dam stared at the black triptych of monitors, listening to the noise in his headset, first imploringly, then anxiously and finally angrily.

But however fervent his expressions, they weren't about

to perform miracles. The screens didn't suddenly spring to life, nor could a peep be heard through the speakers. The group down in the caves was completely cut off from the outside world.

'Professor Friedemann?' said van Dam regardless, clicking all over the control display, even though all the signal-markers were red. He stood up quickly and removed his jacket and tie. The stress was making him sweat.

Think, he urged himself, stroking his handsome moustache repeatedly. He paced around, circling his desk, constantly running his fingers through his greying hair.

The satellite link could be down, or the transmission could be being blocked by spotty Wi-Fi. Or perhaps the upload from the Mercedes was being hindered by some modem error. Or Professor Friedemann had forgotten to place enough signal-boosters.

There were all sorts of possible reasons behind this technical silence.

'I'd checked everything so carefully,' muttered van Dam as he booted up a diagnostics programme.

His chauffeur Matthias was still not contactable, which meant he couldn't try to fix the disruption – but should he not have returned long ago with his special cargo? Had he had an accident? Had he been stopped by the police? How could he possibly explain to the average police officer that he was driving an unconscious young woman whose eye colour kept changing to the man who probably wasn't her father?

Van Dam had just sat back down at his desk when a chorus of angry shouts erupted downstairs, closely followed by a loud clattering sound. He lifted his head in surprise and looked over the edge of his monitors towards the entrance.

For several seconds nothing happened, then there followed a timid knock at the door.

It was definitely not Ella Roth, his private secretary; she would either knock far more decisively or dispense with the pleasantries altogether. Perhaps Matthias had finally arrived with his counterfeit daughter?

'Come in.'

The door swung open forcefully, in sharp contrast with the diffidence of the knocking that preceded it.

A tall, slim woman entered the room.

For a brief moment he thought it was the actress Tilda Swinton.

'Good afternoon, Mr van Dam.' The stranger's features were striking, her eyes emphasised by heavy brows and kohl. She was wearing a white suit with fine, dark pin-stripes, complemented by a pair of black high heels. She moved elegantly towards his desk and took a seat in the armchair on the right. 'We need to talk.' Her tone was business-like, tinged with a hint of indignation, as if he had forgotten about a meeting they had arranged. 'About your grandfather.'

Van Dam looked over at the open door and through into his PA's office.

Ella Roth was lying on the floor, a pool of red spreading out onto the carpet from the centre of her body.

Van Dam grew cold. He would have loved to reach into his drawer and pull out a pistol, but he didn't have one here. His protection consisted of surveillance systems, cameras and bodyguards: expensive measures which were proving to be utterly ineffective against a lone woman showing no signs of exertion, nor bearing even the tiniest of bloodstains on her white suit.

So Van Dam sat quietly. Histrionics wouldn't bring him any closer to solving the mystery. 'Who are you?'

'And of course your next question will be, "What have you got to do with my grandfather?"' The stranger smiled with insincere friendliness. 'I'm in a bit of a pickle. If I introduce myself as Archangel, that makes me sound ridiculous. But using my real name wouldn't do justice to an occasion such as this.' She looked contemplatively at the panelled ceiling. 'But what if I were to come up with a new name for myself, just for you?' Then she snapped her thumb and middle finger. 'Call me Allegra. In case you—'

'Fine then. What have you got to do with my grand-father?' Van Dam interrupted the smug repartee that he already loathed, even in more conventional meetings.

Allegra slapped the table with the palm of her hand. 'Oh, very good! We *are* making good time, aren't we?' Her eyes, fixed on him, narrowed. 'Come now. You know perfectly well what your grandfather did.'

Van Dam had no idea what she was referring to. 'What are you talking about?'

'Not all that Nazi shit – this isn't a Hollywood thriller or a Scandi noir drama with exciting jumpers.' Allegra put her left hand into the pocket of her white trousers and raised her right hand, with her unadorned index finger pointing to the wall of folders. 'I can see you've kept all his old things. Your father's father left his knowledge with you.' She winked at him. 'Of course we knew all about that – but we believed you were harmless and left you alone. The Supreme Committee decided it would draw far more attention to move against you, although I should say I disagreed right from the outset. But yes, some things can be changed.'

Van Dam half turned towards the wall of folders. Some of his family's old business records were there, along with a few documents that he should have destroyed a long time ago. A very long time ago indeed.

'As for your daughter, *she's* the one we underestimated.' Allegra raised her index finger in a threatening gesture, then traced it over her heavy eyebrows as if to reshape them. 'You no longer have guardianship over her – the young lady is of age. But how could you just sit there and watch her put herself in danger like that, Mr van Dam? You're her *father*!'

'What have you done to her?'

'*I* haven't done anything to her. She's in the cave labyrinth at our organisation's former headquarters, which we were able to set up thanks to your grandfather.' Allegra removed her mobile phone from her pocket and answered an incoming call. 'No, I'm fine by myself.' She listened for a while. 'Good,' she said. 'Carry on.'

'Your people?' Van Dam, now hearing footsteps on the floor above them, had to force himself to calm down.

'Yes.'

'Tell them to leave my employees alone.'

Allegra pinched her mouth together guiltily. 'I'm afraid my people were a little over-zealous earlier.'

Now more than ever he wished he had a gun so he could

at least shoot their leader and call the police. 'So you're going to kill my daughter. And me.'

'Your daughter?' Oh no, one of my colleagues will see to that. He's roaming the caves with his own team as we speak. Or if not, one of the doors will take care of her. We've already thrown your first group off the scent and the second will follow soon.'

The woman calling herself Allegra rose and walked over to the bookshelves and immediately came across his grandfather's old book and the collection of loose papers. 'Your daughter enlarged these and made some more notes,' she stated. 'Sharp as a tack, that one.'

'Then you're here to feed off my misery and kill me once you're done?' Van Dam was considering whether anything on the table could be used as an improvised weapon. 'Not exactly the classiest of moves.'

'We're global conspirators, Mr van Dam, just like your grandfather. If we had any class, you and your daughter would be living in a far better world.' Allegra blinked and smiled. 'Sate my curiosity, if you will. Why have you never carried out any investigations of your own?'

'About the doors?'

'Yes.'

'Because my mother and grandmother hated them. They said the old mansion with all its secrets was cursed,' he said, trying to stall her. The letter opener was within reach – if he moved fast enough. 'And there were a few deaths as well, or so I heard.'

Allegra nodded. 'We underestimated how much the *Particulae* would malfunction at first.' She flipped through the scanned, annotated notes, looking a little amazed at what his daughter had discovered. 'You didn't want to be reminded about it – but you'd have been forced to do something, wouldn't you?'

'I thought it was all in the past.' Van Dam eyed his opponent. Of course she was expecting him to attack her. It was evident how much she was enjoying this performance. Perhaps there was a way he could use her arrogance to his advantage.

'Your daughter thought otherwise, though.' Her phone lit up again.

'Ah, interesting,' she said after listening for half a minute or so, her eyes never leaving the businessman. 'Mr van Dam, did you know the professor on your team was a fraud?'

'Friedemann?' He suddenly remembered the geologist's email. 'What do you mean, a *fraud*?'

'We've done some background research on your team. For . . . various reasons. And a few little secrets have come to light. Some of them are rather gruesome, like Mr Spanger's.' She carried on listening to the person on the other end of the line, then relayed, 'The fake professor's real name is Vladimir Otschenko, a Russian by birth. He's been living in Leipzig for years now. I've just learned he's been looking for the doors – he has crossed paths with our organisation several times. His research has been responsible for some of the more spectacular disasters we've encountered recently.' She ended the call without a word and put her phone down on the table. 'This Mr Otschenko is pretending to be Professor Friedemann, the geologist you hired to lead the search party through the cave system unscathed. Dear, oh dear.

Hardly a boon for the rest of the team. Fancy hearing about the misdeeds of any of the others you sent down to rescue your daughter? You'd be amazed.'

'No thanks. You're going to kill me anyway. Knowledge is no good to me now. I . . . I . . .' He pretended to faint and collapsed forwards, his arms outstretched. His right hand fell onto the letter opener, as if by chance.'

'Oh, Mr van Dam,' he heard Allegra say. 'Are you really planning to attack me with that thing? That's your master plan, is it?'

Van Dam straightened up, clutching the letter opener in his right hand. 'Yes. Take you hostage until you free my daughter. Or at least buy her some time.'

She gave an understanding nod. 'Very honourable. Asinine, but honourable.' She sat back in the chair, the open folder perched on her knees. 'I really am sorry to have to eliminate you and your little family, but your daughter's the one at fault here, not us.' She closed the folder gently. 'Sometimes the past has to stay in the past. You said something along those lines earlier, didn't you?'

He nodded, his fist gripping the handle of the letter opener more tightly. 'You understand I have to try, at least.'

'But of course.' Allegra put the folder back on the desk and opened her jacket. 'It'll make our scenario of an attack on the famous Walter van Dam all the more realistic if you're found with—'

He thrust the letter opener forwards in a straight line like an epée, smoothly and without standing up. The combined length of his arm and the blade would be enough to ram the metal into his enemy's chest.

But Allegra deflected his attack with a precise hand movement, pushing it slightly to one side. The tip missed its mark and hovered in the air a few inches from her breastbone, quivering.

'. . . a gun in your hands, I was about to say.' Using her other hand, she swept one of the three monitors straight into him. It struck van Dam on the head, the force hurling him backwards. His fall was only arrested by the armrest of the chair. The flat screen crashed onto the carpet, dragging the other two monitors to the floor with it like a hapless climbing team.

Van Dam scrambled up from the upholstery, raising the letter opener above his head and stretching his arm back to land as powerful a blow as possible. No matter the cost, he considered it the least he could do to take her out.

Allegra drew a whitish-brown Glock from its holster and shot him first in the abdomen, then twice in the chest. He fell onto the table, panting. He had never felt such pain before in his life.

'That makes it more realistic – for the police investigation,' she explained. 'A head shot would make it look too much like an execution,' she added, watching his suffering with disgust. The eye-catching Glock returned to its white leather holster. 'I really do loathe getting my hands dirty like this. I'm much more of a planner. I usually just sit at our headquarters and direct traffic.'

Van Dam's strength abandoned him; his legs gave way and he slid backwards off the table and crashed onto the floor, unable to breathe. Freezing cold spread throughout his body and his sight went dark. 'Go fuck yourself,' he managed to squeeze out, spitting blood as he did so.

Allegra looked past the table at the dying man and rose from the armchair. 'As if anything you say could stop me.' She gathered up the documents and stowed them in van Dam's own leather case. 'I'll take these with me as you won't be needing them any more. And we'll be having a bit more of a look around, Mr van Dam.' She looked down at him. 'This is all because your daughter couldn't let go of the past. That's the reason why you'll soon be resting in the ground together. Tragic, isn't it?'

Van Dam was choking on his own blood. His senses were fading, but he forced himself to look over at the body of Ella Roth, his excellent personal assistant. In his imagination her features turned into those of his daughter, Anna-Lena. She too would be dead soon.

His lungs rattled as he gasped for air. He couldn't move his eyes any more, so the people now entering the room were merely black trouser legs and dark grey combat boots. All he could hear of their conversations were mumbles, followed by the sound of tools hammering on the walls. They must be looking for cavities.

His thoughts revolved around Anna-Lena and her disappearance – what was about to happen to her – and the fact that he hadn't been able to protect her. It was his fault, all his fault ...

When the hems of Allegra's white pin-striped trousers and her black high-heeled shoes finally left his study, Walter van Dam's heart had stopped and his pain was no more.

The search for the secrets concealed within his four walls continued thoroughly and apace. No one paid any attention to the dead man, now just one of many inside the mansion.

CHAPTER V

Somewhere in Europe, Early Middle Ages

Spanger looked down at himself. He didn't like how he looked in these white Moorish clothes, despite the fact that they were long enough for him to be able to wear his Kevlar vest underneath. 'It looks like shit.'

'These clothes might not be what we would consider fashionable, but the point is for us to not stand out while we're travelling,' replied Ingo, who was dressed in the same style. The leather clothes, tunic and chainmail belonging to the knights fitted him just as poorly as they did Spanger. You couldn't stretch iron rings.

Friedemann was too tall to find anything suitable, but Coco turned out to be a perfect fit for the dark blue, delicately embroidered robe the professor had found for her. Once she added some of the heavy gold jewellery scattered around, she made rather a grand impression.

The warm wind was filled with the aromas of flowers and earth; swallows swooped low to chase the insects buzzing around them.

'Not stand out?' Spanger pointed at the mangled carcases.

'They were killed *because* they looked like that. I'm not sure this is a great disguise.'

Coco had finally managed to overcome her nausea and, carefully avoiding the sight and smell of the recent massacre, she was now holding the pendulum in her left hand. She focused instead on Anna-Lena's photo. *I simply have to succeed*, she thought. The team was relying on her abilities, which had suddenly become so much stronger – well, not stronger, in fact; they had actually started to *exist*. *It's all thanks to the force fields and the doors*, she supposed.

But the golden artefact was showing almost no signs of movement whatsoever. The slight swings gave no clarity as to where they should start looking for the missing girl and that made Coco nervous. Did her powers have to acclimatise themselves to a new century?

'Well, it's better than our modern gear,' Friedemann told Spanger. 'Let's hope Ms Rentski and Mr Troneg have more success.' Friedemann looked unhappily at the hem that ended just below his knees, revealing a pair of pale, spindly legs. Like the others, he had had to wrap his shoes in rags, the only way to disguise them.

Spanger put on a cloak to conceal the sub-machine gun; he had no intention of relinquishing it. He was still rather excited to be in possession of an MP5. They'd make short work of crossbows and swords with guns like these. He puffed his way up to the top of one of the wagons and looked out in all directions. He thought the hero pose he had struck suited him. 'Nothing,' he announced. 'Just a load of nature.'

Ingo was disappointed at the lack of buildings or other

structures around, which might have given them a clue as to where in Europe they were. Although the travellers had been predominantly Moorish, he recognised plenty of native European vegetation.

Ingo tried to remember everything he could about Islamic expansion in the Middle Ages, but he had learned about it a long time ago. Theoretically, they could still be on German soil, but it was just as likely that they were in what was then the Frankish kingdom. His knowledge of heraldry wasn't good enough to determine the symbols emblazoned on the shields of the slain fair-skinned soldiers.

Coco shook her blonde hair grumpily, the black streak breaking loose from its knot and slipping out from underneath her hood. In frustration, she stuffed the pendulum into her shoulder bag, which contained a few utensils she needed to perform her clairvoyant tricks. 'I can't feel anything.'

'Because you can't do it, or because something's blocking you?' Ingo asked, speaking softly to prevent Friedemann or Spanger from overhearing. He didn't trust this sudden awakening of her powers one bit.

'I could feel it back in the hall – why has it suddenly stopped now?'

'Because you're not really a medium.' He looked at his block of measuring devices, but the displays only showed any readings when he turned them to face the frame, which Friedemann was now examining intently. The professor appeared to be more interested in that door than in finding Anna-Lena van Dam. 'You didn't have a single positive hit in Freiburg when I tested you. Nothing at all.'

'I know.' Coco gestured surreptitiously towards the frame. 'The force field – it's done something to me. It's turned me into a proper clairvoyant.'

'*That's* your explanation?' It all sounded far too simple for Ingo's liking. *Wouldn't the whole team have acquired these powers if that had been the case?* he wondered.

'Have you got a better one?' Coco shuddered and started gagging once more; the wind had changed direction, sending a foul odour of rotting meat, blood and excrement in her direction. The ravens were still feasting upon the carcases, croaking quietly between bites as they hopped around, flapping their wings. 'Do we really have to wait here, Professor?' she called out. 'It's . . . disgusting.'

The gaunt man made a placating gesture, but continued to study the frame with his open notebook in his left hand. He was extremely interested in how this unusual portal operated. It was completely different from everything he had read or learned. The frame was a total novelty to him.

Ingo couldn't see a tree for miles around under which they could possibly take shelter from the rising sun. 'I'm guessing it's early summer,' he said, taking a deep breath. It smelled of grass and blooming flowers, and dandelion seeds were filling the air. 'Millet. They're growing millet and oats.' He pointed to the crops in a nearby field.

'I can see a track,' Spanger announced from his improvised look-out post, happy to have discovered more than Viktor and Dana had. 'It's leading the other way.' He pointed to the west. 'Very small. Could just be one person.'

'Reading tracks from twenty yards away?' muttered Ingo

with little conviction. A deer had probably just trodden down a path in the grass.

'Go and have a look, then, Mr Spanger,' Friedemann ordered without turning away from the frame. 'Doctor, would you be so kind as to scan this force field for me?'

Ingo hurried over to inspect the readings as Spanger hopped off the wagon to investigate his discovery.

'Just like in the chamber,' said Ingo as he moved closer to the frame. There were resonances and measurements that usually could only be triggered by something like the CERN Hadron Collider. He quickly jotted down the recorded values. 'I can't explain it, but they're real.'

Friedemann observed the latent flickering through his glasses. There had been nothing in the notebook about any of this. 'Why isn't it breaking down?'

'Didn't Mr Troneg wedge the door open? I'm assuming the energy will be stored up for as long as the door's open on our side and in our time.' That led him to the uncomfortable thought that the wood in the frame might overheat. He pointed to the notebook. 'What's that?'

'Memos.'

'Who from?'

'Nothing that concerns you.' Friedemann closed it and stowed it beneath his white robes. The length made him look as if he were wearing a dressing gown. 'We might need some of the notes.'

'Is there anything in there about permanent build-up of force?' Ingo touched the carved frame, which, thankfully, was still cool. 'When did you first come across these doors?'

'A while ago. Things are what they are. In any case,

our way back's still open. Good.' He produced a large linen cloth, unfolded it and threw it over the frame. 'We still need to find Anna-Lena van Dam.' He looked at Coco. 'My dear Madame, have you discovered anything yet? You know you're our trump card here, don't you?'

She nodded dejectedly. 'I think I need time to adjust to this new place first, though.'

'There are footprints here,' Spanger called out from a meadow filled with knee-high green stalks. It was he who had made this important discovery – he, no one else – and his sense of triumph echoed in his voice. 'I'm no expert, but . . . this could easily be the girl.' He pointed again in the direction the footprints were leading. 'That way.'

The trio looked westwards towards a cloudless, steel-blue sky.

'This is Troneg,' came a sudden voice over their headsets. 'Ms Rentski and I have found something. We think you all should come and have a look.'

With a wave of his hand, Friedemann instructed them to move off. 'You're in the grove at the top of the hill?'

'Yes. Just follow our tracks.'

'Any sign of our missing person?'

'No. That won't be easy. We'll need input from the whole team.'

'We need to go west,' Spanger insisted as he clumsily stomped his way back to the wagon, tripping over the strong stalks. 'That's where we'll find her.'

The small group hurried away from the site of the massacre and followed the line of trampled-down grass. Spanger couldn't stop himself from anxiously circling the other three like a nervous sheepdog. He wanted to be important, to be taken seriously for once in his life; he was their bodyguard, after all. It was imperative to erase the blot he had left in their collective memory of him after the incident with the G36.

They continued towards the wooded hill, where they found Dana waiting for them, easily recognisable in her black clothing against the colourful backdrop of flowers and leaves.

She was using the sight on her rifle to look beyond them in case there was anyone in pursuit, but there was nobody to be seen. 'Come on,' she said to the doctor and the professor. 'We're assuming our resident academics will be able to read more from this than we can.'

'What have you discovered that's so important?' Friedemann looked back at the recently plundered travelling party, which was now too far away for his liking. He was anxious not to lose sight of the frame. The idea of leaving Spanger behind as a guard had come to him too late.

'It's hard to describe. You'll have to see it for yourself.' Dana led them through the grove towards a steep slope where the ground fell vertically by about twelve feet.

Viktor was leaning against a tree, peering through the sight of his G36. 'We thought it'd be best if you all saw this,' he said, stepping to one side to allow the others to look through the narrow gap in the forest.

Barely a mile away was an enormous military encampment, stretching out before them. Banners fluttered in the wind and now they could see the smoke they had spotted was rising from cooking fires dotted around the site. The camp had been set up in rings, with wagons next to the tents forming barriers in the event of attack. Pavilions, some white, some more colourful, had been erected within the circular wagon forts.

'I tried to get an idea of how many people are down there, but it's bloody difficult,' said Viktor. 'They're not all soldiers anyway. A lot of them are there for supplies. Plus, I think the army's been here for a while now.'

'How did you come to that conclusion?' Friedemann had no interest at all in having a closer look at the camp. It was preventing them from doing their job. And from him examining the frame again. As far as he was concerned, these people could bash their skulls against each other to their hearts' content, as long as they did so a long way away from him.

'Because of how they've set everything up. The clothes lines, the state of the tents and the paths they've cleared; the fortifications with wooden barricades – oh, and the fact that this clearing was originally made quite a long time ago,' he said. 'You can see the bushes they trimmed earlier have started to grow back.' He took off the scope and handed it to Ingo. 'Here, see for yourself. The zoom leaves something to be desired, but it's better than nothing.'

'You were in the Scouts, weren't you?' Dana enjoyed repaying his questions about free-climbing. 'You sound like you used to be one.'

'Exactly.' Viktor was prepared to grant her this small victory.

'Why are we even looking at this?' Friedemann wanted

to go back to the wagon. He was uneasy leaving their passageway home unguarded, especially with a huge army encampment in the immediate vicinity. 'Or have you found Ms van Dam in there?'

'No. But we found ourselves needing two scholars to help to shed some light on the matter,' said Dana. 'I mean, there could be thousands of people down there. That could help us to work out when and where we actually are – how many battles were there in the Middle Ages where forces of this size fought against each other?'

Ingo looked through the lens, disappointed at how little detail it afforded him. He would have liked nothing more than to climb down and inspect the real-life Middle Ages up close. 'There are two things I can see,' he said softly. 'And those are siege equipment and Moorish troops.'

'So some of them got mixed up with our travelling party from down there?' Spanger concluded hurriedly. 'Oh man. Then our supposed disguises are more like an invitation for a sword through our stomachs.' He started to pull the robes over his head. 'Not on my watch. There are a few too many of them for me and my sub-machine gun.'

'Leave them to it,' said Friedemann. 'Let's go back to the baggage train and secure the frame. We should have done that at the start.'

'Great idea! I'll go on ahead and guard our portal,' announced Spanger, immediately turning to trot off. 'The rest of you can come once you've finished counting.' He crashed his way back through the undergrowth.

'They're preparing for a pitched battle.' Ingo handed the scope back to Viktor. 'Fascinating!'

He estimated there to be around a hundred and fifty thousand soldiers, roughly twenty thousand of whom were mounted. That was a truly incredible figure and not just for the Middle Ages, especially given that it exceeded the population of even the cities of that era.

He thought about the Moorish clothing and Frankish longswords found among the remnants of the baggage train. The leather and chainmail armour was simple, with basic leg and arm braces – not at all comparable with the full metal armour worn during the High and Late Middle ages. He was glad to finally be able to narrow down the options.

'I can think of one famous battle of this magnitude,' said Ingo thoughtfully. 'It was the first time opposing groups of Christians had fought on such a large scale, slaughtering one another mercilessly. If I recall correctly, some forty thousand died.'

As if suddenly inspired, Coco raised her left hand holding the golden pendulum and stretched it out towards the encampment.

The metal didn't move. Either she was too far away from Anna-Lena, or their quarry wasn't there amid the throng of soldiers. However, Coco could now clearly feel a tug on her temples as she was concentrating. Her gift hadn't abandoned her after all.

'I said, we're going back to the wagon,' Friedemann barked. 'We can't afford to leave our return ticket unaccompanied in a place like this.'

The group turned away from their viewing spot and slowly made their way back.

'Well? What was the battle then?' asked Dana.

'I can't remember everything, but I'm vaguely familiar with it,' Ingo explained as they were walking. 'It was ultimately the origin of France and Germany as we know them today, well, more or less. The dynasty of the Frankish emperors. Or something like that.' He dodged a low-hanging branch. 'It must have been around 840, in France.'

Coco sighed. This was probably the most dangerous part of the ninth century and they had hit it bang on the nail: she and Anna-Lena had been caught up in the midst of this gruesome war. 'But what's all this about the Moors? What were they doing in France anyway?'

'Not a clue.' Ingo shrugged and emerged from the grove at the rear of the pack. 'They didn't have any business being this far north. They were mainly active in Spain – Córdoba and the surrounding areas. That's where all their major successes had been after being defeated at Tours and Poitiers.'

'Now we can see the true worth of a classical education.' Coco grinned at Viktor. 'Not bad at all, Mr Physicist and Parapsychologist.'

Viktor signalled to them to stop. 'We've got visitors.' He raised his G36 and swung it eastwards towards the path. 'A small group of riders,' he announced. 'Lances, shields, helmets. With armour.' He adjusted the eyepiece. 'I could be wrong but ... what can you see, Ms Rentski?'

'The same thing.' She tracked the movements of the mounted men through her scope. 'A third of them are women and it looks as if their leader's one as well.'

The armour glistened in the summer sun, reflecting light far off into the surroundings, while the clattering and rattling of weapons and armour was carried across to them by the wind. They could make out a standard borne on a spear waving in the breeze.

'It's a *scara* – a group of elite soldiers.'

Viktor swung in the direction of the baggage train, where Spanger, crouching behind a wagon, was holding his MP5 in both hands. He appeared to be waiting for an opportunity to fire. 'Elite soldiers,' he repeated softly. That could end badly for Spanger, who certainly appeared to have underestimated the advancing troops.

'Yes – for storming fortifications,' replied Ingo. 'They never give up. Ever.'

'Mr Spanger, we've no need for a dead hero on our hands,' Viktor warned over the radio. 'They may not have guns, but they're still an elite unit.'

'Mr Spanger, you're only to defend the frame,' added Friedemann. 'Hold fire and wait for us to join you.' He stalked off, stooping in an attempt to conceal himself within the tall grass.

Dana and Viktor took the lead; together they hurried over to the wreckage to help Spanger.

Frankfurt, Lerchesberg

The silence prevailing in Walter van Dam's estate was one of omnipresent death.

Servants and bodyguards lay where they'd fallen in beds, in corridors, on floors and on staircases, stabbed and shot. Their blood had dyed the stone floors, the parquet and the carpets, the blood-flow patterns streaming from each dead body creating bizarre works of art.

Nothing in the mansion was in its original place. The intruders had ransacked the facility inch by inch: cushions and pillows had had their stuffing removed; pictures had been separated from their frames; vases and trunks had been smashed; drawers and cupboards had been emptied and the wall panelling had been hacked apart. The house had not been allowed to keep any of its secrets.

The metallic, strangely sweet odour of blood and excrement swirled throughout each floor, overpowering the fragrances that had once been created by the scent sticks dotted strategically around the estate.

The telephone rang occasionally, almost as if trying to perform an act of collective resuscitation. Business partners and employees from law firms, offices and large corporations left urgent messages for Walter van Dam, who was lying dead next to his desk, killed by three shots to the chest and stomach. Emails piled up in his inbox; video calls remained unanswered. Not even the most modern means of communication could bring him back to life.

A sudden groan rang out, chasing off the oppressive silence.

The suppressed sound of agony was followed by a small movement: Ella Roth, the young personal assistant who had led the team to van Dam's office earlier on in the day, wobbled slowly to her feet. She pressed a palm to the left-hand side of her stomach, which was host to a nasty-looking slash. The knife attack had caused her to pass out, losing a significant amount of blood in the process.

But somehow, she was alive.

With a moan, Ella braced herself against the door frame and stumbled into her late employer's office. She opened her blood-stained blouse and reached for the stapler on the desk. She groaned as she pressed down the edges of her severed flesh and inserted several staples to hold the wound together. It didn't work very well; she knew she'd have to have it seen to by professionals in due course, but the main thing for the time being was to not bleed to death. Next she cut a large piece from the thick curtain and pressed it against the wound, using the ripped-out telephone wire to hold her makeshift dressing in place.

Trying to suppress the pain, Ella looked down at Walter van Dam's lifeless body. His broken pupils left her in no doubt that any attempt to resuscitate him would be in vain.

And it was a good job at that.

She bent down slowly and removed the polished letter opener from the dead man's hand. Then she placed his thumb across the edge of the chair leg and skilfully severed the top. Only a small amount of blood trickled out from the stub, as his heart had stopped beating. She wiped the thumb tip on carpet and straightened up, cursing softly.

Ella had applied for the job as his personal assistant specifically to gain van Dam's trust – so she would be able to search the room – every nook and cranny – whenever she wanted, without raising suspicion. She knew all the peculiarities of the heating system and was familiar with all the building's idiosyncratic noises. She had made herself utterly indispensable and her work was impeccable. At all hours.

She wasn't there so that she could have a lucrative job for life, though: she was there to make copies of the markings on the doors that the intruders had scratched with their nails during the raid.

Ella staggered towards the open safe next to the cupboard where van Dam had his bar.

Of course it had been discovered by the attackers, hidden behind a picture. The control panel was hanging out, the loose wires revealing it had been outwitted by the burglars' electronic devices.

There was nothing inside. There had been nothing in it except for a coin collection and hard drives containing financial data about van Dam's business ventures; they had obviously taken the stuff to maintain the pretence of a brutal robbery.

But Ella knew a secret.

Ever since she had discovered it, she had been looking for ways to acquire her employer's thumbprint. But no matter how hard she tried to make sure it was she who cleared away the crockery and checked all surfaces, the prints she found had never been complete.

Now Ella supported her weight using the open safe door and stretched the severed thumb towards the scanner hidden beneath the manufacturer's logo. She flipped the label up and pressed the skin against the glass.

Light flickered as the unique patterns and grooves were scanned.

Ella hadn't even tried to resist when the attackers stormed into the house. The physical superiority of the masked men left no room for effective resistance and in any case, she had sensed this might just present her with the opportunity she had been awaiting for such a long time.

As soon as the blade had been thrusted into her she had contorted herself into a position that allowed the metal to slide into the lower left-hand side of her body, where there were fewer vital organs to rupture. She had not expected to fall unconscious, however.

The scan finished and the light behind the matt screen turned green.

With a click, the entire rear wall slid to one side, revealing a separate chamber containing the items for which van Dam had wanted extra protection.

Ella let go of the severed thumb and fumbled around inside the secret compartment, which contained, among other things, a small notebook. She pulled it out with a groan.

She could feel the blood rushing to her head, and black spirals swirling through a grey mist appeared before her eyes. She sank into an armchair and opened the notebook – only two of the pages had been used; the notebook clearly came from another century. She decided to postpone deciphering it, as there was something specific *inside* that she wanted to find.

Still feeling dizzy, she carefully pulled out the small pocket concealed within the spine. She could feel the tiny splinter inside it and shook it gently onto the palm of her hand.

As flat as a pre-historic arrowhead, matt black and slightly shimmering, the shard felt cool on her skin; it was so inconspicuous that if anyone were to find it by chance, they'd discard it without a moment's consideration – just one of a million such items, or so it seemed.

Ella's face was one of boundless rapture, despite the dull pain in her side and with loss of consciousness lurking just around the corner.

She knew van Dam's grandfather had stolen one of the *Particulae* when the old headquarters had been abandoned. This fragment in her hand had never been used: it was still powerful, not at all dangerous or fickle like the those ancient specimens which had been built into the structure of the doors beneath the abandoned mansion – and which were soon to disintegrate in the not-too-distant future, with unimaginable consequences for the surrounding area.

Ella's elation suddenly subsided when she noticed that something inside her had opened immediately behind her poorly stapled wound. Warm liquid was pouring out of her from the edges of the gash and her circulation instantly began to deteriorate.

Shivering, she managed to pull out her phone, and using all her remaining strength, unlocked it.

'Select . . .' she began to say, before passing out. She tipped forwards onto the desk with her phone in one hand and the *Particula* in the other.

While she was unconscious, her panicking heart pumped the rest of the blood out of her body, soaking her trousers and the carpet beneath her. The transition from unconsciousness to death was quick and effortless.

And silence reigned once more in Walter van Dam's estate.

Frankish Empire, June 841

Sitting behind the wagon, Spanger could hear the dull clattering of hooves rapidly approaching up the road, accompanied by the rhythmic clinking of weapons and armour. Forty men were coming: an elite unit, a *scara*, according to Viktor.

The sub-machine gun and its spare magazine wouldn't be enough to take down all of them, but Spanger was hoping the heavy-duty firearm would at least act as a deterrent; they'd certainly view it as nothing short of the devil's work in the ninth century, bringing death in ways they could never have imagined. He had never been particularly strong at history, but he suspected the invention of gunpowder in Europe was still a long way off. In that respect he was the king: uncrowned, but undisputed.

'They're carrying bows and crossbows,' Viktor warned over the radio.

'Understood. Does anyone happen to know if Kevlar's good against those?' He looked down at his light kaftan. He had the wrong skin colour to be a real Moor, but the mere fact that he was wearing a robe like that was not likely to endear him to the advancing troops.

'I wouldn't count on it,' said Dana. 'A blade cuts through material in a different way to a bullet.'

Clouds of dust blew across, enveloping the wagon Spanger was crouching behind. Beside him stood the veiled frame, their ticket back to the modern age, with energy still crackling and shimmering underneath the sheet.

The roar of hooves finally reached him as the *scara* stopped. The commands issued sounded strange to his ear, but he was surprised to find he understood them. It looked like the force field had been gracious enough to adapt the language skills of the visitors to the period they were in.

Several people dismounted and began to walk among the bodies, but they were speaking too quietly for Spanger to make anything out. He checked the safety on his gun to ensure he'd be able to pull the trigger at any moment.

There came an excited cry.

'Spanger, the troops have found us,' Viktor said hurriedly. 'Stay where you are. We'll do everything we can to find a peaceful solution.'

'Right you are.' He looked out curiously beneath the wagon.

The majority of the *scara* were still mounted, some holding bows while others had spears in their hands, looking ready to attack. Seven of them were standing between the corpses and turning over bodies with their feet or spear-tips so they could see the faces.

Despite their helmets, he could see the group consisted of both men and women, which he found impressive. Hadn't he seen in films that women in this period just stayed at home and looked after the children?

He wiggled his toes and thought about what he could do to help. His instructions had been clear – keep a look-out and wait – but doing nothing felt wrong.

He was itching to prove his worth. All the others had areas of specialism, thanks to knowledge, training or special abilities, like Coco. He, however, was the bloke who got picked last at games because no one wanted him on their team: an unintentionally comical failure, easy to dismiss.

And that's how it had been throughout his entire life, regardless of what he took up or how hard he tried. That's why he'd trained as a bodyguard; that's why he'd applied to work for van Dam. But even here, on this most exciting and intense of adventures, he was surplus to requirements. They simply didn't need him, not one jot – and that pissed him off beyond belief.

The mediaeval elite unit were discussing what to do about the unknown people they were approaching.

He turned his gaze back to the frame. He would have loved to be able to defend it, to scatter the attackers and prove to the others that having him with them was worthwhile – that he wasn't just ballast and they really did need him, meaning it would be a shame if they were to lose him. But Friedemann and the others were trying to find a 'peaceful' solution.

'Hey! Who are you? Why are you wearing Moorish clothes when you're clearly not one?'

A *scarita* had appeared next to his hiding place and was pointing her spear at his throat. A dark streak protruded from beneath her mail coif, and the dust on her robe attested to the length of their journey.

Of course: the precise thing he had been trying to avoid had happened. 'I've been kidnapped,' he said slowly. 'They forced me to serve them.'

The soldier frowned. 'You're lying – and very badly at that.'

'I'm not!' he retorted stubbornly.

'Good. So you can tell me whose entourage this is, then?' She nodded in the direction of the dead bodies.

'They . . . never told me their names.' Spanger thought this was the worst he had ever lied in his life.

The soldier laughed at him. 'Enough with these little games. Confess: what are you and your friends doing here, dressed as Moors but not followers of Aysun al Arabi?'

Spanger didn't reply. *Followers of Aysun al Arabi* – was that some religious denomination or cult? Who or what on earth could Aysun be?

A second warrior appeared, her helmet tucked under one arm, with her coif pulled back to reveal her short, black hair. She hadn't drawn the sword at her side. 'Who's this?'

'A liar, Duchess Sigrid.' The *scarila* kept her spear raised. 'I don't know what he and his friends are up to. They might have laid an ambush for us?'

'Or could be one of Empress Ermengarde's spies.' Sigrid, who was undoubtedly the leader of the group, looked at Spanger. 'Who are you working for?' Noticing the bluish iridescence coming from beneath the sheet, she jerked it away from the frame. 'By the Almighty!' she exclaimed. 'What is this thing? Is it the work of demons?'

Spanger had no idea what to do – just pull the trigger and mow down his two questioners? That struck him as wrong.

'It could be some diabolical weapon to put our troops under a hex,' suggested the first soldier. 'Perhaps they plan to use it before the battle to ensure a quick victory.'

'Duchess, the others are sending a negotiator,' one of the mounted men called out.

'And the rest of the pretend Moors?'

'They're staying where they are.'

'Good. Allow him through.' Duchess Sigrid turned to Spanger. 'I'll ask you once more what this thing does.' She drew her longsword and touched the top of the frame with it. 'If you don't reveal its secrets, I'll cut it to pieces.' The blade pressed into the wood, creating a small notch. The force field hummed and glowed in protest.

Sigrid made the sign of the cross and took a step back. 'Lord protect me! What Satanic work is this?'

The soldier next to her pushed her spear forwards, until the tip was pressing right up against Spanger's Adam's apple. He gave a small yelp of pain as the iron scratched his skin.

'It's nothing evil, I swear,' Spanger stammered. Perhaps it would help if he spoke to the people of this time as if he were in a mediaeval market? 'Verily, most handsome of ladies, it is naught but nonsense. A childish gimmick. The product of a drunken alchemist who sought to keep boredom away, thereby delaying the time of day at which he would so wretchedly sup from the tankard of insobriety. Lend me your ears, sweetling, and just imagine: the old billy-goat was in fact trying to create a mirror without glass ... without ... polished metal. For his long and arduous journey through all seven lands. To make it easier ...' his tongue was tying itself in knots in his attempt to talk like a con artist. 'It's no work of evil, I promise, with the Lord and all his saints as my witness.' Not knowing whether his words were having any effect, he slowly released the safety from his sub-machine gun with his thumb.

'Why has your speech gone stilted all of a sudden? Afraid we'll see through you and your ilk?' Duchess Sigrid pounded on the frame again and her sword tip struck a small stone embedded in the wood.

This time the force field reacted with a warning whir. A dark-bluish flash of lightning erupted from the black stone and into the sword, causing the duchess to cry out. She was forced to let go and her weapon fell to the floor. Her hand was burned, her skin a deep red colour.

'With God as *my* witness, this is an unholy artefact,' said Sigrid with astonishment, quickly picking up the sword with her uninjured left hand. 'If it shoots those sparks into our lines, our people will scatter in terror and confusion.' She pointed to Spanger. 'You'll come with me for interrogation. Empress Judith will want to find out which of her enemies has sent you – whoever you may be: assassins, wizards or conjurors.' She raised her hand to hit the frame again.

Spanger had to intervene: this was his moment. Now was the time for heroic deeds.

He grabbed the spear with his left hand, preventing the warrior from thrusting the tip through his neck; at the same time he swung the barrel of his MP5 out from underneath his kaftan and aimed it at the duchess.

And pulled the trigger.

The submachine gun rattled its bullets against the tightly woven chain mesh. The rings broke under the impact of the projectiles, which penetrated the leather and entered her body. With a scream, Sigrid staggered backwards and crashed to the ground.

The sudden burst of fire had made the soldier in front

of Spanger flinch, but she made no attempt to escape. As Spanger was blocking her spear, she dropped it and drew her sword. 'Your dark arts won't help you here!'

'Spanger!' Friedemann shouted over the radio, 'what the hell are you doing? Doctor Theobald's almost there to start negotiating.'

Tumult had erupted among the *scara*; horses were whinnying in terror as a great hue and cry rang out.

'They were trying to destroy the frame.' Spanger swung the muzzle into his opponent and squeezed the trigger again. 'I had no choice.'

The bullets tore into the warrior's arm, shoulder and neck, shredding tissue and veins. Before she could stretch out her arm to stab him, she collapsed in a heap, dead.

Two more enemies appeared before him, their bows drawn. Spanger didn't have time to turn the gun around; the arrows whizzed towards him, tore through the kaftan and into his Kevlar vest – yet even at this short range, they did not completely break through it.

He raised his weapon, hoping they understood how powerful it was. 'Put your bows down!' he shouted at the men, who were already nocking new arrows. 'Get out of here!'

The distant crack of gunshots revealed that Dana and Viktor had also opened fire to provide cover for the doctor.

As the archers in front of Spanger hesitated, a roaring shadow threw itself from the wagon. The blade of a sword flashed in the sunlight, then whirred downwards onto Spanger's collarbone.

He instinctively fired the sub-machine gun again before it fell from his hand, but the force of the impact had dropped him onto all fours. The Kevlar vest had not withstood this last blow.

As Spanger ran out of air, all he could see was his opponent's chainmail looming over him; he could smell the sweat and dust emanating from his clothes. A blazing pain ran through him from his shoulder to his lungs; the hot blade was eating into his flesh, rendering his right arm inoperative.

His upper body swayed as the sword was pulled out of him, sending blood spurting everywhere. 'Take that,' his assailant shouted, 'for the Duchess!' He swung the wet, red blade.

Spanger didn't even consider giving up. He had to be a hero – defend the frame – keep their path back open . . .

In spite of the pain, he fell to one side and grabbed the MP5 with his left hand. Another burst of fire and the armoured man in front of him lost both his kneecaps in a cloud of blood. He screeched and fell backwards, rolling around in the pool Spanger had created.

There came a series of bright fizzing sounds that Spanger couldn't identify – not until the pain arrived. Arrow after arrow tore into him, piercing his torso, shoulders, arms and hands – then, finally, one stabbed through his neck, which abruptly stopped his screaming.

When one of the arrowheads penetrated his brain, Spanger's life finally ebbed away. His last not altogether maudlin thought was that at least he had perished defending the frame. He was finally a hero.

A dead hero.

What he failed to notice was the force field dissipating at the same time as his life force left him for good.

CHAPTER VI

A Secret Location

Ritter was sitting in the meeting room of the headquarters. It showed no sign of the chaos that had prevailed until recently. In his impeccably fitted pin-striped suit he looked more like an ageing male model who was still trying to get work for more youthful collections; his black hat lay on the chair beside him, revealing his gelled hair.

He stared at the countless monitors, large and small, on the sterile walls, displaying broadcasts from cameras all over the world. Some of the images were from ordinary news channels and online media platforms, but there were others from private homes and inside corporations; needless to say, the people being observed had no idea, let alone where these particular cameras were recording from.

He found the recent furore about internet giants and social media providers secretly eavesdropping on their users rather amusing, as that's precisely what the Organisation had been doing since the invention of the internet.

Since the invention of the telephone.

Since the invention of telegraph machines and the invention of written communication and whispered messages.

Nothing had ever escaped their notice.

Thanks to the doors, they could be anywhere in a matter of seconds – from one end of the world to the other – representing their own interests.

Ritter was unhappy.

He needed only hand movements to flick through the broadcasts, as there were sensors in the room to record his gestures and control the displays accordingly. It had been a mistake to abandon Anna-Lena to what had appeared to be her certain doom – because she was no longer where he had trapped her.

It was inevitable that the young woman would eventually start sniffing around the old headquarters, but he hadn't taken the threat seriously enough. The fact that she had found her way into the new headquarters thanks to a few malfunctioning doors was nothing short of a catastrophe.

Ritter looked at the collection of fresh *Particulae*, the energy-laden stones that, according to the most common theory, had been brought to earth by comets. They were lying in a bowl covered with velvet, just as before, and he had been just about to inspect them when the young Miss van Dam stumbled in and started taking photos of the facility as if she were on a factory visit.

Ritter had tried to apprehend her there and then, but she had managed to escape from him and flee the area – through a door to somewhere else, though not the old headquarters, where it would have been easy to find her. Since then there had been no trace of her.

And since then one of the *Particulae* had been missing – and that made him incredibly nervous.

Management's attention had been aroused and Archangel was now on the scene. If there was anyone who hated Ritter to his core, it was the woman who headed the Organisation.

Ritter had intended to move himself up in the Organisation, using his particular advantage to do so – the advantage which, in this instance, was in the form of a living being, well hidden in the old headquarters underneath the abandoned van Dam estate. This was where he had sent a unit to make Anna-Lena disappear, along with eliminating the two rescue teams her father had despatched. So far they had had only moderate success.

Ritter flicked through the channels, annoyed. Presidents, corporate executives, stock-exchange regulators, union leaders – their people had seats at every table, steering fortunes in their favour – and of course in favour of mankind as a whole, allowing it to continue to progress and not simply wallow in what it had already achieved. Dissatisfaction was a powerful driver: dissatisfaction, and envy.

That's why the Organisation stoked it all around the world, in various nations and on various continents, sometimes on a small scale, sometimes larger. Uprisings, skirmishes, market slumps, strikes, revolts – when carefully meted out and used deliberately – prevented humankind from becoming sedate, or eventually forming a community that might act collectively against social ills.

The door to his right swung open.

In strode Archangel, as most people called her, in her inevitable white suit with its tiny black pin-stripes, white blouse and braces. She was a woman beyond human imagination – and only two people in the world knew her real name.

'Oh, Ritter. I hadn't expected to find you here.'

He knew she was lying. She had tried to arrange a meeting with him on several occasions, but he had always managed to ignore the request, have another equally urgent appointment, or be on a job, it didn't matter wherever it might be. The main thing was to not be anywhere in her vicinity. 'What an unexpected pleasure.'

'Well, perhaps *pleasure*'s too strong a term.' Archangel threw a folder down on the desk in front of him, out of which slipped an ancient notebook containing a collection of loose pages.

'What's this?'

'The fruits of my labours.' Archangel gestured to him and sat down in the armchair opposite. They were sitting absurdly apart, as if the desk's designers had been ordered to ensure all participants would be kept as far away as possible from one another in case they ended up at one another's throats. 'Care to have a look?'

He couldn't hide from his superior any longer. He leaned forwards and pulled the folder towards him. Leafing through the little notebook, he recognised the notes compiled by van Dam's grandfather, along with a few sketches and plans of the old headquarters and annotated copies of certain historical documents.

'Was it worth the effort?' he asked at last.

'I'd say so. We've finally got everything.' Archangel put her feet up on the desk, revealing her white-soled black high-heeled court shoes. 'And by a stroke of fortune we managed to eliminate van Dam at the same time. The loophole's been closed for good.'

Ritter knew precisely what she was about to ask him. 'I'm working on it.'

'On *what*?' she asked smugly. 'Tell me: tell what you're working on while you're sitting in the meeting room, staring absently at all these channels, Ritter. It's a rare talent indeed to be able to lounge around and work at the same time.'

'On finding his daughter.' He didn't react to her provocation, instead focusing on one entry in the book: the word *Arkus*, crossed out, with a note beside it saying *TOO DANGEROUS*. Interesting.

'Ah, yes, that I do know.' Archangel gave a sympathetic smile. 'Not with much success, though. Might be because of all this inactivity.'

'There have been some complications.'

'What sort? Or have you recently starting calling your own laziness a complication?'

Ritter hated her for that. She knew perfectly well the young woman had escaped through one of the doors into a foreign world, time, dimension – wherever. They couldn't track her any longer because of how unreliable the *Particulae* had become. 'We're waiting for her in the caves.'

'You mean your men are,' Archangel corrected, asking him with nothing more than a look to hand the documents back. 'Tell me, are we missing a *Particula*?' She indicated the velvet cover. 'Or have I counted incorrectly?'

Ritter's hatred burgeoned. The fact that Archangel knew

the precise number and had counted them all in secret made his wretched situation with respect to the higher-ups even worse. He hadn't yet admitted to them that he'd lost one of the shards, as he'd hoped to return the missing *Particula* without anyone noticing.

'Oh, really?' Feigning ignorance, he started to count the fragments. 'You're right. There should be one more.'

'I don't suppose you've got an explanation for this?' Archangel put the notebook and loose sheets of paper back into the folder. 'Has the *Particula* become invisible, perhaps? Has it dissolved? Or maybe *someone* has stolen it?' The amusement in her voice failed to hide the fact that she was merely waiting for him to lie, exposing his duplicity in the process. 'Who would possibly dare to take one?'

Ritter cleared his throat. 'I'm afraid it must have been Anna-Lena van Dam.' He gestured to another door. 'For some reason the old headquarters—'

Archangel raised her hand to silence him. She had heard enough. 'You don't need to explain.'

'I thought—' he started.

'No, you really don't. I'm the wrong person for that.' Archangel unbuttoned her white jacket and it fell open to reveal her hand-tooled holster, made of white leather, of course. She had even had her Glock dyed white. What a strange fetish. 'But we don't have to worry, do we, Ritter? You'll take care of it. As soon as your men have caught the child, the fragment will be secured. Problem solved.'

Ritter attempted a smile. He didn't trust her in the slightest. Such a brief display of goodwill after her ruthless performance earlier was highly suspicious.

The monitors around him went out at the same time; a moment later they lit up again to reveal Ritter's face – some far away, some in close-up, zoomed in all the way to his pupils. It reminded him of the Voight-Kampff test from *Blade Runner*.

'What's all this?' he asked, alarmed.

'A record. Our conversation today will be highly relevant.' Archangel's posture remained casual as her feet started bobbing to the tune of an inaudible melody. 'You've been given a once-in-a-lifetime chance here. I don't want you to lie to me any more, Ritter. I'll ask the questions, you answer them.'

'What?' A sense of panic rose inside him.

'If your answers are honest, there's still some hope left for you,' she continued. 'You've been working to preserve the old headquarters for years, correct?'

'Yes, but—'

'To what end?'

'I don't understand.'

She stopped tapping her feet suddenly. 'The reason, please, Ritter. You were there quite a lot, so I hear.'

'Oh – right, yes. I've been studying how the *Particulae* have changed.' Ritter fiddled with the shards lying in front of him. 'I thought it'd be important, since we know this phenomenon will happen again.'

'And just how did you do that?'

'By observing.'

'No measurements? No devices, perhaps like the ones Doctor Theobald brought down with him? Have you collected and evaluated any results so you can present them to us?' Archangel inclined her head slightly to one side. 'Theobald's a professional physicist. He understands how matter works. What have you done to prove the validity of these observations of yours?'

Ritter tried to gloss over the facts with a plausible truth. 'No, I left it at observations and . . . field studies.'

'In which you used the five doors, contrary to your clear instructions not to do so, I suppose.'

'I had to.' Ritter knew where this conversation was going. The woman had been interrogating him from the start and her judgement would come at the end. He didn't have a gun on him – only his ring with the *Particula*, which he could use to escape if he was fast enough.

'And the results? How would you summarise them?' Archangel looked at him coolly across the desk. How many times she had had conversations such as this. How many times people had tried to escape, like fish from an ever-tightening net. But this was more than just a net; it was a trap, with barbed tips.

'Poor.' He raised his smartphone apologetically and made to stand up. 'A message! I'm going to check up on my men down in the caves. Maybe they've already found the girl.'

Archangel motioned for him to stay seated. 'You can save yourself the effort.' With a single gesture she set running a film on the largest monitor, taken by a helicopter camera. It revealed an area of forest, smoke rising in several places, which had sagged extensively.

'That's what happened after we set off the explosives: the tunnels caved in. Van Dam's old estate and the factory next to it are also things of the past. The explosions turned the whole area into rubble – along with the dead chauffeur, that thing that looked like van Dam's daughter and our esteemed employee.'

Ritter stared at the news report, where seismologists were blustering about earthquakes and methane explosions. Most of the area had already been cordoned off.

'You blew up the old headquarters?' he breathed. His thoughts immediately went to another being – one who she hadn't yet mentioned. But his one advantage was gone. Archangel had blown up all the bridges he had built to pursue his own plans.

'I had no choice, given what was down there. The doors themselves had become dangerous. None of the laws we created applied to them any more; the anomalies had started to range from shifts in time to alternate realities. I could no longer guarantee the safety of our Organisation,' she explained, without a single note of regret in her voice. 'Our specialists will publicly support the theory of it being a methane explosion setting off an earthquake. We've already prepared the expert opinions and distributed them among the press and relevant authorities. There won't be any awkward questions.'

Ritter stayed silent, contemplating his next move.

'Anything you'd like to say?'

He shook his head. At least Archangel couldn't read minds – or so he hoped.

'Perhaps you made unauthorised visits to other dimensions and worlds on your field studies and brought a guest back with you?' she ventured. 'A highly dangerous guest? One you wanted to use to take control of the Organisation?'

Ritter met her gaze. Everything was out in the open now. Why bother to hide it any longer? 'If you already know all this, why are we even having this conversation?'

'I want to hear you say it.' Archangel gestured to the monitors. 'A confession – that you've been playing us false.'

Ritter swallowed and played with his *Particula* ring. 'You destroyed my people.'

'Quite right. *Your* people. Whom you would have used to strike against us.' Archangel began to tap her feet again. 'The old headquarters, your people, these guests from foreign worlds, the van Dams and their two teams – they are all history. Extinguished. And that eliminates a minor risk for us.'

'I don't know what you want me to say.'

'The truth. Think about the opportunities I promised you. All isn't lost quite yet.'

Ritter laughed. 'Yes, I wanted power – to improve the world and liberate it from the corset the Organisation has put it in – to allow the world to breathe again, to release it from captivity and the rules humanity's been forced to obey,' he said. 'I'd have created something good from all this.'

Archangel laughed out loud. 'Amazing! You're really rather refreshing, Ritter. Do you truly believe what you're saying?'

'You wanted the truth, and you got it.' Ritter suddenly stretched his hand out to grab the *Particulae*. Escape was no longer an option – they'd find him wherever he went and he had no allies left. At any given moment, anywhere in the world, he would be in danger of a door opening next to him and being eliminated once and for all.

Ritter didn't want to end up like that.

'You're not the only one who can destroy a headquarters!' His finger bearing the ring with the stone embedded in it raced downwards to slam into the remaining fragments and release an uncontrolled ball of energy.

Before Ritter's hand could hit its target, Archangel had drawn her white Glock and shot him twice in the face.

Frankish Empire, June 841

Dana stood alongside Viktor in the midst of the slaughter that had suddenly become significantly greater, much to the delight of the crows and other scavengers. She swore loudly at the sight of the recently departed souls lying on top of and between the bodies of the dead travelling party.

They had won their mismatched battle with the *scara* thanks to their excessive firepower. The numerical superiority of the unit had been quickly erased in their attempts to protect the doctor after Spanger had started shooting. The *scara* had fought to the bitter end, undeterred by the cracking and all the devastating effects of modern weaponry like G36s and pistols.

It felt very much like a defeat to her.

Spanger and the soldiers had been needless victims of a misunderstanding. What's more, the energy field had collapsed, making the frame nothing more than a simple wooden rectangle. And a few ricochets had turned Ingo's measuring devices into mere scrap.

Ingo was attending to a warrior who had not yet

succumbed to her injuries, trying to stabilise her. She had been hit in the right-hand side of her chest by a bullet; blood was pouring out of the entry hole and jagged pieces of metal had pierced her flesh. He didn't want to let the woman die, but the medical knowledge he had acquired for taking his driving test was of little help. You didn't see these sorts of wounds in a car accident. He looked down at his bloody fingers and the gunshot wound. 'Ms Rentski? Can you help me?'

'Of course.' Dana hurried over to him.

Friedemann was inspecting the frame for damage. He didn't care about the deaths; for him the real catastrophe was of a different nature. They had no way of returning. He had laid the linen cloth over Spanger's body so he didn't have to look at it.

Coco sat at the side of the road with her back to the corpses, her face bathed in the summer sun as she breathed in the wind blowing across from the fields and flowers. Unlike the *scara*, this view was timeless.

Viktor looked around at the dead bodies, both men and women, which bothered him. There had been no female warriors in the Middle Ages. Battlefields were the sole province of men. And yet the leader of the *scara* had been a woman – and not just a soldier, a duchess.

'We can still use the frame,' announced Friedemann with relief. The notches hadn't caused too much damage and the stones were all in their rightful place. 'Once we've figured out how to trigger the force field from this side.'

Viktor looked at the linen cloth covering Spanger's peppered body. 'We've got him to thank for that.'

'Perhaps.' Friedemann saw no reason to grant the man any glory. 'In any case, he was the one who picked a fight with the *scara*. Let's not lose sight of that.'

Viktor wondered how best to dispose of the body, or at least to hide Spanger's modern equipment. Burying him would be best. He smiled wryly to himself. That would give the archaeologists a real puzzle later on, finding a Kevlar vest buried alongside people with gunshot wounds in the vicinity of a major mediaeval battle. They had probably already changed the course of history anyway.

Friedemann was only interested in the frame, which he was now examining with the aid of his notebook, going over each engraving in turn. 'Very, very different,' he muttered.

'Different from what?' Viktor took a step closer. He wondered whether their leader's emotional coldness had more to do with his dislike of Spanger or the professor's own solitary nature.

'Different from anything I've seen before.' Friedemann pointed to a couple of decorative elements. 'These signs and symbols don't match what's in here.' He tapped the notes in question and tucked the notebook back under his Moorish robe. 'Wherever we go, the frame has to come with us.'

'Do you have any idea as to why the force field went out?' Viktor asked.

'Overheating – overload. Or maybe the door in the chamber we went through shut.'

Friedemann walked over to those riderless horses which had stayed and were now snorting patiently or cropping grass. He grabbed the reins of two of them and tied them to the wagon. 'The wood's in a pretty bad state. We'll have to handle it carefully when we move it. If the frame breaks' – he pointed to Spanger's covered body – 'his sacrifice will have been in vain.'

Viktor raised an eyebrow and the professor relented in an attempt to avoid confrontation. 'I know what he did for us. It won't be forgotten. And I'll make sure his relatives receive his pay once we've found Anna-Lena van Dam.' He now considered the matter settled. He placed his hand on the cart. 'We can use this to transport the frame.'

'Both of you come over here,' Dana called out. She had tried everything to stop the bleeding, but the soldier's destroyed blood vessels and organs couldn't be saved without modern medicine. 'If you want to interrogate the woman, best do it now. She won't be alive for long. Her name's Josepha.'

Friedemann and Viktor rushed over to the seriously injured woman.

The dark-haired soldier looked at her opponents wide-eyed, her gaze wandering several times to their modern pistols and rifles. 'What . . . what are those weapons you're carrying? The cracking, those wounds – all that *death*. With your weapons that roared and breathed fire upon us you destroyed my *scara* as if it were the easiest thing in the world.' Tears leaked silently from Josepha's eyes, but the shock and adrenalin were saving her from the true extent of her pain. 'What demons has she created?'

'We're looking for a young woman, aged around twenty, with long red hair and a glimmering gem on her nose,' said

Friedemann. He didn't have time for conversations that didn't go anywhere. 'Her name's Anna-Lena and she'll probably have been wearing clothes that looked strange to you.'

Breathing quickly, Josepha turned her head to face the slaughtered travelling party. 'Why did you attack Aysun – where have you taken him? He's a good man – he hadn't done anything to you.'

Friedemann touched her on the arm. 'We had nothing to do with it.'

'Did Septimania send you to kidnap Aysun?' A bead of blood trickled from the right-hand corner of Josepha's mouth and landed on the ground. 'Oh, of course! He's the one behind this treachery, the swine. He's always looking to pursue his own agenda, never able to forget his feud with the old Moor.' She moved her head back to its original position. The blood pouring out of the hole in her chest was slowing. 'But this act of treachery won't prevent my empress from winning the battle,' she breathed, her lips quirking in a confident smile.

'What empress?' asked Ingo, before he could stop himself.

'Empress Judith – the one true empress to rule over all nations. And that's despite Ermengarde trying to stir up the nobles in rebellion,' she spat at them. 'It's all clear now – you *have* been sent by Septimania! I can see it.' She gave a bitter laugh and slumped to the ground. 'The alliance won't break up just because you've killed us. Guerin will come. And then . . .'

The light in Josepha's eyes faded and her body went limp.

Viktor felt just as bad. Ingo, Friedemann and Dana all looked bemused.

'She didn't know,' said Coco from the side of the road, not bothering to turn around. 'I could see into her mind. She was thinking about completely different things – her family, her two sons, her empress. But there was no sign of Anna-Lena in her head.'

Ingo cleared his throat and walked over to her. 'Don't overdo it,' he said quietly.

'I was in her mind.' Coco closed her eyes, feeling the sun's kiss on her face. 'The force field – it's changed me. It's turned me into a real medium. How many times have I got to tell you before you start believing me?' She *needed* to convince him, for her own sake as much as anything. It really had been precisely as she had described. It was confusing and exhausting, but exciting at the same time. Her temples were throbbing and she could feel a migraine coming on. Would she be able to do even more soon? What other gifts might have been awakened in her?

'Well, if that's the case then it's good news for us.'

Clearly Ingo didn't believe her.

'Can you tune in to Anna-Lena van Dam?'

'No. She's too far away.' Coco pulled herself up and stood in such a way that she couldn't see the bodies. She hated the sight and stench of them, not to mention the vicious cawing of the ravens presently congregating on the corpses. 'She mentioned a man named Aysun – he's a Moorish scholar. If I've interpreted her thoughts correctly, he's a friend and advisor to the empress.'

'Well, none of the dead men is an old Moor,' interjected Dana.

'So they've taken him with them to . . . what, demand a ransom?' Friedemann speculated. 'And perhaps they bagged Anna-Lena while they were at it. The young lady must have stepped out of the frame just as the attack was taking place.'

'That would be the trail of hooves, then.' Viktor indicated the tracks on the path. 'We can follow them. If we find Aysun, we'll free him and take him to the empress; in return she'll help us to find Anna-Lena.' The spontaneous plan was a bit slapdash, but he didn't have any better ideas.

'Just what I was going to suggest.' Friedemann gestured at the dead *scara*. 'We'll change clothes. Ms Rentski, you can take the duchess' stuff and be our official leader. That'll be less conspicuous than this Moorish clothing and will give us some authority, if we need it.'

It took them a while to find enough stuff that wasn't overly torn or bloodstained and fitted over their modern kit. Using a little water from the barrels of drinking water on the wagon, they rinsed the blood off the armour and by the end most of them could pass plausibly as being from that period – except for the professor, who stood out thanks to his beanpole of a physique; even the biggest chainmail was too short on his lanky body.

Unfortunately, Coco was the only one of them who could ride a horse. She went around each of the beasts, unsaddling those they weren't going to take with them. They were the only living beings she took pity on here.

They would have to learn how to handle their mounts very quickly if they were going to pass as a *scara* unit – and keep up with the fleeing robbers. Coco showed them all the basics – how to sit, how to make the animal go and stop – while Ingo attempted to drive the wagon. They had hidden their modern equipment in the back, as well as the frame, which they had padded with straw and scraps of clothing.

'All ready?' Dana really looked the part now. Her G36 was concealed beneath her light coat. She and Viktor had a magazine each, plus two for the pistols, but one more battle and they'd have to use sword and spear like everyone else in this era. 'Off we go,' she ordered, 'and stay close to the tracks.'

Coco led off confidently, her mount readily obeying her commands. Her clothes reeked of sweat and iron and everywhere itched. As they travelled, she tried several times to get in contact with Anna-Lena using the pendulum, but still the young woman's whereabouts remained a total mystery.

The group rode in single file, having to use every ounce of their concentration to guide the horses and not fall out of the saddle during the fast trot Coco was insisting on. Each of them employed their own *ad hoc* technique in an effort to stay on the animals' backs, with varying degrees of elegance.

The landscape remained unchanged as they passed row after row of fields with oats and millet growing in them; wheat was becoming a less common sight. Every now and again they took breaks beneath brightly blooming fruit trees, accompanied by the uninterested buzzing of the local bee population. Soon a forest could be seen in the distance, nestled among the gently sloping hills.

As evening fell, they found themselves approaching a

farm with several horses tied up outside. They stayed at a generous distance away, discretion being the better part of valour, and Dana raised her G36 and looked through the scope.

'One in chainmail; the rest have got leather armour. Looks pretty torn up,' she informed the others. 'And it looks as if they've got Moorish clothing tied up in a bundle.'

'So they *did* loot the corpses, then.' Viktor inspected the robbers as well. His thighs and buttocks ached from hours in the saddle; he was looking forward to the prospect of being able to dismount soon. In the glow of the torches and oil lamps carried by the farm workers, he could see a very old, dark-skinned man being supported by a young man. His skin colour and overall presentation clearly set him apart from the other figures. 'That's got to be Aysun.'

The robbers guided the two men from the barn to the main house adjoining it, where they could see lights flickering in the windows.

'Any sign of Anna-Lena?' Friedemann looked at the frame for the umpteenth time. It was lying on its bed of fabric, which had spared it from the worst of the jolts during the bumpy journey.

Ingo, on the other hand, had had a most uncomfortable time on the uneven path and his back was now in agony. Shock absorbers must have been nothing more than a faraway dream for coachmen in this period. 'Be— Is the young lady in there?' he asked Coco, stopping himself just in time from using her real name. That would just elicit unwelcome questions.

Coco pulled the golden pendulum out of her pocket. The metal pendant was hanging limply from the chain and no matter how much she focused on Anna-Lena, nothing happened. 'I don't think so.' She had enjoyed being on a horse again, though the situation itself was most unwelcome: there was too much pressure, too many expectations and absolutely no certainty that the frame would be able to bring them back home at all. She stroked the horse's neck, soothed by the feeling of its warm hide under her fingers.

'Fine. We'll go and have a look.' Friedemann remained calm. 'How shall we go about it?' He looked around the group. 'Any suggestions?'

'We're wearing the colours of the empress and they've taken her Moorish friend captive,' said Ingo. 'If we turn up in the farmhouse looking like this, they'll attack us on sight – they'll know they've got nothing to lose.'

'So we're in the wrong disguise again,' said Coco. Another fight was looming, with yet more death.

'Not necessarily.' Dana grinned. 'We're representing the power of the state, aren't we? The farmers won't dare to defy us and we'll kill the robbers in no time at all.' She pointed to the stable. 'There are no more than five of them.'

'How could they kill the entire group like that, then?' Ingo asked.

'Simple – they had the element of surprise. Aysun and his people wouldn't have been expecting to be attacked like that out in the open. Maybe they were hiding in the fields, ready to spring an ambush.' Viktor looked around at the rest of them, disconcerted by what he could see through the polished scope. 'There are more than five horses.'

'Stolen after the attack?' suggested Friedemann.

'But if not?' Viktor lowered the rifle. 'We haven't got enough ammunition.'

'This lot aren't part of a *scara*, though – they're not likely to fight tooth and nail to the last man,' Ingo pointed out. 'I'm sure they'll surrender after the first burst of gunfire.'

'That's a brave assessment coming from someone with no combat experience.' Dana was less optimistic. 'I'll sneak up on them, get a closer look.'

'Ah, classic reconnaissance work, as practised by all free-climbers,' Viktor goaded, not expecting a response, which was just as well, for it never came.

Friedemann was already leading his horse towards the farmhouse. 'Let's just set this Aysun free and ask him if he's seen our missing girl. She did stumble out of a frame, after all, and that's not the sort of thing that generally goes unnoticed. He might have some information.' *About the portals at least.* 'Why would he be carrying an empty frame around with him if he didn't know anything about its powers? The Moor might be able to help us to rekindle the energy field.'

'Professor, wait!' Viktor tried to stop the man, who was relying solely on his armour, Kevlar vest and pistol, but his damned horse refused to go in the direction he wanted, while Friedemann's steed trotted merrily towards the stables as if eager to greet its equine brethren.

Dana rode past him in an attempt to stay close to their leader. 'Hang on,' she told Viktor as she slapped his horse on the back, causing it to start running immediately.

Ingo rumbled along behind her with the wagon.

Coco kept level with the wagon, the pendulum in her hand and her thoughts focused on the dilapidated court-yard in front of them. She was not a fighter and she had no desire to put herself in harm's way. And no matter how hard she tried, the only thing she could feel was her relentless headache. 'Anna-Lena's not here,' she said softly. 'I'm absolutely certain.'

Ingo was trying to steer the horse, although now it was moving, it was perfectly content to trot along, keeping up with the others. *Herd instinct.* He was having great difficulty believing in the sudden abilities of his former lover. He was a scientist and as such, he required evidence. 'Let's hope Aysun's got some information for us,' he replied evasively.

The unexpected arrival of what was apparently a *scara* caused a great commotion on the farm. A few shouts rang out and some of the inhabitants stepped outside, holding lamps and torches.

Friedemann was pleased to see there were no weapons drawn or bows nocked; perhaps they were all waiting to see what Empress Judith's elite unit was looking for. He noticed one of the peasant boys quickly removing an elabo-rately embroidered cap from his head and hiding it behind its back. The hat appeared to be of Middle Eastern design.

'God be with you,' he called out, considering this to be the most neutral expression. He had no idea how people greeted each other in the Middle Ages.

Dana appeared at his side. 'Let me do the talking. I'm the duchess, remember?' she whispered.

'In the name of Empress Judith,' she declared from her saddle, trying to control her horse as it waltzed nervously back and forth in front of the small crowd, adding a certain drama to proceedings, 'we're looking for the outlaws who dared to attack the entourage of Aysun the Moor. Release him – or we'll burn every last building to the ground.'

'Bit much?' whispered Friedemann. He was afraid they might attack them out of desperation. 'We should probably have tried being conciliatory first.'

Viktor finally joined them, followed by Ingo and Coco. He had to admit they didn't look in the least bit military or authoritative. He could see the very same doubts in the people standing uncertainly outside the door. They were clearly waiting – but for what?

'Keep an eye out in all directions,' Viktor whispered to the group.

'Make way,' came a voice from inside the house, and the crowd parted immediately.

A man aged around twenty appeared, flanked by several armed guards. He was clean-shaven, with blond hair falling just off his shoulders. Judging by the embroidery on his clothes, his expensive-looking jewelled belt and the two gem-encrusted rings he was wearing, he belonged to a wealthy family and didn't live on this farm. He was carrying a long dagger rather than a sword. He was followed by a man and a woman who both looked to be of lower status. 'Let's end this farce.' He stopped four paces away from Dana and the group and put his hands on his hips. 'If you want to leave with your life, Duchess, turn back with your *scara* and pretend you never saw us here.'

Friedemann began to reply, but Dana waved him away. She had decided to maintain her aggressive persona.

What had worked for her in the field should be fine for the Middle Ages as well. 'And you are?'

'William of Septimania. And I have every right not to hand Aysun over to you, for reasons I'm sure are obvious to you.' The young man looked affronted. 'And politeness goes a long way, Duchess. I'm in no way inferior to you.'

'Whoa, not so fast! The Moor isn't yours yet,' intervened one of the men in the background; he certainly didn't appear to be a farmworker – they could now see he was armed. 'We still haven't agreed on our price.'

Dana looked around her. Why the young man considered himself entitled to hold this Aysun captive was a mystery still. 'I can't do that, William of Septimania. And your family history is of no interest to me or the empress.'

Viktor found it remarkable that they took Dana's being in charge as a given; contrary to the history books, it appeared that women were no less valuable to men in this period, which was not at all how he had imagined the Middle Ages to be.

William's face darkened. 'How dare you talk to me like that? The empress would do well to—'

'The empress wants her Moor back.' Dana was thoroughly enjoying putting this arrogant little man in his place. Being on a horse was giving her an increased sense of authority.

'But she banished him from Aachen, so—'

'She's changed her mind.' Dana put a hand on her longsword, intending to make them think she wouldn't hesitate one second to strike if she so decided. On some of her previous operations there had been certain occasions when she had had to talk to corrupt customs officials; those sorts of people understood both threats and bribery. In this case she had only threats available. 'I'm not here to argue with you about the will of the empress. Release Aysun, William of Septimania, and I'll forget I ever saw you and your people. Fail to do so, and I'll have you charged.'

'On what grounds?'

'Incitement to murder and pillaging.'

Ingo thought Dana was doing very well, but he was keeping a close eye on the farm's roofs and windows, just as Viktor had advised.

Coco had little confidence in either the chainmail shirt or the Kevlar vest she was wearing. She would have preferred to crawl underneath the wagon and wait until the dispute had been resolved in their favour.

William lifted his head back and laughed. 'Very well, Duchess. I gave you a chance to clear off.' He gave a command signal to the armed robbers. 'Kill them.'

None of the men or women moved.

This time it was Dana's turn to laugh, as she drew her sword from its scabbard in a single slow, deliberate motion. None of her opponents knew she couldn't wield it properly, so it was just a case of displaying as much self-confidence as possible. That had spared her from a fight more than once in the past.

'My lord, this is a *scara*,' said one of the robbers. 'If we kill them, the empress won't—'

'If you kill them, the empress will never hear about it!' barked William.

'What a wonderful idea it'd be, to attack elite warriors

like us,' Friedemann remarked condescendingly, as if he possessed swordsmanship equal to the god of war himself. 'You know how well we can handle a blade.'

Dana pointed her sword at William. The situation had turned in their favour. 'Since you've admitted to have the Moor in your possession, I order you to surrender him to us. In the name of the empress. Do this and there'll be no need for her to ever learn of your involvement in this matter.'

Ingo noticed an outline behind one of the illuminated windows. The person was crouching down, but had clearly underestimated the revelatory effect of the light. 'Right-hand side, outside,' he whispered to Viktor.

He looked up. A figure with a crossbow was ready to fire. 'Duchess, look! If that man dares to attack us, we'll show no mercy.'

'And if it's the last thing I do,' Dana added, 'I'll burn this whole farm to the ground.'

William raised his hand to stay the fire of the assassin behind the window. For now. 'Don't make me kill the Moor. That would achieve nothing. Let's—'

'Whoa! You won't kill my prisoner!' exclaimed the robber. 'You'll cough up first, William of Septimania, else I'll be fighting on the side of the duchess and the *scara*. And if you die, I'll just negotiate face-to-face with your father.' He took a step away from William. 'Agree a way out of this with the duchess that benefits us all.'

Dana was growing impatient. The longer a situation remained unresolved, the more likely the risk of it esca-lating. She had the impression that William was not a strong leader: the mercenaries would happily rip him off in their negotiations, or maybe just kill him to get the money, then go straight to his father – whoever he was – and earn double.

'I know why you were sent: to prove to your father that you can be a reliable son and skilled negotiator. Let's just say you had a good go at it, William.' She released the reins and was relieved that the horse did as it was bid. 'Send him the empress' regards and release Aysun. Now.'

William's beardless face was unmoved as he considered his options.

'The night's going to waste. I've got better things to do.' The leader of the bandits hooked his thumbs under his belt, which he was wearing over a leather harness, and turned to Dana. 'Duchess, I don't care who pays me for the old man. Make us a fair offer and Aysun will soon be in the hands of the empress.'

'How dare you,' shouted William. 'You promised him to me!'

'That was before I knew a *scara* was going to turn up,' said the man breezily as his men laughed approvingly.

'I know who you are,' came an old voice from inside the house. 'You're from the same place as the young red-haired lady. The land on the other side of the frame. And you're looking for her.'

'Shut your toothless mouth, you filthy Moor!' snapped William over his shoulder. 'You're talking nonsense.'

Dana exchanged glances with Viktor and Friedemann; Ingo sat up in the coachbox and gripped his pistol a little more tightly.

They clearly needed Aysun to find Anna-Lena, but William wasn't about to abandon his task – and the robbers were all too aware that they were in possession of a valuable prisoner, wanted by both sides.

They could see there was no way of de-escalating the situation.

CHAPTER VII

Near Frankfurt

Time and time again he had listened to Ritter's promises and assurances and believed the man would turn them into reality one day soon. That was why had had stayed down in the cave system, guarding it and hindering any curious people who had stumbled upon it – all because Ritter had asked him to.

His real name was unpronounceable in this world, but he had learned that everything on Earth needed a label, so he had given himself one as well: Friend, because Ritter had always referred to him as 'my friend'.

After a while, a few doubts about Ritter's intentions had begun to creep in. And he had started to learn certain things, helped by the items he had taken from dead adventurers. He had learned the languages and history of this strange world, its rules, its nature, what made its inhabitants tick and what they had in common despite their differences.

And how to manipulate and kill them.

His self-confidence had grown at the same rate as his doubts about Ritter's promises. His rebellion was the natural successor to his doubts, showing Ritter that he was under no obligation to adhere to his promises by neglecting his tasks.

Just as he had done with the young redhead and the two search teams who had followed her down.

He had clung to their heels in the passages, but left them unmolested, just to annoy Ritter – to send him a message.

He enjoyed playing the role of watchman.

The first team had quickly fallen victim to the doors and the *Particulae*, while the young woman had disappeared into one of the chambers and hadn't been seen since.

Friend was a little disappointed about that, if truth be told. He had even allowed the second rescue team to return to the surface. To his great surprise, they came back – and he had allowed them to disappear through one of the doors.

Ritter hadn't come down himself, however, choosing instead to send his subordinates to search for the intruders.

And then the other people turned up, equipped with new types of weapons and boxes of bombs. He didn't want to draw their attention as they appeared to be both diligent and very well trained. They belonged to the Organisation, same as Ritter, but were clearly not under his command.

Friend noticed the anomalies in the old headquarters were increasing day by day. The *Particulae* were disintegrating uncontrollably, creating enormous shifts in gravity and altering people's perceptions and their ways of thinking, not to mention the extra-terrestrial radiation penetrating and re-coding DNA.

The humans hadn't noticed it, but he had.

So Friend had decided not to wait for Ritter any longer, choosing instead to be the master of his own fate.

He wouldn't follow the dangerous-looking bomb squad, for they would spot him and kill him immediately. But thanks to the half-burnt records he had found in the abandoned rooms, he knew there were other doors, portals and crossings that still functioned perfectly.

All he had to do was find them.

Friend had come to understand that the Earth's solar radiation would disintegrate him if he were exposed to it for too long. He had heard members of the bomb squad saying they wanted to complete their final investigation and preparation of the caves the next morning, so he waited for nightfall, then set off on his attempt to escape from the maze and the mansion.

On the way, he appropriated the clothes of one of the dead members of the first search party, rather than travel around naked: as a stranger to this world it was imperative that he avoid attracting too much attention.

Friend pulled himself easily along the rusty old steel cable into the villa's basement. It was dark outside, so he could leave the safety of the property without hurting himself. He crept up the stairs quietly, stalked through the cellar and headed for the front door.

He looked through the window onto the porch and drive, where a man in uniform was lying motionless alongside a car, while another was crawling across the gravel to another car which was parked a little further away. He was hurt; Friend could smell the blood seeping from his body.

The scene piqued his curiosity.

He left the house and walked with a bouncy gait towards the uniformed man. From what he had heard, he guessed this must be the chauffeur Matthias. He had a slender knife lodged in the back of his neck and his eyes were wide and lifeless. He was holding a blood-smeared ice scraper in his hand, which he had obviously tried to use as a weapon.

Friend stepped over the body and caught up with the injured stranger, who had blood pouring from a gash in his neck.

'Good evening,' said Friend politely. 'Do you need a first-aid kit?'

'Who ... who are you?' the man managed to squeeze out. 'You ... weren't ... with the group ...'

'Ah, you've been watching the house?' Friend looked inside the car and saw a miniature laptop open with photographs of Viktor, Spanger and Coco on the screen. 'Most interesting.'

He opened the door and picked up the portable computer. He quickly worked out how to change the screen and with a few swipes, he scrolled through the files, skimming all the information about the team members, as well as Anna-Lena and her father. The injured man obviously worked for Ritter's organisation.

Friend looked down at the man, who was still crawling painfully across the gravel an arm's length away. 'You were assigned with eliminating the second search party?'

'How do you know ... ?' He had slowed down, losing strength by the blood continuing to drain from his body and hindered by the slippery stones.

'Ritter brought me to your world. I know as much as I need to about him, you and the Organisation.'

'Then call headquarters – I need . . . a team. The prisoner's . . .'

Friend placed the laptop on top of the car and grabbed the man around his neck. With one hand he lifted the man high. His arms fell limply to his side: he had lost consciousness.

'I'm afraid there's been a misunderstanding. I'm not part of your organisation.' Friend shook him a little, like a cat with a shrew, trying to get him to respond, but it didn't help – so he dropped the insensible man and stepped on his neck, crushing it. He didn't dare leave behind any witnesses to his successful escape. Curious, he strolled across the drive and looked inside the others cars.

Anna-Lena van Dam was lying on the back seat of one of them.

Friend felt a strange sense of kinship with the young woman. There was something different about her.

He carefully put his ear to her chest.

Her heart was beating strongly and regularly, her breathing calm and deep.

Friend was struck by a feeling of connection – familiarity, recognition. There was an aura about her, as if he were aware of something in her that only the two of them shared. He could think of one reason for that: she wasn't from this world either. She had come through one of the doors and assumed Anna-Lena's appearance, a glamour, in order to be brought to safety.

'Can you hear me?' Friend shook her gently by the shoulder. 'Come on, I know you're not van Dam's daughter.'

The doppelgänger remained motionless, as if fast asleep.

Friend gave a grunt and thought hard. He glanced over at the laptop on the roof of the car and decided to read through the files and messages first, to get a better understanding of the group. Perhaps he could wait for them here and force them to help him. They should be rather familiar with the doors by the time they returned.

But what if they weren't?

Friend leaned against the car, picked up the miniature laptop and began to scroll through.

A quiet sound heralded the arrival of a new message. It said that Ritter no longer needed to be taken out, for he had already been liquidated.

Friend grinned as he read about the fate of his mendacious prison guard, praising himself for not having stayed down in the labyrinth.

A low rumble sounded and immediately afterwards, flames several feet in length shot out of the windows of the villa as fire consumed the estate in a spectacular explosion. It continued to blaze, rushing towards the people carrier, as the ground collapsed, swallowing the house whole.

The bomb squad had clearly had a change of plan.

Friend tucked the laptop under his arm, before turning and running down the drive. He would have loved to have saved the sleeping doppelgänger but he didn't have time, not with the unnatural fire hurtling after him. It enveloped his body, burning skin, hair and clothes. Friend held his breath and rushed through the inferno while he still had muscles to propel him forwards. He shot out of the gradually dissipating ball of flame, taking long jumps to avoid the subsiding terrain.

When he finally stumbled and fell after what had felt like an eternity, his battered skin ruptured in several places and burst open. Friend collapsed onto the cool, wet grass and lost consciousness.

'. . . nine, ten! Ina? Are you hiding?' a good-natured, female voice rang out. 'Ready or not, here I come!'

Friend winced, blinking and gasping in pain. He had instinctively rolled into the shade of a tree; the sun was shining all around him but it couldn't penetrate the thick green leaves.

He sat up against the trunk and leaned back.

A girl squeezed through the bushes in front of him and saw him sitting on the floor. She stopped suddenly. 'Mummy! There's a man over here – he looks hurt!'

His clothes were scorched and torn, his features barely visible underneath all the soot and blood. He was breathing erratically, panting as if he had just completed a marathon. He admired the girl for not running away immediately. 'It's all right. I've just got to . . . have something to eat,' he breathed in a scratchy voice. 'This sun – it *hurts*. It's burning me worse than the fire I've just escaped from.'

'Ina, where are you?'

'Here! I'm over here!'

Friend cleared his throat. 'Have you got any food on you?'

Ina nodded. 'A chocolate bar.' She took it out of her pocket. 'Would you like it?'

'Ina? Stay away from that man, do you understand?'

'Chocolate. Chocolate is good.' Friend liked chocolate.

'Do you know, little Ina, I think I'm dying. At least I'll have something sweet on my tongue before I go.'

Ina looked up at the sun, which was obscured by the dark smoke from the fire. 'Like Superman, but the other way around?'

'Superman?'

'You don't know Superman?'

'No.'

'Oh. Well, he's a superhero from another planet who gets special powers from our sun.' Ina gave him a pitying look. 'But our sun's killing you.'

'Yes, I'm afraid that's exactly what it's like.'

'Oh. That's a shame.' Ina didn't look afraid of him any more.

'I agree.' Friend smiled beneath the layer of dirt and soot. 'Would you bring me the bar, please?'

Ina raised her tiny hand holding the chocolate bar.

He stretched out his bloody, battered hand, which protruded from the shredded sleeve. His burnt, soot-covered fingers drew closer to her, trembling, then moving slowly, he grabbed the chocolate bar. 'Thank you, little Ina.'

'You're welcome.'

'I haven't got much time left,' he said after a moment. 'Let's get your mother to hurry up a bit.' His injured fingers suddenly dropped the chocolate bar and with lightning speed he grabbed the child's wrist.

Ina screamed loudly with shock.

'Ina?' her mother called out in alarm, cracking through the undergrowth as she rushed over to where she thought her daughter was. 'Ina, where are you?'

'Don't worry. I'm not going to hurt her,' he called out, grabbing the chocolate with his other hand. He tore the wrapping open with his teeth and started wolfing it down greedily.

The girl's mother, dressed in practical outdoor clothes, arrived at the tree and pressed her hand over her mouth at the sight of the seriously injured man. 'Oh my God!' she exclaimed. 'What's happened to you?'

Friend released his grip on Ina, who took a couple of steps back into the sunlight. 'I was out for a walk when all of a sudden there was this explosion.' His body felt as if it were on fire, but he knew his skin had already started to regenerate. It cracked and crackled as the burnt layer crumbled away, replaced by new pink skin.

'That was the earthquake,' said Ina. 'And there was an explosion afterwards – they said so on the radio.' She pointed beyond him. 'It destroyed that haunted castle. And our house shook as well. All my elf figurines fell over.'

Ina's mother looked at Friend. 'You really need to go to hospital.' She patted her pockets, trying to find her phone. 'It's a miracle you're still alive.'

Friend didn't want to draw any attention to himself. He was recovering some of his strength thanks to the chocolate. He stretched out his mental feelers and penetrated the woman's fluttering, startled mind, placating and calming her so she'd be able to interpret his words. 'Did you come here by car?'

'Yes.'

'Then it'll be fine if you just take me home.' Friend got up slowly and the layers of skin he had shed tumbled off him. His clothes were nothing more than scorched rags. He needed some new ones. 'I just need a bit of rest.' He must have looked a frightful state.

At the last moment he remembered the stranger's laptop, which was lying a few steps away, and took it with him.

'Good. Let's go. Though I still think you'd be better off in hospital.'

On their way through the undergrowth, Ina was flitting around unabashed, chattering about the earthquake. She said the forest around the old sawmill was still on fire – that she had heard it on the news. Experts suspected an underground bubble of methane had been dislodged during the quake and had ignited, with spectacular results. Ina didn't know what 'methane' was, but she knew it wasn't good and it smelled funny.

Friend could smell it: that wasn't methane. The stench was coming from the bombs that had been detonated in the old headquarters; all this talk about methane and earthquakes must have been put about by Ritter's conspirator chums.

They reached the car, a slightly dented and dirty family saloon: pleasantly unremarkable.

Friend got in the back and threw a blanket over himself as protection from the sun. It stank of dog, but it was worth it to keep him out of sight of the prying eyes that a man in his condition was bound to draw.

While they were driving he had a quick look at the laptop underneath the blanket. It might look in a bad state, but it did still appear to be working. The battery level had dropped to around a third. He scanned the most recent messages in the inbox and came across another interesting death report, this one relating to Walter van Dam and his household.

This opened up all manner of new possibilities for Friend. The property would almost certainly be deserted, meaning he could use it as a base until he recovered and worked out a plan to return to his own world. Perhaps he might even find references to other portals and passages while he was there.

'I've changed my mind,' said Friend from beneath the disgusting blanket. 'Please would you drive me to the house of a friend of mine? He'll take care of me.' He rattled off the address listed in the dossier.

'Of course.' Ina's mother turned on her indicator and changed the destination on her satnav.

Frankish Empire, June 841

One thing in particular concerned Ingo about their impending conflict with William of Septimania and his people: the moment they used their modern weapons, they'd have to ensure they didn't leave any witnesses behind. The danger of a handgun from the twenty-first century being recorded in the annals of history was too great. It would be a feast for conspiracy theorists everywhere.

Ingo grinned, in spite of himself. Ever since he had come into contact with the doors, he could no longer rule out the existence of time travel or aliens. Perhaps the conspiracy theorists weren't so wrong after all.

'Are you laughing at me, Duchess? That's your answer?' William of Septimania placed a hand on the handle of his dagger. 'Do you really want to take that chance?' He gave a signal and a woman handed him her sword. 'Get down off your horse and I'll teach you some manners.'

'I'll take my chances.' Dana jumped from her saddle and walked towards the young nobleman, estimating that the robbers weren't about to turn on them if they suspected they'd get a better deal with the *scara*. To the amazement of her opponent, she sheathed her sword.

'What are you doing? I'll grind you into the dust!' William reached out to strike her. 'Don't expect me to go easy on you. The—'

Dana grabbed his sword hand and pulled it towards her, hurling the man over her hip and onto the ground. Modern combat techniques had their advantages. She over-rotated his joints to prise his fingers from his weapon, then picked up his sword and pointed the tip at his throat. 'See how easy that was?'

William lay in the dirt and looked up at her, his eyes wide with shock. He was no fighter at the best of times; now he looked as if he had given up all resistance. His two companions hesitated, not sure whether to intervene, while the bandits merely stood around, smirking.

Dana tore the pouch of coins from his belt and threw it to the leader of the robbers. 'There. Your reward. Now the Moor belongs to us and the empress.'

The outlaw caught the bag and burst out laughing. 'You see, William? That's how it's done.' He pocketed his bounty and gave his people a signal to depart. 'Send my regards to your father. He's been out-bidden – all thanks to you.'

Laughing darkly and with a last few derogatory comments aimed at the noblemen, the bandits left.

Dana allowed William to get to his feet, then shoved the sword into a gap between the stones in the wall and bent it with a powerful jerk. 'Here. It belongs to your people now.' She threw the curved blade at his feet.

The young nobleman paid it no notice, just walked wordlessly to his horse, flanked by his two companions. Their expressions gave no indication of what they might be thinking about this whole affair. The woman looked regretfully at her broken sword, then they climbed into their saddles and rode off.

'You've got an enemy for life now, my lady,' said one of the farmers, removing his hat. 'Forgive us. We had nothing to do with all this, but they forced us to put them up.'

'The empress won't find out.' Dana motioned to her group to dismount and enter the house with her.

'I'll stand guard here,' said Viktor. 'There's every chance our little Hotspur might come back with reinforcements, looking for revenge.'

'Fine.' Friedemann's dismount was more akin to a fall than anything else. 'Let's go and find Aysun.'

Ingo leaped down from the wagon, while Coco slid elegantly off her horse. A farm boy walked over to take care of the animals as the group entered the farmhouse. He stared after the professor, who towered over all and sundry.

It was dark inside and there was a strong smell of molten fat from the tallow candles, combined with the smoke from the fire burning in the fireplace. The farmer's family had positioned themselves against the wall in height order. Eight children and five adults shared the tiny room; roughly constructed ladders led up to bunks that could be closed off by cloth sheets. Thirteen pairs of eyes looked at the *scara* in wonder; no one dared to speak to them.

Coco shuddered at the idea of having to spend a night in a place like this; it must be riddled with vermin.

Aysun was leaning heavily on the table. There were bruises on his right temple and above his left eyebrow. The outlaws had clearly mistreated him despite his advanced age, which might have been well over a hundred years. With his wrinkled skin and sunken features, he resembled a re-animated mummy, looking around with open eyes. He held a clay cup in his ossified left hand, but the skinny fingers bore several glimmering rings bedecked with precious stones. The value of just one of those alone must have exceeded that of the entire farm.

Next to him stood his servant, a young man in Moorish robes, with long, curly hair and a bold expression that belonged more to a soldier than a steward.

When the old Moor caught sight of the group, his pupils gleamed. 'Good evening,' he said in a croaky voice. 'You have my thanks for freeing me from Septimania's clutches. William's father owes me a debt, but I thought perhaps he had decided not to pay it.' He motioned for them to join him on the bench.

The peasant family remained motionless.

Dana sat down opposite the Moor and pointed to Friedemann. 'This is our leader,' she said softly. 'You can talk to him.'

Ingo kindly asked the farmers to leave them alone so

they could speak without being disturbed. 'We'll call you back in once we've discussed everything we need to.'

The family disappeared, barely able to take their eyes off the professor.

Aysun gave a broad smile, which turned his emaciated face into a wrinkled landscape replete with bumps and deep furrows. 'Women aren't leaders where you're from, I take it?'

'We're working on it,' replied Dana, 'but it'll take some time.'

'I didn't think that was the case in your time either,' added Ingo. 'I was amazed when I heard people talking about empresses.'

'Where do you come from?' Aysun looked at each of them in turn. 'I am right in thinking from a time yet to come?'

Friedemann nodded. 'You assume correctly. We're looking for a red-haired young lady by the name of Anna-Lena van Dam. She came out of your frame.'

'Have you brought it with you?'

'Yes.'

'Allah be praised!' Aysun looked relieved. 'And the sphere's still doing its job?'

'No. It's disintegrated.' Friedemann could barely suppress his curiosity. 'Where did you get this artefact from? What do you know about its function? Please share what you know with us. That's the only way we'll be able to return.'

The Moor looked at him with his wise, old eyes. 'You're not just here to save your friend. You're in search of knowledge.' A slight smile played on his lips. 'So these passages will still exist in the centuries to come.'

'They will.' Friedemann noticed the odd looks the rest of the team were giving him. His thirst for knowledge would be impossible to quench with just a few sentences. He had to talk to Aysun for longer – make notes and add it all to his book. 'What would you say to coming along with us while we look for Anna-Lena? We can speak more on the journey.' He gave him a winning smile. 'We've got the wagon with us, so it would be reasonably comfortable for you.'

'That sounds like a great idea,' Ingo agreed enthusiastically. 'I need to find out what's going on with all these empresses. They don't appear in any of our history books.'

'And you said you know where our friend is,' said Dana emphatically. She understood the professor's academic interest in all this, but they still had a contract to fulfil. There was a young woman wandering around somewhere who had nothing and no one in this century.

'It's a difficult time for an old Moor like me, so I accept your proposal,' said Aysun. 'All my people are dead except for my servant. My interactions with the common folk are plagued with suspicion and violence and I know Septimania will try to get his hands on me again.' He sighed. 'I'd be more than happy to accompany you if you will take me to Empress Judith. She's been kind to me and I can count on her support. I was her advisor for a very long time, you know.'

'Of course!' Friedemann pounded the table with joy. 'I want to learn all there is to know about the frame.'

'So you should. There are some notes among my

possessions, concealed in a secret hiding place in one of the chests. I found them at the same time as the frame. Unfortunately, they're all encrypted and rather convoluted.' Aysun looked at him kindly. 'You're making me feel like a learned man here. You can help me to translate them. That way we'll each get something out of this.'

'Anna-Lena,' Dana interjected a second time. She wasn't about to let Friedemann ignore the true purpose of their mission. 'Where is she?'

'I'll tell you as soon as we've recovered my things.' Aysun took a sip of his drink. 'But I can assure you she's in capable hands.'

'So were you, in a manner of speaking.' Dana gave Friedemann a look that suggested in no uncertain terms that he shouldn't be satisfied by the Moor's reply.

But the professor wasn't about to start pushing Aysun. 'I accept your conditions. Consider it a symbol of our appreciation.'

Aysun thanked him with a slight bow.

While the conversation at the table was in full flow, Coco occupied herself by looking around the room. She noticed an elegantly embroidered leather bag next to a basic cupboard, which had previously been concealed by the peasant family's legs. It certainly didn't belong to them – it looked far too valuable for that. Coco rose and removed the bag from its hiding place. It weighed very little. 'Do you know who this belongs to?'

Aysun turned to look at her. 'It's William's. He put it down on the table and must have forgotten all about it in the furore caused by your appearance.'

'The farmer obviously wanted to keep it,' said Ingo suspiciously. 'It didn't find itself in that corner by magic.'

'Shall we see what he was carrying?' Coco opened the bag and turned it upside-down. A pile of letters fell onto the table, all bearing a seal.

'We can use all the historical information we can find,' said Ingo, and immediately picked one up to read.

He was untroubled by the Latin script used among the educated in this century, but the contents were rather dull, on the whole: instructions to tenants; a dispute with an abbot regarding taxes for a monastery. Then, finally, he came across a letter to someone called Guerin, whose name bore several aristocratic titles.

'Listen to this!' exclaimed Ingo, interrupting the low conversation between Friedemann and Aysun.

Most Noble Guerin, Count of Mâcon, Auvergne, Chalon, Autun and Arles,

I am writing to you to inform you of the threat facing our nation and Christianity as a whole, so that you may come to the correct decision.

The armies of Empress Judith and Empress Ermengarde will soon join in battle. Each side will be host to one hundred and fifty thousand brave soldiers, all good Christians and of outstanding honour.

We nobles have been advised to pick a side.

For my part, I prefer to wait until the battle is over and pledge my loyalty to the victor. Were I to show my hand too early, the consequences would be dire.

You will be aware that I have already been sinned against

and, based on false allegations, been forced to withdraw from the court at Aachen. My enemies did not shy away from accusing me of fornication with Empress Judith, from the loins of which base union her son Charles is said to have sprung. Now she is at war for the sake of that very son. Her husband at that time, may God have mercy on his soul, believed this arrant falsehood.

If I throw my lot in with either side before battle is joined, the conclusions drawn would only be to my disadvantage. I am writing this to you in the hope that you will understand my state of mind.

My dear Count, my friends have informed me that Empress Judith has asked you to assist her in her cause.

I am aware of reputation and consider you to be an honest and honourable man. And I daresay you are considering responding to the Empress' request.

To the best of my knowledge she intends to send a scara in the coming days, bearing her imperial standard and with her offer.

It is no secret that you and Lothair, Empress Ermengarde's consort, have shared a deep hostility for each other ever since the incident at Chalon-sur-Saône. That might encourage you to lead your soldiers into battle on the behalf of Empress Judith.

But I am proposing an alternative arrangement, most esteemed Guerin.

Each of us has been stripped of our pride and honour by the empresses of this world. Why, then, risk our lives for these dishonourable rulers?

If you will agree to do as I am asking and to avoid

participating in this slaughter, I will offer you co-dominion over my own holdings.

After the battle we shall approach the victor together and offer our support, as the conflict will have inflicted heavy losses upon the nobles. Whichever empress wins will be weakened and in dire need of our assistance.

On our terms.

If our negotiations with the victorious empress do not go as planned, I will surrender Toulouse to you.

And if they do, you will still receive Toulouse.

You see: either outcome will be to your advantage. And you will have saved your soldiers from certain death.

Do this for me and we can impose our will upon an empress.

Bernard of Septimania.

'Shit,' remarked Dana. They had just wiped out Empress Judith's negotiators. 'We've changed the course of history,' she murmured to Ingo. 'What will happen now with these negotiations? And the outcome of the battle?'

Ingo thought hard. It had been too long since he had studied history. 'I'm not convinced this is our history anyway.' The thesis of this being a fictional Middle Ages was playing havoc with his mind; he'd consider it properly afterwards. 'But if I recall correctly, Guerin's emergence was decisive in the fight over the Carolingian line of succession.' He looked around him.

'Which we might well have prevented.' Coco gathered up the letters. 'We've got to undo it.'

'We've got to find Anna-Lena,' said Dana sternly.

'Looks like we've got more than one mission now.' Friedemann was considering how he could tie all this in with his research. 'Let's sleep on it, then in the morning we'll go back to find what's left of Aysun's possessions.'

The Moor bowed his head in gratitude. 'I'll be certain to tell you immediately afterwards where to find your missing girl.'

'We'll rescue her, straighten out history and then use the frame to disappear,' said Dana. 'I'm not about to end up in the crosshairs of this particular battle.' Three hundred thousand fighters. A gigantic number for any century. And in the Middle Ages the fighting would be nothing short of wild hand-to-hand combat when the two sides met.

'And I've got to find out as much as I can about this time – about the empresses and how they came to power,' Ingo added. He rummaged through the depths of his memory for anything about Carolingian history. The battle was considered a great tragedy, one which claimed the lives of thousands of people, but it heralded a new era for France and Germany, sealed by a Carolingian treaty laying out how each territory would be divided up. But there was nothing in their history books about any empresses.

Aysun laughed heartily. 'Women have ruled your world for more than two hundred years of the Christian calendar. They cleverly manoeuvred themselves onto the thrones of kingdoms by marriage, then changed the laws and took the place of the men.' He stood up and his servant immediately rushed over to support him. 'It was a great pleasure to see nations blossom under their guidance and wisdom – until these unfortunate ruptures between the empresses.

Their enemies will take advantage of it. According to what I heard in Aachen, they're planning to overthrow female rule throughout the whole of Europe.' He shuffled towards the door in his exotic pointy shoes. 'Well, goodnight, my mysterious friends. May Allah watch over your dreams.'

Friedemann looked around with delight. 'What an adventure this is turning out to be. We'll be off first thing tomorrow.'

'We should take it in turns to stand guard. I don't trust the peasants or Septimania,' said Dana. 'I'll sort it out with Troneg.' She left the house.

'And I'll tell the family we'll be staying the night in the barn.' The professor departed as well.

Coco and Ingo exchanged looks.

'We've changed history,' she said, still horrified at the thought. She couldn't believe this was happening. 'What if we can't make it right? Will we still exist in the future – or will we simply disappear?'

Ingo stood up and took her in his arms. 'Of course we'll be able to put it right. And you'll be the first to know, my clairvoyant.'

They held each other in silence, savouring the warmth and closeness.

A short while later they fell asleep side-by-side, holding hands.

CHAPTER VIII

Frankish Empire, June 841

Ingo skimmed through his notes as he guided the horse back along the track they had taken to reach the farm. He had been talking to Aysun since early morning, writing down everything the Moor had told him about the mediaeval era they had arrived in. 'This is . . . unbelievable. The women have prominence in everything – it's the complete opposite of all our historical records!'

Dana led the way as the duchess and leader of the *scara*, with Coco alongside her. Friedemann remained in the wagon, where Aysun, worn out from all that talking, was sleeping on a bed of straw with a blanket laid over his body, his servant beside him, guarding him.

Unlike the clear sunshine of the day before, it was a cloudy, hazy morning. The high humidity was making them sweat heavily underneath their layers of fabric, Kevlar and chainmail.

Viktor brought up the rear of the party. He had overheard Ingo's discussion with Aysun and was also surprised to learn that women were in prominent positions, at least for the most part. The pope and the Church were stubbornly defending their male dominance, with Rome and the Vatican acting as a virile bulwark against the queens and empresses of Europe.

'Has anyone heard of the Phantom Time Hypothesis?' Ingo asked, receiving only shakes of the head in response. 'It was proposed a few decades ago: it suggests that the period from around 600 to 900 anno Domini was subject to historical falsification – and that this had been done immediately afterwards, in the tenth century.'

'Where did they get that idea from?' Viktor looked around for pursuers, afraid William of Septimania would return with a few mercenaries in tow to take revenge and retrieve his letters, but there was no one to be seen.

'Well, on the one hand, people point to a few dubious sources, claiming that many of the better records had been destroyed. And they say they used calendar reform to hide these missing three hundred years.' Ingo pushed his round glasses back up his nose; he was only wearing them when the group was alone. 'Of course it's all been rejected by experts, who point to the rings on ancient trees, for example: when you combine these with a whole host of un-doctored records, you can see that those three hundred years *must* have existed.'

'I know what you're getting at,' Friedemann interjected. 'You're suggesting there was a coup by a group of men in the tenth century, who then had all the records of female dominance erased.'

'Spot on. This period was completely reinterpreted.'

'To what end?' Viktor thought about the debates raging in his own time: oppression and exploitation of women by men; unequal pay and higher costs for women; systemic disadvantage, denial of female intellect and leadership abilities, plus all the other battlegrounds on which equal rights were being fought. Who would have thought that these had been going on all the way back in the Middle Ages?

'My theory is that they did it to stop women from ever seeking power ever again.' Ingo closed his notebook, which was now full of notes. 'The patriarchy bases its claim to power on the tradition that that's the only way society has ever functioned, with history acting as an argument to assert the dominance of masculinity.'

Friedemann was only half-listening. He had no interest in Ingo's ruminations and certainly didn't share his fascination. He would much rather wake up Aysun and talk to him about the wooden frame. Discussing history was all well and good, but without the force field, they'd accidentally become part of the Middle Ages themselves. And he still had matters to take care of in the present.

'We'll be there soon.' Dana put the scope of her weapon to her right eye and scanned the ground in front of them. 'Everything's still there,' she announced. 'Looks like this road's hardly ever used.'

'It's going to stink,' muttered Coco, looking disconsolately at the ravens bobbing and fluttering around on the now-feathery carcases. Every single piece of meat had been torn off by beaks and the larger scavengers, which had clearly been down overnight to feast. 'I'll ... keep my distance.' She reined in her horse and let the rest of the group overtake her. 'I don't want to see it.'

'Don't hang back too far, though,' said Viktor gently.

They reached the pile of bodies, which had been pecked

and gnawed on, torn apart and scattered everywhere. Arms and leg bones, ribs and heads were lying across the grass, victims of predators like badgers, foxes, wolves and birds alike. The stench of decomposing tissues, ripped-open entrails and excrement lingered over the site. Ingo choked, while Friedemann waved his hand around as if the foul stench could simply be wafted away.

Aysun had woken up when Ingo stopped the wagon. Now he sat up and let out a long lament in what sounded like Arabic when he saw his dead companions. Again and again he bowed low, offering his prayers to the fallen.

'That won't do them any good.' Friedemann slipped out the saddle. 'We'll look for his notes in this mess. The sooner we find them, the—'

He broke off, suddenly aware that he had almost revealed his true intentions. 'The sooner he'll tell us where Anna-Lena's gone,' he said instead.

Ingo helped Aysun's servant to lift the feeble old man down from the wagon. 'We're going to look for your belongings and start loading them onto the wagon.'

'Thank you.' The Moor looked at the massacre and the stripped carcases with tears in his eyes. 'My beliefs require me to bury my servants.' He pointed to the dead *scara*. 'I'll leave it up to you what to do with the empress' soldiers. You're Christians, like they are, so you can decide.' He pointed east. 'Then you can take me to Empress Judith and I'll release you from any further obligations.'

Friedemann had to bite his tongue – he didn't consider them to be under any obligation whatsoever, but they were relying on this man's knowledge. Contradicting the old Moor might make him stubborn; he wasn't about to make the mistake of underestimating Aysun. Anyone who lived to his age in this era must have been clever.

Dana dismounted as well. Her legs were wobbly from all the riding and her buttocks still hurt from yesterday. 'I don't mean to sound like a broken record, but I'm going to keep asking about Anna-Lena's whereabouts until I get an answer.' She met Friedemann's warning look defiantly, then looked at Aysun. 'And we won't take you to your empress until you tell us where you saw her going.'

'Look at this.' Aysun gave a weak smile. 'Yesterday this man was introduced to me as your leader' – he gestured towards Friedemann – 'but it's taken just one sunrise for a woman to take over. She's adapting to her circumstances quickly. Keep this up, Duchess Dana. It becomes you.' His brief foray into amusement vanished. 'I promise to tell you as soon as my possessions have been retrieved.' He covered his face with his hands, his rings glimmering in the watery sunlight. 'My poor friends.' Tears streamed along his wrinkles and dripped onto his elegant robes.

'We need to work out which are the Moors and prepare a burial site for them.' Friedemann's face was pale as he looked at the human remains, still being gnawed on by mice and ravens. This wasn't a job for him. 'Let's do as the old man asks. We need his information about the frame, otherwise we'll be stuck here for ever.'

The team began their unappetising task, wrapping their hands in cloth before they started pulling the Moor's men to one side.

Coco watched them from horseback. She was not

prepared to put a foot inside that ring of death. She was racked with despair, overwhelmed by everything around her. Having Ingo so close to her the night before had done her a world of good, quelling her fear, at least for a time. What she was most afraid of was not being able to return to her own time.

The frame lay innocuously on its bed of material, still without its shimmering force field.

Coco had been keeping a surreptitious eye on it. She had sworn to herself that as soon as the energy began to flow again and the passage re-opened, she'd go straight through it without hesitation, regardless of what the others were doing. Nothing could keep her here, as she had made perfectly clear to Ingo. Van Dam had not paid her to spend the rest of her life under these conditions – not to mention the fact that any payment received so far was utterly worthless here.

The unsavoury burial process continued, using spears and shields to dig through the turf. The first of the bodies were placed in the shallow graves while Aysun prayed over them.

Their clothes were soon coated with blood and dirt, making them look like they had survived a bloody battle, cutting down hundreds of opponents. They decided to bury the murdered *scara* as well – although they would be exhausted, it would at least deal with the atrocious stench.

Black clouds loomed over the horizon, threatening an imminent downpour, and the wind changed direction again, this time driving the smell towards the medium. She immediately threw herself from the saddle and emptied her breakfast of honey-sweetened porridge into the dust. 'God, that's foul,' she whined.

She needed to distract herself from the noxious stink, so after spitting to clear her mouth, she took out her pendulum to try to find Anna-Lena again. Her attempt earlier that morning had proved unsuccessful and she was beginning to fear that her star as a successful clairvoyant was fading rapidly, threatening to dissipate into insignificance.

The heavy golden pendant hung vertically, the slight swing thanks only to the cool wind. She looked towards the horizon, where the rain was already changing the texture of the air, as if it were washing it clean. The stink receded as freshness blew all around her.

Coco closed her eyes, calling Anna-Lena's face into her inner eye and concentrating hard on her. The blood coursing through her temples felt hotter all of a sudden, accompanied a low whistling in her ears as she broke into a sweat.

Then she felt the chain tug and looked down.

The pendulum was pointing to the right, at an unmistakeable forty-five-degree angle upwind.

'I've got her,' cried Coco, standing up in her stirrups to see where the gold pendant was pointing and hoping beyond hope that this was not a mistake.

Frankfurt, Lerchesberg

It was evening by the time Friend had been dropped off a few yards outside the entrance to the van Dam estate.

He said goodbye to Ina and her mother, before climbing over the wall in his tattered clothes. He had manipulated the minds of his two helpers to prevent them from ever mentioning him, so Friend would remain a secret.

His skin had completely regenerated by now, pink and pure, like that of an infant; the black hair on his head had grown back as well. It had a different structure from human hair, as any DNA analysis would have immediately revealed, but at first glance there appeared to be no difference, apart from the fact that it shimmered a little more, as if he were using some specialist haircare product.

Friend hurried across the large garden.

There was nothing to suggest the presence of the police; it looked as if all the events on the other side of the wall had so far gone unnoticed.

Friend carried the laptop in his right hand; the battery was practically empty, so the first thing he'd do when he got inside was look for a charger – a password might be required if it had to be restarted.

He could smell the blood from the moment he opened the unlocked front door. A small pool had collected around the corpse of someone he assumed to be one of van Dam's employees.

Friend could see brilliantly in the dark; his eyes were more than accustomed to having very little light to work with. He had concocted a plan that he'd be able to put into place as soon as he managed to charge the stolen laptop.

His search took him through a series of rooms containing the bodies of all the men and women who must have worked in van Dam's household; their outfits suggested a cook, two gardeners, a housekeeper and three security guards.

Finally Friend found the office, and van Dam, lying dead beside his desk, with three bullet holes in his body. A woman wearing a suit was slumped in the chair with her head resting on the desk and her glassy eyes facing the wall. Her left hand was holding a flickering smartphone, while her right hand was balled into a fist.

Friend would have a proper look around in his own time later, but first he needed to find a suitable lead from the jumble of cables around van Dam's computer. He found one that fitted and quickly connected the laptop, causing a little green light to come on. So far, so good.

'My new base.' Friend gave a slight nod to Walter van Dam and walked over to the destroyed flat-screen monitors. He bent over the dead man and examined him carefully, memorising his features, wrinkles and eye colour.

Then he picked up the marble paperweight from the table and smashed it into his own face. A series of heavy blows broke his cheekbones and shattered his nose bone with a sickening crack. He tore off a piece of his nose, ignoring the pinkish blood gushing out of the wound.

Friend breathed the pain away and concentrated on the healing process, which he could feel as a tickling, tingling sensation. As he healed, he altered his facial structure, shaping bones and flesh to make him look identical to van Dam. He had to grow the moustache and sideburns, but that would only take a day; the rest of his hair would adjust to van Dam's colour as well.

He needed to keep up his strength – the exertion was

making him feel nauseous and hungry. He quickly found the kitchen and buttered most of a loaf of bread; after devouring half a dozen butter sandwiches, he followed up with all the eggs he could find, not bothering to cook them, just pouring them down his throat.. He left the meat untouched, instead consuming a heap of vegetables, peel, seeds and all.

At last, his hunger assuaged, his head stopped spinning. And he had refined his plan.

He'd never be able to provide a plausible explanation for all his staff disappearing at the same time, so he would have to go to the police – as Walter van Dam – and report the raid. That left him needing only to dispose of the real van Dam's remains.

Friend went back upstairs, picked up the businessman's corpse and quickly carried it into the spacious basement, where he hid it in the freezer beneath large bags of frozen vegetables. There'd be no reason for the police to look in there.

Then he rubbed off the last of his loose black skin and checked his appearance. His metamorphosis into van Dam was nearly complete. He pulled some of the clothes out of the washing basket and smeared blood on them, deciding to postpone his shower until later, lest he look too clean. He was a victim of violent crime, after all.

Then he went back to have a closer look at the half-undressed woman in the office – van Dam's personal assistant, he guessed – who had been killed by a stab wound to her stomach. She had tried to staple the hole in her flesh, but her makeshift surgery attempt had failed. Why hadn't she rung the emergency services? Her mobile phone was blinking, but he was more interested in her clenched fist.

It took a little while for him to prise open the dead woman's fingers.

'A *Particula*!' He was genuinely surprised.

An old notebook lying on the desk in front of her had a concealed pocket within the spine, which had been left open. He pocketed the blinking mobile phone, keen to meet whomever she had called after finding the *Particula*. It was beginning to look as if van Dam's employee had been keeping secrets from her boss.

Friend put the shard in his pocket, secure in the knowledge that his mental powers would ensure no one tried to search him, then carelessly shoved the woman to the floor and sat down in the armchair before calling the police. Panting, he began to gabble: a robbery that had got out of hand – he had passed out for a long period of time . . . The friendly voice at the other end of the line promised to send assistance immediately. Friend hung up and started to read through the information on the laptop while he waited for the police to arrive.

What he saw was curious and alarming in equal measure. He thought it was a pity the second group van Dam had sent down had disappeared so quickly. He had only had the opportunity to engage with the medium – he would have loved to rifle through their heads and reveal the secrets they were hiding from one another..

Ritter's organisation had been remarkably thorough in their evaluation of the team, unlike van Dam himself.

Meanwhile, the laptop had connected to the internet via

its integrated modem and was merrily pulling data from a host of cloud servers. None of the clever encryption in place was of any use on this side as long as the laptop was running.

The first police cars rolled up outside the estate, followed by the ambulances. Blue lights flickered up the drive and danced over the office walls.

Time for some drama.

Friend had left the bruises on his face from the paper-weight. Now he stabbed his hand and forearm with the letter opener to undo some of his regeneration. He stowed the laptop in the cupboard and was about to stagger out towards the officers when he caught sight of the severed thumb next to the open safe.

Footsteps sounded from down the hall; the police were advancing quickly. 'Mr van Dam?' Lights were switched on in each room they passed through.

'Here.' Friend picked up the thumb and put it in his mouth. He chewed quickly, shredding all the meat, skin and bones and swallowing it all quickly. 'I'm in here.' He stumbled towards the uniformed men. 'I'm so glad you've come—'

Frankish Empire, June 841

Coco and Viktor rode towards the forest from where they had inspected the camp the day before. That was where her pendulum was now pointing. 'Straight on,' she instructed.

Viktor kept his horse on course. He wasn't a fan of

riding; if he was honest with himself he'd admit he was a little afraid of horses. On previous jobs he had always avoided using animals for transport, but someone had to accompany Coco on this reconnaissance mission and Dana had stayed with Friedemann and Ingo to guard Aysun and the frame.

Coco loved being back on horseback, though she'd have preferred to be riding under different circumstances. The golden pendulum had changed tack, moving away from the hill and the copse towards a grassy area next to it. 'She must have moved,' she said as she immediately redirected her horse.

It took Viktor a little longer to manage the same. 'Not too fast!' he called out to her. 'We're about to reach the ridge – it's a steep slope down.'

They reined in the animals at the edge of a steep embankment which had an almost vertical drop of several yards. A handful of men and women were walking in single file below them, surrounding a cart bearing a few more people in the middle. They were all surrounded by armed guards.

Viktor had a closer look through his scope. 'Prisoners, I think,' he said quietly to Coco, transmitting his voice over the radio to the others at the same time. 'They've loaded the wounded onto wagons and anyone who can still walk are . . .' He suddenly leaned forward in his saddle. *Is that red hair?*

Coco grabbed his reins. Her own horse was clearly well-trained; it was tensing its muscles in anticipation of having to go down the hill. 'Sit still and don't let your heels touch its flanks, otherwise it'll just hurtle down the slope.'

'We've found her,' said Viktor excitedly. 'I can see Anna-Lena.' The young woman was on foot, dressed in what looked from there like a simple dress.

'As one of their prisoners?' enquired Friedemann grumpily. His voice was crackly; the batteries in his radio must be dying. 'What unbridled joy.'

'Any chance of freeing her quickly?' Dana asked.

'No.' Viktor looked at the steep, overgrown slope at his feet. He trusted the horse to dash down it safely, but not with him on it. 'Even if I got down safely, they're too close to the main camp. As soon as they realise they're under attack, they'll send soldiers out.'

Coco was following the movements of the prisoners and the guards without the use of the scope. A signal sounded, alerting the camp to the new arrivals. 'Ms Rentski, please would you ask Aysun why he thought Anna-Lena was in safe hands? Because she's obviously not.'

It took a while for her to respond.

'He says Anna-Lena was with Empress Judith's host at first – or at least she had gone to their camp,' came Dana's voice. 'That's the other reason why he wanted to take us to his empress. He thought we'd find her there.'

'She's been picked up by a scouting party,' he guessed. 'They'll need helpers in camp – washerwomen, cooks, that sort of thing.'

'Or they think she's one of Empress Judith's spies.' Coco pointed to the wagon bearing the wounded soldiers. 'Maybe they're going to interrogate these prisoners.' She pocketed her pendulum.

Viktor lowered the scope and looked at the medium.

'We need to split up,' he said. 'Some of us should ride to Count Guerin on behalf of Empress Judith to tell him he'll be needed in the battle to come.'

'And the others can look for Anna-Lena,' added Ingo over the radio. 'It's doable.'

'We're not splitting up,' interjected Dana angrily.

'Haven't we already done so?' Viktor replied with mock innocence, causing Coco to laugh.

'And we're not going to discuss it like this,' decided Friedemann, whose signal was becoming weaker and weaker. 'Madame Fendi, you and Troneg come back and we'll talk about it properly when we're all together.'

'Understood.' Viktor turned his horse around. 'Would you have believed this?'

Coco followed him. 'What?'

'That we'd be riding through the year of Our Lord 841 . . . that a simple rescue mission would turn into such an enormous adventure?' He laughed. 'It's just struck me that it's a bit mad to ask a clairvoyant that sort of question.'

'It's not. And if I'd known, I'd never have answered van Dam's advertisement.' Coco considered her mountain of debt. No fortune in the world could make up for what she had been through ever since stepping foot in those caves – twice. She should have stayed upstairs, just refused to go back down after the first time. 'But how was I supposed to know?' she muttered to herself.

'You're a proven medium, aren't you?'

Coco forced out a smile. It was hard to admit she had been nothing but a charlatan before the mission began. 'I suppose my gift let me down on that occasion.'

'What do you think we should do now?'

'Are you testing to see if I can see better into the future now?'

He grinned. 'No. I'm just interested in your opinion.'

'I'm the wrong person to ask. It's for the professor to decide.' Coco stroked her horse. She decided to take advantage of question time. 'What's going on between you and Ms Rentski?'

'We've met before. I'm sure of it.'

'At a climbing event?'

Viktor hesitated. How much did he want to reveal about himself? About his past, which he had deliberately kept secret? 'Yes,' he said, not sure if lying to a medium was a good idea. 'I'm afraid we were opponents.' That part at least was true when he and Dana were in Darfur: he'd been a Special Forces operative, she, a mercenary.

What he still didn't know was whether Walter van Dam had come up with the lie about her being a professional climber, or whether Dana had used a fake CV to keep the businessman in the dark about her true profession. And if so, what was in all this for her?

But it was unwise to brood over Dana and his former occupation; it was dragging him back into his past ... He could hear Coco speaking to him, but he couldn't detach himself from the images swarming through his mind. This was the job that had first given him post-traumatic stress disorder and now the smells, scenes, noises and screams all felt horribly real: he was suddenly right in the middle of it all again.

The American Special Forces had seconded five people

from their German counterparts to act as tactical observers on this mission in Darfur. Their target, Wes Bestman, a US businessman and senatorial candidate, was pulling the strings of the burgeoning drugs trade, working with two Mexican cartels. They wanted to take him out in Darfur, as it would have been impossible in either the States or Mexico, where there were too many prying eyes.

Viktor and his four men had accompanied the American team to the Jebel Amir region in the east of North Darfur, where there were several rich gold mines. Thanks to the rather opaque situation in the war-ravaged area, several thousand foreigners had gained access to the mines and Bestman was one of them. He had fought off opposition from the Beni Hassan tribe with the aid of mercenaries and his allies from the Abbala tribes so he could smuggle cheap gold through Chad and Libya to sell on at an enormous profit.

They were deployed to the city of El Sireaf. Tens of thousands of refugees had flooded into the city environs after fleeing their homes and the fighting in Darfur, but this was where Bestman was planning to meet a Beni Hassan chieftain, intending to reach an agreement to end the skirmishes, as he was in the stronger bargaining position.

All had gone well initially.

Viktor and his Special Forces team accompanied the US troops, driving through the city at night at high speed in armoured vehicles. None of them wore uniforms or insignia; no one was ever supposed to know about the mission.

Bestman always turned up early to negotiations, hoping

to use the element of surprise. Knowing this, the Americans launched their attack before the Beni Hassan had arrived.

But they had underestimated the firepower and professionalism of Bestman's mercenaries, who fiercely defended the drug dealer-cum-bullion robber, buying him time to escape. Eight of Bestman's fighters died in the battle, along with three Americans.

Viktor would have brought the operation to a halt there and then, but his commanding officer ordered them to make chase, seeking revenge for his lost men.

The breakneck journey across El Sireaf rapidly degenerated into chaos: local militias started interfering, firing machine guns at the vehicles – and killing more than fifty bystanders in the process – while thirty or more houses went up in flames.

By morning both the fleeing party and the pursuers found themselves at an abandoned trading post out in the desert. The situation changed in an instant, the hunters becoming the hunted as the Abbala came to liberate their business partner.

The rattling of automatic weapons, the clinking of shell casings, the booming of shotguns, the explosions of grenades.

And screams – those endless screams . . .

'Mr Troneg?'

He could hear Coco's voice, far away.

Nothing he had been taught during special ops training was of use, not against such odds. They had watched *Black Hawk Down* more than once, each time voicing the hope they would never find themselves in a similar situation.

This was even worse.

Viktor unleashed round after round, then he was reduced to stabbing his enemies with the knifes and daggers he pulled from the bodies of the dead men around him; his Kevlar vest was struck several times by bullets and he received countless minor injuries from flying projectiles, blades, ricochets and shrapnel from grenades. The air was filled with the screeching cries of stricken fighters and the crashing of gunfire; the whole place stank of powder and blood and faeces.

He and his people finally took cover in a small room while their opponents approached from all sides as a sandstorm raged around them, knowing their only chance of survival was for the wind to pick up even more, giving them a little cover while they made their escape.

Two of his own men had been killed immediately, while a third was dragged out of cover and had his leg hacked off, causing him to bleed to death.

And through the swirling haze of sand he had seen Dana – behind a wall . . . with a sniper rifle at the ready.

'Mr Troneg? Hello?' Coco's voice intermingled with Dana's face.

There was an ear-splitting bang as the attackers fired grenade-launchers at the room. The blast blew Viktor and the charred remains of his final comrade out of the door – but he fell against a wall that shielded him from his opponents. He could never forget the dark thought he had had about how his dead comrade's intestines looked like a nest of bloody, sludgy snakes.

And even as he did so, his eyes fell on the door—

The door to the ruins had a knocker and a lion's

mouth – and for some reason, the door frame was suddenly shining brightly.

And he could see outlines of people moving around within.

Despite the panic which had set his heart racing in his chest, Viktor could sense that this was a new memory: he had never seen it before, nor had he talked about it during counselling. It must have been shaken free by the events down in the caves.

Or was he simply imagining it because of everything that was happening now?

A sudden violent wind blew into Viktor's face and something ice cold started pelting him. He blinked and snorted as his mind returned to the present: a thunderstorm had come upon them and rain was drenching him and Coco. When he looked around, he could see the wagon, standing underneath a tree just over a hundred yards away.

'Are you awake now?' Coco was looking at him with concern. At first she hadn't had the faintest idea what could be afflicting him so powerfully that he would completely ignore her – until she had used her powers, that was. 'That looked pretty grim.'

'What did?' He wiped the water off his face, grateful for the downpour.

'What I could see in your memories.'

Viktor froze in the saddle. Until now he had barely given her abilities a moment's thought. 'You were *spying* on me?'

Coco had tucked her head onto her chest, as if that might help to protect her from the pelting downpour. Thunder rumbled loudly above them as a flash of lightning struck the grove on top of the hill. The amount of wet metal on her body was beginning to make her nervous, especially as she was still deeply affected by the echoes of the strange memories she had experienced. 'You weren't responding to any of the radio messages – I had to find out what was happening to you.'

Viktor returned her gaze. 'Please, don't tell anyone about it.'

'I won't.' Coco smiled, pleased that her unexpected powers were working so effectively. 'You know, you're not the only one here who's got secrets. But I'm not going to be the one to reveal them.'

'Thank you.'

'Not even to Ms Rentski.'

Viktor breathed in deeply, enjoying the fresh air as the images of Africa, the attack and the dead men began to blur and return to their place, shut up in the corners of his memory. 'She knows perfectly well what happened in Darfur. That's why she's being so vague about it.'

'Do you think she knew who she was working for?'

'Would that change your opinion of her?'

Coco nodded slowly, sending the water streaming from her blonde hair and oddly, making the black streak appear even darker. 'I'm not sure I could be friends with a mercenary who knowingly worked for a drug dealer and gold thief.'

'She'd have considered it purely a business transaction.' There was a long tradition of using mercenaries in war and the cause was rarely important; it was getting paid that mattered.

'How did it all end?' Coco wished she had a modern raincoat, fully waterproof and nice and warm underneath. These clothes would take for ever to dry out – although at least the rain might make her smell less of old sweat afterwards.

'In Darfur, you mean?'

'Yes.'

Viktor's hands immediately began to tremble. 'It was the sandstorm that saved me and two of my Special Forces colleagues – well, for a while, at least.' He swallowed hard, his mouth dry. 'Everyone else was killed.'

'And Bestman?'

'Still alive and kicking to this day, as far as I'm aware.' Viktor and Coco had almost reached the others. 'And now not another word about it.' He avoided looking at Dana, who was sitting atop a tree, keeping an eye out over the surrounding area.

The traumatic scenes, smells and noises had been suppressed for now, but they were now accompanied by the image of the door and the silhouettes within it.

Whether he was imagining it or not, it scared Viktor – a lot.

CHAPTER IX

Frankish Empire, June 841

The heavy rain continued to hammer down, as if trying to bring about the Ogygian Flood. It clattered and pattered, dripped and deluged the heads of the group, who were huddling underneath the tree and waiting for the storm to blow over.

Far away, lightning flashed occasionally, its crackling resonance revealing how much energy there was in the world that could not be harnessed – neither in the Middle Ages, nor yet in the modern day.

Nor would it be of any use in operating the frame that Aysun had carried with him for many a year, as he told them while they were waiting. Sitting up in the cart, leaning against the side, he told them, 'I found it in the land of the Euskaldunak, also known as the Basque Country. Along with the records.'

Friedemann had not expected this. He hadn't encountered anything about the Basque during any of his earlier research.

Aysun's servant passed him the parchment as the old Moor continued, 'Their language is unique, and difficult to translate.' He looked at Friedemann and Ingo. 'But you're both learned men. You will achieve what I failed to do and discover the secrets of the frame.'

'Could you tell us what you've observed since it came into your possession?' Friedemann was crouching on the edge of the wagon like the Grim Reaper, looking down at the old man through his steamed-up glasses. Fortunately, the Moor's belongings had been protected from the rain, so no damage had come to the parchment. 'Who's been through the force field?'

'Oh, for the most part it just flares up from time to time.' Aysun placed a bony hand on the carved wood and stroked it as if it were a sentient being. 'It felt as if the shimmering were calling to me, trying to lure me through it, but I didn't dare. I was afraid of not being able to return. What could a man like me do if that happened? Stay lost for ever? Would it really be worth it?'

Coco was fiddling with the golden pendulum, which was still pointing resolutely towards Empress Ermengarde's encampment. Anna-Lena was in enemy hands: one hundred and fifty thousand of them. What madness.

Dana kept an eye out on the area from her elevated position in the tree. She could see very little through the grey veil of rain that also served as their cover for the time being. She thought carefully about what their next step would be, and how best to go about it.

'Was it only people who came through the frame?' Ingo wished he had his instruments with him, so he could properly investigate the force fields and record the results.

Aysun shook his head weakly. 'I can't tell you everything

I've seen – but the creatures who came through weren't friendly. I lost two servants to them as they were fighting to defend me. And sometimes lumps of meat would fall through, which I suppose must have once been human. The transition had killed them and turned them into shapeless clumps, which only served to reinforce my fears.' He looked back and forth between Friedemann and Ingo. 'But there were also a few clever visitors who came through and talked to me before returning – but that was a very long time ago indeed. It wasn't until your friend climbed out of the frame that I knew it was working again.'

Anna-Lena had reached the Middle Ages shortly after the attack on the baggage train had ended, Aysun told them; he had noticed her hiding behind a wagon before she started running towards Empress Judith's camp.

The travelling party had been wiped out on the orders of Bernard of Septimania. The farmhouse had been chosen as the meeting point where the prisoner would be handed over. But during the transaction they decided to renegotiate with his son – and it was at that moment that they arrived on the scene.

'You'll be able to return,' said Aysun with a smile. He touched two different places on the frame with his bony finger. 'But be careful! When your friend stepped through there was some sort of discharge. It hit her in the back, and it tore off some of the wood.'

Friedemann leaned forwards and carefully examined the place Aysun was pointing at. 'Yes, I can see that.' The first time he'd inspected the frame he had not realised it was damaged; he had believed it to be deliberate, part of the carvings. There was now a very real risk of the frame falling apart the next time the energy built up. He tapped his chin and straightened the frame. 'We'll have to stabilise it.'

'Perhaps we should decode those records first?' ventured Ingo.

'How long will that take?' asked Dana from the tree.

Viktor looked at the parchment. He doubted it would be a quick process. After all, it wasn't as if there were any libraries around, nor any modern research methods available to them.

Ingo scratched his head; he could feel something moving around in his hair. Fleas and lice were common in the Middle Ages and they had been there long enough for the parasites to have taken up residence. 'Hard to say. It might take weeks, even months, without anything to assist us.'

Coco groaned. 'Oh, don't say that. I just want to get out of here.'

Aysun raised a hand to attract their attention. 'One of the visitors told me how to trigger the shimmering.' He pointed to the inconspicuous little stone embedded in the upper part of the frame. 'If you hit this hard, a wall of energy will build up, which you can then pass through. I can't say for certain whether it works or not, though. I've never tried it.' He closed his eyes. 'And he told me about something he called "Arkus".'

'Arcus is Latin for *arch*,' Ingo translated for them.

'The man said he was looking for comets that had fallen from the sky,' Aysun added quietly. 'He and his friends wanted to build an arch out of them – a frame made only of *Particulae*, which is what he called the fragments.'

Friedemann licked his lips nervously. This was new information. He had come across the Arkus Project in the notes already, but hints about what it was were vague at best. 'Where did he come from?' he demanded. 'When was this?'

Aysun's breathing became shallower.

'Where did this man come from?' Friedemann repeated authoritatively. 'Where were these people from? How far away?'

Everyone understood now that Friedemann was more than simply an expert in geology and speleology. His knowledge of the stones and doors, combined with his suspicious behaviour and possession of that unusual notebook, had made that abundantly clear.

The Moor was smiling softly, his eyes closed.

Viktor leaned forward and felt for his carotid artery. 'Dead.' He looked around, shocked. 'He's just died – out of nowhere. The old man used up the last of his strength to warn us, to tell us what he knew about the frame.'

The scholar's servant began to weep silently. The group exchanged concerned looks, but Friedemann was truly upset. He had been cheated of yet more invaluable knowledge.

The rain was gradually losing its intensity. The black clouds on the horizon were rolling away, revealing a beautiful clear sky behind them, as if to make way for the passage of the dead man's soul.

'We should bury him, as he'd have wanted.' Ingo looked at the old man's face, now devoid of tension. How old *was* he? How much knowledge had he possessed? How much wisdom had departed from the world with his passing?

Dana looked down at Friedemann from her bough. 'Any suggestions, Professor, as to what to do now?'

Friedemann had one ready. 'We'll split up – whether or not you think it's a good idea, Ms Rentski,' he said to fore-stall any protest. Arguments took time and time was of the essence here. No one knew what would happen to the frame if someone activated the force field in the cave beneath the villa. Would it withstand the strain, or would it collapse? For how long would the wall of energy remain stable?

'Doctor Theobald, you know some Latin—'

'Up to a point.'

'Good. Please write a letter from Empress Judith to this Count Guerin, asking him for his help in the upcoming battle.' Friedemann pointed to the chest at the front of the wagon, where Aysun's writings and belongings were stored. 'There's bound to be a royal seal in there that we can attach or copy.' He turned to Theobald and Coco. 'Once that's done, you two can toddle off and make sure this chap actually turns up.'

Coco didn't like this plan one jot. 'But . . . we don't even know where Guerin is.'

'I do,' said the servant – much to Coco's astonishment. 'The count lives in Mâcon. I can take you there. It's not as if I've got a master to serve any more and a Moor without a Christian master will be a dead Moor before long in this part of the country.'

Friedemann laughed with delight. Things were working out perfectly. 'And what should we call you, my friend?'

The servant gave a small bow. 'My name is Wahid, my lords and ladies.'

'Fine. As the women seem to be in charge around here, we'll give Madame Fendi the title of duchess: that will give her access to Count Guerin.'

Dana climbed higher up the canopy to see further afield, but there was no one around, she was relieved to discover. 'Then I assume, Troneg, you and I will be the team who rescues Anna-Lena from the camp at night.'

'Spot on, Ms Rentski.'

'Not the worst plan in the world,' agreed Viktor.

'And it'll succeed,' the professor announced firmly. 'We'll meet up again, bring the traitor's letter to Empress Judith, which will convince her to lose faith in this Bernard of Septimania, then, once we've gained her confidence, we'll be able to stay close to the empress – and while we're under her protection we'll have time to devote ourselves to translating the documents Aysun has left us. We'll disappear as soon as possible afterwards.' There would almost certainly be a skilled carpenter at court who could repair the damaged frame. Problem solved. 'The course of history will continue as before, since we'll have corrected what we inadvertently changed. Right then, everyone. We need to bury Aysun – his servant can hold the Muslim ceremony for him.'

They started to dig with spears and shields, aligning the pit in the direction of Mecca, as required by the rite. By evening Aysun's feather-light, already mostly ossified body had been laid in eternal rest, with his servant leading the prayers.

Immediately afterwards, everyone turned in, foregoing a fire to avoid attracting any unwanted attention before their missions began in the morning.

Dana took first watch as Viktor and Friedemann pulled blankets over themselves and quickly fell asleep.

Coco lay awake for a while, listening to the sound of Ingo's breathing and enjoying their close proximity. The sounds of the night were different from the twenty-first century.

When Dana looked into the clear night sky, she was amazed by the number of stars she could see. Without the light pollution prevalent in present-day cities, the spectacle was truly breath-taking, with the Milky Way appearing as a bright band, surrounded by other stars, all glowing intensely down at humanity. The Moon was a wafer-thin crescent, which would soon fill out over the coming days.

Dana had resigned herself to staying in the Middle Ages for the time being. As a mercenary she was used to adapting to new circumstances. What worried her most was not knowing how to use a sword or spear correctly – she was skilled at mêlée combat, with or without a knife – but if she had to fight soldiers, or even another *scara*, hand-to-hand, things might get a little hairy.

She noticed Wahid was also gazing up at the stars, his lips moving in a silent prayer. 'Can I ask you something?' she whispered once he had finished.

The young man looked at her in amazement. 'Are you talking to me, my lady?'

'Yes.'

He grinned. 'Forgive me. I'm but a humble servant – I am not used to be spoken to so politely by a duchess.' He inclined his head. 'How may I be of service?'

Dana found this adherence to class distinction baffling,

but if she was to make a good impression on the empress, she needed to learn more about the warring factions – more about the conflict, their relationships with one another. Ingo and Friedemann had the advantage of a good education, but she had only questions.

She started, 'How has it come to be that two armies of one hundred and fifty thousand soldiers are about to clash?'

'My master Aysun would say it was because of greed and intrigue.' Wahid was whispering so he didn't disturb the sleeping members of their party. 'Empress Judith and her husband Louis had a son called Charles. Her husband had previously been married to another, and when she died, the empress was free to marry Louis – but Louis died a year ago and his two sons from his first marriage pushed a claim to their father's inheritance.

'And Empress Judith views *their* son as the sole heir to her late husband's estate,' guessed Dana.

'Exactly, my lady. Lothair, one of Louis' sons, is consort to Empress Ermengarde and has convinced her to take up arms in support of his claim,' said Wahid. 'Ermengarde is as ambitious as she is fair and she's had her eye on the lands to the east for a long time now. This inheritance dispute was a convenient excuse to declare war.'

'Hang on.' Dana's head was spinning. 'Isn't Charles rumoured to be the son of Bernard of Septimania?' She'd never understood how historians managed to keep track of all these names.

'That's what people *say*. But it's not true.' Wahid shuffled over to Aysun's box and took out a wax tablet on which to draw a rough family tree. 'We've got Empress Judith and her son Charles, along with her sister Hemma, who's married to Louis' other son from his first marriage.

'And he supports his stepmother?'

'Yes.' Wahid separated them with a line. 'Empress Ermengarde and her sons Lothair and Pepin are on the other side. The East Franks versus the West Franks.'

'And it is looking as if battle is inevitable.'

'It would appear so.' Wahid pointed to the grove, on the other side of which lay Empress Ermengarde's camp. 'The empresses have been mustering their troops since November last year. The locations kept moving. At Orléans, when they were less than six miles apart, they sent out negotiators. Lothair and Charles negotiated on behalf of their wife and mother respectively, but the agreement they made in May never came to fruition: Ermengarde didn't turn up, which Judith perceived as a declaration of war.'

'You know a great deal about all this.'

'My master ... my former master Aysun was well acquainted with the various plots that were going on. For a long time he lived at the court in Aachen, where he made an enemy of Bernard of Septimania – an enmity that's carried on ever since.' Wahid laughed. 'Aysun had warned the empress that some of the richer and more influential nobles were getting ideas above their station: with papal support, they were seeking to overthrow female rule. They want their power back.'

'And where are we now, precisely?' Dana still had no idea what part of France – if it was France – they were in. 'On a map, I mean.'

'We're near Auxerre. Empress Judith and her allies have made camp near Thury, on the hill at Roichat,' said Wahid. 'My master predicted the armies would finally face each other at Fontenoy, which would be the best location for three hundred thousand armed men to fight each other.'

Dana had never appreciated modern reconnaissance techniques more – maps, aerial photographs, drones, satellite images, the lot. Here in the year 841 all they had were rough estimates and vague information, while their maps didn't even hint at anything like terrain.

'Then we need to be as far away from Fontenoy as possible when it all kicks off.' She motioned for Wahid to lie down. 'Get some rest. Tomorrow's going to be exhausting for all of us.'

'Yes, my lady.' The young Moor curled up and pulled Aysun's old blanket over himself. 'I miss him already, you know,' he said softly.

'Goodnight.' Dana rested her head against Aysun's chest, listening to the sounds of the night – and the silence that permeated this century.

A deep, true silence.

Frankfurt, Lerchesberg

Friend was enjoying his new temporary residence, which had now been cleaned of all traces of the robbery by a top-rate cleaning company. The employees' bodies had been taken to a forensic laboratory for autopsy and the crime scene had long since been re-opened.

The house's shutters fit perfectly, allowing no direct sunlight into any of the rooms; if Friend ever needed to leave the house during the day, he made sure to move around only in the shade. This was an entirely new existence for him.

Friend had reset all the electronic passwords, allowing him access to van Dam's data so that he could continue to live this stolen life for the time being. He had delegated everything related to the business empire to van Dam's managers until further notice. Of course everyone was understanding about his desire to take some time for himself.

He hadn't employed any new staff, needing only himself, the mansion and delivery services. The television remained on in the background. What he had missed most during his time underground was noise – of any kind.

Friend sat in the office, drinking an exquisite cup of hot water and sifting through the data he had downloaded from the conspirators' cloud servers. A few minutes ago the main server had denied him access and the stolen laptop had apparently had its privileges removed too.

But it looked like the Organisation had worked out who the imposter Professor Friedemann really was: a Russian called Vladimir Otschenko, who'd been working under a series of assumed names to undertake his own investigations into the doors.

Friend laughed and sipped at his hot water as he read through the file.

It looked like Otschenko had been responsible for a great deal of misfortune over the years. Several photos had captured the Russian in a number of guises, sporting a variety of beards, wigs, glasses and a wide range of different outfits.

There was also a video file, taken by a CCTV camera.

Friend leaned back and played it.

Vladimir entered a large shop selling antiques, rarities and home furnishings. The high-end Berlin boutique was called *Frills & Furbelows.*

'Good afternoon,' he greeted the shopkeeper politely, relying on his glued-on beard, wig and peaked cap to render his face unrecognisable. The tattoos on his neck and hands had been painted on and he had bulked himself up a little using some padding. There was a sign on the door informing customers about the use of CCTV cameras, so Vladimir had come prepared.

A pierced, tattooed woman in dungarees stood fiddling with her phone behind the counter, which must have once been an altar until brutally repurposed. Her short blonde hair was covered by a red headscarf, making her look like a workers' poster from a bygone era. She had just taken a selfie and didn't even look up to acknowledge his presence. Standard Berlin service.

'Hashtag boredom?' Vladimir approached her.

She finally tore her eyes from the screen. 'Hilarious.' On her name badge was written *Annika*; maybe she was named after the prim little girl from the *Pippi Longstocking* books. 'Feel free to have a look around.'

'I'm looking for—'

'I'm just watching the shop. Mario's not here,' she interrupted. 'I know fuck-all about this place.'

'Okay, then.' Vladimir put his hands in his pockets and started on the indicated route through the shop.

He had discovered something interesting in the online *Doors, Gates, Temple Artefacts* section. For half his life he had been chasing the doors – those magical doors that were in fact portals, if you knew how to activate them.

Many years ago, during the commission of a burglary, he had stumbled upon a small notebook from the early twentieth century which had belonged to someone in opposition to the so-called 'Band of Conspirators', a group who guided global events from the background by apparently using doors that granted them access to anywhere in the world. Vladimir hadn't believed any of it until he started investigating the clues himself. On his forays he had discovered some of the doors, which existed all around the world in various guises, but they had refused to allow him through – and the series of tests he'd undertaken had had disastrous results.

Now Vladimir had reached the section of the shop he had been looking for.

The proprietor of *Frills & Furbelows* had compiled an enormous smorgasbord of doors, gates and temple artefacts, ranging from pigsty gates to destroyed doors from Second World War bunkers. Many more were hanging from chains attached to the ceiling that could be slid back and forth like clothes in a dry cleaner's.

Vladimir began his search.

Various doors described in the notebook were extremely special, according to the author, who had provided detailed drawings, analysis of the symbols, recommendations for use and the locations where they could be found.

Vladimir had visited some of the places listed and had had some strange experiences there, but there were plenty of occasions when he hadn't been able to find anything at all. Decay, fires, vermin and other misfortunes had destroyed several important doors, or they had gone missing, like the one he suspected was in this shop.

Vladimir's greatest wish was to find the headquarters that the conspirators had been using around 1920: it had apparently had access to five doors, with other portals nearby. *Five!*

'More haste, less speed,' he muttered, setting frames and doors crashing and clattering against each other as he went through them.

Vladimir had previously financed his lifestyle with scams, burglaries and petty theft, until the day he found the notebook and set out on his search. He'd discovered two very old doors, though sadly so badly damaged they were unusable, but he'd also found some Roman and mediaeval gold coins and other precious items, which he sold on the black market for a tidy sum. Now he had set his sights on the big ticket, the door that would make him a multi-millionaire. A door leading to a treasure trove: gold, money, safe deposit boxes – all for him!

'Oi, not so rough with my babies,' came a man's voice from behind him.

Vladimir looked over his shoulder. 'Apologies. They're moving around by themselves.'

Mario wore the same overalls as his assistant and had just as many tattoos and piercings, along with two-day-old stubble and a shaven head. He appeared to be in the wrong line of work. 'Lookin' fer sumfin'?'

'Doors.'

'You've found 'em awright. Anyfing in particular?'

'Yep. A door I saw online.' Vladimir pulled out his smart-phone and showed him the door he believed to be special. 'The one from the basement of that demolished house in Frankfurt.'

'Fuckin' 'ell. You've come for that old fing?' Mario laughed. 'Yer need yer head lookin' at, mate.'

'It's a lovely object.'

'Why din't yer just order it online, then?'

'I needed to see what it looked like in real life. There's not a photo in the world that could properly replicate it.'

Mario nodded. 'Looks like we've got ourselves a conn-ay-soor.' He walked over to a keypad on the wall and pressed a few buttons. The chained doors were raised towards the ceiling and replaced by a second selection with a loud rattle. 'It's one've these, I fink.'

Vladimir cocked his head, admiring the dozens of doors dangling enticingly, swaying back and forth before his eyes. 'How many of them are there?'

'Lost track.' Mario gestured to the new batch. ''Ave a butcher's anyway.'

Vladimir had already found the one he was seeking: definitely mediaeval, severely warped, a later paint job almost completely gone and the wood covered with water stains and teeth marks where rodents had gnawed on it in times past. The proprietor was right: it was in terrible condition – but the knocker was still intact. Despite the devastation inflicted upon Frankfurt in the Second World

War, it looked like its residents had managed to keep hold of a few of their older heirlooms during the reconstruction.

Including this door, which had allegedly come from the old town hall.

Vladimir had arrived too late to ransack the late antique collector's house, but he had managed to locate the original buyer's address and, after some digging, tracked it to Mario here in Berlin.

'There it is.' Vladimir pulled it closer to get a better view of it in the harsh glow of the floodlights illuminating the room. He ran his fingers over the frame, then he took out his notebook and felt beneath the peeling layer of paint for the areas it had specified. He could feel where the stones – these so-called *Particulae* – were located. They were apparently responsible for the force fields. 'Looks good to me.'

'I'll say. Two grand.'

Vladimir stopped dead, then turned to face Mario. That was definitely not the price he had seen online. 'Hang on a minute.' He checked his phone. 'It says five hundred here.'

'That was before you come in 'ere all hot and heavy fer it, mate.' The dealer grinned. 'But I'll cut yer a deal: eighteen hundred, cash, and yer takes it wiv yer today.'

Vladimir had the money, but it was a matter of principle. A con artist and thief couldn't allow himself to be ripped off, especially not by some jumped-up market trader with ideas above his station. He turned back to the door and examined the knocker carefully. He noticed a few cracks in the corners of the frame which urgently needed to be reglued before the whole thing fell to pieces; it was the only thing stopping the lower crossbeam from springing out of joint. 'Oh dear, oh dear.'

The smell of stale cigarette smoke told him the dealer had moved closer. 'Seen summing, 'ave yer?'

'Just checking it's all okay. Everything's a bit loose.'

'Ah.' Mario tapped the wood with his knuckle. 'But it sounds bootiful. Still eighteen hundred knicker, mate.'

There was a sudden crunch underneath Vladimir's right foot. When he looked down he saw a small stone – a *Particula* – that had come loose. He could hazard a decent guess from where. 'Oh, hello.'

'You've broken it!' said Mario angrily. 'Back up to two grand now, mate.'

Vladimir ignored him. He bent and picked it up, then carefully pressed the fragment back into the inlay on the door knocker at the point where it would hit the plate. Any attempt at activating the force field would fail without this stone so it was a good job he had been paying attention.

Just as he was about to start haggling with the dealer, the man walked over to where he was standing. 'Go on, mate, give it a whack. I ain't tried it yet.' Mario's hand closed around the ring.

'No, best not.' Vladimir tried to push himself between Mario and the door.

'Go on—' Mario refused to let go, instead, setting the weather-beaten door swinging – which caused the lower part of the frame to slip. 'Just let me bang it, awright?' At the same time, he brought the ring down hard onto the plate. 'It should—'

The sound of the impact was like a church bell being

detonated. With a hum, the flaring energy field tried to build up within the battered frame, blowing out the lower cross-beam as it did so.

The force discharged itself uncontrollably, gouging an enormous hole in the brick floor; thin streaks twitched their way around the shop, burning lines onto the walls, severing chains and sawing pieces of furniture in half. Doors, suddenly free from their brackets and singed by the balls of energy, began to rain down about the two men while fires began to break out at various points throughout the shop. Reddish brick dust and grey smoke made it almost impossible to see.

The door, which had survived from the Middle Ages, even through twentieth-century bombing raids, was abruptly blown off its hinges and shattered into thousands of tiny fragments which went whistling off in all directions, embedding themselves everywhere – even into Mario himself, who was thrown backwards into Vladimir. He died in a matter of seconds with chunks of the destroyed metal knocker lodged in his skull.

Vladimir lay on the floor as a fire alarm rang out overhead. He could hear Annika screaming like a stuck pig somewhere far off, but he was mostly all right. The dead man had saved him from the worst of the impact.

He got up and escaped through the smoke and dust, dejected at the sudden end to his search and the destruction of another door. But he had no intention of giving up, because the headquarters with its five doors and more lying in wait was still out there somewhere.

*

The recording ended with nothing but thick veils of dirty smoke that hid Vladimir Otschenko's flight from *Frills & Furbelows*.

Friend finished the video and took another sip of water, but it had gone cold. He went into the kitchen and as the kettle was boiling, he considered how his existence as van Dam's doppelgänger would give him another decisive advantage: at some stage the conspirators would come to find him.

News of Walter van Dam's survival would inevitably pique the curiosity of those who had assumed the businessman was dead, so sooner or later, another team would turn up to finish the job that the first lot had apparently failed to complete. But they would soon discover he wouldn't be as easy to kill this time.

But he would be able to find out what he needed to know about the doors directly from the people who knew the most about them.

Friend thought carefully about his next move.

Let himself be captured?

Remove all but one of them from the equation?

Pretend to be one of them and sneak into the new headquarters?

The kettle boiled and turned itself off.

He poured the boiling water into a fresh mug and inhaled the steam. He had never known such a delicacy before; his survival depended on tastes and aromas that were imperceptible to humans. The next thing he wanted to taste was pure water from a spring or glacier, just after it had boiled – the hot vapours such a liquid produced would surely be utter bliss.

Friend moved into the lounge. Through the window he observed the plant shadows growing longer, which meant he'd soon be able to sit outside, light a fire and enjoy the surroundings. And drink as many gallons of hot water as he wanted.

His research would also involve the Arkus Project – an arch apparently made entirely of *Particulae* – which had been mentioned a couple of times in the old notebook. That would create such a portal as had never before existed.

Friend recalled the video of the detonation at *Frills & Furbelows*. What would the explosion look like if it were not just tiny splinters but a whole mass of large fragments instead?

He sipped his water, considering. An arch like that would surely do more harm than good, that was certain. He looked over at the large television, which was now showing reports on the earthquake and the so-called methane explosion. They were much briefer than those from a few days ago.

'The area will remain closed to the public until the specialists have completed their investigations,' said the newsreader importantly. 'Experts believe there is still a significant risk of further explosions and sinkholes. State authorities are considering imposing an indefinite ban.' The man smiled into the camera. 'Rescue workers have announced that a woman has been saved from a wrecked vehicle found near the scene of the incident. She's currently in hospital with severe burns and her condition is said to be critical but stable. There are no deaths to report so far.'

Friend slowly lowered his hand that was holding the cup.

He knew precisely which car they were talking about: it contained the mysterious woman he had discovered outside the house.

Who had come from the labyrinth.

It would appear he had another item on his agenda now.

CHAPTER X

Near Auxerre, June 841

Viktor scanned the detached scope from his G36 over Empress Ermengarde's encampment. 'I think we'll be able to sneak in at night.' He tried to make himself sound more confident, wanting to hide the fact that he thought this was a highly dangerous operation. They had defensive positions formed by wagons, a partial outer palisade and guards outside each gate, and there were scores of tents of various sizes, not to mention very few landmarks to use as orientation. Among all that, the camp was teeming with people, soldiers and civilians alike, from traders to cooks to camp followers. 'There are a few places where we could slip through,' he said, hoping he sounded confident.

He and Dana were sheltering among the trees at the top of the escarpment, from where they had an excellent view of Empress Ermengarde's gargantuan camp. They were both memorising tactical positions that might prove important and risking the battery usage to record their observations on their phones' drawing software so they wouldn't have to rely on memory alone.

Coco sat behind them; also now dressed in military black. Their borrowed armour and insignia belonged to the wrong faction, and in any case, their modern gear would give them an advantage in the undergrowth. She looked at the golden pendulum, which continued to tug on its chain to confirm that Anna-Lena was somewhere among the chaos of tents and wagons, waiting to be found by them.

The morning had started with Friedemann changing his plan: he and Ingo had hurried off to see Count Guerin, accompanied by Wahid, as they would be of little assistance in infiltrating the enemy camp. The rescue team needed Coco and her pendulum to act as a compass and point them to where the young woman was located. The camp was far too large and crowded for them to have much chance of stumbling upon her by chance.

Coco was missing Ingo terribly. His presence had a soothing effect on her, like an intensified echo of their former fling. Her feelings were becoming deeper, more mature.

'Any sign of her?' she asked.

'No.' Dana picked up her phone to jot something down. 'Everything's so close together – it's almost impossible to tell anything apart.' She was astonished at the muddle spread out below them. Their whole system was entirely different from anything she was used to.

Coco suddenly had a moment of inspiration. She took out a pen and some paper from her pocket and made a rough copy of the drawing from the display on the screen.

'What are you doing?' Viktor sat down and looked at her.

'Saving us a job – if it works, that is.' Coco concentrated on the pendulum, trying to redirect the energy flow, hoping that instead of continuously pointing at the camp, it might be able to show Anna-Lena's location on her sketch-map.

'Go for it,' said Dana, re-attaching the scope to her G36. It was a rather decent idea.

But the pendulum was being stubborn: it jerked and bucked around, flitting between the camp and the drawing as if it couldn't make up its mind. Coco began to feel nauseous, the tugging feeling in her temples turning into a burning sensation. Then the golden tip finally descended upon a spot on the map, hopefully revealing Anna-Lena's whereabouts.

Coco made a mark on the map. 'Please check if I'm right,' she gasped, trying to suppress her sickness. She felt entirely drained, as if she had just finished sprinting up a thirty-degree hill.

Dana peered over the barrel through the scope. Finding the spot in question among the raft of tents was no mean feat and she had to shift position along the edge of the embankment several times, trying to get a better view.

'I can't see her, but ... *yes*! There's some red hair – in the large open tent with blue and white stripes. It could well be her!'

Viktor looked for the tent, breathing a huge sigh of relief. Friedemann's change of plan, with Coco as the ace up their sleeve, had proved to be a masterstroke. 'Now we know where we need to go tonight.'

'You don't need me for that.' Coco looked down at the circular camp with its circles within circles. 'I'll wait for you on the hill.'

'Hmm ...' Viktor wasn't convinced. 'If Miss van Dam moves, we'd have to start our search anew – and then we'll need you and your pendulum again.' Dana looked at Viktor, who nodded in agreement. 'And what if something goes wrong and we have to find another way out? You'd be stuck up here by yourself.'

'I understand all that.' Coco had no desire to be any closer to thousands of hostile soldiers than absolutely necessary. She tapped the map with the tip of her golden pendulum. 'We can do it over the radio. I'll guide you from up here if Anna-Lena changes location. I'm not a fighter,' she added. 'Honestly, I'll bump into things and make a load of noise. You won't want me with you. I'll just ruin the whole operation and everything will become far more complicated than before.'

Viktor could see the fear etched on her face. There was no denying she'd become a hindrance as soon as they were crawling among the tents. 'We can make that decision tonight.'

'I've already made my decision.' Coco approached the edge and looked down at the camp. Wild horses couldn't drag her down there. Another idea came to her as she observed the people milling around the tents and fires. 'Can I borrow one of your rifle scopes?'

Viktor handed her his. 'Another piece of inspiration to save us some work?'

'Very possibly.' Coco searched for the tent, which took a little while, even though the red curls she sought stood out between the lines of striped canvas. The nausea and burning sensation in her temples had subsided: she was ready to undertake a second mission. 'I'm trying to talk to her,' she announced, without putting down the glass, 'with my mind.'

'Blimey! I didn't know you could do that.' Dana was impressed.

Coco just managed to stop herself from letting slip her former charlatanry. 'Well it's only an attempt. We'll see if it actually works or not.'

Some movement could be seen in the tent as several people moved around inside.

Anna-Lena van Dam appeared in the scope's field of vision. She was wearing a simple linen dress with a rope around her waist, a makeshift belt, Coco assumed. She still had her nose piercing. She was walking among a throng of young men and women, each carrying a bucket, who appeared to be receiving instructions from an older woman.

'She's being sent to fetch water.' Coco concentrated hard on Anna-Lena and said out loud, 'Don't be alarmed, Miss van Dam. Carry on as if nothing's happening.' She hoped she really was projecting the words into the girl's mind. She tracked the route the youngsters were taking through the camp, afraid her plan would fail if her visual contact with Anna-Lena broke.

It was only after the tenth attempt that Coco spotted a reaction on the redhead's face – one of amazement, with not a small hint of joy. 'Good. Very good. Nod if you can hear me clearly in your head.'

Anna-Lena nodded hesitantly.

'My name is . . . Beate.' It made more sense for her to use her real rather than her stage name. 'Your father's sent us to bring you home.'

Anna-Lena laughed out loud, which made her companions turn to look at her in surprise.

'We're sitting on the little wooded hill – I'm looking at you through a telescope.'

Anna-Lena promptly turned her head and appeared to look Coco straight in the eye, though this was obviously just her imagination.

'We're going to infiltrate the camp tonight and get you out of there,' said Coco, a little disappointed that Anna-Lena wasn't able to communicate back to her. Head movements and gestures would have to suffice.

'Ask her if she's still got her watch with her,' prompted Viktor.

There was a sudden tug on her forehead and the medium was struck by a bout of dizziness. She relayed the question.

Anna-Lena gestured in the negative.

'Pity. That would have made everything far easier,' said Viktor.

The group was approaching a row of tent walls, where a barrier of carts had been piled up one alongside the other. That would be where they'd break through. 'Hang in there, Miss van Dam. Only a few hours to go.'

Anna-Lena nodded with a relieved smile playing on her lips, then mouthed, 'Thank you.'

'Good. I . . .' Coco quickly handed the scope back before vomiting violently over the edge. She hadn't been able to contain it any longer.

Dana reached out and grabbed the medium, preventing her from falling down the slope. She pulled her back a couple of paces. 'Back you come. We still need you.'

Viktor's confidence rose considerably. The rescue mission had gone from being an almost impossible task to being entirely feasible. His eyes roamed across the vast camp. With the mercenary at his side, he now truly believed they could succeed. 'Let's stay up here and keep our eyes peeled. Some larger gaps might appear during the day.'

They still needed luck on their side. Any carelessness, any alarm raised and they'd have a hundred and fifty thousand men on them in a flash.

'How long is this going to take?' Ingo was relieved to discover that Wahid couldn't ride very well either, so at least the three of them were all suffering equally. Their style was more reminiscent of a series of hops and jumps on top of a horse rather than actual riding, as the aching in their legs, crotch and posterior testified.

'Two or three days, sir,' said the young Moor. 'It depends on where we decide to wait for Guerin. He and his people will be on their way to see the empress.'

'I'd try to make my horse gallop if I could, but I wouldn't stay on for long,' Friedemann groaned.

Ingo grinned. He had finished his letter and was hoping his Latin would be passable. From what he recalled, classical Latin was rather different from the version used in the Middle Ages, but with the best will in the world he didn't stand a chance of imitating that.

The weather was set fair: a mild, early summer's day, but they had still broken into a sweat, a combination of the effort of riding and their numerous layers of clothing and armour.

Ingo wore a ducal badge, while Friedemann was playing the role of an old veteran, his pennant lance bearing Empress Judith's banner. Wahid rode slightly ahead of them, following landmarks, for they'd left the road and were travelling cross-country to make better progress.

Suddenly Friedemann brought his horse to a halt. He patted himself down in a panic, then swore loudly.

'What's the matter?' Ingo and Wahid stopped as well.

'My notebook – I've lost it.' Friedemann's face wore an expression of horror. 'No!' Then he checked himself. 'It's all right, I haven't lost it – it's in the grass, next to the wagon.' He was already turning his horse around. 'I've got to go back.'

'We can go back for it later.'

'It might rain later, or someone could find it,' the professor retorted. 'You wait here with Wahid. I'll be back soon.' He set off in the opposite direction. 'I'll be as quick as I can. If I don't return, ride on to Guerin. Correcting our intervention in history is more important than finding me, Doctor.'

'Right you are, then.' Ingo dismounted as Friedemann hastened away, and Wahid followed suit. They walked over to a small clump of trees and loosely tethered their horses so they could graze.

With a groan, Ingo did a few stretches in an attempt to soothe his aching muscles. The weight of the chainmail pressing into his back was making riding almost unbearable. 'I must say this is a welcome break,' he said, leaning against the trunk of a birch. He brushed his hair back; it felt horribly greasy and dirty, and his body reeked of sweat, old and new. The mediaeval world was no place for people with sensitive noses.

'Do you think he'll find us again, sir?' Wahid watched the professor as he disappeared into the distance. 'He's not a tracker, is he.'

'Our prints are clearly visible. He's also an experienced . . .

speleologist. He's more than capable of finding his way.' Ingo noticed a shrub on which blue-black berries were growing. 'Whinberries! I haven't had those in ages. Plus, they're guaranteed to be organic.'

'Organic, sir?'

'Oh, never mind.' Ingo plucked a handful of the dark berries and wolfed them down. They were delicious, a refreshing combination of sweet and sour. Dark spots remained on his dirty fingers after he had finished, but that didn't bother him. 'Ambrosia.'

His mind drifted to Beate, to peaceful nights lying beside her. Although their history hadn't exactly been glorious, he now longed for more such nights: to be calm again, bathing in their deep connection.

He silently scolded himself. Like any old fool, he was just pleased to have won the favour of a younger woman. And as soon as word got out that he and Beate were an item, the derision of the sceptical community would inevitably follow, casting aspersions on both his competence and her abilities.

But crossing through the force field had turned Beate into a true medium; he didn't need to take any measurements for he had seen it with his own eyes. She'd amazed them all.

'Sir!' Wahid had approached him. 'Sir, I went to get some food ready for us—'

'And?'

'Something's missing from the saddlebags.'

'Oh, well, it must have fallen out. Whatever it was, it's a shame, but—'

'No, sir, the straps were still closed tight, as when we left.' Wahid was looking perturbed. 'All my dead master's records have disappeared – everything he wrote about the door and the Basque Country. But I don't understand how – I myself stowed them away safely after you'd finished looking at them.'

Ingo frowned, wiping his hands on his breeches. Together they searched through the bags once more. 'The professor,' he concluded. 'He's got them.'

Friedemann had lied about losing his notebook – and he had never intended returning to them. He had taken the documents with him.

Ingo clumsily hauled himself back into the saddle. 'Come on, Wahid. I think he wants to go back through the force field – without us.'

'Who, sir?'

'Friedemann.'

Wahid climbed onto his horse. 'Why would he do that? He's your friend, sir.'

'I wouldn't be so sure.' Ingo was annoyed with himself for having believed Friedemann's lies. The professor had always paid far closer attention to the doors and the frame than to the group or rescuing Anna-Lena. He should have taken that as a warning.

The pair rode back as fast as they could, which resulted in both Wahid and Ingo falling off their horses. Apart from a few cuts and bruises they weren't badly hurt, but it took them a while to catch up with the skittish animals and continue on their journey.

To make matters worse, another summer storm was imminent. Thunder clouds rolled in menacingly as forked lightning flashed in the distance; the deep, sonorous boom of the thunderclaps sounded far louder than those he was used to in the twenty-first century.

Ingo tried several times to re-establish radio contact with Viktor and Dana so they could stop Friedemann from escaping, but the batteries were getting weak and they were out of range.

'He's gone the wrong way.' Wahid indicated the fresh tracks on the ground. 'Look, he took a wrong turn here; he's ended up on the road.'

'Then we've got a chance of catching up with him!' Ingo could no longer feel any pain, thanks to the adrenalin and excitement pumping through his veins.

The tree where the wagon had been left appeared on the horizon, next to which he could make out the gaunt professor fiddling with the frame. Friedemann, with a bag slung over his shoulder, noticed the two riders approaching and turned to face them.

'Stop that at once!' Ingo called out through the rumbling of the storm. 'How dare you, Friedemann?'

'Go fuck yourself, Theobald,' said the man, drawing his pistol. 'I've got what I need. There's nothing that can keep me here in this shit-hole for a second longer.'

'The frame, though – it's damaged. You might break it.'

'It'll be enough for me.'

'And what about the rest of us?'

Friedemann straightened up and released the safety on his semi-automatic pistol. The wind was beginning to pick up and the first drops of rain fell upon them as the thunder and lightning chased each other across the sky.

'Don't move, ghost-hunter, or you'll find out once and for all whether there really is life after death.'

Ingo stopped his horse. 'You really are a prick, Friedemann.'

'My name's not Friedemann.' He grinned. 'And I'm not a fucking professor. Enjoy what's left of your life, dickhead.'

A particularly loud thunderclap startled the horses, and cursing loudly in Arabic, Wahid struggled in vain to get his mount to stop; it galloped towards the false professor, despite Wahid tugging bravely at its reins.

'I warned you.' Without a moment's hesitation, Friedemann aimed and fired off two shots, striking the young Moor in the chest and neck. Gurgling and spitting blood, he fell backwards out of the saddle and landed in a heap on the ground. After one final gasp he lay silent.

'No—!' Ingo cried. 'You're a madman!'

'You see, I don't believe in jokes, as the real professor might say.' Friedemann pointed the pistol at Ingo once again. 'I do actually like you – and the rest of the group – but collecting some stupid It-girl was never my true concern.'

Ingo couldn't believe how this man had suddenly turned into a cold-blooded murderer. 'But you too saw the energy field collapsing in on itself – that means something's happened back in the chamber in our world,' he shouted. 'Something that's closed the door—'

'I don't care. I'll find a way.' Friedemann gestured with the mediaeval dagger he was holding in his other hand. 'The portal works a little differently from the models I'm familiar with, but I've figured out how to open it.' He pushed the tip of his blade against a small black dot embedded in the frame. There was a bright clicking sound. 'If you give it a whack at three different places, it activates the in-built

Particula. Watch and learn – you want to get out of here as well, after all.' He raised his arm to land the first blow.

Ingo slid out of the saddle with his hands in the air. The rain was now falling so heavily that it hurt his skin. It was so dark you could almost believe it to be night. 'Friedemann – or whoever you really are – *please*, don't do this!'

'Weren't you listening? Stay where you are.'

'I'm unarmed. You're not going to shoot an—'

'Wahid was unarmed as well, remember?' He raised the dagger again. 'So I wouldn't bet on that.'

Ingo took a brave step forwards. 'You're not going to—'

Friedemann suddenly pointed the pistol and fired. '*Tada!* Don't say I didn't warn you.'

The bullet shot through Ingo's right thigh. Gasping, he fell to the floor, clutching the wound as blood bubbled over his fingers. The projectile had hit an artery – he'd be dead in a matter of minutes if he couldn't find a way to bind his leg.

'Consider that a warning. Now you can focus on saving your own life.' Friedemann tapped the smoking barrel to his forehead in a macabre salute before tucking the pistol back into its holster. 'Good luck, Doctor.'

Groaning, Ingo pulled off his baldric and with trembling fingers, he tied the belt around his thigh as a makeshift tourniquet. As he did so, he glanced up through the veil of rain at Friedemann.

Ignoring the water soaking him, the fake professor gave the frame a quick tap at three different places. A flickering hiss emanated from inside the frame and sparks emerged at each corner, at the points where the carved wood was most damaged. The entire structure was clearly unstable, but

Friedemann sounded unperturbed. 'Send my regards to the others, Doctor. I truly hope you do make it through to the other side of the looking glass – just like Alice.' He cocked his head and stepped purposefully into the shimmering glow.

The buzzing became an uncomfortably bright whirring – and the frame tore itself apart at the damaged areas.

Myriad bluish-white discharges flew off in all directions, shooting into the black, stormy sky and digging into the ground, sending clumps of dirt spurting up all over the place. There was a strong smell of scorched earth and burnt grass; steam swirled around everywhere.

Ingo, blinded, covered his face with his blood-soaked hands and rolled to one side as the ground shook. The hooves of his whinnying horse missed him by inches.

Then the whirring stopped as suddenly as it had started.

All was quiet, apart from the struggling of the terrified mounts and the sound of the rain as it continued to hammer down.

Ingo quickly turned his attention back to his tourniquet, still trying to staunch the bleeding. He held it taut in one hand and sat up straight. Somehow, he had to find out what had happened to the frame – their only way out of the Middle Ages and back home.

The wood was not much more than a pile of smouldering remains, scorched in several places, destroying the elaborate carvings. There were only burnt-out holes where the *Particulae* had once been.

Friedemann's right leg, lower back, left arm and parts of the back of his skull lay on the scorched ground among the smouldering blades of grass. They had all been smoothly severed by the collapsing energy field. The blood seeping out of the disembodied limbs was soon washed away by the downpour. Whoever this pretend professor of geology was, he was history now.

The bag was lying next to him on the ground.

Ingo really hoped it contained Aysun's records. The leather would have offered the parchment some protection from the rain, at least.

His vision became blurry and his surroundings started swimming before his eyes. He didn't know how to defend himself against this sudden grim mixture of shock and blood loss. He tried once again to get through to someone over the radio, but his device was proving obstinate.

Darkness gathered gently in the recesses of his mind like a welcoming blanket. It quenched the pain, soothing his thoughts as Ingo allowed himself to sink into the soft ground beneath him. His fingers released the tourniquet and he began to bleed again.

Weak and exhausted, he closed his eyes. He could no longer feel his teeth chattering.

He needed to rest, just for a little while.

Then Ingo could start in earnest again.

Dana and Viktor advanced through the pouring rain, fog and darkness between the tents of Empress Ermengarde's camp. They had taken some of their modern equipment with them, but used more ancient techniques to camouflage themselves, blackening their faces with ash and soot, which had started to streak in the rain.

They had found it easier than expected to avoid the

guards, find their way through the palisades and dried thorn bushes and crawl underneath the keep made up of wagons. Infiltration apparently wasn't much of a concern for people in the Middle Ages. There had been just a couple of hairy moments, when they had almost collided with the metal plates on the guy-ropes – the ringing would have given them away.

They were only planning to use their weapons in an emergency. Regardless of what century they were in, a gunshot was still a gunshot, and here it would certainly attract attention.

They had left Coco sitting on the hill as they had agreed, where she would be of most use as a scout, ready to report the moment Anna-Lena van Dam left the tent.

Viktor crouched in the shadow of a square tent, looking at the sketch of the camp in the weak light of his phone. 'Here's where I think we are,' he whispered to Dana, pointing to a spot on the map.

'You sure? I thought we were four rows further up.'

The mist rising from the surface, created by a combination of warm soil and cool rain, was a double-edged sword. On the one hand it was providing them with excellent cover, but it was also making orientation incredibly difficult. The tents all looked very similar, for the flags, pennants and banners were barely visible. The scope wasn't of much assistance either right now, although they had left one of them with Coco so she could direct them from atop the hill – in theory, at least.

'I can't see either of you,' came Coco's voice over the radio, 'but Anna-Lena's still in her tent.'

Viktor swore under his breath. 'Okay. Let's see if we can

work out where we are.' He walked on with Dana close behind.

They had observed the camp all day, noting down landmarks such as certain tents, flags and firepits which would help them to find their way around, but the dense fog clinging to every surface had put a rather hefty spanner in the works. It was already obvious that the mission would take longer than expected.

After half an hour Viktor and Dana still had no idea precisely where they were.

'We could try some sort of light signal?' suggested Dana. All this wandering around aimlessly was irritating her immensely. 'Then you could tell us where we are, Madame Fendi.'

'But what if someone sees you?'

'We might have to risk it – otherwise we run the risk that we'll be running around blindly till the sun comes up,' Viktor replied. He liked Dana's idea. 'They'll just think it's a will-o'-the-wisp or something.' He took out the light he had removed from his helmet earlier and pointed it up towards the hill. 'Ready?'

'Hang on,' said Dana beside him, grabbing his arm as she listened closely to snatches of conversation from a nearby tent. 'Listen – this might be relevant for us.' She opened the radio channel to allow Coco to hear what was being said too.

'. . . swear to you, my Empress, Guerin and his troops won't turn up to fight alongside your enemies,' came a man's voice.

'I have every faith in you, Bernard. How did you manage it?' asked a woman they assumed must be Ermengarde.

'I sent him a letter to nudge him in a certain direction: a load of nonsense about alliances and common interests, combined with a few false promises,' Bernard of Septimania summarised. 'My son took the letter to her himself.'

'Just so,' came another voice – William's.

Dana and Viktor exchanged glances. The young man had apparently neglected to admit to his father that he had lost the letter: clearly he'd said not a word about his encounter with the supposed *scara*.

'And what did he say in reply, William?' the empress asked.

'He . . . he said it was a good deal. I shall meet the count as soon as the battle is over and your victory has been ensured, my Empress.'

'In any case I want him brought to me, Bernard, do you hear?'

'Certainly, my Empress.'

'Then I bid you good night. May the Almighty bless you for your works on behalf of me and the Empire. After everything Charlemagna achieved, it absolutely must not be allowed to fall apart under the rule of an idle opportunist.' Several armed bodyguards emerged from the tent, bearing torches and lamps, followed by a woman in her forties, with a purple cloak over her white dress, with a black hood to protect her from the rain.

Their supposition that this was the empress was confirmed by the man trotting behind her.

'When will battle commence, my Empress?' Bernard looked to be fifty or older and his embroidered brown robe was a little tight on him, which was not helped by the drenching that followed when he stepped outside into the pouring rain. 'Have you come to a decision yet?'

'Yes. Our forces will pitch at Fontenoy in a week. As soon as Judith and Hemma's troops see how strong my army is – and realise there's no sign of Guerin – their people will start to abandon their cause. And that's when they'll feel the full force of my brave Lothair and his troops.' Ermengarde held out a ringed hand. 'You've chosen the right side, sir.'

Bernard knelt down in the mud before her and kissed her rings. 'I have indeed, my Empress.'

Dana and Viktor were lying flat on the grass, using the shadows as cover.

Ermengarde had not yet bidden the count to rise. 'Tell me, is it true that the boy Charles – my enemy's son – is *your* bastard?' She looked at William, who was standing by the tent flap, his gaze lowered. 'Do you not find it strange, fighting your own flesh and blood?'

'If that were truly the case, then so be it. It would not be the first time that such an event has happened in human history, my Empress,' Bernard replied, giving absolutely no indication that the question had affected him.

Ermengarde smiled. 'As clever as ever.' She withdrew her hand, allowing the man to stand up again. 'I'll see you and your son tomorrow for further discussion.' Then she turned and walked to her part of the camp at the top of a gentle incline, in the centre of the cluster of wagons.

Dana and Viktor stayed where they were, curious to hear what father and son would talk about. Anything they could find out would be to their advantage once Guerin turned up.

'Have you gone mad?' Bernard hissed. 'You've lied to the empress!'

'She'll never find out – I'll ride over to Guerin and stop him. Just give me a new letter, Father, and I'll be on my way.'

'Where did you lose it?'

'I . . . don't know. Somewhere. It must have fallen out of my saddlebag.'

A loud slap could be heard clearly through the thin walls. 'You imbecile! It bears my seal – my *signature*! If someone finds it and understands what it entails, we're lost – all of us, our entire family—!'

'Father, no one's going to find it. And it has been raining for ever – it'll be completely illegible by now. Empress Judith has no evidence against you.'

'You can't possibly know that.' There was the sound of William receiving a second slap. 'That's for your negligence. Now sit down there and don't move until I've finished writing a new message.'

Silence fell inside the tent.

Dana signalled to Viktor to move on. Time was running out; they had less than two hours until dawn broke.

'What about the Moors?' Bernard asked suddenly; evidently he hadn't forgotten about Aysun. 'I told you to intercept them.'

'We . . . had them. But our men were killed by a *scara*,' William replied diffidently.

'A *scara*? Empress Judith's personal guards?' From his rising tones, they could tell Bernard was losing his temper again. 'You're only telling me this *now*?'

'It doesn't make any difference. No one knows you're the one behind—'

Viktor and Dana grinned as William was slapped in the face for a third time.

'I'll tell you for free where my letter is: with *them*!' he shouted at his son. 'Lord God Almighty – if the empress loses the battle and Judith's people are victorious, I'll lose *everything* – *we'll* lose everything. She's got written proof of my betrayal! You will go to Guerin immediately, you wretched fool, and make sure he and his soldiers stay put, or you will never again set foot in my presence.'

'Yes, Father. Can I have the letter once—'

'There won't be another letter! You must convince him with words and promises,' Bernard replied angrily. 'The world doesn't need any more evidence against me. Now get out of my sight!'

Viktor and Dana watched William tumble out of the tent, wrapping a heavy cloak around himself, and hurry over to the horses. Only a few minutes later they saw him dashing out of the camp at a swift gallop.

'What if he finds Guerin before Ingo and the others do?' came Coco's anxious voice over the radio; she had heard everything. 'We've got to go as well to—'

'We need to find Anna-Lena first,' said Dana. 'Friedemann and Theobald have got a head-start.'

'Don't worry. It'll be okay,' said Viktor reassuringly. 'Any update on the missing girl?'

'Still in her quarters.'

Dana had the map in front of her and began to give the light signal up towards the hill. 'Can you see the blinking?'

'Yes. One sec. I'll check.' Coco was silent for a few seconds. 'Head down the main path and turn right. Eight wagons along, then take a left. She should be in the large area with all the washing and trading tents.'

Viktor and Dana advanced, crouching, using the shadows

cast by the linen walls and making sure to avoid the guards and the firepits dotted around.

They quickly found the area Coco had been talking about. A few of the tents were lit from within, and they could hear the moaning of men and woman in the throes of passion. That was obviously one of the services available to those travelling without their family.

'We're here,' breathed Dana. 'How's it looking, Madame Fendi?'

'I . . . I can't go on,' came her weak reply. 'It's too tiring. I've got a constant nosebleed and I keep vomiting. I'll break down completely if I don't get some rest.'

'Fine. Let us know as soon as it's passed.'

They completed the final few yards without any supernatural reconnaissance, helped by the illuminations coming from all over the area. As they crawled underneath the wagons, they could see all manner of repair works – sewing, cobbling, patching – being undertaken in the glow of a motley assortment of oil lamps, candles and firelight. An army needed logistics, no matter what era they were in. Thankfully, there didn't appear to be any guards around.

'In there,' whispered Dana, pointing to a large, round construction of painted canvas. Within it, they could see a dim light was burning. She compared it once again with the sketch she had made. 'It's got to be.'

They crept quietly through the mud, Viktor considering how much tougher rain made everything, especially compared with desert operations. Sand could simply be brushed and shaken off, but mud burrowed its way everywhere, even into the very fibres of his clothing, making them unbearable once they had dried.

Dana knelt by the entrance and peeled back a flap. She peered through, then scurried inside. Finally there was something for her to do: a job she had mastered, regardless of what century they were in.

Viktor stayed close behind her, enjoying how well they were working together, almost as if they had always been part of the same unit, even though the opposite had been the case.

Thirty-odd people were asleep on the floor, straw pallets or makeshift camp beds, some of whom were snoring loudly. An oil lamp hanging from the centre pole cast a dim light over the tent.

Viktor was still looking around for a sight of long red curls when Dana stepped in front.

'Fifth from the left,' she whispered. 'I'll get her. You secure the entrance. If anyone wakes up, just knock them out.'

'Right you are.' Viktor grinned. As if he needed to be told. The mercenary knew precisely what he was capable of.

Voices were coming from outside, an outraged male voice followed by a woman's throaty laugh. 'I provided you with a service. Now pay up,' said the man.

'That limp old thing? That was of no use to me. I didn't even feel it inside me,' replied the woman contemptuously. 'And you dare to ask for coin for *that*?'

Viktor stole a glance outside, where a slender man dressed in a loincloth was facing a female soldier who stood there in only her underwear with her chainmail slung over her shoulder.

'You were moaning and everything.' He held out his open hand. 'Hand over what we agreed.'

'Out of boredom, you cretin. I almost fell asleep.' The warrior pushed him to one side. 'Now get lost.'

'Hey!' He grabbed her by the arm. 'I'll report you for theft.'

But she just punched him, hard, laughing as he went reeling down into the mud. 'Poor bunny.' She left him lying there and trudged on.

'You swine!' he called out, struggling to his feet. 'I hope they slit your throat in the battle!'

A man looked up from his straw bed next to Viktor. 'For goodness' sake,' he berated the man. 'Quieten down, will you?' Then he noticed the intruder crouching alongside his bed. 'Who by all the saints are—?'

Viktor drew his knife and brought the handle down hard onto his forehead, knocking him out cold.

Dana gave him a thumbs-up and shook the redhead by the shoulder; she mumbled grumpily, clearly unhappy at someone trying to wake her.

'Abort – abort immediately,' said Coco furiously over the radio, adding, 'Is that what you're supposed to say?'

Viktor furrowed his brow. If their medium was being attacked, they were too far away to help her. That had always been the flaw in their plan. 'What's going on?' he whispered.

'Anna-Lena's with me – someone threatened her so she couldn't wait any longer. She used the fog to escape—'

At that very moment, the red-haired woman opened her eyes and looked straight at Dana in her mask. Before the mercenary could put her hand over her mouth, she let out a loud, terrified scream.

CHAPTER XI

Munich

Archangel sat in the back of her black Audi limo, reviewing the data that had been downloaded from the Organisation's cloud server over the last few days – data that had no right to exist, seeing the man in question was dead.

She was wearing a state-of-the-art earpiece that wouldn't be available to the general public for several months. 'I'm looking at it,' she remarked to her colleagues back at headquarters. 'How has this happened?'

'Our IT department spotted it too late,' replied Frisk, also an Organisation director. 'Partly because they hadn't been told the account was no longer supposed to be active.'

'I reported the employee's death at the time.' Archangel was fuming at the level of incompetence on display. Relying on other people drove her mad, especially if basic protocol wasn't being followed.

'Yes. We know. But the message . . . slipped through the cracks.'

'Holiday?'

'Holiday.'

Archangel gave the front seat a violent kick to stop

herself from screaming with rage. She'd make sure to abolish holiday time in the near future, or at least make it a capital offence for anyone to take holiday without providing sufficient notice. 'And have they been able to track the IP address? Or the location? Or is the employee in charge of that sunning themselves somewhere as well?' she added caustically.

Laughter could be heard at the other end of the line. 'It's been coming from Walter van Dam's house in Lerchesberg.'

Archangel checked the date. 'That can't be.' She double checked it, just to be sure.

'We had IT confirm it several times.'

'But . . . that's after I'd paid him a visit.' She was baffled. How did the laptop find its way into the house of a dead industrialist after one of their employees had died? And who from there would be interested in information about his second team?

'Have you been watching the news? About what happened after the earthquake and your raid?'

'I've been busy with our new projects in Munich. The documents we took from the house have led me to a new door.' She looked down at the folder containing the records. 'As far as blowing up the old headquarters is concerned, our experts are in no doubt that—'

'Walter van Dam's alive,' Frink interrupted.

'No.' Archangel looked out the window, trying to process what she had just learned. 'I killed him. No doubt about it.'

'He hasn't given any interviews yet, but we've discovered that he received treatment at hospital and is back at home now.' Frisk cleared his throat. 'Did you just shoot him in the leg or something? I remember you being a better shot than that.'

This time the laughing was directed at her.

'Three shots. I watched him die.' She managed to shake off her crippling sense of shock. 'Something's not right – it's *not* van Dam.'

'How could anyone else possibly pretend to be van Dam?' Frisk audibly poured himself a drink.

'I'm going to go back to the villa to find out.' Archangel planned to seize the laptop, as well as this man pretending to be van Dam. She had a few questions for him. She turned on the news. Various transmissions cycled through by themselves at three-second intervals on the screen embedded into the headrest in front of her.

The detonation in the forest had ceased to be a sensation and if it was mentioned, it was only in passing. The Organisation's experts had done a good job of ensuring the events were now considered a closed case.

'Best of luck.' Frisk ended the conversation.

The fact that Archangel had been sent on her own to Lerchesberg was clearly a punishment for her having made a mistake. The conference call would certainly continue without her but about her, because of her negligence. *Alleged* negligence.

She considered herself blameless.

She slid the pane separating her from the driver down a crack. 'Airport, please,' she said. 'I'll need a private jet. As quickly as possible.'

'Yes ma'am,' he replied calmly.

The glass whirred back up.

'For fuck's sake!' Just as Archangel was about to switch

off the news, she heard someone talking about some sort of miracle that had happened in the woods near the old carpentry workshop. An unidentified woman had been rescued from a car crash. She had sustained severe injuries, but was still alive.

She waited, her finger hovering over the off button, then leaned forward and enlarged the image, trying to see more detail. The car in question – now entirely destroyed and partially melted – was the Rolls-Royce in which van Dam's chauffeur had laid the Anna-Lena clone, ready to take her back to her father, according to her man on the ground; at least, that was what he had said before the connection broke off.

'No normal human could survive an inferno like that,' said Archangel softly to herself. 'So what are you?' What had the lost team dragged up from the old headquarters?

She'd visit the injured woman in hospital before heading to Lerchesberg.

The vaguest hint of an explanation for the businessman being alive and well was beginning to ferment in her mind.

And she didn't like it one bit.

Near Auxerre, June 841

Dana knocked the red-haired woman unconscious and she fell silently to the floor.

Viktor quickly dropped down next to the man he had just knocked out and half-covered himself with his body, trying to stay hidden.

'What's going on?' a dark-haired woman muttered, sitting up from her furs.

Three more people had awakened and were blearily looking around the tent to find the reason behind the disturbance. Thankful for the dim light from the oil lamp, Viktor and Dana held their breath anxiously in their hiding places.

Outside the tent, the cheated man was still complaining about the soldier.

'Shut up, Eckhard!' the dark-haired woman called out. 'We're trying to sleep in here.'

'Fine, fine,' came the reply from outside. 'But I'll get my money from that woman.'

Grumbling, those who had woken up hauled their thin blankets back over themselves and tried to go back to sleep.

'We'll wait here for a bit,' Viktor radioed quietly to Dana. 'Then head straight off.'

After fifteen minutes, they broke cover and slowly eased themselves out of the tent. They got out of the market-like area and sneaked from wagon ring to wagon ring through the thickening fog. At least the rain had stopped.

It didn't take them long to find their way out of the camp and with a sigh of relief, they saw the hill, its peak protruding out of the fog.

Coco and Anna-Lena were visibly pleased to see them.

'I've already explained everything – who we are and where we are. And how to get back,' said Coco, relieved that her nausea and nosebleeds had subsided. 'So we can—'

'Why didn't you wait for us?' Viktor snapped at Anna-Lena. 'We put ourselves in danger for you for nothing!'

Anna-Lena's eyebrows twitched. 'No more danger than if I'd been there too. And I'd have made your escape harder, wouldn't I?' she retorted, tying her long, red hair back. Her desire to not be blamed for what had happened was over-riding her naturally friendly nature. 'One of the traders threatened me – pretty violently. So rather than lashing out and risking drawing attention to myself, I bit my tongue and escaped as soon as I had an opportunity. I wasn't going to sit around waiting for ever, Mr Troneg, and I knew where to find you, so it was better to leave immediately.'

Dana grinned. This young lady wasn't turning out to be the spoilt brat she had expected her to be, considering her father's wealth and the life of luxury she had led up until now.

'Someone could have spotted you!' Viktor's dander was up. 'Then we'd have had to free you from chains.'

'But they didn't, did they?' Anna-Lena gave him a con-ciliatory smile, her nose piercing glittering. 'Thank you for everything you've done. You've achieved what you set out to do – I'm here.'

Dana patted her on the shoulder. 'Well done.' She indi-cated the way down. 'Now let's get out of here and wait for Theobald and Friedemann by the wagon.'

Viktor was looking forward to putting on the dry clothes he had left there. His trousers and shirt were caked with mud and smelled even fouler than the other clothes from the ninth century. 'Good. Let's go then.' He shook hands with Anna-Lena. 'Sorry for over-reacting earlier. It's been a long night.'

She returned his handshake. 'No problem. I understand.

By the looks of you, you must have dug up half the field down there.'

Coco led the way, glad that they had accomplished this portion of their mission. 'Hopefully, our academics have figured out how to get back by now.'

The trio caught up with her.

'Or maybe you know something about them?' Dana gave Anna-Lena a sideways glance. The simple dress suited her, despite it being a little baggy around her hips and chest. 'About the doors – any idea how they work?'

'Only vaguely. I've read a lot about them, though.' Anna-Lena brushed an unruly strand of hair behind her ears. 'I think they've got something to do with my great-grandfather. He was the one who discovered the catacombs underneath the house in the forest. I still don't know how he was connected to the Organisation, though.'

'We're more interested in the portals, to be honest. How to trigger them and . . . make them work,' said Viktor.

'If I knew that, I wouldn't have found myself in this position.' She tossed her hair back angrily, stuffing it under the hair band. 'I'm going to cut this all off one day. It's getting on my nerves.'

'You've probably got lice or fleas by now,' remarked Coco.

'So do we all.' Dana overtook the medium as they reached the edge of the forest. This was no time for carelessness. Bandits could be lurking anywhere and an abandoned wagon laden with goods was sure to arouse people's greed. She surveyed the surroundings, waving the barrel of her G36 back and forth. 'Can't see anyone – not through this fog at least.'

'Let's keep going, then.' Viktor took the lead, with Coco

and Anna-Lena walking behind him and Dana securing the rear. As they walked, Dana and Viktor told the others what they had overheard in the camp.

The grass around them rustled constantly as the wind picked up, chasing the grey curtains of mist away from the meadow. Stalks of wheat waved around, rubbing against one another amid the background noise of whistling wind, barking foxes and the hooting of owls emanating from the copse they had just left.

Viktor considered it all rather peaceful and allowed himself to be swept away by the tranquillity. They had found Anna-Lena, after all. Now they just needed to get back to their own time.

The fog lifted, revealing the cart.

Ingo and Wahid were lying beside it, lifeless, while the frame was scorched and in pieces. They were also met by the horrific sight of the ripped-apart human remains that had doubtless once been the professor.

'No!' cried Coco, running over to Ingo in a panic. She put her head to his chest and listened closely. 'No, it . . .' Then she shouted for joy, 'His heart – it's still beating!'

Dana rushed over to their wounded colleague and examined his condition in the glow of her light. 'Gunshot wound, damaged artery, but not too badly. Looks as if he closed it himself after binding his leg. Massive blood loss,' she remarked, checking his pulse: all part of the routine. 'Weak, but still present. Blood pressure low. The ground's absorbed most of his blood, so it's hard to tell how much he's lost, but I'm pretty sure he'll need a transfusion if he's to stand any chance of pulling through.'

They pulled out disinfectant swabs, bandages and compresses from their backpacks; Dana quickly applied a pressure bandage.

They all knew a transfusion would be impossible under their current circumstances – not only did they not have the equipment for it, they didn't know the parapsychologist's blood type. And if the femoral artery were to split open again, or the wound were to widen, it would be all over for him.

Viktor looked down at the destroyed frame. Wahid had been shot and the professor was lying in pieces on the grass. 'You've got to be fucking joking!' He had run out of ideas. 'What happened here?'

Coco pulled Ingo's head into her lap and caressed his face.

Dana rubbed her bloody fingers on the wet grass and searched the doctor's clothes. She retrieved his letter in Latin and held it up. 'Looks as if they never made it to Guerin.' She started to inspect the professor's assorted body parts and his bag dispassionately. 'The notebook and the notes Aysun left for us,' she announced. 'If you ask me, I'd say Friedemann tried to leave and decided to take out Wahid and the doctor in the process.'

There was a slim chance that the notebook and the documents could show them another way home – but their sole remaining academic was unconscious and very likely to die of blood loss, septicaemia or gangrene.

'Fuck!' Viktor's good mood had well and truly departed. 'Why did Friedemann want to leave?'

'Because he never intended to find Anna-Lena.' Coco was

still by Ingo's side. 'He was only ever interested in the doors.'

Dana leafed through the notebook, then handed it to Anna-Lena. 'Better for you to have it. You know more about all this than we do.'

'Not really.' Anna-Lena took it nevertheless, her eyes now fixed on the broken frame. She had never come across anything like that in any of the records. The damage was serious: the *Particulae* had been destroyed, so the frame was useless to them now.

Ingo's eyes flickered open for a moment. He recognised Coco and felt for her hand. 'The letter,' he gasped. 'I couldn't . . .'

'We've found it.' She smiled at him, trying to conceal her concern. 'Mr Troneg thinks you're going to be fine.' The lie was necessary to reassure him – to reassure herself. Could she use her gift in any way to help him? Maybe she could relieve his pain, or heal him somehow?

'You have to deliver it,' he said weakly. His mind was so addled that forming clear sentences was proving difficult. He wanted to tell them everything that had happened, but he didn't have the strength for it. The letter was the most important thing for now. 'Otherwise the course of history will be changed.'

'I don't care—'

'But I do.' Ingo could feel himself close to fainting again. 'The whole of Europe will be different if the wrong empress wins.'

'Which might not be the worst thing in the world,' commented Dana, once again cleaning her hands of blood on the grass; this time it was Friedemann's. 'Having women in power in the twenty-first century might be nice. Less macho shit and fewer pissing contests.' She grinned briefly. 'But who knows what else might have changed in the process?'

'Please, Beate! Take the letter to Guerin. The consequences are unimaginable otherwise. I . . .'

Ingo blacked out.

Coco was scared Ingo had died in her arms, but the vein in his neck was still throbbing; he hadn't given up the ghost yet. Shedding silent tears, she kissed his forehead. It occurred to her only too late that she could have read his mind to find out what had happened. She couldn't get through to him while he was unconscious.

'What if we took the doctor to Empress Judith?' suggested Viktor. 'We can tell her about Bernard of Septimania's betrayal, that he tried to warn Guerin off and then joined the other side. We've got his letter as evidence.'

'And then what?' Coco folded her scarf and placed it beneath Ingo's head as a rudimentary cushion. 'Are we going to tell her we killed her *scara*?' she pondered.

'Of course not. But maybe the empress will help us to take care of Theobald.' Mediaeval healing methods might be backward, but the empress would have the best medical professionals of the time around her. 'Without the frame we haven't got a chance of getting him to a modern hospital for the time being.'

'He'd be better off in that farm,' retorted Coco. The empresses would soon be at war, making an army camp a dangerous place to be. And they couldn't stay out here in the open, underneath a tree. Her intense concern for Ingo had triggered something inside her, which she was starting to feel as a tingling sensation just above the bridge of her nose. Was a new gift awakening?

'Hmm.' Dana folder her arms. 'Let's tell Judith the *scara* was dead when we found them. Then she can write another letter to the count.'

To everyone's surprise, Anna-Lena took Ingo's letter to Guerin out of Dana's hand. 'The traitor's son is already on his way to Guerin. The game will be up as soon as he gets there.' She walked over to the horses grazing nearby. She suspected Ermengarde's counsellors would be pressing her to deploy her army soon now spies had infiltrated the camp and released a prisoner. There was no time to waste.

'Wait. I'll come with you.' Dana stripped to her underwear, then slipped back into the duchess' battle garments. She hid the G36 under her overcoat and picked up the spear with the pennant on it.

'We'll look through these notes while we wait here.' Viktor handed Coco a simple robe and started to change his clothes as well. 'If we're not here by the time you get back, come and find us at the farmhouse.' He turned off his radio. 'Only check in briefly – on the hour – to save battery life.'

'Agreed.' And Dana dashed off, looking, Viktor thought, like an older version of Joan of Arc, albeit one with less competence on a horse.

Anna-Lena, however, was clearly an accomplished rider. 'We'll blag our way to the count. Wish us luck.' She urged her grey into a gallop and shot past Dana, who struggled to keep up.

Viktor saw the dawn was rising, heralded by the chirping of the birds all around – and interspersed with a noise he couldn't at first identify: a constant grinding and roaring sound coming from the distance. Then he realised Ermengarde's camp was being dismantled. One hundred and fifty thousand soldiers would soon be marching to Fontenoy to meet their opponents on the field of battle.

Coco stroked the dirt-covered face of the motionless doctor, whom she was protecting as if he were a baby. As soon as she worked out what this new gift of hers was, she was sure it would help her immensely. 'The battle's going to start soon,' she mentioned.

Viktor quickly climbed the tree to keep an eye on the road.

No matter which army appeared, no matter which empress they belonged to, they couldn't be discovered. If they were, there was every chance he and Coco would be forced into the army and Ingo would be left to die.

Neither of those things could be allowed to happen.

Dana's concentration was mainly focused on keeping her feet in the stirrups. They had slowed down a little to spare the horses. As they travelled they had asked the various itinerant merchants they'd passed where to find the count, and they'd all said they should head south, 'Keep following the road – past Mâcon.' So they kept heading south.

'How long have you been here, Miss—?'

'Please, call me Anna-Lena.'

Dana grinned. 'Very well. I'm Dana. How long have you been stuck in this time?'

'Only a few days – but anyone who says they'd like to live in the Middle Ages should be made to suffer what I've had to endure.' Anna-Lena had plaited her hair with a leather thong to stop it from falling over her face, but she knew it probably wouldn't hold for more than a few miles.

'Was this century the first place you came to?'

'No, the first place I went to was this nightmare world with sirens and a forest and howling wolves – that's where I found a second passage, which took me to the year 841 . . . well, after a bit of a scrap with some guy in a suit.' Anna-Lena shuddered. 'All I wanted was to find out a bit more about all those stories my grandmother used to tell me – and whether the records in my father's office were accurate.'

'Well, you've certainly done that,' said Dana drily. 'Do you think there's any way back for us?'

Anna-Lena recalled the sight of the destroyed frame. 'We just need some gaffer tape,' she replied, grinning. 'We can just bung the wood back together. And *Particulae* are two-a-penny here.'

Dana laughed. She liked this young woman. 'Seriously, though.'

'I don't think so.' She straightened herself in the saddle and looked ahead. Another hamlet. No sign of an army yet. 'Our only hope is finding something in the notebook – or those documents.'

'If only I'd paid more attention in history.' Dana's buttocks ached from all the riding and her back was beginning to mutiny.

'Why? How would that help?'

'Well, I could use any knowledge I had to get ahead in

life. If I'm going to be stuck in this Godforsaken place I might as well thrive.'

'Sadly, we never did the Middle Ages at school,' remarked Anna-Lena. 'But one thing's for certain – no one ever said *anything* about women being in charge – or that there were empresses who ruled by themselves. What little I know about the Franks and Charlemagne is *completely* different – and it's not even Charlemagne here: they were all talking about *Charlemagna* – or Carla Martell – who defeated the Arabs at Tours and Poitiers.

They'd reached the hamlet, which consisted of four huts, but there was no one around, other than the people who were working in the cornfield beside the path.

'But that's not true,' Anna Lena continued, 'so either we're in a parallel Middle Ages or . . .' She couldn't actually think of an alternative. 'No idea.'

'Doctor Theobald mentioned a theory he had, about some of the Middle Ages being fabricated,' said Dana. 'He said the men might have staged a coup against the women in around 900 or thereabouts, then the records were deleted or re-written to hide the fact that there was ever a matriarchy.'

'Oh?' This was the first Anna-Lena had heard about such a thing. 'That would explain something I overhead as I was escaping yesterday. There was a group of men acting rather suspiciously . . .'

'It was foggy,' Anna-Lena started, and at Dana's nod, went on to tell her what had had happened. There was enough noise around to drown out the sound of her foot-steps, so she had been making good time. But then a few figures appeared and she scurried into the closest tent, where she hid behind some storage chests to avoid being discovered.

As luck would have it the figures entered the same tent, but oddly, no one lit any of the candles or oil lamps.

'This isn't the best night to do this,' said a muffled male voice. 'The empress is too well protected. We need to consider the best way forward before we meet our venerable ally. He's already in camp – incognito, of course.'

'What about the assassin we hired to kill Judith? Young Charles is nothing without the empress' leadership – and her sister will have to surrender as well,' ventured a second man.

'Don't underestimate Empress Hemma,' the first voice warned.

'She's got a strong husband in Louis and there's no doubt he'll be able to convince her to take over her sister's inheritance,' added a third.

'Our killer got nowhere near Judith,' growled a fourth voice.

Anna-Lena had been shocked to realise they were conspiring against the empresses.

Another figure entered the gloomy tent, stopped at the flap and spoke, 'The Lord God said unto the woman: thy desire shall be to thy husband.'

'And he shall rule over thee,' replied the quartet.

'Amen.' The newcomer walked over to the conspirators and shook each of them by the hand. 'We must cancel our plans. The camp's in turmoil about the upcoming battle.'

'I knew it!' exclaimed one of them. 'Why can't we just go straight for Ermengarde now?'

'There'll be another opportunity,' said the newcomer.

'And just allow the battle to happen? This is madness – insanity! The losses sustained will ruin countless farms and villages – they won't have anyone in charge, no protection or income,' interjected another. 'The blood of the noblest men in the land will flow like water.'

'I said right from the start we needed to speed this along,' growled another. 'And now we're stuck in this mess. If the Moors change their minds and launch an attack after seeing these women tearing one another to pieces, only God can save us.'

'God helps those who help themselves,' the newcomer retorted piously. 'I've received a missive from Rome: Pope Gregory hasn't forgotten how he was used as a puppet by the empresses and now he fears for his life for daring to express his displeasure aloud. He urges us not to tarry too long with our endeavours.'

'The holy fart's afraid of losing his power. We told him not to interfere,' said one of them dismissively. 'He'd better hope his cardinals can save his arse.'

Most of the men laughed, but the newcomer said, 'Don't be so hasty. My spies report that at the request of both empresses, Gregory will be followed by a female pope. They've already sent their abbesses to Rome to take part in the selection process. The curia's made it clear they'll comply with their wishes. Gregory suspects they're plotting to depose him completely.'

The other four were outraged; remarks such as 'mockery', 'the Byzantine Empire will never allow it', 'this last bastion will never fall' and 'God created us first' were bandied around inside the tent.

'Quiet! We'll stay our hand for now,' said one of them. 'And in the name of all the saints, keep your voices down. If the guards catch us we'll have some explaining to do.'

'We could say we were praying loudly for the health of Empress Ermengarde?' suggested one caustically 'What else could bring us together at a time like this?'

'Or worrying about the battle ahead,' added a second, amid the sound of the men laughing.

'Why refrain from carrying out the assassinations, though?' ventured the third man. 'Do you mean to say we shouldn't kill Judith and Ermengarde at all? Is that how we should interpret all this?'

'Absolutely: we need the battle to take place: it will weaken both of them,' the man by the flap explained. 'There will be slaughter as never seen before in these lands, and the spilling of so much noble blood will fall squarely on the dainty shoulders of our rulers. It is their lust for power that has brought about such a state – we'll make sure that's fully understood by sending travelling tinkers and bards throughout the country once the massacre has taken place. We'll stir up resentment. The seeds will take longer to grow, but they'll be strong, with deep roots.'

'What about the Emir of Córdoba? Could we persuade him to—?'

'Never!' howled one of the others. 'The devil take the Moors – and Aysun first, that unholy bastard! If he hadn't crawled beneath the empress' skirts in Aachen I'd have finished the job there and then.'

'The emir is Aysun's enemy, as far as I'm aware, Bernard,' replied one of the men with a placating tone. 'It'd be in your best interest to—'

'No Moors! *Never!*'

'Fine. We'll leave the emir out of it then. My lords, I hereby call off the attack on Empress Ermengarde,' announced the ringleader. 'We'll instead use the tragic, bloody outcome of the battle to our advantage. The rule of women will be over – if not today, then tomorrow. Three hundred years of their futile, patronising aspirations is more than enough.'

'Amen,' replied the conspirators, shaking hands as they parted. Anna-Lena, still concealed by the shadow of the chests, waited for the last of the four men to leave the tent.

'I have no idea who they were,' she said by way of ending her story, 'but it was obvious what the men were planning.'

Dana had been listening attentively, recalling what Ingo had said. Bernard's letter to Guerin contained evidence of Septimania's betrayal, but there was nothing about any conspiracy to remove the empresses from power. This meant they had interfered in history once more, though perhaps this time it was for the good?

Anna-Lena pointed to a spring bubbling up between the houses that trickled down into a small pond. 'Time for a break. The horses need a drink as well.'

They brought their mounts to a stop by the pond and dismounted.

No one appeared to ask the strangers what they wanted or whether they could do anything to assist a duchess, but a rhythmic clang of hammer on anvil could be heard from the annexe next to the barn, punctuated on occasion by the dragon-like hiss of a bellows. There was work to be done, guests or otherwise.

Dana groaned in pain. Her buttocks, thighs and back were agony personified. 'Why would anyone do this voluntarily?'

Anna-Lena grinned. 'It's just a question of technique.' She took the reins and led the horses to the water. They drank deeply, snorting happily between gulps. 'And practise.'

'Ho! You there!' A woman emerged from one of the cottages, holding a wicker basket full of washing. Her hair was concealed beneath a hood, her dress simple and fastened by a broad, leather belt. 'Who are you? You should introduce yourself if—'

She recognised the duchess' insignia and stopped, then put down the basket and bowed low. 'Forgive me, my Lady. My eyes aren't what they used to be.' She moved closer, bowing a couple more times for good measure. 'Are you hungry? I've only bread and lard to offer, mind. The beer's stale but I can rustle up an infusion of lemon balm if you prefer.'

Dana wanted to refuse, but her stomach growled treacherously. 'Bread will suffice. Thank you.'

'Follow me inside, my Lady.'

'No, we'll not put you to more trouble. We'll stay out in the sunshine, thank you.' There was no way she'd step foot inside such a dilapidated building, which was almost certainly riddled with lice, fleas and scabies. 'We'll eat out here.'

'As it please my Lady.' The peasant woman hurried back into her hut. Several small children peered through the door and windows to gape at the visitors, jostling and thumping one another to get a better view.

Anna-Lena took a sip of the spring water. 'Tastes amazing.'

After what she had experienced on earlier operations, Dana would have preferred to toss in a purifying tablet. Catching cholera in this time would be a death sentence.

The farmer returned with a loaf baked from rough, dark flour. The smell was enticing and the visitors began to devour it hungrily.

The farmer appeared delighted that it was going down so well.

'This is the best bread I've had in a very long time,' said Anna-Lena as she slathered some lard onto a couple of slices.

'Thank you, my Lady. I bake every day to provide for my family working in the fields.' She bowed low again. 'Feel free to take it with you if you like.'

A small group of people emerged from the other side of the track, carrying scythes and rakes over their shoulders and bearing a cart full of grass cuttings. It looked like the morning's work had been completed.

'That's very kind of you.' Dana thought it only right to pay the woman for her kindness, so rummaged through her pocket and took out a handful of silver coins. Not knowing how much they were worth, she hoped she had enough. 'Thank you. For your trouble.'

The peasant woman stared at the money. 'You're too kind, my Lady. But that's . . . that's . . .'

'Take it. Please.' Dana patted her black horse, who had just finished drinking. 'Right, shall we carry on?'

'One sec.' Anna-Lena felt her horse's hind leg and lifted up its hoof. 'Ah, just as I'd feared. The shoe's loose: it's hampering my gelding.'

The farmer immediately pointed at the annexe next to the farmhouse. 'My husband's in there and he'll sort it out right away.' She hurried off. 'Gerard! Another job for you,' she roared.

Dana tied her own horse to a tree and followed Anna-Lena to the barn. The clanking sounds became louder and yellowy-white smoke stinking of burnt keratin billowed out of the forge's open door.

When the smoke subsided, they made out a leather-clad blacksmith adjusting the shoe of a dapple-grey rouncey. A man was sitting next to him on an upturned bucket. It was William of Septimania.

Dana raised her eyebrows. 'Well, look who it is.'

The young man stared back at her. He hadn't forgotten the woman who had thrown him into the dirt in front of his men. His hand reached for his sword.

'Are you sure you want to do that?' Dana took a couple of quick steps towards him. 'After what happened last time?'

'You two know each other?' Anna-Lena looked back and forth between them.

'William of Septimania, sent by his father to correct his mistakes after losing his letter to me,' Dana summarised. 'Lovely to see you again, although I'm afraid this is where your mission ends.'

'I don't think so.' William rose. 'You must be out of your mind, Duchess. And you have no authority in this place: as one of Empress Judith's vassals, you're not welcome here.'

The returning field hands had entered behind Dana and Anna-Lena, announced by the sound of their rattling tools and loud footsteps.

William reached for his belt and took out a small pouch that gave a metallic jingle. 'Thirty pieces of silver to kill both of them,' he snarled.

'This is unfortunate,' Anna-Lena murmured, shrinking back from the confused rabble. She had nothing to defend herself against scythes and hoes.

'You'll receive twice that if you arrest this traitor,' announced Dana.

'*I'm* not the traitor here, Duchess. These peasants follow a feudal lord sworn to Empress Ermengarde. In their eyes it's you who is in the wrong.' William was enjoying being the one on the front foot this time. He walked behind the forge, using the glowing brazier and the blacksmith as cover. 'Well, what are you waiting for? Kill them!'

Dana drew her sword, hoping the *scara* armour would be sufficient to deter the peasants.

The farmer picked up the pouch of silver and weighed it in her hand. 'You heard him, boys: for our empress!'

The first of the men lowered their scythes and rushed towards them.

'Anna-Lena, run,' Dana ordered, her eyes not leaving the enemies before her.

'Absolutely not.' Anna-Lena took two large steps towards the forge, grabbed a small shovel and loaded it with glowing coals, which she hurled at the attackers.

The men cried out, ducking to avoid the projectiles, which were closely followed by a shovelful of glowing ash. A few of them were hit, burn marks left on their clothes and red spots on their skin to show for it. The red-hot lumps landed on the floor.

'Get away from there!' The smith raised his hammer.

Anna-Lena slammed the hot shovel down on to his right foot; there was a loud crack and the man limped away, wailing.

The farmer poured a bucket of water over the coals, hoping to prevent fire from breaking out and spreading to the farmhouse.

Dana swung her sword violently in the direction of the peasants. It made a buzzing sound as it whizzed through the air and they backed away, intimidated, their scythes raised in defence. 'Go inside and stay there till we're gone,' she ordered. 'No one here needs to get hurt.'

'You two do!' shouted William as he broke cover with his own sword drawn. Aiming a blow at Anna-Lena, he shouted, 'Death to the traitors!'

Anna-Lena fended off the jab with her shovel but was unable to avoid the punch that followed. She staggered and fell back into a pile of straw behind Dana.

One of the farmhands found his courage again and swung his scythe, its edge hissing as it made a large, semi-circular arc through the air.

Dana intercepted the blow with her sword, grabbed the handle and slammed the blade into him.

Her opponent had not let go quickly enough: he lost three fingers to the scythe, which landed on the floor like fat caterpillars. Blood spurting from the stumps, the man screamed and ran off.

Sensing an opportunity, William tried to stab Dana in the neck while she was distracted, but the crackling of coal underfoot betrayed his attack.

Whirling around, Dana knocked her enemy's weapon out of his hand with the scythe and immediately thrusted her sword into his side with all her strength.

The chainmail might have prevented the blade from entering his body, but the force of the impact threw him to one side and a loud crack emanated from his hip. With a screech he smashed into a supporting beam, clutching his pelvis as he sank to the ground. 'Something's broken!'

'No chance of you riding anywhere soon, then.' Dana dodged another scythe attack, then turned her attention to the two who were jabbing at her legs with wooden rakes in an attempt to knock her to the floor.

To make matters worse, several children were now running out of the house, picking up stones and throwing them at her, calling her names as they did so.

Anna-Lena stood up and wiped off the blood oozing from a cut on her chin. She shook off her dizziness and grabbed William's sword. 'We've got to go.'

'I know.' Dana sliced through the rakes with a single swing of her sword. She pointed to the nobleman's grey rouncey. 'You take the stallion. I'll clear the way so you can ride out. Then I'll run over to my horse.'

Anna-Lena ducked under a handful of flying stones, which instead struck William as he lay on the ground, whimpering. 'Reckon you'll make it?'

The thundering of hooves could be heard approaching from the road; a dozen or so armed riders in leather armour rode through a cloud of dust to the peasants and stopped directly behind them with their spears lowered. The whole area was covered with a layer of fine powder.

'What's going on here?' demanded the commander as she rode up down the semi-circle formed by her soldiers with her sword drawn. 'How dare you threaten a duchess? I'll have you all executed!'

The riders advanced slowly, their spears aimed directly at the farmer and her family.

'Stop! Stop!' exclaimed Dana, relieved at the unexpected assistance, though she didn't recognise the coat of arms on their shields. 'They were deceived by this man.' She pointed at the groaning William, who had tears streaming down his face. He appeared to be in agony; a broken pelvis in this era would probably render him permanently disabled. 'He paid them to attack us.'

The farmer's wife immediately flung the small pouch of coins to the floor. 'Forgive us, Duchess!' she pleaded, sinking to her knees. The others followed suit, holding out their hands plaintively to first the armed riders, then to Dana and Anna-Lena in turn. 'We were fools, is all. I beg your forgiveness!'

The children wailed as the farmers begged repeatedly, whispering 'mercy' and 'leniency' as they grovelled on the floor.

Before Dana could speak, William interjected. 'You, Countess. Take me to Guerin,' he croaked. 'I have a message for him from—'

'Don't listen to him,' interrupted Dana. 'I've been sent by Empress Judith for a meeting with the count. This man' – she looked contemptuously down at William – 'is a traitor and a double-crosser, just like his father.'

'Let the peasants go inside while we talk.' Anna-Lena

lowered her sword, but did not drop it. She liked how it felt in her hand. 'They don't need to hear any of this.'

The countess gave orders to her companions, who promptly escorted the family back to the cottage. 'My name is Margaret, Countess of Digne,' she declared. 'Guerin sent me to learn more about the dispute between the two empresses – and it would appear I've come across two parties seeking an audience with the count himself.'

'Greetings. I am Diana, Duchess of Misnia, emissary of the Empress,' replied Dana politely, hoping she had remembered Meissen's former name correctly. Hopefully, they were far enough away for no one here to know much about who ruled in Germany. 'This knave's only intention is for your lord to commit treason. He's been sent to whisper falsehoods into Guerin's ear, to serve his own ends.'

'She attacked and injured me!' William complained. 'All because I've got this message—'

'My master has not forgotten what Emperor Consort Lothair did to him at the behest of his wife Ermengarde. So you'd do well to hold your tongue.'

Margaret looked at Dana and Anna-Lena. 'If you come with me I'd be glad to accompany you to my master. Then you can present Empress Judith's offer.' She looked down contemptuously at the wounded man on the floor. 'If meeting Guerin is that important to you, I'm sure your injuries won't prohibit you from riding. Follow the road. It's a two-day ride for a team of four or five.'

Dana was most unhappy to hear this, for it meant it would take them at least four days to get back to Viktor,

Coco and an ever-weakening Ingo. The battle might be over by then.

'We're in a bit of a hurry, so we can swap.' Anna-Lena led the dapple-grey past the seething William. 'You'll need to have this one re-shod before you leave. But you're more than familiar with the blacksmith here, so that won't be a problem for you.' She picked up the pouch of coins and tossed it into his lap. He gasped angrily. 'Here. At least you'll be able to pay for their services.'

CHAPTER XII

Near Fontenoy, June 841

'His fever's getting worse,' Coco said helplessly. She was
perched on a stool beside the straw pallet Ingo was lying
on; they had stashed their belongings, including what
remained of the frame, beside it.

Viktor had managed to load Ingo onto their wagon and
get him safely past the enemy forces to the outskirts of
Empress Judith's camp. They had left a message for Anna-
Lena and Dana in the crook of the tree.

Their chainmail and *scara* insignia had granted them
access and the duty guards had referred them to the large
tent at the edge of the camp where the wounded and
sick were being cared for. The upcoming battle meant no
one took the time to take a closer look at the returning
party. Preparations were in full swing inside the ring of
wagons: soldiers recited prayers and checked their armour
and accoutrements, weapons were being sharpened. The
smallest thing might save a life in battle; even a torn strap
could bring you down.

'There's definitely no gangrene,' murmured Ingo, trying
to keep Coco calm. The skin around the bullet wound had

turned red and hot, with greenish-yellow pus oozing from the hole. 'It's probably just an allergic reaction.'

Coco bit her lip, dabbing sweat from the injured man's face. There hadn't been time for her to investigate her new powers, nor did she have the focus for it now, so her latest gift, whatever it was, had so far remained unexplored.

In truth, Viktor knew perfectly well what infection looked like. In any modern army camp, doctors would have sorted a wound like this in a flash, thanks to the wonders of modern medicine. But in the year 841 all they had were prayers, obscure tinctures, infusions and poultices, and honey – oh, and a red-hot piece of iron to cut out and sear the infected area. It was a complete lottery as to what would help and what would make it worse. 'I'll be right back.'

He walked past the rows of pallets provided by the empress; she obviously expected a great many casualties.

Viktor stepped outside and looked across the busy camp at the men and women preparing to offer what passed for medical help on the battlefield after the fighting had finished. They were stuffing sacks with knives, pliers, bone saws and tourniquets, as well as a variety of herbs and potions, ready to help the survivors while they waited to be brought back here for treatment.

He was surprised to hear a cheerful melody being played by pipers and drummers nearby, and all the faces around him were happy and carefree. He suspected that was because they weren't the ones who had to fight; they were there to tend to the wounded – and to loot the enemy corpses.

'Hey,' he called out to one of the healer monks hurrying past him, 'my friend needs help.'

'Is that the *scaritus* with gangrene?' At Viktor's nod, the man stopped and opened his bag, rummaged through the contents and pulled out a bottle of powder and a clump of dried herbs. 'Boil these into a broth, cut open the wound and pour this over it.' He looked at Viktor. 'And then pray for him.'

'Can't you—?'

The man shook his head. 'I've got to go. The battle's about to begin.' He pressed the ingredients into his hand. 'Shouldn't you be with your unit as well, *scaritus*?'

'The duchess has asked me to attend to my friend. I'm not one of the elite troops,' he lied.

'If you were you'd be in the vanguard, I suppose.' The monk rushed off, but just before disappearing between the tent walls, he called back, 'Don't forget to pray. He'll need it – just like all those other poor souls on the battlefield.'

Viktor, depressed, returned to the tent and presented them with what he had been given, repeating the instructions. He rubbed the herbs, then uncorked the bottle and sniffed the contents. 'No idea what this is either.'

'It could kill him,' whispered Coco desperately. 'First the blood loss, then the inflammation and now . . .' She held Ingo's hand tightly. His eyes were closed, his breathing laboured. Her skills as a medium were of no use; probing his brain wouldn't do anything about pus. She'd have to figure out what her new ability was all about – but how? 'Is there nothing else we can do?'

'I'll give him another dose of our own pain medication

for now.' Viktor exposed the wound, where pus was starting to collect again. 'Cutting and burning it out is probably our best bet.'

'But what if that tears the damaged artery?'

'The heat'll seal it back up.' He toyed with the idea of fetching one of the monks, who must have done this sort of thing countless times before. 'If we don't do anything, he'll die of blood poisoning.'

Coco put a hand over her mouth and began to sob quietly. She reached out with the other hand to wipe Ingo's forehead.

Ingo coughed weakly and murmured, 'I'm not about to die.' He shifted slightly on the hard straw pallet. 'Not before we've repaired the course of history. Actually, no, you know what? Not even then.' He felt awful for putting Coco through all this. 'And I'll take the hot iron option.' He tried to open his eyes but could do no more than flutter his eyelids. 'I'm not going to put a gloss on it: it can't stay like this for much longer.'

Coco kissed his feverish forehead, still shedding silent tears. 'The painkillers will make it more bearable.' *Using hot iron for curing an infection? Barbaric.*

'I'll probably just pass out – that'll be far better.' Ingo gestured blindly to one side. 'If I don't make it, there are the translated documents, or as much as I've been able to decipher, at least.'

'You'll get through this!' snapped Coco, putting a hand on his chest, knowing she would trade all her powers in a heartbeat in return for his life.

'Look for fragments of the destroyed *Particulae*,' he said.

'We can still use them, although they won't be easy to find. The frame itself is useless now.'

'How do you know?'

'The notebook – the one stolen by the guy pretending to be Friedemann? There's a warning in it about trying to repair damaged artefacts.' Ingo gritted his teeth as heat coursed through him; he felt as if he were roasting beneath a merciless desert sun. 'We need a new structure.'

Viktor prepared the syringe with the opiate and carefully inserted it into a vein in the doctor's arm. 'So we're stuck.'

'No. Not necessarily. It . . .' Ingo tightened his grip on Coco's hand. 'Shit – shit, that hurts.' His leg was throbbing and burning as if it were about to explode. He wanted to tear it off with his bare hands. He felt faint, and utterly exhausted.

'The pain'll be over soon.' Viktor didn't want to wait a moment longer to perform the procedure; he guessed the infection was starting to spread throughout Ingo's entire body, poisoning his blood, shutting down vital organs. 'You said we weren't necessarily stuck. What have you found?'

'A story.' Ingo relaxed as the twenty-first century drug took immediate effect, relieving most of the pain. But the fever was still addling his mind and sweat was pouring from his body. 'A story about brave knights . . . who hunted . . . a beast . . . to lock it up . . . for all time . . . in the portal . . . with no way back . . . portal . . . no way back . . . no . . .' His thoughts were engulfed by the heat.

Ingo babbled on, but the only thing Coco and Viktor could make out was how important it was for them to not change the course of history.

'Is he saying we should look for another door?' She looked at Viktor. A door with no way back didn't sound like a particularly desirable option – but then again, she had no desire to return to this place.

'Apparently so.' It was time for him to find a branding iron and a forge. He thought he had seen something useful not far from the tent.

'I . . . I'd like to try something first,' said Coco. She could feel her new gift swelling inside her, as if it finally wished to reveal itself.

The flap was unexpectedly swept aside and six soldiers, four men and two women, entered. 'So it's true, you're here! I recognised your coat of arms,' exclaimed one of the women, heading straight for Coco. 'Good job you're back. You're needed, Duchess.'

Coco's eyes widened in alarm. 'No, I've—'

'You've been asked to join the *scarae*. We need a woman like you in the battle, Duchess.' The woman bowed before her. 'Your skills are the stuff of legend.'

Viktor had quietly put his hand on the handle of his G36, but then he relaxed. If this person knew Coco wasn't the real Duchess, they'd have already been seized, charged with being spies and doubtless executed on the spot.

'No.' Coco clung to Ingo's hand. 'No, I won't leave him here alone.' She concentrated hard, trying to penetrate the soldiers' minds and dissuade them from pursuing this course of action.

'Your concern for a sole member of your unit commends you, Duchess, but now is the time for heroic deeds.' The armoured woman stepped slightly to one side, gesturing towards the exit. 'And bring your companion with you. We need every sword we can get, as Count Guerin hasn't turned up. And every prayer, for that matter.'

'Of course.' Viktor leaned close to Coco. 'We've got to play along. We'll find a way to give them the slip on the way over.'

'We've got to – we're not warriors.' Coco stroked Ingo's forehead again. 'Well, I'm not, anyway.'

'At least you can ride.' He put a hand on her shoulder. 'Trust me. I want to save the doctor as much as you do, but if we resist we'll make matters worse for ourselves and we might not get the chance to treat him at all.'

Coco kissed Ingo, now unconscious, on the forehead and stood up. *Trust.* That was stronger than her abilities. 'You won't leave my side?'

'I won't, Madame Fendi.' Viktor fell in beside her to demonstrate that he was her bodyguard and confidant. He was still concealing the rifle beneath his coat. 'Put on your hood and helmet. We just need them to recognise your coat of arms.'

Coco did as he'd instructed. The helmet wasn't fully closed but the mask-like visor meant she would be hard to recognise, especially at first glance.

The escort took up formation around her, but what was intended as a guard of honour felt more like a human prison; one they couldn't escape from without causing a tremendous fuss.

The camp followers' yard was adjoined by the enormous, ring-shaped tent city belonging to the main army, which was now eerily deserted. Only a handful of men and women were scattered around the tents; the only activity was injured soldiers being treated.

As Coco's breathing quickened, the nose piece of her helmet meant her hot breath rebounded into her face. Her fear for her own life was increasing in parallel with her concern for Ingo, waiting helplessly in the hospital tent with a festering wound. 'What are we going to do if we can't get out of here?' she whispered?

'Improvise. And not ride into battle,' he replied quietly. 'I'll stay with you.'

The further the group travelled, the louder became the booming sounds of war until they found themselves looking down from the top of a small hill onto the plain where the two armies had assembled. A sea of flags billowed beneath them, accompanied by an overwhelming number of mounted knights, foot soldiers, archers and crossbowmen, not to mention weapons of war like catapults and ballistae. Only now did Viktor believe that a hundred and fifty thousand people would truly be lining up on either side.

'Dear God,' said Coco, stopping dead in her tracks.

This was a far cry from the romanticised versions of battles she had seen in the movies. The majority of the troops below them had simple boiled-leather armour worn over their normal clothing, while the horsemen wore chainmail and were armed with shields and spears – there weren't any longbowmen that they could see, which made the mail an effective option. There were crossbowmen, but the weapons looked fairly basic and cumbersome to use. Once the horsemen charged into the ranks, the fighting would be nothing but brutal hand-to-hand combat.

Viktor took a deep breath, inhaling an unpleasant smell of mud and iron.

'Then speak your truth: God help us all.' The soldier pointed to the right. 'Your *scara*'s over there, Duchess. I'll bring you over to the horses at once.'

The little group swung towards the banner where the elite troops had assembled.

Coco wanted to run away and hide with Ingo. She knew she wouldn't be able to bring herself to do what was expected of her.

Viktor also felt incredibly anxious. He had never seen a battle like this before and watching it up close was rather arresting. 'Go on,' he whispered to Coco. 'We'll have an opportunity soon. I swore I wouldn't leave and I don't plan to break that promise. You won't be alone.'

Coco was going to use whatever supernatural ability she had inside her to save herself from death. There would be no greater challenge than this, for death in a hundred and fifty thousand forms was waiting for her on the battlefield of Fontenoy.

Frankfurt

'Of course you can come in, Commissioner Angel. But she's still unconscious,' said the nurse gently.

'No problem. I just want to see what condition she's in for myself.' Archangel's police ID had granted her instant access to the hospital ward. She had reluctantly swapped her pin-striped white suit for a more generic grey one so as not to draw too much attention. It was a pity, as that suit had always brought her luck.

She had started to push open the door when the nurse asked, 'I hope you don't mind my asking, but why are the police interested in her?'

Archangel opened the door and stopped at the threshold.

'I don't,' she said, with a wink. 'Ah yes, Sister . . . Inga,' she read from her name tag, 'tell me, has our burned woman had any visitors?'

'Apart from our own staff and the hospital chaplain to say a few prayers over her . . . ?' Inga thought for a moment. 'Well, her father, of course. Walter van Dam. Bit of an old fogey. Born in the wrong era, I'd say.'

'How many times has he been?'

'Every day.' She looked at the clock. 'Usually at around 10 p.m. It's out of visiting hours, of course, but he has special permission.'

'Hmm. But how could he identify his daughter if her face is burnt and she didn't have any belongings with her?' the false commissioner wondered aloud.

Inga shrugged. 'I assume she must have had specific features he recognised. In any case, it was his car they found her in – plus he's paying for her private treatment.' She looked at Archangel with mild surprise. 'Shouldn't you know all this if you're with the CID?'

'I was never here, Sister Inga.' Archangel grinned at her conspiratorially.

'Understood. But it'll cost you a cup of coffee.' Inga smiled, then looked serious, to show that she meant it.

'I'll pay up on my way out.' Archangel entered the patient's room.

'On your honour! My shift ends soon, so I won't be here to make sure you do,' Inga called out before Archangel closed the door behind her.

The patient was wired up to several machines which were monitoring her vital signs. There was a ventilator on hand, just in case, but the young woman, presumed to be Anna-Lena van Dam, was breathing independently. Her pulse, blood pressure and oxygen saturation were all healthy.

Her face and body protruded from beneath a layer of bandages, and several cannulas were draining the fluid from an assortment of wounds. The reddish-white liquid dripped into a small plastic bag dangling from the edge of the bed. Her copper-red curls lay haphazardly over the clean white cotton pillowcase. Archangel sniffed. Surely the lustre of the young woman's hair should have been cause alone for suspicion on the part of the hospital staff.

'Hello there, whoever you are,' Archangel said softly, stepping towards the sleeping woman. 'Let's see just how quickly you heal, shall we?'

She took out the scalpel that she had secreted up her sleeve and tore open the packaging, then skilfully unwrapped the bandages around the woman's head.

The face of Anna-Lena van Dam was revealed, even down to her nose ring. The skin beneath the peeling layer of charred flesh was fresh and pink, like that of a baby.

'A perfect imitation,' Archangel said, admiration in her voice. 'Mimicry adaptation and deception.' She leaned over the sleeping woman and pulled up one of her eyelids. 'Or is it?'

The pupil contracted, first assuming the shape of a seed

before becoming round again. Her eye colour was changing rapidly, almost as if it were searching for the right one – or wasn't prepared to commit yet.

That wasn't normal for a human.

But it was possible for a being from another world – from behind one of the doors.

Archangel looked over her shoulder at the monitors. The readings hadn't changed, nor had the sleeping creature responded to her examination in any way.

'Those sodding *Particulae*,' she muttered. What else had they brought to Earth?

The old headquarters should have been destroyed long ago, along with those unstable splinters that Ritter had used on his solo ventures to cause no end of trouble. This creature was probably another of the innumerable playthings he had hidden among the corridors. Hopefully they had all turned to ash now, with the exception of these van Dam clones.

Archangel searched the room. She rummaged through a wardrobe containing some dirty washing, but found nothing out of the ordinary. It was only when she opened a drawer in the wheeled side table that she made a discovery.

Beneath the woman's hospital records was a slip of paper containing a few notes about a television programme as well as remarks about hospital meals and the facility as a whole. It looked like the product of boredom, presumably notes van Dam had made while he was sitting and waiting next to his daughter. Or perhaps the two imposters had actually talked to each other.

She turned it over and a sketch of an arch-like portal jumped out at her. It looked to be made of countless small stones. Next to it were a few handwritten notes:

- Arkus // Arcus // Ark Project
- Basque?
- never implemented, only theoretical
- warning about excessive energy from the Particulae, uncontrollable
- maybe a way back for us?

So it looked like van Dam had told the sleeping woman about what he had found and the notes he had made. Where had he got the information from, though? Clearly she and her team had overlooked something during their raid, which was highly irritating.

She'd search the Organisation's archives to see if they had anything about this 'Arkus' or 'Arcus' project or whatever, then turn the house at Lerchesberg upside down again. Archangel pocketed the slip of paper and walked over to the sleeping woman. She pressed a button to turn the monitoring devices to stand-by, preventing them from recording anything else.

Then Archangel covered the woman's mouth and nose. For a long time.

She closed the woman's airways for several minutes until her chest stopped rising and falling. Then she checked her pulse. Nothing. Her pupils were fixed and non-responsive to the light she shone in her eyes.

Satisfied, she pulled the visitor's chair into the corner that couldn't be seen from the door and waited. Van Dam was due to visit and Archangel didn't want to miss him.

Fontenoy, June 841

'I'm going to die.' Coco was startled to hear the words coming out of her mouth, as she hadn't intended to say them aloud. The statement echoed dully inside her masked helmet; her breath smelled sour and fearful.

Viktor sat beside her. They were waiting on the left-hand flank of the army, alongside a lot of men and women on smaller, swifter horses than the great draught horses the heavily armoured knights rode. They hadn't had a chance to sneak away yet, but he was sure the opportunity would arise. 'We're not anywhere near Empress Judith.' He pointed to the centre of the army, where her banner was waving. She was surrounded by several *scariti*, presumably for her personal protection. 'That's a good thing.'

'Is it?'

It was clear to Viktor that, as an elite unit, they would be given some special task. Forty mounted men and women in chainmail surrounded Coco and him. Behind them were three times as many soldiers, bearing shields and bladed weapons, and some were also carrying long barbed spears. There were a couple of dozen archers in the rear.

Coco looked over her own lines. She didn't know the first thing about strategy and tactics, could see no particular structure and had no idea what was going to happen next. Her entire body was soaked through with sweat.

Then she looked across at the opposing side.

A sea of flags, pennants, banners and streamers waved and swayed above the heads of their enemies in the gentle breeze, giving the scene an impressive, almost poetic element. Beneath the coats of arms, however, was the more prosaic sight of the warriors: archers and soldiers on foot and on horseback.

One hundred and fifty thousand enemies, each of whom wanted to see her dead. They were coming for her with swords and maces, lances and arrows, and there was nothing she could do to stop them.

It was farcical that she, a fake duchess, should be leading a *scara*. The only thing she knew how to do was ride a horse. Her shield was too heavy for her and she didn't have the faintest idea about how to hold a spear or swing a sword properly.

Unless she could find a way to use her mystical powers, whatever they were, she was certainly going to die.

Viktor pointed out a messenger approaching them. 'Looks as if we'll have our orders any minute now.'

The knights had positioned themselves at the centre. Behind them stood foot soldiers and archers in loose formation, with men and women on faster mounts positioned in smaller blocks, doubtless to be used as auxiliary troops as and when required.

To Viktor it looked as if the mounted units would simply collide in a mêlée, supported by the foot soldiers, leaving the archers to fire over everyone's heads. Simple, brutal and utterly confusing. And it would last until one of the empresses fell, one side surrendered or a retreat was sounded, allowing time for the troops to regroup, and then repeat the bloody process all over again.

The messenger stopped in front of them and bowed.

'Duchess, I bring word of your orders from the empress. I am bidden to tell you that you are to wait until after the first engagement has occurred and, using your best judgement, take your *scara* and bypass the enemy lines to attack Empress Ermengarde directly. Your footmen will stay here.' The man raised a finger. 'You are to take her alive: Empress Judith will wish to negotiate a truce.'

'And if we can't,' Viktor interjected, 'what then?'

'Pull back, sir. You'll ride off when the signal is given. Godspeed, and may the saints be with you.' The messenger turned around and rushed off.

Coco was unable to conceal the tremor in her voice. 'I can't do this,' she whispered to Viktor. She was trembling with fear and her heart began to race even faster as the trumpets and horns rang out with the first of the signals. Battle cries erupted from both sides.

'We'll ride off, then try to improvise something from there,' he replied tensely. He'd do whatever he could to get her out of there, but he was concerned about his own lack of horsemanship. If he fell, he'd most likely be crushed to death in an instant by countless hooves.

Even more flags, banners and streamers were raised in the warm breeze, serving as a muster point, or so the troops could rush to their lady or lord's aid.

The hue and cry died down, followed by a deafening silence over the plain at Fontenoy.

Coco looked across at the armoured empress as she kissed her son on the forehead before giving a speech to those around her. She was too far away to hear what she was saying, but her words were conveyed in whispers through the throng by the troops. It was all about fighting for a just cause and God being on Judith's side, as well as that of her son Charles, and Queen Hemma, her sister and ally.

Monks then appeared among the ranks, saying prayers, imparting blessings upon the troops and telling them why it was not sinful for Christians to fight other Christians; that killing on a battlefield would be forgiven, so there was no need to worry about their eternal soul.

'The things they care about in these days,' muttered Viktor.

Coco was shaking uncontrollably and was now in desperate need of the lavatory – or whatever passed for a loo in this era.

Viktor had rested the butt of his spear on his saddle. Things were starting to become rather dangerous and he still hadn't thought of a viable escape plan. It wasn't as if they could just up and leave. Ingo was waiting for them. Dana and Anna-Lena were waiting for them. Walter van Dam was waiting for them.

'Shit.' He licked his cracked lips.

On the opposite side came the first clump of knights on heavy warhorses. They were riding in more of a cluster than a line, at a calm trot. Empress Ermengarde had apparently decided to initiate battle.

The monks hastily brought an end to their ministry and withdrew.

Viktor could see a second wave close behind the first: there were fewer of them, but they were riding in a line. He guessed it would be their job to punch a hole in the battle lines, allowing the foot soldiers to follow them in.

The wind carried the sounds of the clinking of chainmail and the clattering of shields and saddles towards their position.

Viktor pulled the scope out from where he'd concealed it under his surcoat and tried to spot find the opposing ruler. Since he was unfamiliar with heraldry, he looked instead for the more heavily armoured horsemen in the middle of the ranks who would most likely be acting as bodyguards. He ignored the astonished looks of those around him at the sight of his scope. What could he possibly tell them?

'There she is,' he called out, pointing towards the field. 'In the middle, surrounded by a sea of pikemen, just behind the foot soldiers.'

Coco knew they'd never get through to Ermengarde. She looked over at Judith, who was in turn giving orders for her mounted warriors to advance. The empress had apparently decided against employing a second wave, choosing instead to put all her eggs in one basket. Her husband and several *scariti* rode beside her.

'She's fighting,' she said in amazement.

'It's a symbol: to show her people she believes they'll win.' Viktor watched the two formations approaching each other, neither side increasing their speed.

Now the foot soldiers and archers were hurrying forwards across the churned earth. They were still at a distance, but were coming in range of arrow-fire. The ballistae and cat-apults, archers and crossbowmen were all ready to loose.

The horses began to gallop once the opposing parties were around a hundred yards apart.

The armoured riders held their shields at an angle in front of them, using them as cover. Rather than having their spears tucked under an arm, the majority held them out slightly to one side, while others were wielding them above their heads, ready to throw them like javelins.

In the blink of an eye the two bands of knights smashed into each other and pressed together, melding into a single mass of flesh and steel and sending a resounding clatter across the battlefield, followed almost immediately by the screaming of wounded men, women and horses. Wooden poles shattered loudly while flags and banners fell to the ground, disappearing amid the battle.

The archers halted and began to fire arrows across the slaughter into Ermengarde's onrushing second wave. The foot soldiers threw themselves into the mêlée, fighting alongside their knights. The metallic screech of crossing blades grew ever louder.

Coco could no longer stop the nausea rising inside her and vomited to the side, ejecting mostly bile onto her boot and stirrup. Fear – unmitigated, horrific fear – struck her squarely in the stomach.

The archers had done little to stop the second enemy wave, which was thundering into the fray. Their tactics were now becoming clear: the long line was to form a circle around the archers and foot soldiers, cutting Judith off from the rest of her troops.

The catapults starting firing as the lighter horsemen rushed across to support their empress.

'The signal, Duchess,' said a *scarita* from behind her, clearly concerned. 'It's just been given.'

'We've got to go,' Viktor whispered to Coco.

Coco had tears in her eyes from all the vomiting. The sour smell inside her helmet was unbearable. 'We'll never make it through.' She could feel acid bubbling up in her throat once again.

Viktor grabbed her by the arm. 'Look at me!'

She turned to look at him, her face pale.

'We'll survive this. You understand?' His eyes were blazing. 'Think of Ingo. You'll make it back home safely for him – back to our own time. Just follow me when I veer off.'

'Okay. Just give me a second.' Coco closed her eyes and took a deep breath, trying to learn more about her new gift. Anything that might help her to survive. She concentrated as hard as she could.

The trembling of the earth was palpable as the lighter horsemen thundered off; the screaming of the wounded and dying soldiers, the neighing and snorting of the horses, the endless clanking, whirring and thumping of weapons and projectiles and the blaring fanfares filled the air, together with the smell of churned earth, voided bowels, pierced entrails and fresh blood.

Coco breathed out and opened her eyes. She choked off the disgusting taste in her helmet and drew her sword. 'For Empress Judith!' she shouted, although she thought only of Ingo and his plea for them to correct the course of history.

Her decision had been made. If this was what Fate had determined for her, it would be because of *her* decision and not Guerin's. No one would care as long as the outcome of the battle remained the same – and *history* remained the same, just as Ingo wanted. There was nothing more she could do for him.

Coco maintained her concentration and pressed her heels into the horse's flanks. The *scara* dashed off, hurrying past the main battle that looked like an enormous ball of entangled men and women, interspersed with pockets where the fighting was particularly intense.

Viktor leaned forwards and clung tightly to his mount's neck to prevent himself from falling off. His spear and shield were so uncomfortable that he had already thrown them away.

The rest of his unit quickly overtook him and he began to lose sight of Coco. *That was not the plan*, he thought.

Coco, noticing he was lagging behind, reduced her own speed, but even that wouldn't be enough for Viktor to keep up. His horse was following the others purely out of instinct, with no assistance from its hapless rider.

Stay with me, she called to him mentally, knowing there was no chance of her voice penetrating the thumping of hooves and the clatter of weapons and armour. *There's still so much to do.*

Viktor wanted to get to Coco's side, but persuading his horse to do so was beyond his meagre abilities.

They were soon upon Ermengarde's left flank, but they had been spotted by her foot soldiers, who rammed their blunt spear ends into the ground at an angle so that their sharp, polished tips faced the *scara* galloping towards them, ready to impale them. The men and women wore no armour; they were almost certainly peasants, common folk who had been offered up by their feudal masters as a vassal quota.

But a spear was still a spear and would be fatal for anyone who ran into or fell upon it, regardless of who was holding it.

Viktor lifted his visor again, stood up in the saddle and looked out across their unit. An idea came to him. 'Veer off!' he shouted ahead. 'We can go right past them! There's a gap about fifty yards further on. Can you hear me? Don't swing in!'

But Coco couldn't hear his instructions. She had forgotten her fear entirely and was focusing purely on the task she had assigned herself.

The unit thundered through the haphazardly arranged spears, which merely scratched the horses, and struck out with their longswords, sending two or three dozen of the defenders flailing into the mud, either dead or wounded.

They had broken the first line of defence and now, cheering loudly, the *scara* swung towards the larger block surrounding Ermengarde. The empress had made less of an effort to protect her flank, evidently not anticipating a surprise attack.

'Dear God, no! No!' Viktor wished he'd insisted they turn on their radios. This minor victory had clearly made Coco over-confident and she'd forgotten their real plan of escaping the mêlée – they had lost their best opportunity to flee.

A hail of arrows flew into them from the enemy ranks. Whereas the experienced *scara* immediately knew to take cover behind their shields, making themselves as small as possible, the deadly swarm fell directly onto Viktor and Coco before they could react.

He could no longer see what was happening to the medium, for his horse had buckled under the impact of several arrows, finally unseating him while galloping away. A second later, his surroundings were rotating rapidly before his eyes, as if he were being spun around by a washing machine on its highest spin setting.

And that was precisely how it felt.

CHAPTER XIII

Frankfurt

Archangel awoke from her slumber with a start. She was still sitting in her chair in the corner of the patient's now-dark room. The devices she had put on stand-by illuminated the room, as well as the being she had suffocated, with electronic twilight.

She started again when she saw the silhouette of a man standing next to her with his hands behind his back, watching her. He was the spitting image of Walter van Dam, but she knew it couldn't really be the businessman.

'You sleep remarkably well,' he said slowly. 'For a murderer.'

Archangel remained relaxed. If he had wanted to kill her, she wouldn't have even been allowed to wake up. 'Who are you really?'

Van Dam gestured towards the bed. 'Why did you do that?'

'She had no right to be on this planet.' Archangel smiled coolly.

'Just like me?'

'Just like you.' She remained seated, opening her grey jacket. 'You're an intruder here.'

'I was kidnapped – by someone from your organisation. You can hardly blame me for that.' Van Dam walked over to the dead woman. He had completely exposed her face and cleaned off the charred remains of skin, leaving Anna-Lena van Dam lying in her bed, flawless but dead, surrounded by her long red hair. 'I still don't know who she is.'

'No one from this world, anyway. Her eyes.' Archangel pointed to her own. 'They kept changing colour. And they looked as if they belonged to a predator.'

Van Dam picked up the scalpel. 'You looked at my notes on the Arkus Project. What do you want with those?'

'What do *you* want to do with them? To use them to escape?'

'As you've so accurately pointed out, I don't belong in this world.' He pointed to the dead woman. 'And since I have no intention of ending up like her, I need to find another way out.'

'You yourself have written that building a door out of *Particulae* was just a theory.' Archangel wondered why she was still alive. The fact that he had only just picked up the blade meant he wanted something from her.

'I admit it was a struggle to know what to do – for a while I thought I could become accustomed to living in this reality. But then I thought to myself: theories are there to be tested.' Van Dam sat down next to the dead woman, the machines lighting up his stolen, fifty-year-old face, complete with sideburns and a moustache. 'You will take me to your headquarters. To the heart of your organisation.'

Archangel laughed out loud. She would never have thought him one for cracking jokes.

'I'm sure you've got a list of all the doors you use,' he continued. 'I'll review them all, so that should keep me busy for a while. How many *Particulae* do you think I'll need to tear off to create a portal?'

Her laughter stopped abruptly. 'You want to *destroy* the doors?'

'No, just remove the stones. The doors can stay where they are.' Van Dam toyed with the scalpel, the blade shimmering in the artificial glow. 'How do you propose we go about it, then?'

Archangel pulled out her white Glock from its holster. 'Well, first I'll find out if shooting you will kill you. If so, great. If not, I'll have to come up with something else.'

'I see. So you won't take me to your headquarters voluntarily.' He reached into his jacket pocket and pulled out first the magazine from her semi-automatic, followed by the knife she normally concealed in her waistband, then the note and finally the *Particula* ring she had until very recently worn on her left-hand ring finger. 'I thought as much.' Van Dam pointed at her gun. 'I've already been through it. The barrel's empty.'

Archangel was astonished. How had he disarmed and robbed her while she slept? She nevertheless released the safety, aimed the muzzle at the man and pulled the trigger. *Click.*

'I quite understand. It was worth a try, I suppose.' Van Dam raised the scalpel, allowing the blade to gleam in the light. 'Where's the closest door that will take us back to your headquarters? Once we're there, you'll get your ring back.'

Archangel couldn't stand the thought that her only option was fleeing. Fleeing, or fighting him to the death. She rose from the chair and buttoned up her grey jacket. 'You're right. You're holding all the cards here.' She walked slowly towards the exit. 'Come on.'

Van Dam didn't move. 'First tell me where the door is.'

'Why?'

'In case something were to happen to you.'

'Then you'd better make sure nothing does.'

Van Dam's laughter gave Archangel goosebumps. 'Either you tell me where we're going or you die. In this room. And I'll use your ring to find a way to the headquarters. It might take a while, but I can live with that. It's up to you.' His sombre laugh rang out again. 'I've always preferred to give people choices.'

Archangel slowly turned towards the creature who had assumed the businessman's features and was now living his life. 'What did you find in the villa? What did my people and I miss when we ransacked his office?'

'Oh, there was a safe within the safe.' Van Dam was still holding the scalpel in his hand. 'I think one of his employees was a spy – not for you, but for someone else. I found her bleeding to death in the armchair, along with the contents of the safe you missed.'

Archangel swore. The fact that there was someone else looking for the doors was not good news, but it was crucial that she tell her superiors about it now they had a new, secret enemy to contend with. 'And did you find anything interesting inside?'

'Another *Particula*. And another notebook.' Van Dam

grinned, his moustache suddenly appearing bushier. 'Rest assured I'll find a way to your headquarters. I'd just rather speed matters along.'

Archangel turned on a sixpence. As the old adage went, if you can't beat 'em, join 'em. 'Why not team up with us, van Dam? You could be part of—'

Anna-Lena van Dam jerked up with a sudden gasp and started to cough. Her eyes turned first to the unsurprised businessmen and then to Archangel, who glared back at her in consternation. Anna-Lena's eyes narrowed, her pupils changing shape, and before either of them could react, she had leaped out of bed and grabbed the scalpel out of van Dam's hand. She landed in front of Archangel and moved her arm in a rapid semi-circular motion.

Blood spurted out of Archangel's slit throat, hitting the young woman, the floor and even the ceiling, and continued spilling out of the cut.

Archangel's vocal cords had been severed, so she couldn't even scream in pain. She clutched her wound with one hand and reached out with the other to try to grab Anna-Lena's bloody-spattered neck, but shock had knocked all the strength out of her and her fingers slipped off the girl's wet skin.

Archangel collapsed into a pool of her own blood at the bare feet of the woman she had believed to be dead.

'If it were that easy to kill me,' said Anna-Lena to the dying woman, 'I wouldn't have survived the cave or the fire.'

Archangel's grey suit had been re-painted by the glittering red puddle surrounding her blonde hair like a halo. With a final wheeze, she perished.

The blood-soaked woman turned to van Dam with the scalpel now in her left hand. 'And who are you?'

Walter van Dam smiled. 'Someone who's just had a very good idea.'

Fontenoy, June 841

Ingo was feverish and weak. There had been no one around when he woke up – Beate and Viktor had gone, according to a monk who told him they had left with a handful of soldiers.

To do what? Ingo couldn't imagine they were going to be part of the battle. Or had he said something in his fever dream that had changed Beate's mind? Had he insulted her? He vaguely remembered talking about putting history right again. Had that set anything in motion?

His leg was on fire, sending scorching heat down to his toes and up to his head. The painkiller Viktor had given him was wearing off and the pain was almost unbearable now.

Occasionally a monk would appear to dab the sweat off his face with a vinegar-soaked rag, say a prayer over him and then leave. There were far more important preparations to be made for the imminent influx of wounded soldiers.

Ingo didn't need a doctor to know the prognosis for him and his leg wasn't the best. Gangrene, infection, inflammation – in the Middle Ages even one of those things was almost certainly a death sentence. There was no way of avoiding having it burned out, or perhaps even having the leg amputated. And then there would still be the risk of it becoming infected once more.

Ingo closed his eyes and found himself praying to God – for Beate, for the others. And yes, for himself. He understood why some people found faith in times of great need. In a situation such as this, you'd take any support you could get.

As a scientist, he was a little ashamed of himself.

Ingo opened his eyes again, thirstily looking around for something to drink. He had insisted on any water he received being boiled, which had surprised the monk who had been caring for him, but he had granted his request nevertheless. The cup was on the edge of the stool, along-side his notes about the doors.

He had trawled through the imposter professor's note-book, looking for any reference to other doors they might be able to use, but all he had come across was a legend about a group of knights who had been chasing a fierce beast and had vanished through the Arches of Eunate in northern Spain with a blazing flash and were never seen again. It appeared they had sacrificed themselves, as the beast disappeared for good as well.

Ingo wanted to investigate further. Perhaps the Arches of Eunate were the key to returning to the twenty-first century.

He had to lean a long way to reach his water and the notebook. His fingertips only made it as far as the edge of the stool, so he tried to make himself as long as possible – but he and the rough blanket covering him fell onto the straw-covered floor, his head smashing into the stool and he moaned in agony as his leg gave him a vicious reminder of its current condition.

The cup of water wobbled, threatening to spill all over the priceless notebook. Ingo grabbed it quickly, sending only a few harmless droplets splashing onto the cover.

Hasty steps approached and two people came into the tent.

'Do we have to do this now? The battle's about to start. My *scara*'s waiting for me,' a man complained. 'If we're caught, we'll be sent to the gallows.'

You'll be back with them soon enough,' replied a muffled male voice. 'Listen: Empress Judith must not die today. We need her to remain as Ermengarde's adversary – otherwise our coup will come to nothing.'

'To hell with your doubts,' hissed the other soldier angrily. 'We've got the perfect opportunity: she'll ride into battle and I'll make sure I'm close by. I've got two arrows from the enemy stash; a quick stab with one of those and Judith's history. Without the empress, young Charles will be putty in your hands. He'll be sure to bring about the reforms we need to put men back in charge.'

'Nothing would come of it. Judith's sister Hemma will assume the throne after she's dead. Louis supports her and he's a strong ally to have,' returned the other man. 'We'd still be miles away from our overall goal. Now, promise me you won't do anything.'

Ingo lay stock-still underneath his blanket, then lowered his arm holding the cup as slowly as possible, so as not to be spotted.

'How long must we endure this female dominion over us?' cried the *scaritus*. 'I've been saying right from the start that we need to stir up rebellion in our lands faster than we have been. Our ancestors allowed themselves to become chattels and we're the ones who've got to clean up the mess.'

'You weren't at our meeting last night,' said the other man. 'We've had word from Rome: there's going to be a female pope after Gregory – at the request of *both* empresses. Their abbesses have already arrived in Rome to undergo the tests and the result of the battle will decide which one will be declared pope. The curia's too afraid of their armies and the likelihood of Rome being sacked for them to refuse.'

A fanfare sounded from outside: the battle lines were drawing ever closer together.

'I've got to get back to my unit,' said the soldier, 'but doesn't this new information give us even more cause to kill Judith? If the women win the papacy, all is lost.'

'No. We'll use this slaughter to weaken the empresses in other ways,' replied the conspirator. 'There's no time for a proper explanation. Just lead your troops hard into battle and make sure as much noble blood is spilled as possible – all of which will be blamed on our rulers. Leave the rest to me.'

'I am your humble servant, Bernard,' replied the *scaritus*, departing the tent.

Ingo hadn't dared to stick his head out from beneath the cover and only now sank back on the pallet with a groan, closing his eyes in attempt to fight off dizziness. His leg throbbed in abject agony.

'Where have you come from?' came a surprised voice from the entrance.

Ingo's blood turned to ice. He hadn't noticed the conspirator was still in the tent. He turned his head to see a middle-aged man wearing a dark brown robe covered with expensive-looking embroidery and a sword hanging from his belt. 'I've been asleep, in a fever dream.' He indicated his wound. 'I'd love to join the battle, but . . .'

'Bernard,' came a voice from outside, 'it's starting. We've got to go.'

The conspirator looked at Ingo intently. 'May the good Lord grant you a speedy recovery.' Then he hurried out.

Ingo knew he had just come face-to-face with Bernard of Septimania – and what that meant for him.

The nobleman was surely a master of intrigue: he would not allow a sniff of his betrayal to get back to the empress, for his coup would end before it had even started and months, maybe years, of preparation would all be in vain.

Ingo vowed not to fall back to sleep again, lest Bernard be presented with an easy opportunity to kill him.

As the arrows whizzed towards her, Coco could feel a tingling above her nose, as if her gift finally wanted to reveal itself. Was she now able to stop projectiles coming her way?

She bent down low on one side of the horse, with her shield tilted to form a canopy over herself. A second later, several arrows embedded themselves in the heavy wood, two metal tips even protruding through it. But it withstood the onslaught.

She returned to an upright position to see her *scara*

looking at her in astonishment. Perhaps they hadn't expected to witness riding of that sort. Four of them had already been unhorsed, while two others had received wounds but were still in the saddle.

'Where's—?' Coco turned her head to look for Viktor, and found him lying in the mud at the broken first line of defence, several yards behind her, alongside the other fallen *scariti*. He was motionless. Helpless. *Dead?*

The enemy foot soldiers were rushing over with a great hue and cry to seize the wounded and fallen troops; their belongings would be divvied up as loot, and any injured nobles could be ransomed after the battle.

Coco's mind was racing as she wrestled with her twin obligations of her promise to Ingo to restore history and her responsibility to help Viktor. One of those things was ultimately more important to her than the other, though.

'You,' said Coco to the one she thought was her second-in-command, 'lead our forces, keep them advancing towards Ermengarde. Seize her and bring her to our camp. I'm going to help our wounded.'

'Duchess, you—'

'Those are your orders. See it done.' Coco dropped back. 'And may God be with you!'

The *scara* raced towards the second line of defence, which had already formed up, ready to repel their assault. The way the soldiers held their pikes and spears towards the onrushing cavalry looked far more professional, while the hail of arrows flew in a significantly more co-ordinated and targeted manner.

Coco turned her horse around and rode back to Viktor as quickly as she could.

It had become a race between her and the enemy soldiers. Cries of alarm rang out as they noticed a *scarita* returning. Coco deftly avoided several hastily fired arrows, concentrating on the twenty or so men and women assembling from different directions to bring her down.

Meanwhile, the main battle was raging, the screaming and neighing, screeching and crashing and clattering continued to build in a gruesome crescendo. Surely anyone who found themselves in the eye of this storm of lethal steel would inevitably suffer hearing damage. Boots and hooves pounded the earth, which had been turned into a putrid mud by the blood and other bodily fluids of slain people and animals, partially covered by falling flags and banners. Much of the fighting took place on top of the dead bodies, or occasionally even among them.

Coco paid no attention to the relentless brutality all around her. She had almost reached the motionless Viktor when four archers lined up in front of her.

There was no time to dodge and her shield was hanging on the wrong side.

She felt that strange tingling above the bridge of her nose once more. With a final roll of the dice, Coco gathered all her powers of concentration and directed them at each of the four bowmen at the same time, willing them to miss their shots. There was a fierce throbbing in her temple and a coppery taste rose inside her dry mouth.

The arrows fizzed past her harmlessly.

Coco allowed herself a short whoop for joy before pulling on the reins to bring her horse to a halt next to Viktor. Her confidence, at least about leaving the battlefield alive, had increased after that minor miracle: in fact, confidence and self-belief would be her weapons now.

Coco dismounted and crouched next to Viktor. His helmet had flown off and he had a pronounced bulge on his head. His armour was caked in mud, as if he had tried to camouflage himself. She checked the pulse of his carotid artery, relieved to find he was alive. 'Troneg! Troneg, wake up!' she cried. She quickly glanced at the enemies approaching. 'Up you get!'

A bolt fired from a catapult hurtled towards them.

Coco concentrated her mental powers on the first man she could see running towards her and forced him to fling himself in front of the projectile. The tip pierced his breastplate and threw him back several yards, where he crumbled to the floor.

The enemy soldiers slowed down, all of a sudden uncertain.

Viktor groaned and opened his eyes. He couldn't remember the last few minutes at all. 'What's happened?'

'You've fallen off your horse.' Coco helped him up, feeling blood trickling from her nose as she did so. The tugging sensation behind her forehead was still there.

While their adversaries agreed upon a new course of action, they fired off more arrows in Viktor and Coco's direction.

There was no time to manipulate the archers, so she concentrated on the three whizzing projectiles. Grasping them was harder than she'd hoped, but with a great effort, she diverted their flight, turning them around so they were now flying back towards the approaching soldiers.

What was evidently nothing short of a demonic attack was enough to make the men and women turn tail and run for their lives, screaming.

Her plan had worked.

'Thank you for helping me.' Viktor staggered to his feet. He didn't think anything was broken, but his whole body was in agony. Battered and pummelled, his head was throbbing incessantly from the impact. Bruises had appeared everywhere, several of which had been caused by the G36 hanging around his neck. From a brief inspection he could see the barrel had bent and was clogged up with dirt. It would be of no more use to him. He looked at Coco, mightily impressed. 'You actually tried to carry out your orders! I hadn't understood what you were doing at first.'

'Yes. I thought it was our duty – after all, we're the ones who changed history.'

They could see the *scara* had been stopped by the second line of defenders and were now engaged in a vicious mêlée. There was no chance Empress Ermengarde would be taken prisoner. The plan had failed.

Viktor moved his right arm. His shoulder ached as if it had been dislocated and popped back. 'That was brave of you.' Of course it had been more than brave – it had been utterly insane and extremely dangerous. He was impressed.

'Back to the camp,' said Coco firmly. The pain in her temple and behind her forehead was subsiding and she no longer felt as if she were about to throw up. She felt well, apart from some slight dizziness and the continuous nosebleed. 'We've got to leave while the battle's still raging.

If Ermengarde wins ... I don't know what will be done to the losers.'

'You're right. Let's get out of here.' Viktor looked around for a horse.

'I'll take you. It'll be safer that way.'

Two hundred horsemen, foot soldiers and archers approached them in a loose formation on their way to the main battlefield.

Viktor climbed uneasily into the saddle and pulled out his pistol from beneath his robe. It was still intact. 'We'll make it through.'

Coco allowed herself a smile. 'I'd be careful about making any more promises if I were you. Not that you're about to fall of your horse again, mind.'

Trying to break through the scrum would be dangerous, even if Viktor managed to fire an initial volley into the crowd with his pistol. Given all the noise on the battlefield, it was questionable as to whether the blast would have any disruptive effect on the mediaeval soldiers at all.

Coco climbed on to the horse's back as well and sat in front of Viktor. 'Hold on to me,' she ordered. 'Hold on tight.'

'Will do.' He held the loaded P99 in his right hand with the safety off. 'Give me yours as well. So I don't have to reload.' That would give him two rounds of fifteen bullets.

Coco handed it over. 'Woe betide you if you shoot me.' Then she closed her eyes, focusing her powers. If they wanted to escape, it was time for another miracle.

She opened her eyes with a jerk, now focusing intently on the throng of approaching enemies. Then she suddenly unleashed her power – and was instantly struck by another bout of dizziness.

Viktor reached out to grab Coco as she swayed back and forth, holding her in place in the saddle as he watched the people in front of him, open-mouthed.

The soldiers had suddenly stopped and were now sitting down in the mud, rubbing it all over themselves and singing loudly, as if taking a bath. They thanked their comrades as they were handed clumps of earth and began to lather themselves up.

'That should do it!' Coco was struggling to control the swirling in her head, tilting it back to stop another stream of blood from pouring out of her nose. The greater the effort, the bigger the side-effects. She wouldn't be able to do any more without passing out. The horse dashed off, with Coco looking for a gap in the lines.

'That was amazing! Look right.' Viktor was clinging on to her waist. He hadn't used his pistol yet, as their opponents were harmless for the time being. 'We'll be able to get through there.'

Coco directed the black horse through the small group of addled soldiers, who were gradually regaining their senses, unable to believe what they were doing down in the dirt.

As soon as they saw Viktor and Coco, they threw down their arms and turned to flee.

Viktor grinned. 'They're scared of us,' he said excitedly in Coco's ear.

Then he realised what Empress Ermengarde's troops were actually running away from.

With the force of a freight train, a large mounted unit was thundering from the flank into the middle of the raging battle. The armoured horses tore open the ring that had encircled Judith and her soldiers. The deafening clank of blades on armour, the rumbling of arrows and maces on shields and the breaking of lances and bones were now the loudest sounds across the whole battlefield.

Foot soldiers poured in behind them, while their accompanying archers unleashed a shower of arrows towards the enemy to keep them at a safe distance.

'Those must be Guerin's people!' Viktor shouted into the bracing wind. 'Anna-Lena and Dana must have made it!'

Coco brought their horse to a stop, not wanting to get caught up in the stream of soldiers rushing across them. She looked around, desperately searching for a way out.

Then she spotted a head of wild red curly hair in the horde of riders, and recognised Dana alongside.

We're here, still alive, she sent to Anna-Lena as a mental message. *Meet us at the tent they're using as a hospital.*

'That way.' Through the dust and chaos, Viktor was keeping an eye out for signs of danger. He kept his P99 in one hand; the other was wrapped around Coco.

'I've got through to Dana and Anna-Lena. They're here and they know we're here too.' Coco diverted the horse around the count's troops; he had arrived with at least ten thousand fresh warriors to turn the battle in Empress Judith's favour. Just as history dictated. She couldn't wait to tell Ingo all about it.

Viktor observed the fray with the requisite curiosity of a former soldier coming face-to-face with the brutality of war from more than a thousand years ago. Swords, maces, clubs, spears, lances, bows . . .

He looked at the pistols in his hands. The tools of death had become more efficient over the centuries, but the degree of brutality hadn't changed.

And that was precisely why he had abandoned his former profession.

Viktor hoped he wouldn't have to fire a single shot or kill anyone before they returned. *This is enough*, he thought as he gazed upon the slaughter. *This is enough*.

Ingo was struggling to stay awake, but he was aided by the persistent pain in his leg. He could hear loud cheers through the tent walls, proclaiming Empress Judith's victory. The fact that Guerin's name was also being lauded led Ingo to assume that Dana and Anna-Lena had been successful in their task.

Now all that was left was for Beate and Viktor to return.

Ever since Bernard of Septimania had left, he sensed that the monks were looking at him differently. They felt hostile, lurking, as if they were simply waiting for him to doze off before slitting his throat.

Hoof-beats stopped immediately outside the tent, then Coco flew in, together with Dana and Anna-Lena, while Viktor hung back by the entrance.

'Thank God,' exclaimed Ingo. 'Quickly, load me onto one of the wagons.' He hugged Coco, who was now kneeling beside him. A combination of relief and pain brought tears to his eyes. He never wanted to part from her again, but right now he had to let go. 'We've got to go – now!'

The quartet looked at him in surprise.

'Don't you want to hear what happened?' Coco kissed his forehead, which was hot and tasted of salt and vinegar. 'You're burning up! The fever's getting worse.'

'For now all that matters is you're alive. But my temperature's not the problem. And the wound's healing.' He lowered his voice to tell them about the conversation he had overheard.

Once he had finished, Anna-Lena augmented his story with her account; the two reports gave a clear picture of the conspiracy.

'Septimania's got people everywhere throughout the camp.' Ingo looked around anxiously. 'Please. We've got to leave.' He indicated the documents. 'I know where we need to go.'

'Okay, then. I'll handle it.' Viktor turned to leave, with Anna-Lena close behind. 'We'll find a cart.' They hurried off, while Coco began to pack up their things.

'What do you mean?' she asked.

'I've got a decent idea of where we can find a door to take us home.' Ingo gritted his teeth as a stabbing pain shot through his leg. 'We've got get to the Basque Country, where Aysun found the frame.' He looked at Dana. 'You found Guerin in time. Well done.'

'We got lucky. He and his people came to meet us, which saved us a lot of faff. Otherwise the battle would have gone very differently.' Dana grinned. 'It wasn't easy pretending to be a duchess, but Anna-Lena played the role of a humble servant so convincingly that Guerin believed us. We told him about the Septimania family's betrayal and gave him the letter containing Bernard's offer. That should hopefully spell the end for that prick.'

Coco was delighted that their plan had worked. That meant they wouldn't have to approach Empress Judith; they could simply disappear once and for all. After they had found Ingo's door.

'And what about your leg? You said the inflammation had gone down.' Dana pulled back the sheet before Ingo could stop her. She looked at her doctor's wound and her good mood instantly dissipated. 'Oh, shit.'

Coco leaped to her feet. She had believed Ingo's assurances unquestioningly. 'Oh, God, no.' She closed her eyes and held her hands over the wound, feeling the heat of the red gash and focusing with all her might.

But no matter how hard she tried, she couldn't find a way to cure him. Performing a miracle of that nature was beyond her abilities, even her new ones. 'I can't,' Coco exclaimed in desperation. 'What . . . what can we do?'

'Get back to the present as quickly as possible.' Dana looked at Ingo gravely. 'Or we'll have to remove your leg.'

'Fuck,' he murmured, trying to conceal his terror. In his weakened state there was no guarantee he'd survive such an operation. It had become even more important for the others to learn what had to be done.

Anna-Lena entered the tent again. 'We've found a wagon. Viktor's waiting there and we can go while the final skirmishes are still raging. It looks as if a few of them are refusing to give up.' Without hesitation, she grabbed the bags and carried them outside.

'Up you get.' Dana supported Ingo, who hopped along

beside her. She seriously doubted the parapsychologist would survive for long without modern medicine. 'Where to, then?' A bit of optimism couldn't hurt.

'Spain.'

Her optimism was burst immediately. 'Spain's a pretty big place, Doctor.'

'More or less in the northwest corner, at the French border. Or thereabouts.' Ingo knew it was very far away. 'Based on where we are now, I'd say it's just over five hundred miles.'

'Five hundred!' echoed Coco with dismay. With a wagon. They wouldn't be able to do more than twenty miles per day. 'That would take almost four weeks! We . . . I . . .' she stammered in shock, realising there was almost no chance Ingo would survive.

'I know. It's going to be tough,' he said with a wry smile. He had assumed it would actually take six weeks, at least. The Middle Ages had too many unknowns, and nor was it known for its quality of roads. 'I'll explain precisely what you need to know – in case you need to find your way without me.'

'That's out of the question, Doctor.' Dana helped him out of the tent and with Viktor's assistance loaded him onto the small two-wheeled horse-cart he'd appropriated.

Anna-Lena had already stowed away everything they needed to take with them, plus a few sundries for the journey she'd found somewhere: a barrel of provisions, bread and several boxes of dried medicinal herbs. 'We'll need these.' She smiled at Ingo. 'Can't have you dying on us.'

Panting, trying to look confident, he made himself as comfortable as he could on the straw bed.

Coco and Anna-Lena mounted up and raised the pennants while Viktor took over the reins, glad to not have to sit astride a horse. Dana joined Ingo on the cart. They had hidden the last G36 and its magazines within easy reach underneath the straw. They had also retrieved their modern equipment from the tree and packed it into linen bags.

Their small retinue began to move off. No one stopped them as they left Empress Judith's camp.

The cheering and chanting of the victorious returning troops resounded behind them. Guerin's rapid advance had taken their opponents utterly by surprise and annihilated Ermengarde's forces.

'And what's been written down will come to pass. Or at least something close to it,' murmured Ingo on his lumpy bed. The straw was cushioning the jolts better than he had expected, though his fever made it feel as if he were sweating out his soul. He reached out to take a sip from one of the waterskins – which turned out to be wine, sour and unpleasant, but he drank it nevertheless, as the alcohol helped to ease the pain.

Anna-Lena looked back at the plain. She hadn't forgotten the conspiracy. 'Assuming we're not in a parallel universe and this is the real Middle Ages – our Middle Ages,' she began, 'can we allow the conspiracy to go ahead?'

'What do you mean?' Once they were out of sight, Dana checked her automatic weapon and dismantled it to give it a good clean, placing the pieces on the blanket next to Ingo.

'Such a violent shift back to patriarchy – the fall of

women. Can that be allowed to happen?' Anna-Lena turned to Coco, looking for an ally. 'Think about it. If we tell Empress Judith, she can warn the other rules and—'

'And we'd have changed history. Again – and for good,' said Ingo weakly. His tongue had grown weary from the combined effects of his fever and the wine. 'It's not our job.'

'But we'd be sparing centuries of oppression for generations of women,' said Anna-Lena. 'Even in our time we're still miles away from real equality. And why? Because of a mediaeval coup, after which the men will doctor history to keep us in our place.'

Dana continued to clean her gun, contemplating Anna-Lena's words.

It made no difference to Coco. Her only concern was Ingo, lying there numbing his pain with wine.

'I know it's shit,' said Viktor, 'but it's history – it's happened. We tried to fix our mistake by getting Guerin to intervene, but going by your logic, we might as well have not bothered.'

'He's right,' agreed Dana. 'I'm the last person to stand in the way of equality.' She gave Anna-Lena a kind look, recognising that she was struggling not to protest. 'But we wouldn't just be changing the position of women, but the course of all the centuries that followed as well.'

'Which would mean no world wars. What would be so wrong about that?' Anna-Lena knew the rest of the team were right, but that didn't make it any easier to accept women being disempowered by the epitome of emasculated, reactionary gammon. 'Shit,' she said disconsolately. 'We could have done something great here.'

'Or we could have started another war,' replied Viktor. 'It would be an experiment with the entire future of humanity and I'm not prepared to be responsible for that.'

Coco nodded absent-mindedly. 'At least we know how it really happened.'

Ingo laughed, choking on his wine. 'I'm looking forward to arguing with my colleagues about who used to rule the Franks – emperors or empresses.' The alcohol had put him in a good mood; the throbbing in his leg had become less agonising.

'That's not going to make you any friends, Doctor.' Viktor let the cart horse ease into a comfortable trot. 'Let's get a move on.'

Dana had been thinking about the route they needed to take. 'To get to northern Spain we need to go southwest to Bordeaux, via Bourges, and then head south from there.' She began to reassemble her G36. 'Depending on the roads, of course. I don't know how things used to be in the Middle Ages, but in any case the Pyrenees are still in the way.'

'Going by the description, the place we need to find is near the Way of St James, on the other side of Pamplona,' Ingo explained, looking for the notebook as they rumbled along the track. 'Here it is: near the Aragonese Way at Navarre. They've also provided the longitude and latitude.'

Dana gave a bitter laugh. 'As if we could get our hands on such a precise map in this era. Or a compass.' She paused. 'Did they have compasses in the Middle Ages?'

'No – at least, not at this point in time,' Anna-Lena said helpfully.

'And this portal's just going to be lying around there?' Viktor enquired doubtfully.

'No. There's a church there dedicated to Saint Mary of Eunate. Its entire outer wall is surrounded by arches,' Ingo read out from the handwritten notebook. '*Eunate* is a Basque word, meaning something like "*a hundred gates*" or "*of a hundred gates*". There's also a note about the church not having been built until 1150, but it says that the arches were much older.'

'Is there any evidence that we'll be able to find a door to take us home?' asked Dana.

'Well, the name's a good sign. Did you say Aysun had brought this frame back from the Basque Country? That fits quite nicely, don't you think?'

Ingo thought the most decisive part was something else. 'There's a legend about a band of brave warriors who were hunting a hideous monster nearly a hundred years ago. It had swept across the country, terrorising the people wherever it went. They chased it to the plain where the arches stood. At that time the arches were said to contain doors, each of which was secured by a large key and a box lock.'

Anna-Lena listened. Something in her memory was stirring.

'The warriors – male and female alike – fought the beast tooth and nail, more viciously than had ever been seen before by humankind. The fight was not going their way, however, and if they lost, they would put the entire country in danger. But one of the injured men found an inscription saying that anyone who stepped through one of those portals without permission would disappear for good,' Ingo continued. 'In their desperation, the warriors opened a door and lured the beast through it, knowing it would mean that they too would disappear for ever. And with a tremendous flash of lightning they all vanished inside and the portal closed, never to open again – because the key was missing, you see.'

'Well it's a lovely fairy tale.' A few days ago Coco would never have believed a word of that story, but now those words represented hope.

'It really sounds like one of our doors,' remarked Viktor.

'A key.' Anna-Lena recalled her grandmother telling her a similar story a long time ago, but she couldn't remember the details. 'Is there a picture to go with it?'

'I'm afraid not.' Ingo drank deeply again; he had already drained half the wineskin. 'We'll find out what it looks like once we get to Eunate. He lifted the container. 'My friends, let us drink to our plan. And to my surviving this fucking injury!' He took another sip and passed the wineskin around.

The toast became a silent oath between the five of them.

None of them dared to question the existence of the church and the arches aloud. The prospect of finding a way home was all that kept them moving forwards.

CHAPTER XIV

Commune of Navarre, Puente La Reina, End of August 841

Annà-Lena rode back to the group, her horse's hooves sending plumes of dust into the oppressive afternoon air, and pointed enthusiastically down the track through the cloud she'd raised. It hadn't rained here for a very long time. 'The arches are over there! We're less than a mile away from Eunate,' she called out happily. She had been chosen as their scout as she was best rider among them. 'And the doors are still there as well.'

'Hear that, Doctor?' Viktor looked at the bed where Ingo was lying, delirious, his eyes closed. The parapsychologist's body was still fighting off the gangrene as it sought to migrate from the dead tissue to the rest of his body. He had resisted any suggestion of amputation, but he had been unconscious since they'd crossed the Aspe Pass in the Pyrenees. 'We'll take you to hospital straight away. Stay with us.'

Coco was sitting with him and doing everything in her power to care for him, despite her lack of healing abilities. She hadn't left his side for a moment, tirelessly ensuring he ate and drank periodically, as well as giving him the herbs and continually cleaning the wound in his leg. Necrosis had spread throughout his lower leg; a foul smell was now emanating from the swollen flesh and the swelling in his skin had formed cracks out of which yet more pungent fluid was seeping. It was a miracle he was still alive. All the excess fat had disappeared; his clothes now hung loosely off him.

Dana rode alongside the wagon. 'We'll be back home in no time,' she said reassuringly. Under Anna-Lena's guidance, she had learned to ride properly over the past six weeks, even using her thighs to guide her horse, just as Coco had taught herself to excel as Ingo's nurse and the group's mystical compass.

Everyone knew Ingo was practically dead. Although he had occasionally rallied and the swelling in his leg subsided from time to time, it always returned more intensely than before. The whole of his right leg had swollen to twice its original size and was somewhere between dark red and purple in colour.

Viktor adjusted the reins to speed the cart-horse along.

After a slight bend, they emerged at the edge of an open plain where myriad arches were arranged in a perfect square. The church Ingo had spoken of, however, had not yet been built.

Dana instinctively raised her G36 and viewed the area through the scope. 'Nothing. We're alone. These last few yards shouldn't be dangerous.'

'Then I suggest you and Anna-Lena ride ahead to find a portal that might work,' said Viktor. They couldn't afford to lose any more time than was necessary. 'Check the inscriptions.'

Coco leaned from the cart and handed the notebook and Aysun's documents to Dana. 'Find something,' she whispered. 'Anything that'll take us home.'

The two women set off at a gallop and reached the arches in a matter of minutes. They slowly rode around the colonnade, astonished at the architectural masterpiece. The joints of each interlocking element in the supporting columns and the semi-circles above them had been plastered clean, while the carven symbols were so delicate that Dana and Anna-Lena couldn't help gazing in wonder. Only ten wooden doors remained, where once there must have been dozens. Some of the arches still bore broken remnants hanging from hinges, while several others had nothing left inside at all.

Anna-Lena dismounted and tied up her horse. She rattled several doors. 'Locked.' They'd need to generate an energy field. She inspected the elaborate box locks, which were made from some metal, not one she recognised. Although they shimmered with a silvery-coppery gleam, they smelled of iron, which she remembered from sharpening her grandmother's old kitchen knives. 'If only I'd brought my key from back then,' she muttered.

Dana guided her mount through each arch that didn't contain a portal, looking for clues about why they had been destroyed, but she had no success. She was able to push open two other doors with her foot.

'I suggest we look at the locked ones first.' She dismounted next to Anna-Lena. 'Did you say something about a key?'

'Yeah. My grandmother once told me a story about dead

knights and a door that had a beast locked up behind it –
no, not a beast, a demon,' she recounted. 'She gave me the
key to make sure the devil never left its prison.'

'And what have you done with it?'

'I hid it in my father's library.' She leaned forwards and
peered into the mysterious keyhole. 'I bet it would have
fitted.'

'May I?' Dana looked at the box lock. 'It's only attached
on one side.' She knelt in front of it, drew her knife and
pried the cover off.

'What are you doing?'

'Looking at the mechanism to see if we can turn the
lock without having the right key.' Dana pointed to the
symbols. 'Try to decipher what those characters mean.' She
handed her back the notebook. 'You'll be better than me
at that. I don't know enough about all this.'

'Rubbish.'

'Fine then. I don't have the patience.' Dana thumped
the panel with the doorknob.

Anna-Lena looked back and forth between the notes
and the arches, starting with the vertical columns up to
the five semi-circles arranged one above the other. They
didn't match.

'They don't look alike,' she reported, after she had finished comparing them. 'I'll have a look at the others.' She
began to move off.

'Right you are.' Dana had removed the cover with a
combination of skill and brute force, revealing a far more
complex mechanism than she had expected to find in the
Middle Ages. 'Let's see what this baby can tell me.' She
illuminated each of the corners with her torch.

There were five cylinders for the key bits to engage with, each of which pressed a pin into a metal plate. If Dana had understood it correctly, the plate would be pushed back to release a filigree gear, in the centre of which was an uncompressed spring made from thin wood.

And at the end of which sparkled a tiny *Particula*.

'Shit.' She looked over at Anna-Lena, who was walking along, carefully examining the arches that had locked doors. 'Well?'

'Nothing yet.'

The other three arrived with the cart. Viktor leapt down to join the mercenary while Coco remained with Ingo.

'Ah. That looks rather complicated,' he said, after a brief inspection of the mechanism.

'It really does.' Dana pointed her knife at the stone embedded deep within. 'A *Particula*. I think if you turn the right key, the spring is compressed like clockwork, then released with an additional turn.'

'Meaning the stone hits something hard, creating a force field,' Viktor completed the thought. Then he noticed something concerning. 'There! Look – the wooden spring's cracked. It looks as if it's been done recently, as well. What do you think?'

Who had sabotaged their way out?

An unwelcome thought crossed Dana's mind.

She turned over the box lock cover she had removed. 'Look: a fuse.' She showed Viktor the thin blade that she had initially considered to be a bracket. 'This is what cut it. It destroys the mechanism if you handle it forcefully.'

'Do you think we could—?' he began, but there was a sudden *crack*.

The spiral broke, the *Particula* fell through a wafer-thin vial, causing it to shatter and release the liquid inside, which dripped onto the stone. Its pungent vapours were so strong that Dana and Viktor had to draw back, coughing violently.

The acid dissolved the *Particula* in a matter of seconds, rendering the door utterly useless.

'Now we know how the fuse works,' said Dana darkly, wiping the tears from her irritated eyes. 'Can you pick locks?'

Viktor said no. 'Still nine more doors to try, though.' And they didn't know where any of them led.

'Seven. Two aren't locked.' Dana waved over to Anna-Lena, who shook her head. There was still no sign of the door described in the notebook. 'What happens if we blow all the fuses?'

Viktor didn't want to think about it. 'Madame Fendi,' he called, 'we need your powers.'

Coco gave Ingo a kiss and got down from the cart to join them. 'Is that it?'

'No. We've got a problem with the locks.' Dana briefly explained how the mechanism worked. 'Can you use your skills to rotate each of the cylinders in turn?'

'Hmm.' Coco thought about it. She had been trying to train her telepathic abilities on the journey, sensing that she might be able to do more with her new power, even telekinesis.

But there was a cover over the mechanism, meaning she couldn't see what she was doing. 'It might be tricky.'

'We've got seven doors for you to practise on,' replied Viktor. 'Then it has to work.'

'Or else we're stuck.' Coco looked back at the cart. That

would spell the end for Ingo. There could be no greater motivation than that.

'I've got it!' shouted Anna-Lena with excitement, jumping up and down, her red curls bouncing around. 'The same symbols as the ones on the frame.'

'Excellent,' Dana called back. 'See if you can use the notebook to find out where the portal's going to take us.'

'Will do.'

Viktor gave a sigh of relief. 'That's one down.' He looked at the medium as she concerned herself with the broken lock. 'Reckon you can do it?'

'Hang on.' Coco concentrated hard, her mind straining to reach the mechanism. She gently tried to engage one of the locking cylinders.

The pins rattled against the metal plate and chased their way through the lock housing, eventually smashing into the gear wheels.

'Shit.' Coco sniffed the first drops of blood back up into her nose. She needed to be more sensitive – figuratively, that is. 'How many attempts have I got?'

'Seven,' replied Dana. Or nine, if they used the unlocked doors to practise.

'I'll check on the doctor in the meantime.' Viktor walked over to the wagon and jumped in alongside a delirious Ingo.

It broke his heart to look at him. A swarm of flies circled the emaciated, heavily bearded man, trying to find their way underneath the thin linen robe to lay their eggs in his suppurating flesh. His pulse was throbbing rapidly as sweat dripped from his face in thick droplets.

Viktor wiped his forehead and dabbed his cheeks. The smell of the burnt tissue was horrendous. 'Hang in there, Doctor,' he said with a sigh.

Coco tested herself on the locks, but only succeeded in ruining one after the other. From her position nearby, Dana could hear the clinking and rattling from inside the metal boxes, shortly followed by a thin trail of caustic mist that inevitably rose from each hole.

Coco then turned her attention to the unlocked doors in an attempt to gain increased sensitivity to the pins, which she had to move blindly. She held a handkerchief under her nose to staunch the drops of blood that continued to tumble from it. Giving up was out of the question. She was doing this for Ingo.

Then there was only the tenth door left.

Her door.

Dana beckoned Viktor over from the car. 'This is it. Bring our not-so-walking wounded over, Troneg.'

Anna-Lena was sitting on the grass in front of the colonnade, making notes. 'The symbols here are identical to the ones on Aysun's frame,' she told them. 'I've found an inscription in Greek up here. Something about times and changing locations.'

'You can read Greek?' Coco stopped. This was the moment of truth. It could take weeks for them to find another location in the notebook – or even months. Or years. Ingo barely had hours left.

'I went to a school that taught classics. My father wanted me to have a broad education.' She tossed her hair back. 'There's a sort of cuneiform writing inscribed into the arch underneath, followed by a warning in Latin.' She cleared her throat. '*Beware, wanderer, of sinning wherever you find yourself. See, marvel and return.*'

'Nothing else?' Dana indicated the fifth arch, which hadn't been mentioned yet. 'And this one? What's on here.'

'It's in Basque, I'm afraid. I can't understand a word of it.'

Viktor stopped the cart in front of the colonnade and with Dana's assistance, removed a panel from the wagon's side wall to use as a stretcher. They placed Ingo onto it, then heaved him down and laid him on the grass next to the final door, before unloading the boxes containing all their equipment and releasing the cart horse.

Dana noticed Ingo was barely breathing any more. 'Hurry up, Madame. We've brought him all the way to Eunate – I don't want to see him die here.'

Coco resisted the urge to kneel down beside Ingo and cradle him. That wouldn't help matters at all. With fierce determination, she turned her blue eyes towards the lock. 'You will bend to my will,' she whispered, as if the mechanism could understand her.

Anna-Lena took a step back while Dana and Viktor readied themselves to bear the injured man onwards.

Coco closed her eyes.

She hesitated; a bold thought had just struck her.

The technique she had been using up until now had ruined the locks before the spring caused the stone to strike the plate. But if a key were used correctly, the *Particula* would be preserved and could be used to open the door repeatedly.

But they didn't necessarily need precisely the *same* key.

So Coco didn't even try to move the cylinders.

Instead, she grabbed the tiny stone with her mind and slammed it against the metal plate. The fact that the spring broke and the fragment subsequently dissolved in the acid was immaterial to her. She only needed a one-way ticket back to the hall whence they had come.

At that very moment there came a blast that shook the colonnade and resonated all around the building along the arches, causing dust and dirt to trickle down. The tell-tale whirring sound heralded the build-up of a force field, while a crack had formed in the stone of one of the pillars further on.

'It's worked!' Anna-Lena opened the door to reveal a shimmering, pale blue wall of energy. The field was pumping electricity into the air, causing her hair to stand on end as if she were touching a Van der Graaff generator.

'More cracks,' Dana warned, pointing to the five semi-circles belonging to their arch. The crevices within the stone were widening.

Coco decided not to tell them she had destroyed the lock by activating the energy field. They had no choice but to all go through now, with no prospect of a second attempt. If the arch broke before they all got through, they'd end up like the false Friedemann: torn to pieces.

'Go!' Viktor and Dana lifted an emaciated Ingo on his stretcher. 'It's now or never.'

Anna-Lena picked up two boxes of equipment and was the first to pass through the energy field, disappearing before their eyes.

Then Dana and Viktor walked through with the professor.

More and more cracks began to form in the arch; a few stones came loose and fell out. The whirring from the wall of energy changed slightly, its colour turning from pale blue to a deep turquoise.

'No!' Coco threw herself through the force field with a piercing whirring and humming filling her ears.

Dazzled by a glaring, cold brightness, Coco stumbled out in front of an old church wall illuminated by several spotlights. She took a few steps back and recognised an octagonal building.

Saint Mary of Eunate.

She had landed in a period where the church existed. And where there was electricity. She hadn't left the spot – only the Middle Ages.

Her heart pounded with joy. Spitting out the blood that had run down her throat through her nose, she braced herself against her latest bout of dizziness, with no idea whether it was a result of the wall of energy or her gift. It didn't matter. She had done it!

'Ingo?' Coco looked around.

A dozen people in shorts, wearing hiking backpacks on their backs and expressions of pure amazement, stared back at her. One of them raised an old camera; it clicked and the flash turned the dim ambient light suddenly dazzling.

But there was no sign of Ingo, Anna-Lena, Viktor or Dana.

Coco's suspicions were raised further by the clothes worn by the tourists and the type of camera they had. 'Excuse me,' she ventured in English to the young man who had taken her photograph. 'Can you tell me what day it is?'

'Tuesday.' The astonished look on his face had worn off. 'I mean what date.'

The man eyed her, sniffing the air. 'You smell really bad.'

Coco was wearing clothes from the ninth century, replete with chainmail; the fabrics had absorbed an enormous amount of dirt, grime and sweat on their journey through France. 'I'm an actress and I've got lost. We're making a film about . . .' Coco was too agitated to think of anything plausible. 'The date?' she asked again.

'Oh yes. August the twenty-eighth,' he replied, then added as a precaution, '1951.'

Just as she had feared. When the colour of the energy wall changed, she'd feared something like this would happen. But what else could she have done?

Suddenly unsteady on her feet, Coco sat down on a bench and breathed deeply in and out.

The revelation hit her hard.

She had ended up somewhere completely removed from the others, far away from Ingo – from the man she would have followed to the ends of the earth once he had recovered, out of love for him.

Coco put her hands over her face and wept bitter tears.

Frankfurt

There was a brief knock on the door to Ingo's ward and it swung open.

Viktor, Dana and Anna-Lena entered hesitantly, but with smiles on their lips.

Ingo smiled back, trying his best not to look too despondent. All he wanted was for Beate to visit him, but it hadn't happened yet, however, and there was a voice inside him telling him it would never happen, not for as long as he lived. There had been no trace of her since their return.

'Hey, finally – a smile!' Anna-Lena hauled over a heavy bag with a package peeping out of the top. She was wearing a black sheath dress with a dark green belt; the outfit emphasised her fair skin, freckles and red hair. Her cheerfulness was forced. 'Nice to see you looking a little more cheerful, Doctor.'

Dana wore a semi-military outfit. She gave him a curt nod, her hands not leaving her pockets. She didn't have the words to say anything appropriate.

Viktor, dressed in jeans, a polo shirt and trainers, saw the catalogue for prosthetic legs open on the side table. The metallic carbon-fibre model had been ticked. 'You're going to become the Terminator.'

'Yes. I like that one the best.' Ingo pointed to the empty space below his torso, where his right leg had once been. The doctors hadn't even tried to save the leg; all they could do was remove the dead, poisonous flesh from the hip, leaving only a stub. 'Any news?'

Anna-Lena knew the question was addressed to her. 'No. I'm afraid not.'

They moved the chairs in the room into a semi-circle around the convalescent, who was still looking incredibly frail. After arriving in the twenty-first century three weeks ago at Saint Mary of Eunate, a Spanish doctor was actually on hand and able to arrange his treatment. Although they had spent almost two months in the Middle Ages, only a few days had passed in the present, according to the date on the doctor's forms.

'At least our dealings with the authorities are over.' Anna-Lena's smile remained weak. She had just learned that her father and someone alleged to be her had been killed in a private jet crash on the open sea. She had been able to prove her identity quickly and had inherited everything from Walter. Her father's nervous shareholders were calmed for the time being; the van Dam family business would continue to operate smoothly thanks to the team of good managers her father had instructed to run the company after his house had been ominously burgled.

'But I still don't understand what my father was doing in a private jet from Hong Kong.' Anna-Lena drummed her fingers irritably on the bed. 'He'd never have abandoned the rescue mission voluntarily.' But there was no doubt about it. The body had been identified from DNA and dental records, yet there was no sign of the daughter who had supposedly perished in the accident alongside him. At first they said her body must have been washed away by the tide. Now the authorities assumed Anna-Lena had re-emerged after a misunderstanding had arisen about her passport information.

'Do you think it had anything to do with the robbery?' Ingo asked. The burglary had got out of control, with countless valuable items stolen and van Dam's entire staff killed. 'Blackmail? Could someone have wanted him to smuggle something for them?'

'We found something on his desk. It was left there for us to find.' Viktor removed a USB stick from his pocket. He and Dana had helped Anna-Lena to get everything in order. The weeks they had spent together in the Middle Ages had made them pretty well attached at the hip. 'It contains information about us – the fake Friedemann and organisation behind it all, as well as their plans.'

Anna-Lena was certain that the stick with all this information on it couldn't have come from her father. But perhaps it had been left there for him?

Dana looked at the storage device with its explosive content. It also contained details about their incursion in Darfur – she as a mercenary and Viktor as a Special Forces observer on an American military operation. 'We each had links to the Organisation without ever realising it,' she confessed to Ingo.

'Oh?' He sat up in bed. 'How curious.'

'I'd been hired as a bodyguard for a drug dealer called Bestman.' Dana pointed at Viktor. 'And he was part of a German Special Forces unit sent to observe their American counterparts in how to operate in enemy territory.'

'Long story short, shit hit the fan.' Viktor wanted to keep their report as brief as possible, rather than dwell too long on what had happened. 'Bestman fled to a ruin on the outskirts of the city. We thought he and his people had got lost.'

'But we had been instructed to go that way,' Dana corrected him.

'I remember the door to the ruin had a knocker and a lion's mouth carved into it. The frame was glowing.'

Viktor tapped the USB stick with his index finger. 'A shadowy figure emerged and killed everyone while a sandstorm raged around us.'

'A portal,' remarked Ingo. 'Then this Bestman must be one of the conspirators!'

'Precisely. Bestman decided to escape in that direction because he sensed something might go wrong. That's why he chose El Sireaf as the meeting place.' Dana leant back in her chair. 'No one survived on either side. Apart from us two.'

'That's insane.' Ingo reached for his throbbing leg, but his fingers found only the sheet. Phantom pain. The doctors had prepared him for it. He had been given sleeping pills for his nightmares. He couldn't remember most of what had happened at the end of their visit to the Middle Ages, as he had been immersed in one long stretch of delirium, so he had had to hear second-hand how Beate had cared for him – sacrificed herself for him. And how she had even tried to rectify history at the Battle of Fontenoy. Ingo's throat constricted as grief washed over him once more.

Dana saw his change of demeanour and gave him a comforting smile. The father of the young man who had descended into the caves as one of the first rescue team had been just as depressed. Dana had hired someone to find him, as she had to tell her client that there was no hope of finding his son's body, not after the explosion in the caves. There was nothing left of either van Dam's old mansion or the five doors either.

Anna-Lena put her hand on Ingo's arm. Her concern for him, combined with a strong sense of duty, meant she couldn't leave him on his own. 'I'll keep checking your Beate's flat regularly. We'll be the first to know if anything happens.'

Ingo nodded absently, fighting back tears. He couldn't imagine ever living a normal life again. The institute had noted his 'hiking accident', as he had described it to them, and wished him a speedy recovery. All his colleagues had asked him when he'd be back, but he couldn't face it. 'Maybe I'll move in next door – next door to her flat, that is. I can wait there until Beate finds a portal.'

Viktor, Dana and Anna-Lena exchanged glances.

'She could be anywhere,' Dana finally dared to say. It gave her no joy to torpedo whatever faint sense of optimism he might have left, but she considered it far healthier to come to terms with loss rather than clinging on to an imagined scenario that would in all likelihood never happen. 'As in, in any time. In any world.'

'I know,' Ingo replied, more loudly than he had intended. 'I know that.' He couldn't stand to just sit around, hoping. He looked at Anna-Lena. 'Are you still researching the doors' history? From those documents? I'd like to help, if I may.'

She sighed. Unlike Dana, she couldn't bring herself to pour cold water on his hope of finding his beloved again. 'We'll see. I'm quite heavily involved with running my father's businesses now, you know.'

'Basically, I'm out,' announced Dana. She had received a generous pay-out of two million euros and was not about to put herself in danger again. 'Our little adventure was enough for me.' It was time to do something on her own: A restaurant, or perhaps a café. Something without gunfire and the constant threat of imminent death. 'But as soon as there's any trace of Ms Schüpfer, I'll be there. I owe her as much.'

'Me too,' said Viktor. 'I'll be there for our medium any time.' Then he remembered what he had almost forgotten to tell Ingo. 'Besides, the conspirators are history. We haven't got an enemy any more.'

'Right!' Dana nudged Anna-Lena. 'Show him.'

'Oh, yes.' She removed the tablet from her pocket and pulled up a few articles; she scrolled through briefly, then turned the display to face Ingo.

A high-rise of at least a hundred floors could be seen in the centre of Singapore. It was on fire.

Long tongues of flame flickered out of shattered windows, while plumes of smoke billowed around the glass front of the building. The fire had gutted the building completely, as demonstrated by the short film clips showing occasional violent explosions from within.

'What's going on here?' Ingo asked. 'Oh my God! What's all that flying through the air? Is this some sort of bomb plant?'

'*Particulae*,' responded Dana.

Ingo looked up, his eyebrows raised. 'What? How do you know?'

Anna-Lena paused the film when it started to show interior shots of the skyscraper. 'I recognised the headquarters from when I found myself there after escaping from the world with all those wolves. I was only there for a few minutes, but I'm sure that's the place.' She enlarged a few screenshots for him. 'There. You see?'

Ingo recognised an unusually large number of door frames, all piled up in a room. The recordings of the burning building also revealed the remains of numerous doors in their frames.

Dana was sitting with her legs wide apart and her elbows resting on her knees. 'It was the largest skyscraper in Singapore – it was supposed to be completely empty as the lease hadn't been signed yet, but when the emergency services arrived, they found a load of fully equipped offices, as well as all these destroyed doors.'

'Along with dozens of burnt-up computers banks. It looks as if they had enough storage capacity to match any supercomputer,' added Viktor.

'The authorities believe it was a hacking centre.' Anna-Lena swiped through the photos until she came across one of the rooms she had run through – where she had come face-to-face with the man in the pin-striped suit, with whom she had had a violent scuffle before fleeing.

Ingo frowned. 'What really happened?'

'Those splinters were volatile.' Dana gestured to one of the explosions. 'Like that frame that killed the pretend Friedemann. Oh, and you can read about who he really was on the USB stick. In any case, that *Particula* started a chain-reaction, resulting in the doors falling one by one like dominoes, destroying our global conspirators' carefully guarded data in the process.'

Ingo inclined his head as he looked at the photographs. 'I wouldn't rule out some of them making it out,' he said carefully. 'Those doors are the best possible escape route.'

'They found bodies.' Anna-Lena flipped through to find

the article. 'More than fifty men and women, burnt beyond recognition.' She firmly believed it had killed the man in the suit who had slammed the bunker door in her face. 'And even if some of them did manage to escape, there's nothing left for them.'

Ingo remained sceptical. 'Didn't you say earlier your father had crashed on his way back from Hong Kong?' She nodded. 'What if he had travelled to Singapore first? What if *he* was the one who started the fire?'

Dana rubbed her eyes. 'Walter van Dam in full-on Rambo mode? Are we talking about the same stuffed shirt here?'

Anna-Lena had an active imagination, but even she couldn't picture her father waltzing into an office building and shooting up the place. 'How would he have learned about the Organisation?'

Ingo pointed at the USB stick on the table. 'Why shouldn't he have known? He could easily have read this all before we did.'

'I doubt it.' Viktor recalled meeting the older man. They had only spoken in his study for a few minutes but he couldn't imagine him having such a destructive streak. Plus, the Organisation's headquarters would have had the best security available. An individual acting alone would never have made it so far.

'This is all speculation, but I have a strong suspicion that van Dam's unexplained trip to Asia and the fire in Singapore are related.' The air crash would remain a mystery for the time being, as well as the puzzling presence of a second daughter on board, along with Beate's whereabouts. 'It would mean a lot to me, being able to help with the research.'

'I'll think about it, Doctor Theobald.' Anna-Lena stood up. 'Time's getting on. I need to get back to work.' She neglected to mention she had decided a long time ago to continue her investigations into the inscriptions around the doors. Even without Viktor and Dana's help. 'The van Dam Corporation waits for no one.' She took the package out of the bag. 'This is for you, Doctor. From your institute.' She placed it on the table.

'Probably full of sweets. Gummy ghosts or something.' Dana stood up and shook Ingo's hand. 'Hang in there, Doctor. Get better soon. And don't forget – if you need us to get Beate out from wherever she's ended up, I'll be there.'

'Me too.' Viktor rose as well. 'We'll come and visit you.'

'By the way, everything's taken care of – the hospital, rehab, prosthetic leg and fitting. You don't need to worry about a thing,' said Anna-Lena, before giving Ingo a hug. 'Thank you. You rescued me and I swear I'll never forget it.' She looked around. 'That goes for all of you.' She opened the door and went out into the corridor. 'See you tomorrow, Doctor.'

Dana and Viktor followed her out, the door clicking softly behind them.

Ingo looked at the package.

He recognised the writing on the label: it was Corinna, the secretary at the institute. She had drawn a little heart alongside his name to cheer him up.

Even though he didn't much feel like opening the box, at least it would be a distraction from the relentless self-pity, heartache and despair he was currently enduring.

The doctors had warned that amputation didn't just mean losing a limb – for many people it triggered an existential crisis, a suffering soul.

So before Ingo could sink back into bed and start sobbing, he tore open the packaging. Inside was a sealed box with a note from Corinna, saying the package had been delivered by a courier service. There was no sender information.

On the top was written, in scratchy handwriting, *packed on 31.12.2001*, alongside a barcode sticker, as if the parcel had been stored in a warehouse.

Ingo's curiosity was piqued. With a jerk he tore off the flap and opened the box.

Inside were reams of letters, stacked tightly one on top of the other.

They were tied up in little bundles with red ribbon and each bore a number. They smelled of old paper but the envelopes didn't look as if they had even been despatched.

Ingo picked up the letter with the number one and opened it, before beginning to read the cursive female handwriting.

As soon as he saw how he had been addressed, tears began to well up in his eyes.

My darling Ingo,

Time is relative, as they say.

But not for me. For me, time is absolute and it snatched me away from you. I ended up in 1951, in the very spot where we last saw each other, in Navarre.

For a long time I didn't know where it had taken you. I had to come to terms with not being able to find you, or a door that might bring me back to the present – my present. My pendulum was of no use in that respect.

But my psychic powers told me you were still alive – that you were all right. That you survived the journey back to the present and hadn't died from your wound. Even though there was no chance of us being reunited, I was happy.

Years passed. They were cruel, yet still they passed.

I've kept myself busy. Imagine this – Spanger's ghost visits me from time to time. At least he's having fun – not necessarily as a hero, but he loves haunting people and garnering attention from it. Trust me, ghosts really do exist, but you can find the rest out for yourself. You're a specialist, after all.

When I finally reached a time when I knew you were alive, I approached you on several occasions without revealing myself. It was nice to see the course of your career from a different perspective. You should be proud of yourself.

In case you were wondering, it was with a heavy heart that I decided not to intervene in the course of history – in case it ended badly for you. I know how important that was to you and I respect that.

My powers have told me you'll suffer for a while, then rise further and further, celebrating one triumph after another.

I am absolutely certain about that.

When you read the rest of my letters – trust them. Trust me.

Since there was no way for us to talk to each other or spend any time together, I wrote you letters instead. I ended up writing more than I'd intended, as I got rather carried away at times. Please do read them all, though. It was my way of dealing with losing you, of keeping you in my life as best I could.

The lines you're reading now are my last, written on New Year's Eve 2001. I don't have long to live now.

I promise you I've made the best life I could under the circumstances. And all I ask from you is to make the best of yours, dear Doctor.

Smile when you think of me and forgive me for using your feelings for me against you. It became real for me before the end.

And now it's farewell.

With eternal love through the ages,

Your Beate

Ingo sobbed into the package, his vision blurred.

Her final letter to him was numbered 2,400. And he would read them all.

ECHOES

Las Vegas, 11 November 1951

Beate stood behind the stage and smoothed down her white knee-length dress. A black belt subtly emphasised her slim waist. She listened to Frank Sinatra's distinctive voice as he crooned in the limelight, backed by a bombastic big band. The audience in the grand hall of the *Flamingo* went wild. Young women screamed in the direction of the singer, who was clearly adoring all the attention.

Behind the curtain, the stagehands began to move the set into position for the next performance. Every time they passed Beate, they nodded to her with a brief, 'Ma'am,' and she beamed back at them.

Beate's white hair was piled up into a monster hairstyle, accentuated dramatically by the black streak. She had no idea how the make-up artist had done it.

Las Vegas. This was where she belonged. The shows, the stars, the casinos, the lust for entertainment – not to mention all the glamour. Nowhere else in the world held as many opportunities for a medium.

'Seven minutes,' announced the stage manager in all directions. 'Seven minutes.'

She wasn't nervous. She was actually rather happy, in spite of everything.

Beate's first appearance of the night was at the *Flamingo* which, like all the other casinos on the Strip, was enjoying the start of its heyday. Then it was a quick trip over the road to the *New Frontier* to perform a handful of small tricks for the audience while they waited for the next show. Magicians wouldn't be the star attractions for some time, but they were good as filler between the dancing. The *Desert Inn*, which had opened the year before, had also shown a great deal of interest in her.

Sinatra gave it his all once again, adding that incomparable glaze to his voice that, along with his charismatic appearance, had made him such a star.

Beate was looking forward to the years ahead. She'd make sure to catch Elvis Presley's first performance at the *New Frontier*, as well as those of her childhood heroes, the Rat Pack: Lauren Bacall, Humphrey Bogart, Judy Garland, David Niven, Dean Martin and Sammy Davis Junior.

They'd all be singing and dancing right in front of her.

It was a veritable delight to see a fleet-footed, unsurpassable Fred Astaire gliding across the floor as if physics were only for mere mortals. She would buy tickets for as many shows as she could afford, as she couldn't stand to miss any of them.

'Three minutes,' barked the stage manager, looking at the large clock next to the staircase. 'You the magician, honey?' he said to Beate as he passed her.

She nodded.

'Don't forget, you've got ten minutes tops. Then I'll

chase you off, whether you've caught your pigeons or not, sweetheart.'

'I haven't got any pigeons.'

The man stopped. 'What are you going to do, then?'

She looked into his eyes and began to read his memories. 'You had coffee for breakfast – black – and poured half your cup over the newspaper because your cat Miu startled you. You also had an egg, undercooked, and toast with cheese,' she rattled off. 'Your daughters are called Sue and Annabelle and you've seen active service in the Pacific, near Pearl Harbor. Your favourite colour's green and you play the same slot machine every day: a one-armed bandit, dimes only.' She smiled at the man, who was looking rather perplexed. 'Fancy hearing any more about yourself, Mr Ian George Paul Patrick O'Brian?'

'Holy shit!' The stage manager took a step backwards and crossed himself jokingly. 'You're the Devil in disguise, Miss!'

'1963.'

'Sorry?'

'Elvis Presley.' Beate held out an open hand. 'Let's have a bet. Elvis Presley's going to release a song in 1963, called *Devil in Disguise.*'

'Who's Elvis Presley?'

'You'll find out then.'

'Who knows if I'll even still be alive then?'

'You will be, Mr O'Brian. *I* know you will.' She winked at him and wiggled her fingers. 'Well?'

He laughed. 'No, honey. I'm not going to bet against the Devil.' He checked his watch and swore. 'One minute.

Positions, everyone. Let's get that scenery off.' He nodded at her with a new-found respect, with an expression on his face that could only be described as pleasant discomfort.

Beate took a deep breath as Sinatra basked in his standing ovation. In a few years' time, he and the Rat Pack would be thrilling the crowds once more at their summit shows, full of singing, drinking and laughter. They'd be the most popular shows in Vegas.

Everyone knew about Sinatra's Mafia connections. The mobsters were all over Vegas like rats, represented by various families. The first of them had already knocked on Beate's door with an offer to be her manager.

It was a male domain.

And Beate was breaking into this male domain where women were only allowed to be bit-parts.

It was the only conscious historical change she had committed. She would stay out of everything else and allow mankind to make its mistakes while she remained in her little microcosm, this glittering world full of endless possibilities.

Sinatra emerged from the stage, loosening his bow tie, and gave her a wink as he passed, as he probably did to every attractive woman he came across. A smell of after-shave and a subtle hint of sweat followed him in his wake. 'Good luck, little lady. If you're any good I might have you open for me one day.'

Beate raised an eyebrow. 'See you soon, then, Mr Sinatra,' she said without looking at him.

The stage was set, with all but three of the phalanx of spotlights extinguished; those three were focused on a single spot where the tail-coated compère stood. The rest of the *Flamingo* was dark as the punters laughed and murmured to one another, the occasional clinking of glass ringing out across the theatre. The euphoria from the star's performance was still sparkling in the air.

She didn't want to be the opening act – she didn't need to be. Beate knew she'd have her own show in less than a year. An evening-long show.

'Join me in welcoming a new talent who's made the long journey across the Atlantic from Germany for your entertainment tonight. She's following in the footsteps of her ancestor – the great, unforgettable Harry Kellar,' announced the man in the tailcoat. 'Nothing in your head is safe from her. Gents, hide those thoughts about your mistress. Ladies, keep your latest shoe purchase a secret. Please welcome to the stage the wonderful, the magnificent, the unique' – he turned towards the staircase and stretched out an arm in her direction – 'Greta Kellar!'

The applause made the hairs on Beate's neck stand to attention.

For you, Ingo. She put on her most radiant smile and walked onto the stage of the *Flamingo*.

Would you like to know what would have happened to our team of rescuers if you had opened the door marked with a question mark or the door with an 'X'?

Pick up *DOORS ? COLONY* or *DOORS X TWILIGHT* and discover a whole new adventure!

ABOUT THE AUTHOR

Markus Heitz studied history and German language and literature before writing his debut novel, *Schatten über Ulldart* (*Shadows over Ulldart*, the first in a series of epic fantasy novels), which won the Deutscher Phantastik Preis, Germany's premier literary award for fantasy. Since then he has frequently topped the bestseller charts, and his Number One-bestselling *Dwarves* and *Älfar* series have earned him his place among Germany's most successful fantasy authors. Markus has become a byword for intriguing combinations: as well as taking fantasy in different directions, he has mixed mystery, history, action and adventure, and always with at least a pinch of darkness. Millions of readers across the world have been entranced by the endless scope and breadth of his novels. Whether twisting fairy-tale characters or inventing living shadows, mysterious mirror images or terrifying creatures, he has it all – and much more besides.

DOORS is a work of new opportunities and endless possibilities, with each book following our team of adventurers as they choose a different door. Do you dare to cross the threshold and explore the unknown worlds beyond?

WHICH DOOR WILL YOU CHOOSE NEXT?

When his beloved only daughter goes missing, millionaire entrepreneur Walter van Dam calls in a team of experts – including free-climbers, a geologist, a parapsychologist, even a medium – to find her . . . for Anna-Lena has disappeared somewhere within a mysterious cave system under the old house the family abandoned years ago. But the rescuers are not the only people on her trail – and there are dangers in the underground labyrinth that no one could ever have foreseen.

In a gigantic cavern the team come across a number of strange doors, three of them marked with enigmatic symbols. Anna-Lena must be behind one of them – but time is running out and they need to choose, quickly. Anna-Lena is no longer the only person at risk.

The team knew their mission would be perilous – but how do you defeat your own demons? Trapped in their own nightmares, their only hope of escape is DOOR X, which leads to a threatening vision of the future . . .

DOORS: THREE DOORS, THREE DIFFERENT ADVENTURES. WHICH DOOR WILL YOU CHOOSE?

Available in paperback and eBook

WHICH DOOR WILL YOU CHOOSE NEXT?

When his beloved only daughter goes missing, millionaire entrepreneur Walter van Dam calls in a team of experts – including free-climbers, a geologist, a parapsychologist, even a medium – to find her ... for Anna-Lena has disappeared somewhere within a mysterious cave system under the old house the family abandoned years ago. But the rescuers are not the only people on her trail – and there are dangers in the underground labyrinth that no one could ever have foreseen.

In a gigantic cavern the team come across a number of strange doors, three of them marked with enigmatic symbols. Anna-Lena must be behind one of them – but time is running out and they need to choose, quickly. Anna-Lena is no longer the only person at risk.

They little expect door ? to take them back to the 1940s – but this is not the 1940s they know. In this timeline, Nazi Germany capitulated early, the US has taken control of Europe and is threatening the Russian-led Resistance with a nuclear strike. If the team is to rescue Anna-Lena – and survive themselves – they will have to stop this madness – at all costs!

DOORS: THREE DOORS, THREE DIFFERENT ADVENTURES. WHICH DOOR WILL YOU CHOOSE?

Available in paperback and eBook

Jo Fletcher
BOOKS